Risky Business

The door of the flower shop opened easily. Sucking in a careful breath of relief, Chris stepped into the shop—and came to a dead halt. There facing her was a very upset man holding a semiautomatic in a regulation hold.

"You were just about to tell me who you are," the new police chief said, not bothering to lower the gun.

Chris tried her best smile, even with an illegal set of lock picks in her carefully upraised hands. "I'm Chris Jackson. I'm an author."

"And?"

"And I've lived in Pyrite for the last five years. When I need to try something new for a book, the town lets me practice."

The chief hesitated a moment, then finally holstered his gun.

"How about if I explain the whole thing over a cup of coffee?" Chris asked.

By Eileen Dreyer

A Man to Die For
If Looks Could Kill
Nothing Personal
*Bad Medicine**

Available from HarperPaperbacks

*coming soon

Eileen Dreyer

If Looks Could Kill

HarperPaperbacks
A Division of HarperCollins*Publishers*

This is a work of fiction. The characters, incidents, and dialogues are products of the author's imagination and are not to be construed as real. Any resemblance to actual events or persons, living or dead, is entirely coincidental.

HarperPaperbacks *A Division of* HarperCollins*Publishers*
10 East 53rd Street, New York, N.Y. 10022

Copyright © 1992 by Eileen Dreyer
All rights reserved. No part of this book may be used or reproduced in any manner whatsoever without written permission of the publisher, except in the case of brief quotations embodied in critical articles and reviews. For information address HarperCollins*Publishers,*
10 East 53rd Street, New York, N.Y. 10022.

Cover photography by Herman Estevez

First printing: October 1992

Printed in the United States of America

HarperPaperbacks, HarperMonogram, and colophon are trademarks of HarperCollins*Publishers*

❖ 10 9 8 7 6 5 4 3

Acknowledgments

Once again, I've depended on the generosity and hospitality of others to help complete this book. My thanks go to the people of Ironton, Missouri, which, of course, bears no resemblance to Pyrite—except for the jail. Special thanks to Mayor Jack Mayes, Police Chief Joe Wilson, Pat "Who Runs City Hall" Boffman, Sgt. Roger Medley, and Ms. June Haefner of the venerable and delightful Green Roof Inn. I couldn't have finished this book, either, without the help of Lt. John Podolak and his ever-patient wife Michelle, who helped with the proofing. Thank you, Karyn, for holding the proverbial hand; Carolyn Marino, Karen Solem, and Chris Wilhide for giving me such a wonderful home at Harper, and, of course, thank you to the real Bitch Queen for the use of her exalted title. And, as ever, to P. B. It wouldn't be any fun without you.

Happy families are all alike; every unhappy family is unhappy in its own way.

—Leo Tolstoy
Anna Karenina

If you talk to God, you are praying; if God talks to you, you have schizophrenia.

—Thomas Szasz

✦ Chapter 1 ✦

IT WAS AL MacNamara's first day on the job as police chief for Pyrite, Missouri, and he didn't want to fuck up. It wasn't that he couldn't get another job if he did. After fourteen years pounding the streets along Chicago's Area Six, he could walk into damn near any metropolitan area he wanted and get work. He had enough commendations, not too many complaints, and only one ex-wife who still really hassled him. Forty was a year or two away and, according to his medical records, the steel plate in his head would only cause problems in airports.

But when he'd spent his medical leave poring over the ads in the law enforcement magazines, he'd ignored the name of every city big enough to be recognized. If he'd been wanting excitement and challenge he would have just stayed in Chicago. He'd spent all those hours while his eye had been bandaged closed looking for someplace just like Pyrite.

It was Monday evening, and the town was all but shut down for the night. Harry Truman High was in the basketball play-offs, which meant that except for the Pizza Hut, where the victorious champions would

1

return to celebrate, the majority of businesses were locked and empty. Everybody was at the game.

With two square blocks of downtown, Pyrite sported the latest in video stores and the most vintage of hardware stores. It had the obligatory funeral home and used car dealership that labeled it a two-horse town, and three stop lights just to slow down the high school kids on Friday night.

Tucked into the northern folds of the Ozarks, Pyrite had once been a bustling little mining town. Now, though, it was just another struggling county seat a hundred or so miles south of St. Louis, in an area where the unemployment rate hovered in the teens. The town square boasted a Civil War monument, the Rock of Ages Baptist Church was the tallest building in town, and the city hall was housed in what had been Pyrite's only brush with supermarket convenience. After Chicago, just what Mac needed right now.

It was a town to walk, and that was what Mac was doing. He wasn't really used to it anymore, after the years in a black-and-white and then the detective's bureau. His senses were still too keen from surviving the projects to enjoy an easy stroll down Main Street. Last time he had walked a street he had been eyefucked by every gangbanger on the block. Tonight two little old ladies invited him to dinner, and the proprietor of the Kozy Kitchen intercepted him with a free cup of coffee. A long way from Cabrini Green.

For the first time in fifteen years, he could smell the fresh hint of spring on the damp night air. He heard a mourning dove in the tree in front of the barbershop and saw people sitting on their front porches. He was back walking a beat in a uniform, and he felt pretty damn good. Not a bad way to start a new job.

He had just turned from Main onto Elm when he saw it. Or maybe he sensed it first. After this long, Mac no longer differentiated.

"Aw, shit."

A shadow, back in the alley. A faint scratching noise. A very low curse.

A funny itching at the back of his neck.

No mistaking that. Out of place here in Mayberry, but much too familiar from the real world to ignore.

Mac reached for his gun. Damn, not on his first night. Not on his first goddamn day here. He didn't even realize that he was already sweating, or that his gut had automatically curled into a hard knot. When he drew his gun though, his hand was shaking, and it made him curse again.

Carefully, he stepped across the street and back onto the sidewalk. No use taking a bad guy out in the alley. It was a lesson he'd learned a long time ago in Chicago. Attempted got a slap. Catch 'em with their sneaky little toes over the threshold, though, and you had yourself a righteous collar with at least a chance at a sentence.

Mac took one more look around to see the streets still empty except for the appliance dealer across Main who was just locking up. But just his luck, there was somebody on the other side of that door that the perp was testing. There were lights on in the shop and the shudder of movement behind the desk. Taking a deep, slow breath to slow the sudden staccato of his heart rate, Mac reached out with his left hand and opened the door of the How Do I Love Thee Flower Shop.

"Oh, I'm sorry, we're closed," the little lady behind the counter immediately announced before her parchment and peach features folded into recognition. "Oh, Chief MacNamara, how lovely."

Mac lifted a finger to his mouth to silence her as he crept in, the gun held flat against his back where it wouldn't surprise her into really giving him away.

"Ma'am—" he began, sidestepping the horseshoe of carnations that read "To our lodge brother and most devoted bison" and heading for a counter that spilled over with ribbons and cards and charitable donation boxes.

The birdlike woman barely cleared the cash register. She was patting at hair the consistency and color of cotton candy and beaming at him with a coyness that looked well practiced. "I'm Miss Eloise Elliott, Chief. Please do call me Eloise. And welcome to town. No matter what Serita Ruth Patterson says, I'm glad to have you here."

So much for discretion.

"Miss Elliott—"

She waggled a finger, even as Mac saw the lock on the back door tremble beneath the stealthy assault from the other side.

"Eloise," she admonished.

He nodded quickly, carefully bringing the gun around. "Eloise," he allowed very quietly, focusing on the job at hand instead of the shakes that threatened to take over, the liquid heat that seared his gut. "I want you to very quietly walk out the front door. I want you to do it now."

Miss Elliott's carefully penciled eyebrows lifted like gulls' wings. "Well, whatever for?"

She hadn't even seemed to notice the gun yet. Her

hand had stilled against her bony chest, though.

"Because somebody's trying to break into your store, ma'am. Now if you'd just—"

He reached out to take her arm, just to get her going. She flinched away, shaking her head.

"Oh, no," she demurred, that hand now out front where it was shooing him away. "You go on, now. I don't believe I called you. I don't believe I called you at all. That wouldn't be fair, now, would it?"

One eye still on the pitifully inadequate door lock to the back alley, the other on Miss Elliott's now-smiling face, Mac did his best to hold his temper. He'd never been one to deal well with stupid civilians. It was much worse now. Much worse.

"No, you didn't call me," he said, making another try to catch her. "I saw it. Now, come on, before you get hurt."

"Hurt?" she echoed incredulously, looking around the pastel walls and the forest of real and artificial flowers in the little showroom. "Why would you think I'd be hurt?"

"Because somebody's trying to break into your store," he insisted.

Somewhere behind the pots of azaleas on the floor, there was a rustling. A faint hissing. Instinctively Mac spun on it, his gun up, his heart stumbling. The leaves dipped and his finger tightened around the trigger.

Nonchalant as hell, a cat stepped out of the foliage. Fat, nasty, and yellow-eyed, with a tail that stood straight up. Behind him were three more. Mac almost put six rounds straight into the goddamn things.

He tried his damnedest to get his breathing back

under control before he returned his attention to the matter at hand.

The matter at hand had her attention on his out-stretched arm.

"A gun," she accused, pointing at him. "Well, of course. Put that thing away, and we won't have any trouble, will we? After all, I didn't call you. I did not call the police."

Maybe this job wasn't going to work after all. The streets might be quieter, but the denizens certainly weren't any less loony. And the cats were beginning to circle him.

"Listen, Miss Elliott," Mac warned, struggling for control. "I'm not going to tell you again. Either get out of the store now, or I'm not going to be responsi-ble for your safety. You have somebody trying to break into your store."

Unbelievably, she broke into a big smile. "Why, yes," she said with a bright nod. "That's the whole idea, isn't it?"

The alley wasn't in Pyrite, it was in St. Louis. Up in the north end of town around Martin Luther King Drive, where the gang wars were waged. At midnight the streets would be quiet, eerily so, except for the constant ululation of sirens lifting at the corners of the tense night hours. The summer heat would collect close to the ground, pulling at you with clammy fin-gers, even late at night, sapping your energy, your patience. Way down at the end of the alley by the empty rowhouse, a lone surviving lamplight spilled slick rainbows into an oily puddle and betrayed the ragged-toothed devastation of the brick buildings.

The lock picks in her hands were slippery with her own sweat. She was doing her best to look non-chalant, a white woman alone in the worst part of town, just standing there next to a locked warehouse door as if that were a perfectly natural thing to do. If she were a man, she could at least pretend she was taking a leak. For a woman, it just looked like she was too drunk to stand up straight—or she was picking a lock.

Four pins. She heard them snick back into place when she let the tension go. Simple pin and tumbler, so that all she had to do was keep the pressure on, just a little, to rotate the lock, and rake the other pick over the pins, forcing them back above the shear line. Then, voilá, she'd be in.

Except that she'd been raking those damn pins for over seven minutes now. If she had really been in North St. Louis, she would have been caught and or dead five minutes ago. Thank God she was only doing it in Pyrite.

"Son of a bitch."

She let go once more, the pins clicking back down. Wiped her hands against her pants and took slow, careful breaths to ward away the unreasoning panic. It was too damn dark here. There were things rustling behind her in the corners, things Chris wouldn't see when she turned around. She rubbed at her face a little with a hand that shook. And then, her gaze turned to the half block of Pyrite she could see, she slid her picks back in and tried again.

Ed Williams was heading for his car from the Train Wreck Saloon across Main. Early for Ed. Usually he didn't amble home until after midnight, and that didn't take into account the nights of the Fraternal

Order of the Bisons' meeting. Guess he was going to miss another of Ed Junior's star turns at right forward.

"Come on, come on," she muttered irritably to the door, shifting weight. "Either open or I just pull out the Beretta and put a couple of rounds through you."

There wasn't even a snick. The lock just slid around to the right, as if it were the most natural thing to do. Chris took another quick look around and soundlessly levered the lock open. For the first time she allowed a smile of triumph. They couldn't get her now. She was in.

The door opened easily in her hand. Her crepe-soled shoes didn't make a sound as she eased through the door. She imagined that she was even the only one who heard the way her heart hammered with relief at the light.

Sucking in a very careful breath, she moved into the shop—and came to a dead halt. There facing her was a very upset man holding what appeared to be a Glock .40 semiautomatic in a regulation hold. The kind of two-handed hold that went with the uniform and the brand-new gold badge that was pinned to its chest.

Chris took a look at the barrel that was pointing right at her own not-very-considerable chest and let out another oath. "I guess I wasn't as good as I thought, huh, Eloise?"

Just behind the new police chief and to his right, Eloise managed a nervous little smile of apology. "I suppose not, dear."

"You were just about to tell me who you are," the officer said, not bothering to lower the gun.

Chris tried her best smile, even with a perfectly illegal set of lock picks in her upraised hands. Interesting man.

He was younger than she'd anticipated, still balancing right around forty, with a tall, rangy body and salt-and-pepper hair. Chris had heard someone's features described once as "fifty miles of bad road." That, she thought, would describe the new police chief. Except that his road had a very intriguing pothole in it, and not a very old one at that. A jagged, angry-looking scar traced his left temple from cheek to hairline, missing his noticeably unamused eye by a fraction of an inch.

"I'm Chris Jackson," Chris said, hands still carefully held where he could see them. "I, uh, live nearby."

"She owns the store," Eloise insisted, from the tone of her voice, not for the first time.

The chief never pulled his disconcertingly intense gray eyes from Chris's chagrined features. "Then why didn't you come in the front door?" he asked in a gentle voice that belied the steely attention he was paying her. "It was open."

Chris fought the urge to duck her gaze and dig a rueful toe into the tiled floor. "Because I'm practicing."

"Breaking and entering?"

"Is it breaking and entering if it's your own place of business?"

"Until you can better explain that set of lock picks, it is."

For the first time, Chris noticed that she wasn't the only one sweating here. The new chief had a definite sheen on his forehead. And his hands weren't as steady as they could have been. She took another look and saw that what she had mistaken for natural suspicion was anger, and wondered who was the target. Her or him?

"I bought them from a locksmith friend up in Farmington," she admitted. "He's the one who taught me the craft." That didn't seem to be making much of an impression. She tried the rest of the truth. "I'm an author."

Still no noticeable reaction, no easing of posture. "And?"

"And I've lived in Pyrite for the last five years. When I need to try something new for a book, the town lets me practice on it."

Only Chris seemed to notice the agitated nodding of Eloise's head, or the fact that even when Eloise moved with all that conviction, her hair didn't move.

"When Billy Johnson locked his keys in his foreign car last month, Chris was the only one who could get in for him," the little woman insisted. "And she rewired the Reverend Bobby Rayford's security system so she could get in any of his doors with the garage door opener. It was most amazing."

All that seemed to do was make the chief even more uncomfortable. "Handy, aren't you?"

"But harmless. Can you put that thing away, please?"

"Maybe when I see some identification."

Chris let out another sigh as she motioned to the black jumpsuit and knit cap she wore for camouflage. "I didn't carry a purse."

Chris thought she detected a hint of amusement. "No second-story man worth his salt goes out without some phony ID."

"Come on," she insisted, just a little unnerved by the deadly aim of that gun. "Do I look like a burglar . . ." Her protestation died a little when she considered the fact that she had, in fact, made it a point to look just like a burglar.

"It doesn't matter what you look like," he countered equably. "Some of the nastiest mopes I've met have looked like choirboys."

She did at least manage a new grin. "Which means that you could actually be a peeping tom with a badge fetish."

"Oh, no, dear," Eloise chimed in. "He's the police chief." Then she turned on the chief. "And she's the owner. I promise."

"Have you ever had a victim stand up for the perp?" Chris asked.

"All the time." Even so, the gun came up and the chief relaxed his posture. Chris figured it was about time to make those belated introductions she should have taken care of when the chief showed up in town.

"How about if I explain the whole thing over a cup of coffee?" she asked, pocketing the picks and pulling off the knit cap. "You have at least another half hour before anybody makes it back from the basketball game."

The chief hesitated a moment, his eyes zeroed in on hers, although Chris couldn't decide whether in judgment, consternation, or amusement. The chief seemed to keep his better emotions to himself. Finally, though, he holstered his gun and lifted his own cap to run a hand through his hair.

"If coffee'll help things make more sense," he obliged.

Chris nodded and held out her free hand. "Chris Jackson," she reintroduced herself. "I'd promised myself I was going to go by and warn you about Pyrite's nefarious secret right away, but I've been a little preoccupied."

He took her hand in an uncompromising grip, and Chris was damned if she didn't see a twinkle in those eyes. "Burglary'll do that. Al MacNamara."

"Welcome to town, Chief MacNamara." His palm was just as damp as hers, which intrigued Chris even more. Letting go, she turned toward the partitioned area behind the cash register. "Do you take anything in your coffee?"

She assumed he'd follow. He did.

"No, thanks."

"Eloise?"

Eloise waved from where she was bent back over the cash register. "I'm tallying receipts, dear. Go right ahead."

Much better to catch the best dirt from a safe distance, Chris knew. Eloise's head was tilted so that her hearing aid could pick up the conversation like a directional mike.

Chris fought a grin as she hefted a coffeepot that had been brewing since sometime before lunch. "Pyrite must be a change after Chicago, huh?"

The chief hooked a thumb in his belt. "Quieter."

Chris let go with a laugh that echoed all around the high ceilinged old building. "You," she accused, "are a master of understatement."

He accepted his mug and a seat after Chris cleared her tax receipts and one of the attack cats off it. Chris perched on the six inches of free space on her desk. Or rather, Eloise's desk. Chris made only nominal appearances at the How Do, even when she came in by the front door.

"You say you're an author?" MacNamara asked from behind his mug, his attention skipping restlessly around an area decorated in early wallboard and stock overrun.

"Card-carrying. It's kind of the town's little

secret. Nobody knows I live here, and I'd prefer it that way."

"Your pseudonym Stephen King?"

"No. C. J. Turner."

That provoked the most interesting reaction yet. Halfway to taking another sip of coffee, the chief left his mug hanging in midair as he let his gaze settle right back in on Chris.

"The suspense writer?"

She nodded, still uncomfortable with the astonishment that usually met that statement.

"I pictured you older," he admitted. "And a lot balder."

Chris offered a bright grin. "A misconception I work hard to encourage. I find it much easier to write if I don't have to deal with any of the little complications of, um, notoriety."

The chief took his sip of coffee, but his features didn't ease any. He didn't look away from Chris, either, which suddenly made her just a little nervous. She had a feeling she was well acquainted with other varieties of that look, and none of them had anything to do with fame or accomplishment.

"Is there a problem?"

He made it a point to finish his coffee before answering.

"Pyrite isn't exactly the place you'd expect to find a name like C. J. Turner. The book covers all say he lives in Taos."

"I drove through there once," Chris said, her voice hesitant. "I thought it would be a nice place to set an author."

But the chief was looking around the store. "Don't you have a phone?"

"I do here," she said, giving him his lead. "It has an answering machine I check at least once every couple of weeks whether it needs it or not."

He nodded, almost as if coming to some conclusion as he stroked at his upper lip with two fingers, an instinctive action of concentration. Chris wondered distractedly how long it had been since he'd shaved off his mustache.

"At least it makes sense now," he said almost to himself.

She did her best to remain polite as the first tendrils of dread curled through her. After passing acquaintance with bad news, she'd developed an unerring instinct for it. Her tolerance for it wasn't nearly as good.

The chief returned his attention to her. "Call came in about you today. I thought it was a mistake."

Chris saw something she didn't like at all behind those experienced eyes.

"A call?"

As if it had been choreographed, his walkie-talkie sputtered to life.

"Dispatch to the chief, come in."

With an apologetic look at Chris, he unclipped the small mike from his shirt pocket and answered. "MacNamara here."

Chris saw Eloise lean over a little to hear better. Eloise had a police scanner at home and watched every true crime show on television. Chris knew it was because she'd never experienced violence firsthand that the little woman found it so fascinating secondhand. For Chris's part, she could only hold onto her fraying patience as tightly as she did the cooling mug of coffee in her hand.

"Wilson just called in, sir," Tina Elcorn's voice rasped from the receiver on the chief's belt. "He walked into a fight up at the Tip A Few."

MacNamara only allowed a brief tightening of his features to betray his irritation. "Well, tell him to handle it."

"There are ten of them and one of him."

Down went the cup. "On my way. Get the sheriff to back him up."

He reclipped the mike and turned back for the front door.

"I thought it was going to be quiet here," he groused, raking a hand through his hair before resettling his cap as he stalked past the wide-eyed Eloise.

Chris followed right on his heels. "You must have us confused with Utopia," she offered dryly. "It's a couple of counties over."

MacNamara turned to her with the closest thing he seemed to have to a smile. "Mayor Sullins told me the town went weeks without anything happening."

"He's talking about real estate, not stupidity."

Chris lasted until MacNamara opened the front door. Maybe he was already thinking about something else, but she wasn't.

"Chief MacNamara."

A chilly evening breeze snaked in. MacNamara turned just shy of leaving. "Oh, yeah," he said, stopping, his body already geared up for whatever waited for him up across the tracks. "I'm sorry. The call. Seems there's a homicide detective from St. Louis looking to talk to you."

Chris fought to hold onto the cup in her suddenly cold hands. "Homicide?" she asked, her voice carefully neutral, the dread exploding straight into panic.

He nodded. "Name of Lawson. Seems to think

somebody up there copycatted one of your books."

Chris wasn't sure what she'd been expecting him to say. Any number of things, actually. There was so much out there he could have brought to her. That one, though, was probably the single problem she hadn't expected. It froze her into incredulity.

"Copycatting?" she demanded, struggling to catch up. "Like murder?"

"Like murder. She'd appreciate a call as soon as you can so she can compare notes."

He didn't even bother to say good-bye, just loped on down the sidewalk to where his unit was parked. Watching him go from the open doorway, Chris was left with a feeling of stunned disbelief.

"Son of a bitch," she breathed, wedging the coffee cup against a chest that was suddenly tight with surprise. Shutting the door, she slumped against it and gave a little laugh, and was embarrassed to admit it was from relief.

✦ Chapter 2 ✦

THE HIGH SCHOOL basketball team lost that evening, so Pyrite went to bed early. By eleven the only traffic consisted of an occasional parent looking for a late teen, and by one o'clock, it was just Curtis Marshall's police cruiser crisscrossing the empty streets when he wasn't parked over in the Baptist church lot dozing in between calls. Only street lamps illuminated the silent square, and even the Tip a Few was closed and darkened, the earlier contestants either home or nestled down in the county jail down behind the sheriff's office. Most everyone except the sheriff's dispatcher and the night man at the Sleep Well Motel out on Highway V was asleep. Everyone, that is, except Chris Jackson.

By now the town was used to seeing her lights on all night long. Everybody knew that Chris wrote at night. It seemed appropriate, after all, a mystery writer keeping such odd hours. And it wasn't like you couldn't get hold of Chris during the day if you really needed to. She was usually up and around the town bright and early. Girl just never had needed sleep much, from all accounts.

Sometimes she kept the shades up so that neighbors could tap a hello on the way by. Sometimes, like tonight, she kept them down to signify that she was preoccupied.

She was preoccupied all right. She just wasn't writing.

Chris was pacing. From one end of the open, hardwood floor to the other as the stereo gave forth Metallica and the seagull-and-Cessna mobile that hung from the balcony swung lazily above her head, she measured her steps as carefully as she did her thoughts.

The sense of relief at the chief's news hadn't lasted long. Even if he hadn't exactly hand-delivered disaster to her door, the danger was still there.

She was going to have to call that St. Louis cop in the morning. She was going to have to call her editor, who had evidently gotten the notice about the possible murder even before Chief MacNamara, and had been leaving frantic messages on the machine for the last twenty-four hours.

Trey Peterson didn't handle that kind of surprise well. Come to think of it, Trey didn't handle any kind of surprise well, which was why his voice had sounded so panicked on the answering machine. If he'd been thinking, he'd have realized that from a purely mercenary standpoint, if someone really had decided to act out one of Chris's books, it would do nothing but boost Chris's sales. The public relations department at Helm Carlson Publications would express public dismay, and then party when the doors were closed. Trey would be interviewed as a stand-in for his reclusive author, and the world would never question the distress in the handsome young editor's eyes. And within ten minutes the order would go out to reprint every one of Chris's back titles, with particular attention paid to the lucky winner of the atrocity look-alike contest.

And Chris, her privacy so religiously protected through five surprise best-sellers, could very well find her anonymity a quaint footnote in history. The press that had so long wondered about the mysterious author would have a great excuse to camp out at the St. Louis police headquarters, looking for leaks, casting about for C. J. Turner like diviners in search of water. Research departments would chug into high gear digging up every bit of trivia they could find about the mysterious recluse to go with the unfolding story. Eventually somebody would find his way to Pyrite.

To her.

Damn it, anyway.

Chris took a turn through to her kitchen to pop a can of soda, and then headed back out into the living room to raise the sound level just a little on the CD player. She was overreacting, she knew it. It was just one call. One possible murder. One detective with maybe an overactive imagination.

After all, Chris couldn't think of any reason someone would want to pull a stunt like that. She wasn't exactly Elvis, with impersonators showing up at nightclubs everywhere. The press usually relegated her to the eccentrics and oddballs file, and her readers had never struck her as the type to be quite so slavishly devoted they'd flatter her with imitation—at least, she didn't think so.

The vast majority of letters she got from readers were sane, mostly polite, and often enough complimentary. Not one, even the ones from state penitentiaries, had ever expressed a desire to emulate her work. A few wanted to have her baby, and one particular man had expressed a desire to smell her shoes, but that wasn't exactly a class A felony. At least in most states.

All right, so some of the people in her life weren't exactly running on all eight cylinders, but that didn't put them into the psychopathic pool either.

The morning was going to come, and she was going to call that detective up in St. Louis to find out it was all a big, stupid mistake. Not oleander poisoning at all, she'd say with a hearty laugh. It wasn't even the right author. The person she'd meant to get hold of was this Christie character. Know where she lives?

Chris looked at the great-grandfather clock that dominated the front foyer, a grotesque old thing from Germany with sonorous chimes and carved around the face the contorted visages of gnomes that bore a striking resemblance to the CEO of Helm Carlson. If only it were already morning. She was sane in the daylight, reasonable. She could laugh at Trey's distress and defuse the enthusiasm of the detective. She could at least enjoy the absurdity of the situation.

But it was the night, and Chris didn't survive the night well.

Abruptly she whirled around and cranked up the volume on Metallica again so that the crash of frantic music could flood out the stale itch of fear that had taken root in her chest.

It was going to be all right. She'd worked too damn hard for her peace of mind to offer it up because one gung-ho cop had an overactive imagination. She'd achieved a hell of a lot on simple guts and elbow grease. It was going to take more than one lousy phone call to sabotage it.

Chris even managed a smile at that, tilting her head back to drain the last of her soda as James Hetfield shrieked over her head about love and madness. Yeah, she thought, it should be easy. It should if the sun would just come up a little early. If she could just ignore that bubble of anxiety in her chest that had been stealthily growing the past few weeks and months. If she could know for sure that the nightmares were only beginning to resurface because she was tired.

The first time the doorbell rang, Chris didn't even notice. She was standing in the center of the bright, white room, her head back, letting the avalanche of drums and guitar bury her. Heavy metal wasn't music, it was pulverization, and that was just what she needed right now.

The second time, the sound was more insistent. Chris looked over at the grandfather clock.

Who could be stopping by at this hour? Pyrite wasn't exactly the place for all-night socials, and besides, everybody knew better than to bother her when the shades were down. It was the corollary to the rule that if the town kept her secrets, she'd keep theirs.

"Chris, please," the high-pitched young voice hissed.

Chris took another instinctive look at the clock, and her mood fell even farther. Damn, this could only mean one thing, and she wasn't sure she was up to dealing with it tonight. Well, at least it would take her mind off phone calls.

She opened the door to find a wan, dishwater-blond in jeans and an oversized leather jacket standing out on the sidewalk. At first sight, the girl just looked skittish, the way any fifteen year old might, caught out after curfew. Instinct directed Chris's attention to the new bruise along the girl's jaw.

"Come on in, honey," she said, and ushered her inside. She didn't mention the discoloration. That would have pushed the girl right back out into the night.

"I know your shades are down . . ."

"You caught me in the middle of a break. Come on in and have a Coke."

As she guided Shelly over to one of the overstuffed couches that bracketed the freestanding Franklin stove, Chris took a second to regroup. Like a mental exercise, a deliberate realignment. Shove her problem back into the shadows where it belonged right now, shuffle Shelly's forward. Mental doors opened and shut, Metallica off, Debussy on, and Chris settled down to business.

"Did you go to the game tonight?" she asked as she walked on through to rummage in her depleted refrigerator for another soda and grab a half-opened bag of chips from the counter.

"It was a bust," Shelly answered in that tight little voice that betrayed so much.

Chris wondered who had hit her this time. Tossing the bag of chips onto the brass-and-glass coffee table, she handed off the soda and took her own seat in the black leather-and-chrome rocker by the couch. It wouldn't do any good to bring it up. All Chris could do was offer asylum and hope for the best. Again. She knew the game plan much too well by now to either expect more or settle for less.

She waited. It was what was needed with Shelly. Patience and circumspection. Silence. Chris's house was the DMZ in Shelly's life. The compromise between what Chris should have been able to do for the girl and what she'd managed. There was just no lesson like the one about what could happen to a person who accused the judge who controlled most of the county of hitting his little girl. And if there was one thing Chris prided herself on, it was the fact that she only had to learn her lessons once. So she balanced her soda can on her knee and waited for the rest.

"Bobby Lee was supposed to be high scorer, ya know," Shelly finally offered, watery blue eyes focused on her hands where they clutched her own soda can in her lap. Her nails were bitten so badly that her fingers bled. "He was printed up in the *Dispatch* and everything."

The grandfather clock ticked its way toward the conclusion Chris had already reached. Bobby Lee was Shelly's current boyfriend, an impatient, immature headbanger who was looking to take his place on the next turn on the never-ending cycle of violence in Shelly's life.

"I . . . I guess he just had a bad night."

He'd had a bad night all over Shelly. Chris fought the urge to shake the girl until she rattled, the same urge she checked every time the girl made the same mistakes, got herself into the same trouble and then whined her way to a rationalization that would keep her right where she was.

Chris knew all about it. She knew just how the cycle worked, how it fed on itself, and finally fed on the women born and raised in it. It didn't ease her frustration in the face of it. It did keep her from venting it. Instead she focused her own attention on the balcony fifteen feet over Shelly's head where a chorus line of oversized stuffed bears sat with their legs sticking out into the air between mahogany spindles.

"You don't want the judge seeing you tonight," was the most she could say, thinking of those bears. Of the comfort of stuffed animals that never demanded, never hurt, never disappointed. Wishing she could at least offer Shelly that, and knowing it would never be enough anymore.

Shelly let loose with a harsh bark of laughter that seemed almost obscene on such a frail, hesitant girl. "The judge could care less. Except that he can't stand the idea of me havin' a say about anything I do."

Her jaw was clenched now. Her fingers dug at the aluminum until there were a series of dents along the side of the half-full can. Shelly, the once-shy, caregiving younger daughter, the child her mother had always dressed for church and sent along with suppers for sick neighbors. Shelly, raised to be a victim to yet another man who'd beat her. Shelly was going to blow like a pressure cooker one of these days. Chris knew. She just hoped she could be handy to diffuse some of that deadly anger once it let loose.

Finally, Shelly looked over, and Chris was privileged to the silent tears no one else in town saw. It was a burden she sorely wished she could have escaped.

"Why can't I have a nice family like other people?" the girl whispered. "Amy's family looks wonderful. And Krystal's. And you're so normal and everything, ya know?"

Chris could only offer her a sad smile. "Nothing's the way it seems, honey. Just because somebody acts happy doesn't mean they're any less miserable than you. Don't envy anybody."

"Would you mind if I stayed?" the girl asked, sounding so much like a child it should break a person's heart.

Her heart particularly susceptible, Chris gave Shelly her best smile. "I'd mind if you didn't. As long as the lights being on all night doesn't bother you."

Shelly was already getting to her feet so she could make up one of the couches. "Never does."

Chris got the linen.

"Hear you got some interesting news tonight," Shelly said over her shoulder as she unfolded the couch into a bed.

Her hands full of sheets, Chris came to a stop. She guessed she shouldn't be surprised anymore. The grapevine in this town put CNN to shame. Two years ago Thelma Potter over at the EasyLube had known that Chris's second book had made *The New York Times* best-seller list before Chris did. Last year when her house had been broken into, she'd been tracked down way out on an isolated promontory on Preacher's Mountain within forty minutes to get her home.

Even so, she demurred a while longer. "All I know is that I have to call the police department up in St. Louis," she said, shaking out the sheet. "Probably a parking ticket they're trying to get me for from the last time I was up there."

Now that she'd found haven, Shelly decided to thoroughly enjoy the salacious news. "I heard there's a serial killer after you," she informed Chris, her plain face lighting with almost unholy glee. "And that the new police chief—have you *seen* him—offered protection."

"You're going to have to stop seeing those slasher movies, Shel. It's not healthy."

Chris was surprised to see Shelly go still, the pillow she'd brought in clutched tight in white-knuckled hands. "Nobody's gonna hurt you, Chris," the girl said, her eyes glittering oddly. "Nobody. I'd never let them."

For just the briefest of moments, Chris couldn't quite pull together a snappy retort. There they were, alone in her house, the clocks echoing in gentle syncopation beneath the high tin roof that had once covered a general store, the bears looking down with smiling, friendly faces, the setting comfortable and familiar. She shouldn't have felt so suddenly unsettled.

"Honey," she insisted, her voice as soft as Shelly's, just as serious. "Nobody's trying to hurt me."

Shelly's face twisted, just a little. "If you weren't who you are," she said, her voice in deadly earnest, "the judge would have had you by the throat two years ago."

All Chris could do was give her an unconcerned smile. "Well," she retorted as easily as she could, knowing just how true what Shelly said was, "that's why I am who I am. Now, let's get you to bed."

They didn't get the chance. Just as Shelly was heading into the bathroom with an oversized T-shirt Chris kept as a spare nightgown, the doorbell rang again. And again, Chris looked over at the grandfather clock.

"Is there an Open sign on the front door?" she demanded, soda can back in hand as she walked toward the noise.

"Maybe it's Bobby Lee," Shelly whispered, frozen in place.

"If it is, I'll just tell him to go home."

Again, that harsh, too-knowing laugh.

"If you're worried," Chris suggested, hand already on the door, "then wait in the bathroom."

Shelly straightened to attention right where she was. Chris fought a sigh. It was too typical, showing bravery in a no-lose situation. The next time Shelly was alone with Bobby Lee, she'd let him pay her back, just like her father had always done, and nothing would be different.

"What if it's the killer?" Shelly asked now.

"I'll tell him to go home, too."

It wasn't Bobby Lee. It wasn't, as far as Chris knew, the killer. It was the new police chief. She was so surprised to see him standing out in the puddle of light on the sidewalk that Chris found herself caught flat-footed, her hand still on the door. The brisk night air swirled through the screen and raised goose-bumps on her bare legs.

He didn't actually smile. "Tina said you stayed up late."

Chris lifted her hand in an ineffectual wave at convention. "Can I, uh, do something for you?" Then her natural curiosity got the better of her. "What are *you* still doing up?"

He was still in his uniform, too, the white shirt as crisp and creased as if he'd walked right off a recruitment poster. His predecessor, old L. J. Watson, had always carried at least three of his last meals on his uniform shirt, and had blotted reports with his tie.

"I wanted to spend a little time with all three

shifts," he said, not quite standing square on his feet, as if balanced to react. Tensed, even in the middle of the night in Pyrite. "And since Tina said you probably wouldn't mind, I thought I'd give you the note about that situation in St. Louis on my way home. So you can get in touch with them."

He was doing his best to keep his attention on her face but, like everybody who came to Chris's house for the first time, it seemed he couldn't help letting his gaze stray over her shoulder. Chris couldn't exactly blame him. She never had opted for the conventional, and now that she could afford it, she was able to satisfy all her whims. And appease her phobias.

"Come on in," she invited, pushing open the screen door.

He didn't hesitate. When he reached her entryway, his head went right back to take in the stamped ceiling some thirty feet over his head, and he laughed. "Well, they told me."

Chris looked after him, knowing that what she saw was different than what he did. He probably saw the huge rectangular room that had once comprised Pyrite's General Mercantile and now held her living and dining area, the balcony fifteen feet up that edged all four walls with workspace and bedroom, the mahogany cases that had once sported dry goods, and the new two-story greenhouse out the back that served as kitchen and extra dose of sunlight while she worked. Now the addition was shaded like all the other windows, and the track lighting ruled.

"What's your electric bill like?" he asked, eyes following the high white walls back down to glossy hardwood floors.

Chris smiled, hands on hips, seeing every corner in her big, bright house. Seeing the shadows evicted. It still didn't always help, but it was better than anything she'd had before. "Not all mystery writers yearn to live in gothic towers," she said. "I happen to like bright, open spaces."

"It's really excellent," Shelly spoke up from where she stood at the bathroom door. Clad only in the oversized T-shirt that brushed the tops of her thighs, she presented a totally different picture than the waif who'd landed on Chris's doorstep.

Chris went right into action. If there was one thing she could depend on from Shelly, it was inappropriate behavior. Chris was halfway across the floor before either Shelly or the Chief could comment.

"Back inside," she commanded. "The front door's still open."

"But I want to say hello." Shelly pouted, suddenly looking older than her fifteen years, her attention on Chris's latest guest.

A confused adolescent was a dangerous beast. Especially one who'd been abused. Shelly had no idea how to act around men, which was why she ended up with dates like Bobby Lee.

"Say hello," Chris instructed, standing foursquare in front of her and blocking her view of MacNamara and vice versa, "and then get your little butt back in that bathroom or the deal's off."

For just the briefest of moments, Chris was exposed to the anger, the blind, flashing fury that bubbled beneath the surface of that troubled, painfully uncertain child. Fear, shame, hurt, all chased quickly across Shelly's expressive features before she capitulated with no more than a shrug. "Hello, Chief.

I'm Shelly Axminster. Chris says I can't stay to visit."
Then she leaned around Chris and flashed the chief
her best smile. "Maybe later."

To his credit, MacNamara refused the bait. "Hello,
Shelly. If you don't mind, I need to talk to Chris for a
minute."

"Oh, about that mad killer thing," Shelly gushed,
eyes wide, leaning farther around Chris, her expression avid. "Is he headed this way? Are you staying
tonight to protect us?"

Chris grabbed the girl by the shoulders and swung
her back toward the bathroom. "There's plenty of
stuff to read in there. Take a bath if you want. If you
come out before I come in to get you, you've lost
your visitation rights here. Understood?"

That almost pretty face teetered on the edge of
rebellion for just a second before crumbling into submission. "Tyrant."

Chris stood before the door until she heard the click
of the lock. Then she turned back to the chief with a
rueful smile. "I can offer diet soda or regular soda.
Anything else has to wait until my next run to the
store."

He waved a dismissal. "No, thanks. I just wanted to
give you a name and phone number anyway." His
voice dropped just a little. "Judge Axminster's daughter?"

Chris walked on past him to close the front door.
"Sometimes when a kid doesn't get along with her
parents, it's nice for them to know she has a safe
place to go."

She stopped alongside the chief long enough to
get a careful reaction. "Diplomatically stated," was all
he would allow, which meant he had learned a lot

during his first day on the job.

Chris shrugged. "Words are my life."

In her own house, Chris had no problem setting the pace. It didn't bother her that MacNamara needed a few minutes to acclimate to her atmosphere, or that he'd dropped in unexpectedly at two in the morning. As long as he didn't expect her to venture out at this time of night. As long as he didn't demand any explanations she couldn't give.

Unbuttoning his breast pocket, he pulled out a piece of paper. "Sgt. Elise Lawson," he said. "And not the St. Louis Police. It's St. Louis County. The way she talked, I take it there's a big difference."

Chris nodded, already distracted, the sense of impending doom growing again. "The city's independent of the county. It's two separate government systems completely." As he handed over the paper, she filled in the rest for the chief, who had obviously never partaken of C. J. Turner. If he had, he would have already been familiar with St. Louis politics. "My suspenses have all been set in St. Louis County. They feature a psychic English professor, Dr. Livvy Beckworth, and a county detective, Sgt. Frank Stephens."

"St. Louis doesn't really strike me as a film noir kind of town."

Chris tried to smile as she accepted the folded paper and turned toward the furniture grouping in the center of the floor. "You'd be amazed what goes on up there. Did Lawson say why she thought there was a copycat?" she asked, settling instinctively into the rocker, pushing off with her feet.

The chief followed her, but didn't take up a place on the couch. "She mentioned *Hell Hath No Fury*." He was reaching into another pocket when his hand stilled and he looked around.

"Ashtray's on the top of the jukebox," Chris said, her attention on the paper in her hand. "That's the book?" It didn't make any sense. It still didn't make her feel any better.

Instead of going for the ashtray, he settled on the arm of the couch, his fingers straying back to his upper lip. "It's the only one she mentioned."

Chris looked up. "I wouldn't have an ashtray in the house if I minded smoke," she prodded gently.

His scowl was rueful. It made him look more human than his smiles had so far. "I try not to smoke on the job anymore."

"I'm trying to lay off caffeine," Chris countered dryly. "I'm having about as much luck."

"Chris!" came the plaintive cry from the bathroom.

"Read chapter two!" she retorted.

The response was unladylike and imaginative enough to make Chris chuckle. "She really is a good kid," she said. "She wants to be a juvenile social worker. I'm trying to talk her into business school."

"You don't like social workers?"

"I don't think there's any future in it. Lousy pay, worse hours, impossible caseload. It's like being a cop, except you can't shoot back. Unfortunately people who grow up with problems think they can solve them by helping somebody else, and it doesn't work." For just a minute, Chris looked over to the closed bathroom door and thought of the weight of perception. Then she turned back to the chief. "Don't take her advances seriously, and never take them alone."

He seemed surprised, whether by the opinion or

the warning Chris wasn't sure. Even so, he thanked her for the advice. In return she thanked him for the information.

"You'll let me know?" he asked. "When you talk to Lawson. I'd be happy to help."

Chris gave in to a small grin. "Already too quiet for you?" she asked.

He was gentleman enough to smile back. "It will never be too quiet here for me."

"Mind my asking a question?"

He didn't move. Didn't so much as stiffen. Even so, Chris saw the sudden retreat. Minute contractions of the muscles around his mouth, an eerie stillness to his eyes that betrayed his reaction even before she asked the question that was meant to follow.

She immediately wanted to apologize, to ask him to forget she'd spoken, because, of course, he knew. He knew that she'd want more from him than anyone else who would ask about that scar that puckered the side of his face. Other people would be curious about simple logistics. What, where, when, how, why. But Chris was different. She'd want to know implication, impact. She'd mine the darkness beneath that careful wince to know what that scar had to do with his running from Chicago for a place like Pyrite. What the cost had been to his courage, his self-image, his pride. And Chris wouldn't need words for her answer.

It was a place Chris had no right to invade. It was the secret to her writing that she could so easily see in when others couldn't. She sometimes forgot that it was an intrusion.

She'd already raised her hand, ready to rescind her request, when the doorbell rang. Again.

Again Chris checked the grandfather clock. This time Chief MacNamara did it with her.

"Well, hell," Chris groused, climbing to her feet. "That's probably Sergeant Lawson now."

"If that's Bobby Lee," Shelly called, her voice echoing faintly. "I'm not here."

"If it's Bobby Lee," Chris reminded her, "the police chief's here. You won't have to worry about a thing."

The police chief grimaced. "I'm off duty."

Chris waved off his objection. "If you were off duty, you'd be smoking."

It still wasn't Bobby Lee. This time it was Victor and Lester, Chris's next door neighbor. Neighbors.

"Are you all right?" Lester demanded in his high, childish lisp.

Chris battled back a delighted chuckle. This was beginning to look like a conspiracy to keep her mind off her problems.

"I'm fine," she reassured with a sincere smile, but for Victor, whose big brown eyes were wide with worry. "What are you doing out this late, Victor?"

"And Lester," the dummy insisted.

Chris gave in and looked at the dummy nestled in the crook of Victor's left arm. "And Lester."

"We saw the police chief here," Victor finally spoke, his own voice a softer, kinder version of the dummy's. "We wanted to make sure you were OK."

Chris pushed open the screen door. Well, if MacNamara wanted to find out about the town he'd inherited with that gold badge, he couldn't have visited on a better night. "Come on in and ask him yourself."

By the time Chris turned to make introductions,

MacNamara was back on his feet. In fact, he was over by the jukebox retrieving that ashtray. She didn't blame him.

"Police Chief MacNamara, I'd like to introduce you to my neighbor . . . s. Victor Marshall and the incomparable Lester."

MacNamara looked hard-pressed for tact. Chris could read every one of the reactions crossing his mind, every instinctive crack and comment he battled as he studied the frail, serious young man who stood before him holding the red-haired, freckle-faced dummy. All the chief allowed, though, was a fairly controlled, "Nice to meet you."

Chris allowed herself to relax.

"We heard about you," Lester announced, his round hand-painted head bobbing as if in examination.

Chief MacNamara kept an admirably straight face. "Did you?"

This time Victor nodded. "We've always wanted to go to Chicago. Do some of the clubs there. We're up in St. Louis all the time, but it's so provincial there, they just didn't understand our humor. You know what I mean?"

The chief seemed reduced to nodding. Chris did her best to keep a straight face. He was really getting it with both barrels tonight, and he hadn't even met Miss Harmonia Mae Switzer yet.

"Victor has been studying ventriloquism since he was ten," Chris said, wishing, as she did every time she saw Victor, that she could sneak him into one of her books. Considering the fact that he could quote each one chapter and verse better than the Reverend Mister Bobby Rayford could the Bible, it would have been like sneaking Russian words into The Star Spangled Banner." "He's been trying to find an agent who'll handle him . . . and Lester."

"I think it's because Lester looks so much like Ron Howard," Victor said quickly, as he always did. "I was actually trying to make him look like Holden Caulfield, because, of course, he *is* the quintessential young man. I'm afraid, though, he ended up looking like Opie Taylor. A more identifiable social figure, I suppose. But I think agents object to the similarities. Like he might get mad. But he wouldn't. I've written him about it on numerous occasions. And, of course, I've consulted with my good friend Chris." Both of them looked over to her. Only Victor smiled. "Because, of course, she's famous, too—"

"You asshole!" Lester immediately protested, the voice scathing. "That's a secret!"

Victor swung those liquid eyes Chris's way.

"The chief knows," she assured them gently.

It actually looked as if both of them sighed in relief. "Well, that's good," Victor said with a bright smile for Chief MacNamara. "That means you can help us all keep her identity safe. It's quite a job sometimes, you know."

The chief was already taking his first drag off an unfiltered cigarette. "I'll bet."

"She's most ingenious," Victor enthused, now warming to his subject. "Would you care to read her reviews some time? I have them in my home next door."

The chief was going to demur. Lester didn't let him. "My home?" he shrieked. "*My* home? Listen, you dickhead, who's the one who pays the bills?"

Victor damn near crumbled into a little pile. Another of Chris's legacies. Lester saved all the interesting stuff for her.

"Excuse him," Victor begged. "He's had a bad day."

"Can't I even say hi to Lester?" Shelly demanded.

Chris was beginning to get a headache. "He can hear you fine from there."

Greetings were summarily exchanged, and Victor eased himself and Lester back outside. Just to be sure, before she shut the door again Chris took a quick glance up and down the sidewalk. No more company from the looks of it. The only porchlight on was hers, and the police cruiser was darkened and still over on the church parking lot. She wondered if Curtis's chief knew.

"I should probably be going as well," he said from behind her.

Chris didn't close the door after all. "You're sure? Give me five minutes and I can probably scare up the town librarian and a couple of Hell's Angels."

"Not for my benefit, thanks." He stubbed out the half-smoked cigarette in the ashtray, a lumpish green remnant from the ceramics class Eloise had taken after seeing *Ghost*. "Is this the way your nights all go?"

Leaning against the open door, Chris took a contemplative look out toward the silent, darkened street. "Usually I'm the only vampire in town. But Lester worries about me."

The chief stopped alongside her, his own gaze following hers pretty closely. "Lester?"

"And Victor."

That brought him to a bit of headshaking. "He's . . . uh . . ."

"Always been like that," Chris said. "Nobody's seen those two apart for the last ten years. But since Victor's mama left him about half a million dollars, it doesn't seem to matter much."

The chief leveled a slightly bemused look at her. "A lot of material in this town for a book, huh?"

Chris chuckled. "Yeah, but I'd have to wait until they're all dead to publish it."

Still standing there, the chilly night air carrying in the last taste of winter, the two of them went on considering the town outside. The chief finally gave his head one last shake.

"Well, it's unique, I'll give you that."

"And you haven't even seen the Mobile Home Hall of Fame yet, have you?"

There didn't seem to be any appropriate response to that, so the chief just pushed open the screen door. It creaked egregiously, startling somebody's dog down the street.

"I appreciate your stopping by," Chris said. "I'll call Sergeant Lawson tomorrow and let you know what she says."

MacNamara made it almost all the way out before he stopped. "You could do me one favor."

"If you want to book Victor and Lester, you'll have to call them yourself. They do a great Good Cop-Bad Cop routine."

Another scowl, this one a beauty. "I was wondering if you had a copy of *Hell Hath No Fury* I could borrow."

"Chris!"

"Chapter three!" Chris yelled over her shoulder, then turned back to her guest. "You don't want me to just tell you who did it? I happen to be in a good position to know."

Maybe she was the only one who tended toward manic humor along about three in the morning. The chief was just looking tired. Chris noticed his hand stray not to his lip, but his temple to worry at the scar.

"I've never read C. J. Turner," he admitted. "I thought I should at least be conversant with the subject."

"You probably read nonfiction," Chris said. "And occupational magazines."

"Nope."

Chris waited a second for elaboration, but she just wasn't going to get it. Not one for self-exposure, the chief. "Well, I'm crushed that you've missed out on such a wonderful experience," she said, "but I'd be happy to rectify the omission. Hang on."

C. J. Turner lived in the far corner of the balcony with volumes on forensics research, penal codes, first aid and toxicology, and a giant jar of jelly beans. Chris trotted up to C. J.'s corner and unearthed a box of books in the bottom cabinet.

"*Hell Hath No Fury,*" she announced, returning to hand it off to the still bemused policeman. "The story of what finally happens when a long-suffering wife is pushed too far. I'm really sorry if this is the murder they're talking about. It wasn't one of my neater ones."

The chief looked down at the stylized dust jacket, a geometric pattern in fuscia, blue, and black. "I'll let you know how I like it," he said, lifting it a bit in final salutation.

Chris finally managed to get him outside. The house was fifteen degrees cooler, and she was in shorts. And God only knew who else was waiting out there to knock on her door in search of some kind of help.

Injured puppies, she thought suddenly. I collect bruised people like some people pick up injured puppies. A gift. A curse. One of these nights, she just wasn't going to answer the door.

"Good night, Chief."

He nodded one last time as he climbed into his cruiser. "Good night, Miss Jackson."

Out of long habit, Chris waited until he got his car started before turning away. Once she did, though, she just stood there a moment, head now throbbing steadily, the soda her only nourishment since about lunchtime. She looked toward the bathroom and considered what lay inside. Considered what lurked in the corners of her very deliberately renovated house. Considered the fictitious mayhem she would be much happier escaping into than the misery that waited on the ,other side of that door, or, for that matter, the other side of the dawn.

"Come on out," she called and then sighed. She might as well get it over with so she could go back to work. After all, it was a cinch she wasn't going to get any sleep tonight, either. Climbing back up into her loft, Chris collected the stuffed bear who shared her work chair with her and nestled it tight against her chest before heading back to face Shelly.

✦ *Chapter 3* ✦

She was crouched in the corner of the bath-room, huddled against the safety of the cool tile wall, curled so tightly into herself that maybe she couldn't see what her life had become. So she couldn't see in the mirror what she'd become, so long beaten down, so pummeled by fists and feet and words that she wasn't recognizable any-more. He'd find her. He always would. He'd beat her so badly she couldn't leave the house for a week, then beg her forgiveness.

And like every other time, she'd give it . . .

Slipping a marker in the book, Mac shut it and dropped it on the table. He hadn't gotten to the murder yet, but he had a pretty good guess what it was going to be. He'd seen murders with scenarios just like this one. Wife abused so long that she decides there's only one way out. Self-protection all mixed up with desperation and rage, leaving behind a corpse that usually looked like bad hamburger and a perpetrator who met the police at the door with a watery smile.

She had it down, too. The setting, the psychology,

41

the rank smell of futility. He was impressed. No wonder the critics liked her so much. No wonder she'd
been lauded in *Newsweek* and *The Trib* as the new
Chandler.

Mac pulled his cigarettes back out and lit one up.
It was so late by now that the only television on was
the cable shopping network. Even so, he had it on.
The house he was renting from Judge Axminster was
small, boxy, and uninspiring. He'd hung a couple of
Chicago posters in the living room and arranged his
kids' school pictures on his dresser with the shot
they'd taken at Francis's diner the day the other dicks
had sent him off. Even so, it wasn't any more a home
than the efficiency he'd rented on the South Side
after the divorce. A place to hang your hat in
between shifts, same kind of living quarters as most
of the cops he'd hung around with.

He rubbed the beer can against his temple, the
cool easing the constant burning. Mac hated new
places. He'd been born and raised in Chicago, a
product of generations of Chicago cops. His father
had driven for Mayor Daley and his mother had tat-
ted altercloths for Sacred Heart's. He'd gone on his
first drunk over at the old Emerald Isle and been suspended from school for cutting class to attend Cubs
games. The last time he'd left home, it had been for
Vietnam, and look what a success that had been.

But when you can't do the job, you don't hang
around and attend your own wake. So here he was,
five hundred miles away, soothing his shakes with
too much beer and too little activity.

He had no business itching after the C. J. Turner
puzzle. After all, it was St. Louis County's call. He
hadn't been invited to dance. He knew better than to

butt in, especially after getting a load of Sgt. Elise Lawson's voice on the phone. A real little ball-buster, that one. Jayne Wayne with an attitude. She'd come down on him with hobnailed boots if she thought he was even sniffing around her collar.

It didn't matter a whole lot. He was already interested. After all, it was what he'd done for ten years. He could be the police chief of Pyrite until the day they dropped him six feet under, and he'd still be a Chicago detective. It was what he'd been good at and what he'd missed when he left. And the single factor that had made the difference on his arrest and conviction record had been the fact that his curiosity was insatiable.

He finished his beer and tossed the can to join the others. The woman in Chris Jackson's book had probably had a kitchen just like this one, he thought morosely. Old and scarred and weary looking. The woman in Chris Jackson's book would have called the cops eight or nine times to get her husband off her, only to change her mind when it came time to press charges. She'd want him stopped, but not jailed. She'd be terrified of him in a rage, but even more terrified of him not there at all. Until that moment when she couldn't take any more. Maybe he'd hit on the kids, or started looking at her little sister. Maybe a friend prodded her to do something about that asshole that made life such hell for her, and he'd found out and beat her all over again, threatening to find her wherever she was and kill her if she left him. Kill her and all the kids. And she'd believe him, because it was probably true. So she'd wait until he was asleep and sneak up on him and pull the trigger, or plunge in the knife so many times he couldn't be recognized, just to make sure he couldn't still get up and hurt her. Just to pay him back for all the pain. Just to finally, finally stop him.

How had Chris Jackson known? How could somebody who lived in a converted hundred-year-old mercantile that smelled like potpourri and had porcelain teapots cluttering old sales cases and bears ringing the balcony, possibly know what it was like to be that desperate?

It was one of the things that intrigued Mac so much. He'd been hearing about Chris Jackson all night long. A sweet person, an unassuming folk hero who joined in all the town's activities. A shy celebrity who, for all that fame, was just as normal as your neighbor —well, with just a few eccentricities, but heck, she had a right to be just a little different, didn't she? In fact, the town would have been just a little disappointed if she hadn't. But, for all that, bright and open and funny. A nice, talented person with a vivid imagination.

Except that Mac didn't believe it. There was something more there, something the good people of Pyrite weren't seeing, something dark.

She'd faced it. Somewhere in the vague recesses of her past before she'd shown up on Pyrite's figurative doorstep, Chris Jackson, a.k.a. C. J. Turner, had really waded through some shit.

Mac knew the look. He had it. The people he respected back home had it, the ones who'd earned their street degrees. The shadows left behind from all the violence they'd taken part in, the sum of the misery they'd seen. You wade through enough sewers, you're going to smell like them.

A couple of times, Mac had been forced to baby-sit

a writer or an actor researching a role. They'd asked to sit in with him, to dig into his methods and memories, to cull whatever it was they'd need to give back a realistic portrayal of a cop on the mean streets. And each time Mac had looked into their eyes, he'd known they didn't have a hope in hell of getting it right. Cushioned by their safe, comfortable lives, they'd thought they could step into reality for a few days and just absorb it. Get a little dirt on their hands and show the world how well they knew the real streets. But it was bullshit. The look of their eyes had been too shallow going in, and too shallow when they'd left again. They might have picked up the language and the gestures and the lingo. They would never have the ghosts that came with the job. They would never have to wake up in the morning knowing that it really wasn't going to get any better out there. The thousand-yard stare was earned, and they'd never do it.

Chris Jackson liked to laugh. She was smart and funny and bright, just like her neighbors said. Mac would even give her points for eccentricity—even in a town with a resident ventriloquist. But what they didn't seem to see was that behind all that deliberate normality was the darkness. It was as if she'd done it backwards, stepping into their world to see if she could get that right after surviving the sewers.

She might come close, too. Close enough to fool people who didn't know better. Al MacNamara knew better. He had a feeling she wrote nights because she couldn't sleep either.

When the phone rang, he was still sitting at the table. Going on five, the world was just beginning to lighten up outside. Birds chattered out in the big oaks that ringed his porch, and down the street somebody was pulling out of his driveway to go in to work. Mac was in his kitchen, dressed in running shorts and keeping company with Miller and Camel.

"Chief?"

He didn't realize he was rubbing at his head again. "Yeah."

"This is Crystal . . . you know, the night dispatcher?"

Nineteen, bleached blonde and six pounds of eyeliner, hot to have a cop in her shorts. Mac knew all about Crystal. "Yeah, Crystal."

"Well, Curtis is down at the junction of Highway W with a multi-vehicle accident with fatalities."

"Can't he handle it?"

"Well, I think he's part of the accident."

Mac's head hurt worse. His first goddamn day. He'd had no sleep, ached in more than one place from the wrestling match down at the Tip a Few, and was numb in a few others from about half a case of beer. The last thing he needed now was a Chevy sandwich to investigate. "I can assume he isn't one of the fatalities?"

Crystal's high, breathy voice slowed, as if her brain had to gear down for the question. "Well, I don't think so. He's the one who called it in."

"What about sheriff and highway patrol?" Pyrite was the Puckett County seat, which meant Mac had the added privilege of tap dancing around a county sheriff's department on the same block and the highway patrol station over the hill to the west. Back home, all he had to worry about pissing off were his superiors and, occasionally, the feds.

"One deputy headin' that way, highway patrol's over to the other side of the county. Besides, they can't work the same scene without drawin' blood. Should I tell 'em you're on the way?"

Mac tried to remember where he'd tossed his uniform when he'd walked in. "Yeah. Give me a couple of minutes. The paramedics already rolling?"

"Well, Heilerman's sent a crew. The paramedics from the community hospital are tied up."

Heilerman's, Mac thought as he climbed to his feet again. Funeral home. There was some kind of problem there, but he couldn't remember what.

"Um, you maybe want to make sure they got off quick," was all Crystal would say.

Oh, yeah. A slow ride to the hospital was good for business. Now Mac remembered. "On my way," was all he said as he hung up and headed for the sink.

Turning on the cold water, he shoved his head underneath. That and four Excedrin would get him working, anyway.

He was dressed in five minutes. In another five he was guiding his unit through the lightening streets of Pyrite on the way to the highway where he could already see the shudder of strobes. As he passed the corner of Main and Sixth, he noticed that he'd been right. Chris Jackson's lights were still all on.

Chris was in disguise when she dropped Shelly off at school that morning. It wasn't that she was afraid of running into the judge. She was testing out another book situation. Shelly considered it great fun, especially when nobody recognized the graying, slightly bent, frail woman with glasses and a complete avocado polyester wardrobe with matching net scarf as the town's favorite author. Shelly introduced

Chris as her aunt in from over Potosi way, and everyone nodded.

Chris shuffled the streets in her outfit, amazed at
how easily people took to her persona. She'd used
no more than the kind of bad, cheap wig older
women tend to wear to cover their thinning hair,
loose clothes and bad pancake makeup along with
her concave posture to effect the change, and everybody bought it without consideration.

She crossed the street three times just to see what
would happen, and found herself escorted by Pete
Chitwell who ran the gas station, Thelma Potter, and
the new chief himself, who was obviously so distracted by the very lovely Miss Shawntell Malone in her
new Lycra skirt that he didn't look twice at Chris,
even when she gave him a kiss on the cheek as a
thank you for his help.

She didn't get more than a passing glance from
Weird Allen Robertson, which was just as well. Allen
had a nasty habit of staring, which, coming from
those oily, petulant features, sent chills crawling up
Chris's back. At thirty-five, he still lived with his
mother, didn't drive, and worked as a stockboy at the
ShopMart. The town simply put down his unwashed,
overweight appearance to being Weird Allen. Chris
suspected that he'd been standing outside her back
window at night lately. At first she'd meant to report
him. Then she'd begun to see him as the prototype
for a villain in her next book.

Today, he barely noticed her. After all, she was
just a disagreeable old woman. She gave more than
passing thought to dressing up more often, just to get
a chance to watch him unobserved.

The crowd at the Kozy Kitchen was much more

perceptive. It took Luella Travers all of three minutes to demand an explanation.

"How'd you know?" Chris demanded, finally able to pull off the scratchy wig and ditch the glasses.

Luella pointed with the coffeepot that always seemed to be in her hand. "Your purse. Nobody else has one like it."

Hefting the offending article onto the counter, Chris had to agree. The rest of her life might be orderly and organized. Her purse took care of all overflow. Crammed with everything from airline tickets to screwdrivers, it was the size of Georgia and twice as heavy. Useful for survival in airports and defense on dark streets.

"Well, congratulations," she admitted, pulling off the scarf and stuffing it in with the revision notes she had to take to a phone and the other outfit she was going to change into at the store, "you have better eyesight than half the town."

Luella just snorted. "Half the town don't pay attention. The rest pay too much."

"One of my victims this morning was the new chief," Chris announced slyly, knowing perfectly well that her statement would lead the group onto the subject she wanted.

It did.

"Well, I'm not sure," Luella said as she imparted another dose of caffeine with the information Chris had casually requested, "but what I hear is that he was in a gunfight with a drug ring up in Chicago. Almost died. Can't hardly be surprised, considerin' the size of that scar."

"Weren't no drug dealer," Paulie Twill protested from the next stool over. "Gang fight. Chief stopped it single-handed after his partner was killed."

"Well, Eldon told me," Pete Chitwell said, resetting his feed cap on thinning red hair and nodding his head decisively, "and he should know, bein' as how he's the sheriff, that it was a Mafia guy. Had a hit out on the chief for him testifyin' at a trial. That's why it ain't safe for him to be in Chicago no more."

Luella snorted. "If the Mafia can find him in Chicago, what's to say they can't find him in Pyrite?"

Pete swung his fork in Chris's direction. "Nobody's found C. J. Turner yet, have they?"

"Yeah, but she's usin' a different name. He isn't."

Which left Chris with the realization that she should have known better than to go to the town grapevine for accurate information. A serial killer was after her, and the new police chief was running from the Godfather. If life were really that interesting, she wouldn't have to write books.

"I heard it was just another senseless bowling ball accident," came a new voice from the doorway.

Chris turned to find Sue Clarkson sauntering in for her pre-work breakfast. The only reason anybody knew Sue's last name was that she was married to the town's general practitioner, a tall, slow-moving, good-looking ex-jock who liked his fishing and loved his wife. Even though the two of them had only relo-cated to Pyrite from St. Louis five or six years ago, they'd so ingrained themselves into the fabric of the town that people almost considered them natives. Especially Sue, whose success at her job was mea-sured by the fact that instead of being known as Dr. Clarkson's wife, she was simply referred to as "Sue-Who-Runs-City-Hall."

Chris was glad to see her. Sue was her sanity in

the small town, a dry dose of common sense that helped keep the rest of her life in proportion. Sue and Tom were also the basis for some of Chris's most profitable writing, but they never had a clue, and she hoped to keep it that way.

"Well now, you should know, Sue," Luella spoke up, already setting out coffee and juice for the tiny blonde woman, who hopped up on the stool and set down the brace of romance books she always brought to enjoy with her breakfast. "Just how did the chief come by that scar?"

"Shaving accident," Sue informed them all and attacked her coffee. Sue was also the repository for most of the town's better—and better-kept—secrets.

Chris couldn't help a smile, already feeling saner. The sun was up, the world of Pyrite went comfortably on, and Sue was here to sow normality like pumpkin seeds. In the daylight, Chris was always vaguely ashamed of her phobias. In the daylight, she couldn't understand how the night could be so hostile. But in sunlight, it was difficult for familiar things to take on unfamiliar shapes, the way they did under the moon.

"We was just wonderin'," Pete protested diffidently. "I mean, who knows how it might affect him? I hear that he's gonna make everybody in the department take more trainin' and stuff. Have a, like, weight limit or somethin'."

"Wouldn't hurt JayCee a bit," Chris mused.

Pete huffed a little. "A lot of bother, you ask me. I still say that for a mayor who only works an hour or two a day, Ray Sullins sure was full of hisself goin' all the way to Chicago to hire a new chief when there was perfectly good candidates here. I mean, what does a big city boy know about a place like Pyrite?"

Sue never bothered to look up from her coffee. "Exercise'll do JayCee a lot of good, Pete." JayCee being Pete's nephew and the light of his sister Serita Ruth's life. "You know perfectly well he's gotten just a little too fond of those pork rinds."

"It's not just that. JayCee says he's gonna have them all taking college courses and stuff. Refreshers. Well now, JayCee's been on the force here for ten years. He don't need no refreshers."

"Give the man a chance," Sue suggested with a pat on his arm. "I think the chief'll do just fine. Which reminds me," she said, swinging toward Chris. "Did he get in touch with you?"

Chris just nodded, still four cups of coffee shy of a state of readiness. "Introductions were made last night when he caught me breaking into the How Do."

Sue laughed, a sound not unlike air escaping a low tire. "I knew there was something I forgot to tell him."

After another ten minutes catching up on Sue's kids and the vagaries of small town politics, Chris wandered on up to the How Do to make use of the phone system there to get back in touch with the rest of the world. She was still smiling, even humming to herself, the caffeine finally kicking in, the comfort of the company at the Kozy Kitchen settling her. Chris's bonhomie lasted all of about fifteen paces.

"Chris Jackson, have you found Jesus yet?"

Chris winced. "Misplaced him again, have you, Harlan?"

She couldn't help it. With anyone else in town, she could be endlessly tolerant. This was her home, the people as close to family as Chris had—especially the

more unique ones. Chris considered that only appropriate. But her patience evaporated like alcohol over
heat the minute she heard the sonorous tones of the
Reverend Harlan Sweetwater.

Harlan wasn't so much a preacher as he was a
bounty hunter. Souls for Jesus, was his battle cry.
Chris pictured them swinging from his belt like
scalps.

Fifty and florid, Harlan thumped Bibles, tables,
and baby's bottoms with equal enthusiasm. He rant-
ed at aldermanic meetings against textbooks, dancing, and the danger of having Home Economy
classes in school, and once missed his own service
because he was over across the tracks at the tiny
Catholic church slipping little comic books under
windshield wipers alleging not only that the Pope
was the Antichrist, but that he owned the *Los Angeles
Tribune* and *Playboy* as well.

Considering the fact that Chris was usually found
on the opposite side of any of Harlan's intense cru-
sades against the devil in Pyrite—not to mention
the fact that she wrote books starring a psychic,
which Harlan considered witchcraft at its basest—
she was considered fair game for his proselytizing.
Which meant that every time he ran into her, he felt
it his duty to charge for her soul. Chris was beginning to feel like a flag in a game of king of the
mountain.

"You can only be born again in the Lord," he said,
following right on her heels, Bible soundly in grip,
hand out as she picked up speed toward her shop.
"It's not too late."

"Closeout sale?" she retorted instinctively. It didn't
really help to irritate Harlan. It was, however, great

fun to see the various shades his neck could turn when he got upset.

"I know you, Chris Jackson!" Harlan called as she reached the door. "I know you and I'll expose you for what you are."

She had her hand on the door. She should have gone on through. Chris knew better. She kept letting Harlan get to her, and that was no way to start out a day, especially when that day included talking to the police about homicide. "I thought you were going to save me, Harlan."

"How can you be saved?" he demanded loudly enough that Pete, coming out of the cafe, turned to hear. "You have no respect for the Lord's word. Would you submit yourself to the will of a man, like a proper woman? Would you give up your evil ways and take on the righteous cloak of salvation?"

Chris smiled then, a bright answer that sent Harlan from mauve to puce. "No," she admitted evenly, "I guess I wouldn't. Have a nice day, Harlan."

She walked on into the shop.

All she did there was trip over three very large cats and a disgruntled Eloise.

"That woman called," Eloise announced in a huff as she patted at her hair. "And on the store line, too."

Chris sighed. And to think the day had so briefly been promising.

"I'm sorry," she apologized. "I'm sure Dinah didn't mean any harm."

There wasn't any question, of course, that it could be anyone else. Eloise responded the same way every time Dinah called. Eloise was a dear, but she was no match for Dinah Martin. Come to think of it, neither was anyone else, which was what made

Dinah the perfect agent. Dinah wasn't called the Bitch Queen of the Eastern Seaboard for nothing. But then, anyone else might have objected to the term. Dinah had gone out and had a desk plate made with the words embossed in gold.

"Go on and get some breakfast," Chris suggested as she threw her purse onto the counter. "I'll watch the store."

Eloise was already gathering up her paraphernalia. "Should be some business. The Wickersham boy was killed in an accident this morning."

Chris looked up. "I thought I heard sirens." Actually, she'd thought she'd dreamed them. "Anybody else hurt?"

Eloise did enjoy her scoop. She was smiling like a preacher with the good word, which meant it must have been a busy night on the old scanner. "Well now, the way I heard it, Curtis Marshall was answering the call and ended up wrapping his cruiser around a light post tryin' to radio in and miss one of the victims on the road at the same time. Are you going to find out about that crazed killer thing today?"

Maybe the chief would work on driving right after fitness. Chris didn't think to correct Eloise. "Yes, Eloise, I am. If he's heading this way, you'll be the first to know. Are there any more surprises?"

Chris motioned to include the various recumbent bundles of fur in that statement. Widowed for the last fifteen years, Eloise had taken to salving her loneliness by adopting any stray cat in the county. She couldn't talk Chris into sharing the glorious burden, so she settled on letting the good cats be rewarded with visits to the shop. More than one customer had been pounced on during feline maneuvers among the foliage.

"Let's see," the little woman mused, counting off fingers. "Pesky, Frisky, Squeeky, and Lenny. That should be it today, although I'll have to go home to check in on Prissy. She was feeling just the slightest bit irritable this morning."

"PMS?"

"Pardon?"

Chris just shook her head. "Nothing." One encounter with Harlan was enough to threaten her relations with everyone. Chris satisfied herself with a wry smile at the thought of a bloated calico holed up with a box of Moon Pies and a Mel Gibson movie, and headed for the office.

"Thanks, Eloise," Chris said, picking one of the privileged off her coffee machine so she could get started. "I'll take care of it from here."

"Chris?"

"Yes?"

"Isn't that Harmonia Mae Switzer's dress you're wearing?"

"Not anymore. I bought it at the Rock of Ages rummage sale."

"Oh . . . it's, uh, nice."

Chris grinned to herself. It was nothing of the kind.

"Thank you, Eloise."

Pouring herself a cup of coffee, she played back the messages on her answering machine while picking errant cat hairs out of the liquid. Two more frantic calls from Trey, one each from Dinah, the lawyer, and the accountant, and five hang-ups. Considering the fact that hers was an unlisted number whose secrecy was guarded like a Swiss bank account, those hang-ups were getting irritating. Multiplying from singles a few weeks ago, always silent, always the long pause, beep to beep, as if it were Victor trying desperately to get the courage to say something. Chris erased them along with everything else as Eloise reached the door on her way to report to the Kozy Kitchen on the accident.

The bell over the door tinkled and three cats hissed. Chris looked up at the last minute.

"Eloise?"

"Yes, dear."

"Food or flowers for the Wickershams?"

"Oh, food. Definitely food."

"Thanks, Eloise. Enjoy breakfast."

The bell tinkled again and Eloise was on her way. Left behind, Chris found herself reluctant to actually breach the outside world.

It was the real recommendation for Pyrite. Isolation, insulation. For the last five years, Chris had successfully armed herself with the day-to-day simplicity of this small town on the edge of the real world. She'd fought long and hard to get here. She could leave it regularly to venture back out into the real world, where people had more on their minds than weather and ball scores. But it was this town, like a time warp, a bubble in reality where Opie Taylor was reincarnated as a wooden doll with a foul mouth and the main tourist attraction was a memorial to the mobile home, that helped keep everything else in perspective. Here Chris could be, for at least this time, whatever she wanted to be, and everyone here let her.

She'd been feeling the old panic lately, that clutch

of anxiety that couldn't be explained or chased away like an irritating insect. Maybe that was what it had been about. Maybe she'd begun to suspect that even Pyrite wasn't Shangri-La. There were ways over those mountains, and someone was sure to find them. She just didn't want it to be yet.

Business or pleasure, she mused fatalistically, looking down on the crumpled piece of paper with the chief's chicken scratch on it. Editors or police? Chris needed to call the police first, but she didn't want to. She'd had a nightmare again last night, just as she'd known she would. A quick trip into hell on a fifteen-minute nap. Blank, black void. Even waking to the lights, to the soft strains of Mozart, she'd been lost, curled up in fetal position on the floor next to her bed with no idea of how she got there or why her heart was racing and her chest squeezed shut.

Well, at least she'd left the pillows alone. There had once been mornings when she'd spent hours cleaning up. She must have been quiet, too, because Shelly had slept right through it.

Like all nightmares though, it had followed her through to daylight, a stale taste at the back of her throat, an uneasiness that defied explanation.

She should call the police and find out what was going on. After stalling long enough to change from avocado polyester to pink-and-green cotton, she called Dinah instead.

"Weekends been a bit dull in your little burg?" was the answer she got. "You had to go looking for some real fun?"

Chris almost choked on her coffee. "Thanks for the vote of confidence, pal."

The chuckle that met her protest was low and

throaty, the sound of a woman who knew how to use her vocal chords to mesmerize. Chris, who had known Dinah since before her first publishing coup, was immune.

"You sound drearily cheerful at this hour of the morning," Dinah protested.

Chris doodled, sharp geometric shapes shaded in black. "This hour is later for you than it is for me."

"Something that does not even bear considering. I have a hangover the size of the deficit, and you're probably out celebrating sunrise or something vile."

Chris shook her head in wonder. "Was there a reason for your message, or were you just in the mood to whine?"

"On or off the record?"

Chris grinned. "No, I'm not recording." One of Dinah's more quaint paranoias was the fear of being preserved for posterity without her permission, and Chris definitely had the tools with which to do it. Tucked into C. J. Turner's cabinets behind the make-up case and lock picks and firearms catalogues were the phone recorders, taps, tracers, location finders, directional mikes and computer protectors. Chris had collected each one for research during visits to New York where exclusive shops catered to even more paranoid big business. Chris knew how to use them all. She never did, unless she was working on a book. "Now, what's up?"

Dinah's voice loosened up infinitesimally. Only Chris would have noticed. "Oh, you mean about that rather . . . no, that absolutely bitchy little police detective who's been threatening everything short of capital punishment if I didn't give away your address? I want you to know I held off as long as I could."

"The drums have already reached me. I'm calling her next."

"No, dear, call Trey next. He has a migraine and it's not even noon. Tell him you're not knifing people in St. Louis so he can manage lunch."

"And what if I am?"

"Then lie, of course. He's in the middle of editing your next book. You lose him, and you'll be back to Wanda the Comma Commando from Hell."

It was a relief to get in another smile before facing the next call. "That's what I like about you, Dinah. You never lose sight of what's really important."

For just a second, the static from New York was empty. Chris fantasized that the outside world had vanished, that all that was left was Pyrite with its small jealousies and unshaken loyalties. That the only world was the one that ambled along outside her window, and that the worst thing after her was Harlan with his good Book and bad breath.

"Did you hear which book this person is supposed to be pretending to?" her agent asked, and for the first time her voice sounded less than in command.

Chris considered her doodles, a hundred sharp edges that wept black ink. "That's what confuses me, Di. If it were a death by sword, it'd be a pretty easy call. But *Hell Hath No Fury* . . . I've seen that pattern too many times to call it an isolated cause of death. What makes them tie it to me?"

When Dinah answered, her voice was missing its trademark razor-sharp edge. Not ten people in publishing would have recognized the sound as one of concern. "Maybe you should call and find out."

Chris took a very long breath. "Yeah. Maybe."

"And then call me right back."

That made Chris smile. "I'm a big girl, Dinah. You don't have to run right down and hold my hand."

She won a self-righteous snort for that. "Good dear God in heaven. What a horrible thought. Dinner with the Clampetts."

"You never know," Chris taunted. "You might just like it here. I do."

"And I might just sell my condo and join the Medical Missionary Sisters. Now, call that . . . person, and find out what's going on."

"Nothing's going on. Somebody in St. Louis doesn't have enough to do, that's all."

Ten minutes later, she wasn't quite as sanguine about it.

"*You're* C. J. Turner?" asked the voice on the other end of the phone.

Chris wasn't exactly sure how to respond to the delight. It wasn't quite the reaction she'd anticipated. "Yes. Detective Lawson?"

"I want you to know how much I've enjoyed your work. All your work. I've followed you from the very beginning."

Chris knew that voice. It tickled at the back of her mind a moment, stirring emotions like rustling leaves. She wondered if she'd worked with Lawson before. It was certainly possible. She'd have to ask her. One of the few things Chris had little control over anymore was her memory. Notoriously bad, often sketchy. Irretrievably broken so that she spent familiar minutes in just this kind of exercise.

"Thank you," she acknowledged, brow pursed. "Um, what can I do for you, Detective?"

"I'd love to talk to you about your theories sometime, Ms., uh, Turner."

"Jackson. My real name's Jackson."

"Oh, is it really?"

Chris was going to ask then where they might have met, what the detective wanted, when she heard a new voice on the other end of the line. Imperious, furious. Intruding.

"Sorry . . ." The first voice apologized, and then, evidently bowing to the flood of obscenity and command, handed over the line.

". . . well, I'm here now," the new voice snapped in conclusion. Chris couldn't say she was encouraged by this new, more strident tone. Another woman. Unfortunately, the real Detective Lawson. "Sorry," the policewoman said to Chris, not sounding as much sorry as irritated. "That was one of the dispatchers. She has no goddamn business answering phones up here. Goddamn groupies are all alike . . ." And then, abruptly, she sighed. "She's been drivin' me nuts ever since she heard your name. Probably wants an autograph or something."

"I don't mind," Chris tried to protest. It didn't do her much good. Evidently Lawson wasn't anymore interested in her opinions than she was in those of the anonymous dispatcher who'd had the bad taste to answer Lawson's phone for her. Chris didn't like the detective already.

She decided to be just as polite. "Why do you think your murder has anything to do with my book, Detective?"

"Simple," Detective Lawson said in that abrupt, sharp tone of hers, evidently not at all thrown off. "The signature. Remember how Emma stabbed her husband in the shins just to make sure he couldn't get up and run after her, even when he already looked like Alpo?"

Give Chris a cop anytime for not mincing words. "Yeah," she agreed halfheartedly. "But you can't mean to tell me that nobody else has ever done that before."

"Of course not. Maybe coincidence works for writers. It just doesn't cut it for me, though."

The detective wasn't winning any friends on this phone line. Chris could hear the distinctive tonal qualities of a person intent on the cooperation-through-intimidation school of charm, police edition. Everybody plays by my rules, cause I got the gun. Well, Detective Lawson had it bad.

"What makes you think it's not maybe a wife who read my book and kept that kind of pattern in the back of her mind?" Chris tried diffidently, not even happy with that explanation. It would still be a kind of culpability she didn't want. She wasn't writing "how-to" manuals here.

"Because this cookie can't read. Nothing but street signs and beer labels, anyway. She swears she came home from a visit to the tavern with her girlfriends to find her husband sliced and diced by an unknown intruder. That alibi went over about as big here as Ted Kennedy saying he just couldn't find his pants."

"What about forensics? Do they bear her out?"

"Inconclusive. Which leaves the wife cooling her heels in the county jail without enough for bail, and me on overtime."

Like it was all Chris's fault. Chris shook her head, the idea still too alien, the logic forced. The detective was looking for a cheering section, and Chris wasn't in the mood to help.

She tried again to escape. "I still don't see why you're so sure she didn't really do it."

"Because I've read your work. I recognize similarities. M.O., evidence, area of town, even the victim's name. We've almost got a perfect match here."

Chris didn't realize she'd set down her coffee. "The name? The guy's name was Ralph Watson?"

"Not Watson, Weaver. But he was from Affton, just like the guy in your book. Murdered in the middle of the night with a kitchen knife the size of a machete that was dropped back in the corner of the bathroom. And that shin thing, just like I told you. It even happened on a Tuesday night."

For just a moment Chris closed her eyes, sucked in a long breath past the constriction in her chest. The itch had grown into dread. Impossible. This just couldn't be happening.

Chris leaned back in her chair, opened her eyes and deliberately looked out to the forest of blossoms that filled the opening into the showroom. She took a slow, deep breath, smelling roses and chrysanthemums and daisies, reading the messages on Mylar birthday balloons that floated toward the ceiling. You're 40 and I'm Not. Over the Hill. Old Fart.

Normal stuff. Solid, familiar sensations, cats padding back and forth, the sun gleaming in the genuine plastic cemetery bouquets along the far wall, Millie Wyler tapping a hello on the window on her way by. Small, simple everyday things that made sense.

Flower shops made sense. Murder didn't. Even murder that's expected, that explodes from the most violent and primal of human emotions. Chris knew. She was a student of murder, murder by reason of insanity, born of jealousy, revenge, fear. Murder committed as the desperate act of a driven, tormented person.

Not cold-blooded murder. Not the murder of a victim chosen with the deliberate care of a man picking roses for his lover. Not murder without reason.

Chris instinctively retrieved her pen, only to find the sharp-edged, weeping expanse she'd left on her scratch pad. She set the pen back down without using it. She had nothing left to do but stare.

"Why?" was all she could ask. "Why would somebody want to do something like that?"

"Hey," the policewoman protested brusquely. "We got people who like to chop women into totem poles and stand 'em out in the front yard to ward off aliens. Don't ask me about motives. Do you have any ideas about who we might be looking for here?"

Chris laughed. "Why should I?"

"Well, that psychic thing. You know. Livvy Beckworth."

From the terrible to the absurd. "The heroine in my series is psychic, Detective Lawson, not me. I'm just a writer."

She got another stretch of dead air, although this one sounded different than the pause to New York. This one, traveling only as far as Clayton, Missouri, where the St. Louis County police detectives were officed, crackled with activity. Not just physical, like the voices and phones and beepers Chris could hear in the background. She could have sworn she heard mental wheels turning.

"I'm sorry I can't be of any more help to you," she tried, her gaze once again on the doodling, on the jagged peaks of her imagination. "I've never gotten letters from anybody protesting that they wanted to commit murder. Nobody I know enjoys it as a hobby, and I only do it in my imagination." Deep in the night, when her defenses were friable as old skin, when reality lived in dreams.

Could there possibly be someone out there who kept the same hours? Who sought a twisted kind of communion with her? Chris shook her head, took a breath, tried her best to clear the image. To shake off the suspicion. It was ridiculous. She was just a writer.

"Well, you'd better come up with some kind of idea, Ms. Jackson," the detective assured her, "because you have a real problem on your hands."

"Me? What did I do?"

"Who knows if it's something you did? Maybe it's just something you knew. But somebody out there sure likes the sound of your words enough to turn them into three-act plays."

"One murder . . ."

"One?" Lawson retorted sharply. "You think I'd be on the phone if we just had one?"

This time Chris knew her heart had stopped. "What?"

"Nine months ago we had a woman drowned in the bathtub. Blond, real pretty, ran with a real fast crowd out in West County. The P.A.'s going on the assumption that the poor asshole she was married to finally found out she was running around on him. The asshole swears he's innocent."

Chris couldn't even manage an answer.

"Yeah," the detective retorted as if she'd heard something anyway. "I thought it might sound familiar. *Too Late the Hero*, wasn't it? Unfaithful, scheming wife, desperate husband. Her name was Deborah, right?"

Chris could hardly hear her own voice. "Right."

"Eight months before that, a young gay actor was shishkebobbed with a long, sharp instrument in the rehearsal hall of the Loretto Hilton Theatre in Webster. Medical examiner's talking something like stiletto, but I'd bet you money that one of those skinny swords'd fit real nice into the hole in his chest."

"Epée," Chris whispered. She closed her eyes, quelled a sudden lurch of nausea.

"That's the one," the detective agreed. "Now, I admit that I wouldn't have suspected a thing if I hadn't just been reading *Hell Hath No Fury* the day we got the call on the Weaver case—in fact, your favorite fan gave it to me. Anyway, it intrigued me a little. So I started checking back on some cases. I'm finding a real interesting pattern here."

Chris wanted to wash her hands. She wanted to wash everything. Something was crawling all over her.

Lawson didn't seem to notice the silence. "Now, I'm not sure if you just . . . you know, like, anticipated this stuff happenin', like the professor does in your books. Maybe you know more than you think. Maybe somebody's out there screwin' with our heads. One way or another, I'll guaran-goddamn-tee you it isn't gonna stop until we figure out what's goin' on. Now, you gonna help me or not?"

Chris couldn't quite manage an answer. It wasn't a mistake. The murders were real. They were real and they were plotting out just like her books. She'd been having trouble sleeping again, staring into the darkness wondering why she felt chased, and suddenly she knew.

Two years. It had been going on for two years. She felt invaded. She felt assaulted, sitting amid her plastic flowers and orphaned cats. She desperately wanted to get out of there, to run back home, to take off riding through the hills until she could find some new shoots of spring. Instead she sat right where she was and picked her pen back up.

Very carefully, she ripped off the sheets she'd been doodling on and threw them in the trash. Then she turned her attention to the detective.

"What do you want me to do?"

✦ *Chapter 4* ✦

"SHE'S NO MORE eccentric than anybody else in this town."

Mac took another sip of coffee and leaned back farther in his chair as he conversed with Sue through the office door. "I didn't say I called her eccentric, I said L. J. Watson did."

Busy entering tax evaluations into the computer, Sue never bothered to look up from where she was working. She did allow Mac a laugh. "L. J. considers anyone who doesn't vote Republican and own a horse eccentric. Chris is just . . . Chris."

"How long have you known her?"

Now Sue looked up, her expression dry. "Is this interest professional or personal?"

Mac afforded Sue the scowl that question deserved. After only a few days in town he found it necessary to remind himself at five-minute intervals that he wasn't in the big city anymore. "I can't afford personal interest. I'm paying off two wives and two kids. I'm just trying to catch up with that memo on my desk yesterday."

"Five years," she said, going back to her computer.

"We moved to town just about the same time."

"What do you know about her?"

"Other than the fact that she's my youngest's god-mother and the family baby-sitter when Tom and I want to get out of town?"

Mac went back to his coffee, the new budget still unperused on his desk and Curtis Marshall's health forms unfiled. "Yeah. Besides that."

"Nothing very mysterious. She writes a hell of a book, tends to dress in bright colors, and likes her privacy enough that she hides here. Considering the fact that she's not only the most interesting person to hit town since Quantrell but also an active member in almost every town function, it's no big surprise that we let her."

"Does she always take in teenagers for the night?"

Sue smiled. "Teenagers, ventriloquists, old ladies who talk to fish. Chris is a sucker for a sob story. I think it's because she never had a family of her own. She's kind of adopted us."

"No family?"

"Foster homes. It's quite a success story, if she'd just admit it. She finally got out of the system at eigh-teen and worked her way through school . . . schools. She has about three degrees. She's got more useless information stuffed in that brain of hers than a 'Jeopardy' champ."

"Where'd she live before here?"

"St. Louis, around the midwest. I don't know. Why don't you ask her?"

Which meant that Chris Jackson could have more connections to St. Louis than just an itch to set ficti-tious murders there. Which also meant that Sue wasn't the one who was going to give it up on her.

Mac sat in his imitation-leather swivel chair, looking out into the Formica-paneled reception area of the Pyrite City Hall and Police Department, a room brightened by Sue's plants and decorated in aerial photography and aldermanic meeting notices, and thought yet again of the differences here in Pyrite. Of the similarities.

He needed the word on the streets. He needed a snitch. Snitches were a hell of a lot easier to come by in the big city. They were a lot less conspicuous. Besides, the best ones were hookers, and from what he'd been able to gather, Pyrite was a one-whore town. And she resided way out along a dirt road that ended somewhere up the north side of Wilbur Mountain, which meant she couldn't exactly watch the street action on Main.

On the other hand, small towns did have cafes.

Closing the files before him, Mac pushed his chair back. "Think I'm going to get some lunch. You?"

Sue just shook her head. "If you're going over to the Kitchen, make sure they give you an extra Blue Plate. Sheriff's off today, and it's our turn to feed the prisoner."

"From last night? What's he still doin' there?"

"Nobody wants him home enough to post bail."

Mac automatically reached in the drawer for his gun and beeper and came up empty. Habits died hard. He shut the drawer and patted the gun still strapped to his hip, seeking familiar security. "Well, hell, what is it? I'll post it myself."

"For Cooter Taylor? You're the one he tried to bite last night. Do you really want to let him loose in Oz again?"

That stopped Mac halfway to the door. "Oz?"

Sue looked up with a grin. "I swear, they didn't tell you anything when they hired you. The trailers over behind the dump. Been called Oz ever since the tornado of sixty-five, I hear." Her grin grew very dark. "Although, if I were the wizard, I sure wouldn't want to live there."

Mac nodded, running a hand through his hair as he stepped out into the front room. Sue continued to clatter on the computer.

"Have you read her stuff?" Mac asked suddenly.

Sue looked up. "Yeah."

"What do you think?"

She considered it for a second. "I think she's really good. What about you?"

Mac had finished *Hell Hath No Fury* while he'd waited for Curtis in the emergency room. "I think she's spooky."

Mac was retrieving his keys when the front door opened. He was going to just nod a vague hello, the standard response in this town, when he realized that he'd been caught wishing. It was Chris Jackson.

"Sue?"

Mac was intrigued. For a minute she didn't even see him standing halfway across the floor. Striding into the room, attention all on Sue, she looked like a heron readying for takeoff. An agitated heron at that.

Sue swung around at the sound of her friend's voice. After working with Sue for only two days, Mac could gauge the importance of Chris's interruption by the fact that Sue was on her feet before the woman reached her.

"Honey, what's wrong?" She reached up to pat Chris's shoulder, Puck comforting Titania. Chris Jackson was a tall woman, with short dark hair and the kind of body that would have looked good on an athlete. Sue resembled an overripe Peter Pan. An incongruous pair, especially with the smaller woman offering the comfort.

Mac didn't make it out the door after all.

Chris Jackson seemed to be a pacer. She allowed Sue one good pat on the arm before she eased away and turned, evidently needing to give room to her distress. Considering the length of those legs, it didn't surprise Mac at all.

"Oh." Her eyes went wide at the sight of Mac waiting behind her. Hands lifted a little, fumbled a bit with the edges of a lurid puce-and-purple paisley oversized shirt and then dug into jeans pockets.

"You talked to Lawson?" he asked. It wasn't much of a stretch.

She looked as if she wanted to turn away again. Instead, she shrugged, a small, abrupt movement that neatly telegraphed the news. "I, uh . . ."

This must have been uncharacteristic behavior on Chris's part, because Sue was completely at a loss as to how to react. She looked at her friend, and then at Mac, as if searching for somebody to quickly clarify the situation so that she could take appropriate action.

Mac took a careful step forward. "You wanna talk?" he asked.

Chris Jackson looked as if she'd been hit with a stun gun. Wide-eyed, white, rigid as hell. "Later," she managed, not advancing or retreating a millimeter. "Please?"

Mac gave her the same passive smile he gave murder suspects when they asked for water before facing his questions. "You bet," he allowed easily, knowing within a hairbreadth just how close to come to a skit-

tish person. The biggest mistake most new interroga-
tors made was pushing too soon, too hard. Mac
played his targets like very nervous fish.

Chris Jackson was hardly a suspect. But she was
going to give him something interesting to do, and
he wasn't about to blow that off.

"I'm going down to the Kozy Kitchen," he offered
quietly. "Have some lunch. After you talk to Sue, you
want to come on over? I'll save you a spot."

He only waited long enough for her to agree
before turning for the door. So, there had been a
murder. A puzzle, and on his second day here. He
might just survive it after all.

"Three."

"Murders?"

Chris nodded. She was feeling better. Thank God
for Sue, who'd poured her coffee and watched her
pace and listened to her agitated story without comment. Chris still wasn't sure what she was going to
do—what she was supposed to do—but at least the
first shock had died a little.

Walking alongside her, Chief MacNamara shook
his head thoughtfully. "I'm going to have to do some
more reading."

Chris had met him, just as he'd asked. But the last
thing she needed was discussing this with the audience at the Kitchen. Victor and Lester might have
kept the news to themselves, but Luella would have
been down at the *Puckett County Courier* in ten minutes flat. MacNamara made it a moot point by asking
Chris to walk with him to the county jail to feed
Cooter Taylor his lunch.

"I'm not exactly sure what to do," she admitted, hands once again shoved into her jeans pockets as she sidestepped the tree planter outside the drugstore. There were minute buds on the branches, and daffodil shoots poking up through the dirt in the tub. Chris wished she could stop and enjoy them, that she could step into each and every store along the square and waste her time checking the merchandise, visiting with the people, steeping herself in the regular, the routine. It was the special gift of Pyrite, the secret to her sanity. She catalogued the everyday minutiae of this town the way a penitent did martyrs to pray to.

"What does Lawson want from you?"

"Validation, I think. Either that, or she really did want me to gaze into my crystal ball and tell her why my books seem to have started coming true."

"Have they?"

She wanted to close her eyes again. She wanted to run up and down the library steps a couple of times to work off the sudden tension in her chest. "Yeah," she admitted instead. "I think they have."

Ghosts to add to her collection. Responsibility to be piled atop the weight already on her shoulders. She wondered how she was supposed to atone for something like this. Murders committed in her name, maybe to get her attention. Chris had never known how to think of life any way but, "Shit happens, and I'm responsible." Well, this shit was something she wasn't going to get off her hands.

The world had found her after all. That wonderful, magical silence on the phone this morning when she'd pretended that there was no one left out there to get her, had vanished. Whatever was going on up in the suburbs of St. Louis had something to do with her.

It wasn't just the press anymore, or the fact that with one simple intrusion, the entire illusion could shatter. It was the fact that writing was supposed to be an anonymous business. That was why she could do it, why she could dissect her most painful truths and still offer them up to strangers. Because, somehow, she could pretend that no one actually saw them as *her* truths. C. J. Turner carried the burden of fame and suffered the stain of connection in her stead. If that symbiosis evaporated, Chris simply wasn't sure whether she'd have the courage to let Livvy loose on the psyches of murderers anymore.

And if she didn't, she wasn't sure what else she could do.

"What has Lawson asked for?" the chief asked, breaking into her thoughts.

Chris had almost forgotten him, loping along next to her with the tinfoil-covered plate that smelled like meatloaf in his hands. They'd reached the county courthouse, a big, red, square, brick building with a cupola that was badly in need of repair.

Several of the staff were loitering by the side door on a cigarette break. In the summer, the corner would be a perfect place for a little gossip and laughter, lush and shady, with a riot of color from the flowers that the VFW Auxiliary planted and the statue of Grant to keep them company. Now, the trees were skeletal and scratching at themselves in the wind. Chris shivered at the stark sound.

It took some work to concentrate on what the chief was asking. "Pardon?"

"What kind of information did Lawson want from you?"

Chris didn't look up as they walked along the old, uneven sidewalk, automatically matching strides. Instead she focused on the progress of her tennis shoes across the slabs of concrete that had long since begun pushing against each other like tectonic plates. "Um, she wants me to get together any unusual correspondence."

"Threats?" he asked. "That kind of thing?"

Chris looked up to see that his face was carefully passive, the network of crow's feet at the corners of his eyes suspiciously absent. She actually caught herself smiling when she realized that he was fighting like hell to keep his expression nonchalant. "Do you have to be so excited?" she demanded.

He gave himself away in millimeters. "I was right," was all he said. "You are spooky."

"Spooky nothing. I'm surprised you don't have the bends from the pressure change between Chicago and Pyrite. If you're anything like the cops I've known, you can smell a good case a mile off, and don't give up until you have a square foot of pants cloth in your teeth. And I bet you've probably guessed that there aren't that many good cases to go around down here."

He never slowed, never gave in to the amazement Chris knew he felt. "Just how many cops do you know?" he asked.

"I'm a mystery writer," she protested. "It's kind of an occupational hazard. Are you going to help?"

"Depends. Are you going to be honest with me?"

She knew a thing or two about masks herself. "Sure. Are you going to be honest with me?"

Simple barter. Quid pro quo. Chris knew she needed him. There was no one else who could buffer that
carnivorous police detective from the big city. There
was no one else in a position to keep her informed of
progress. And Chris had known the minute she'd said
it that the chief needed her. She had the feeling that
he hadn't left Chicago as far behind as he'd thought.

It took him a second. They both stalled not ten
feet from the sheriff's office, the meal still held in
MacNamara's hands like an offering, the sag of his
shoulders betraying the ambiguities of a man who
wore his uniform like a pledge. Like a challenge. For
a minute he looked out over Chris's head to where
Chris knew the secretaries were watching them. His
eyes narrowed a bit in thought, and his jaw worked a
little.

"It looks like we're already a hot topic on the
grapevine," he said. "That could make it worse."

Chris turned to check the direction of his attention.
She saw the last furtive looks as the women ducked
back into the old glass-and-iron door that had been
installed around the time General Grant had stopped
there to water his horse.

"Nah," she assured him. "They're just trying to get
the scoop on the killer. Besides, most of the town
half suspects me of being a lesbian anyway."

Chris hadn't meant to set him up like that. It was
worth it, though, to see the magnificent restraint in
his reaction.

"Oh?"

"Well, I have lived here five years now, and I
haven't gone after a single one of the local boys."
She shot him a wicked grin. "It only stands to reason."

"Local boys," the chief retorted, casting a telling look toward the prison. "Like Cooter?"

"Not to mention his four sons, Cooter One, Cooter Two, Cooter Three, and Cooter Four."

"They're *all* named Cooter?"

"No matter what you have to say about Cooter, you can't deny that he has a healthy ego."

MacNamara seemed reduced to nodding. "Uh huh. Town doesn't seem overly worried about leaving you with teenage daughters."

Chris hadn't quite lost that grin. "Well, so far I haven't gone after any of the local girls, either. The town figures I'm a little quaint, and mostly harmless, and I haven't seen fit to dispel the myth since it keeps me safe from the Cooters of this world."

All the chief had to do was turn and open the door to get into the station. Through the window Chris could see Marsha, the day dispatcher, watching them instead of the soaps on her portable TV. But the chief didn't move. He simply stood where he was, his expression unreadable, his hands still around the plate.

He gave away his decision before he ever spoke. Chris saw it in his eyes.

"I was going to question a murder witness," he said finally, his posture as sharp as his creases, his words careful. "Turned out he was also protecting a stash the size of Cleveland. I screwed up, and ended up short about four inches of skull."

Quid pro quo. Chris could see everything she'd anticipated, the layers of protection over the too-new wound, the challenge of the bald truth, the tensing for reaction, the deep-down ghosts that hovered around the back of his eyes. She looked away just a moment, uneasy with her own intrusion, wondering at his courage to let her in even this briefly. He'd done his job, offering truth to establish trust. But he hadn't had to offer quite so much.

She had to decide what she could offer back.

What she was able to offer up.

She took a slow breath. Fought hard to dredge up a truth, any truth. One worth even exchange for what the chief had just given.

She couldn't do it.

Dropping her gaze, she fought the familiar surge of shame and gave what little she could. "I, uh, don't live in Pyrite just because it's cute. I don't . . . do well out in the real world. I didn't like it when I lived there, and I don't now. I'd prefer not to have to go back." Finally she looked up and did her best to smile past the sudden, new acid in her stomach. "Which I may have to do if I'm really telling the future in fourteen-chapter increments."

The chief began to walk again. Chris followed, and saw that he had relaxed just a little, not so much a deflating as a resettling. She seemed to have passed some kind of test, though she was damned if she could figure out for what.

"Are you?" he asked.

"What?"

He pushed the door open and held it for her. "Telling the future?"

Chris stopped just inches shy of the threshold. "Oh, no," she protested. "Not you, too."

Caught with his one hand on the open door and the other balancing the dish, the chief considered her carefully, obviously trying to figure out how to play this. "You're pretty convinced that your books are coming true," he suggested.

Chris pulled her hands out of her pockets to settle them on her hips. "I'm not going to explain this again. Livvy's talent is a purely expedient one. I am as much a psychic as Stephen King is a possessed St. Bernard."

That little panicked feeling that had been growing lately had nothing to do with this. The dreams that hadn't really plagued her so much until the last few months. Chris had never considered such a possibility before, and she certainly wasn't going to do it now. Especially now. It was simply too much to be responsible for.

"Any other questions?" she asked sharply.

"Are you coming in?"

Her own shoulders slumped a little. She took her hands off her hips and preceded the chief into the office.

"Cooter Taylor still locked up?" the Chief asked, heading right for the cabinet over the dispatching console to get the keys.

"Can't you hear him?" Marsha retorted. A pleasantly plain, overweight woman with a scratchy, beer-stained voice, Marsha had been manning the mikes for about twenty years. She kept a secret about as well as Victor threw his voice, but very little fazed her.

Chris instinctively looked up toward the heavy iron door that led into the jail. Cooter was definitely back there. She could tell that raw, pit-bull voice anywhere. She could also place most of the obscenities he was tossing around back there with Elvis James, the turnkey. Must have been an intense discussion.

"He been doin' that all morning?" the chief asked evenly.

Marsha just nodded as she buffed at her nails and kept an eye on both the dispatch board and *The Young and the Restless*. The phone rarely rang here. A fairly new office that smelled like coffee, dust, and air freshener, it was decorated much like the city hall down the street, the only difference being that instead of real plants they had silk ones. Sheriff Tipett was allergic. Besides, Marsha killed anything she tried to grow.

"You motherfuckin' sack o' shit, I seen that!"

Marsha pursed her lips at the language. Chris grinned. "He's gettin' kinda musical."

The chief wasn't at all pleased. "I'll be right back."

He slid the big brass key into the lock, pushed the door open, and stepped back across a hundred years.

Chris had been in the jail once when one of the deputies gave her a tour. Built in 1860, it had held slaves, Confederate prisoners, Union prisoners, and moonshiners, in that order. Constructed of solid white-washed granite blocks, the small building was U-shaped, with the cells opening out from the center. Sporadically illuminated by bare bulbs, each cell sported a flat iron-grilled door. The only toilet was set into the lefthand wall by the office, and most of the meals were passed on a tray through a special little door that led through to the sheriff's house where it was attached to the far end. Until the new connecting offices went up, the prisoners had all been admitted through his living room. His wife still cooked for them when she was home.

Chris stood just shy of the door. She couldn't go in there. The lights were blinding against the whitewash, and she knew Elvis was as harmless as he was ugly, but those cells made her break out into a cold sweat. Empty black eyes in a death's-head face, bottomless voids of agony.

The light never reached into those harsh, square cells where the old ring bolts from the time of slavery still protruded from the floor. The sun never even came close. When Chris shut her eyes, she could hear the low, lost moans from all the people who'd been trapped here, in other cells like them, and it unnerved her.

She couldn't go in. Even poised at the very edge, she was clammy and flushed, her chest tight. So she guarded the door with slippery hands, near enough that she could smell the old sweat, thick dirt, and reused motor oil on Cooter, far enough away that she didn't have to see where they'd trapped him.

And then, all hell broke loose.

The chief was just making the step down into the jail hallway, tray in hand, scowl settled over his features at Cooter's inventive language. Elvis, standing right by Cooter's cell, turned to greet the new chief, the gaps in his teeth as stark as the cells he served. The kind of guy who'd do anything for a dollar, Chris was thinking. Suddenly Cooter's hand shot out from between the bars.

Before Elvis could so much as squeak, those beefy fingers with their jailhouse tattoos clamped around his throat and lifted the skinny, vacant-eyed jailer right off the floor. Elvis shrilled and turned purple. The chief, who had so carefully carried that dinner all the way to the jail, promptly dropped it, spattering gravy and corn all over the concrete floor.

Chris was caught in the doorway, unable to step

in, knowing better than to even try going a round with Cooter, her attention fixated on the lopsided blue crosses tattooed into Cooter's hairy fingers where they were curled around Elvis's throat.

"Get me the fuck outa here!" Cooter rasped, the very timbre of his voice invoking the image of little girls spitting up pea soup and spinning their heads. Elvis squeaked again as he slammed into the grate. "Come on, you pussy motherfuckers, get in here and get me out so I can go home and beat some shit outta that cuntface bitch that called the cops on me!"

Chris wasn't even sure whether Cooter knew it was the new chief he'd heard come through that door. She was sure that he wasn't expecting what he got.

The chief never went for his gun. He didn't need to. While Cooter was busy shaking poor Elvis's last few teeth out of his head, the chief reached right in and grabbed Cooter by his throat.

Chris couldn't see Cooter's face, but she heard him. He was built like a tree trunk. The chief had him squealing.

Cooter acted completely within character. He spit right in the chief's face.

"Oh, shit," Chris muttered to herself, frozen in place even as the spittle ran down off the chief's chin and stained his shirt. She should move. She should run like hell, or get on in there and help somehow.

The chief didn't blink. Didn't even bother to wipe his face. He simply yanked as hard as he could. Cooter slammed into the grid with the force of a car wreck. The door, unbreached in a hundred and thirty years, shook with the impact. Cooter made a thudding, pulpy noise, like a watermelon hitting the street, and let Elvis go.

Chris took a huge breath, closed her eyes, and scurried in to get Elvis out of the way. While Mac was preoccupied with Cooter, she pulled the little jailer up off the floor and pushed him back out through the door where Marsha was already calling for backup. Then she turned around to keep an eye on the chief, just in case he needed help—although what help she could be, she wasn't sure.

"Listen to me, you dickhead," the chief was snarling, the sound far more frightening than anything Cooter had managed. "I guess you don't remember me." Yank. Slam. "Well, you sure as shit will now, you stupid piece of wormpiss." Yank. Slam. "I'm the guy you tried to give rabies to last night."

Somehow he'd even gotten Cooter's arm caught by the grate and was exerting pressure on it as he made an imprint of the door on his face. Chris slowly sank onto the office step, propping the door open with her back, too mesmerized by the change in MacNamara to move.

Cooter was gurgling. Chris imagined that even from three cells down she could see the whites of his eyes. That made Mac smile, and it was a terrible smile. Chris had seen a lot in her young years. She had never seen anybody look quite so crazy as Mac did at that moment, with his eyes stark and the smear of spit on his face.

"Now, maybe you scared the people here before," he said, his voice now perfectly calm, delivered in deadly earnest, which made it twice as frightening. "But you haven't dealt with me. And I'll guaran-fuck-ing-goddam-tee you, that if you ever try anything this stupid again, I'll just open the door and beat the dogshit out of you." Yank. Slam. Gurgle. "Understood?"

Mumble.

Chris found herself grinning.

"I asked you a question!"

Cooter managed to answer, even with his nose flattened against the grate and blood trickling down into his mouth. "Yeah."

"You ever try somethin' like this again, and I'll rip off your dick and stuff it up your ass. Got it?"

Pause. Slam. "Yeah."

Mac nodded, his body rigid, his eyes narrowed, focused completely on the suddenly hapless Cooter. "Good. I'd hate for you to make a mistake and think I wasn't gonna keep jumpin' on you like ugly on an ape. 'Cause I'd rather deal with goddamn turtle rapers than one stupid piece of white trash like you."

Cooter must have answered, because Mac let him go. Behind Chris, Elvis was still wheezing and, behind him, Marsha was canceling the call for help. Finally satisfied that he'd gotten his message across to the prisoner, Mac turned away from the cell, and Chris saw what Cooter had seen. Not just anger. Not just power. Madness.

He was shaking. Chris saw it when he lifted his cap to wipe at his forehead. She saw white-hot wildness cool in his eyes. Saw him deliberately fight for control.

It amazed her. This was the man who had been so completely in command the other night when he'd faced off with her. The man who had had the insight to leave her to her friend until she was ready to talk to him. Always calm, always rational. As carefully put together as his uniform.

There was, it seemed, another side to Pyrite's new police chief, and it had nothing to do with simple prisoner control. He'd let something loose in this claustrophobic little room that still battered at the thick old walls, and Chris thought again of that Chicago pension he'd walked away from.

Then he lifted his eyes and found her sitting there in the doorway, her chin in her hand, like a spectator at a ballgame. Mac came right to attention. Chris saw the chagrin, saw the sudden unease. Not just normal police reticence, the idea of civilians being exposed to the kind of reality that cops think only they've ever handled. It was more, as if he'd surprised himself. As if that explosion had caught him as unawares as it had Cooter.

Chris reached over to pick up the napkin Mac had brought with Cooter's lunch. "You know how to speak hooze-fuck," she said, handing it over. "The town will be relieved. They didn't listen to me when I told 'em that white trash knows no jurisdiction."

For a very long moment, Mac didn't move. He was still breathing a little hard, the light picking up the sheen of sweat on his forehead. He didn't say anything, but Chris could almost hear the suspicion and confusion. She wasn't surprised. Mac was an outsider. He was on probation, and she suddenly had the power to hurt him.

But Chris knew exactly how it felt to be an outsider.

Finally, he stepped on up and accepted the offering. "Is all of Oz like that?" he asked dryly, swiping at his face.

She carefully climbed to her feet, masking her own set of shakes, and flashed him a bright grin. "Cooter's the wonderful wizard himself."

Pulling off his hat again, Mac just shook his head and walked on up, finally noticing the pool of congealed liquid that had been Cooter's lunch on the floor.

"And I thought I'd miss home."

Chris laughed. "Like I said. Some things are universal."

She caught that surprise in his expression again. That hesitation that spoke volumes about experience and expectations. He'd lived within an almost cloistered society, where only Chicago cops mattered, where no one else understood or forgave. He'd expected to be the prophet in the wilderness. It made Chris want to laugh all over again.

"You OK, Elvis?" he asked as they stepped back into the office.

Elvis looked like he feared for his life all over again. Chris didn't blame him. That had been an impressive display in there. She had no doubt at all that the new chief's reputation had just been made, and that by dinner the entire town would know.

"I——I'm real sorry, Chief," he stammered, hand still around his sore throat. "I never seen it comin'."

Mac waved off the apology with an offhand gesture. "Surprised me, too. Doesn't say much for my second day here, does it?"

By the time he made it back out into the street, Mac was Elvis's newest idol. One of the sheriff's deputies was pulling around the corner, but Mac deliberately turned the other way, once again matching his stride with Chris's.

"Hooze-fuck?" he asked dryly.

Her attention ostensibly on the dove gray clouds that were massing over the Baptist church steeple,

Chris merely smiled. "It's an endearment I picked up in St. Louis's third district."

Mac didn't say anything, just walked steadily along. And Chris, her eyes still on the slow roil of thunderheads, came to her own decisions.

"All right." She pulled to a stop, eyes deliberately forward, chest once again tight. "I'll admit it. I was a social worker. Case worker for Division of Family Services. A short and sadly uninspiring career spent among Cooter's brethren in St. Louis who, considering the fact that they would procreate with whatever immediate relative happened to be in the room, provided me with a lot of business."

She'd balanced the scales now. An admission of her own to match his. Enough, she hoped, that he wouldn't need more. Her stomach was churning with even that much.

"How'd you end up here?" he asked.

She just shrugged. "I made enough money writing to quit."

Chris didn't realize she'd been holding her breath for his reaction until he gave it.

"So, what else did Detective Lawson have to say?"

Chris knew he heard the low whoosh of relief as she resumed normal autonomic functions. Even so, he didn't comment. He just walked steadily along, affording her the consideration of silence. And she took advantage of it, mentally shutting away images and shuffling others forward. Stepping away from revelation and digging into investigation.

Chris noticed that Elmer Masterson had painted the front porch of his white clapboard house a bright yellow green. She liked it. Kind of like invoking the arrival of spring in his own way. Chris could handle all this as long as there were things like brand-new paint on porches to settle her.

"She's coming down here in a few days. Wants to see any correspondence I might have saved. Especially anything from letter writers who think they're possessed by the spirits of dead kings or such. I told her that dead kings didn't seem the type to copycat crimes, but she didn't seem particularly amused."

"I don't think anything short of capital punishment amuses her." He was nodding to himself now, his attention already back on the problem at hand. A quick, decisive man with brainpower to spare and an evident need to solve puzzles. If Chris had made up a personal grocery list of qualities she'd need right now in an ally, she couldn't have thought of one other, except maybe loyalty; but with her luck, that would just have produced Lassie.

Now, if she could only get the chief to constrain his curiosity to only those areas she wanted examined. Chris knew cops like him, and they didn't have a whole lot of respect for No Trespassing signs. Well, this time it was going to have to be different, or she simply wasn't going to get through it.

"We'll get this thing squared away in no time," he promised, half to himself, like a coach urging victory in the second half. "Probably nothing more than a misunderstanding." And Chris, who needed to hear just that right then, believed him.

Four days later, she found the letters.

✦ *Chapter 5* ✦

SHE'D SPENT THE morning figuring out ways to beat a murder rap. Considering the fact that the crime had taken place rather spectacularly in the suspect's living room, it would be a tricky thing, but Chris was counting on the wonders of the modern forensics lab to finally bail her out. She was hip deep in a treatise on DNA fingerprinting from skin scrapings when the knocking interrupted her.

"Go away," she muttered, making a notation on her timeline for normal lab downtime on fingerprinting. She had a headache that caffeine and aspirin weren't curing, another nightmare hangover, and she wasn't in the mood for company.

"Come on, Chris!" the distinctively high, piping voice insisted through the door a story below. "Victor's out here ready to wet his pants!"

"You live next door!" she yelled back, massaging the back of her neck. "Use your own bathroom!"

Chris really didn't want the company. She was still wiping sweaty palms on her thighs and trying to convince her stomach to stay in place.

If only she had normal nightmares. Falling from a

cliff, showing up at the theater naked. Losing her house in a subdivision where everything looked exactly alike. She could handle those better. She had to have dreams straight out of an Ingmar Bergman film festival. The ones she remembered, anyway. Sometimes those were the easiest to live through.

Silence.

Chris looked toward the door, where she could see the two-headed shadow through the milky glass. "Victor?"

Still nothing. Which meant that either she'd turned him to stone right on the spot, or he really did need to talk to her and couldn't gather the courage to insist. It took a second, but Chris finally dredged up a self-deprecating grin. Poor Victor. He didn't deserve both her and Lester to be in a bad mood at once.

"OK!" she yelled, climbing gingerly to her feet and slipping into a pair of shorts to go with the nightshirt that was standard writing attire. A quick check for leftover feathers from the latest one-woman pillow fight that had taken place in the early hours of the morning, a swipe to dry her hands, and she was sliding down the banister and trotting for the door.

Just as she'd figured, Victor stood stolidly in front of her door, head down, cheeks blazing with embarrassment, Lester somehow looking smug alongside him.

"I'm sorry," she greeted them both. "Must be one of those pesky female things. I'm as cranky as Lester today."

That only served to deepen the hue of Victor's cheeks. Lester chuckled easily. "Is that what all the noise was about last night?"

Chris overcame the urge to look over her shoulder

one more time, sure she'd see a lone feather fluttering down from the loft. Noise, now, too. It was one thing for her to be visited by nightmares. It was quite another to share the experience. If anybody but Victor lived next door, she'd have had her ticket to Fantasyland punched for a one-way ride.

"I had *Gotterdammerung* on the stereo," she demurred. "Lots of tortured-sounding sopranos. You guys are going to have to learn to complain . . ." Her own distress was suddenly lost when she finally took in the change in her friends. "Lester, what the hell do you have on?"

Victor finally got his eyes up to her, big, brown puppy-dog eyes that always seemed to melt in her presence. It was Lester, of course, who answered. And motioned to the spangled, white jumpsuit he wore.

"Like it?" he demanded brightly. "We've decided to try a little tribute to Elvis. It's working for everybody else."

Chris battled back a laugh. A red-headed, freckle-faced Elvis. It made perfect sense. And then Victor slid the tiny sunglasses on the dummy and flipped up the collar, and Chris lost the fight.

"It's . . ." It's a red-headed, freckle-faced dummy in shades and a cheesy jumpsuit, she thought.

"Wanna hear *Jailhouse Rock*?"

She shook her head emphatically. He even had little high-topped patent leather boots on. "No, really, I have to . . . uh, I really . . . oh, Victor, I think it's going to be a hit."

Victor beamed. Lester threw off a few experimental "Hey, baby's" that sounded disconcertingly real. Chris tried very hard to regain her composure.

"We thought we'd try it out on the town," Victor said. "You know, like test marketing. See if they liked the idea before taking it up to St. Louis for our next audition . . . oh, yes, Chris, I'm sorry."

Chris pulled her gaze from the sartorially splendid Lester to Victor's sudden discomfort. "About what?"

"Why we came by."

"You didn't come to show me Lester?"

"Well, that too. But, you see, we were just over at the How Do . . . to get some flowers for Mother's grave, don't you know."

"He's such a good boy," Lester interjected nastily, still in Elvis's voice.

Chris let it go.

Victor shrugged uncomfortably. "Eloise said to get you. That your editor had called twice already, and not on your phone, but the shop's, and it's still only ten o'clock their time, so it must be important, don't you know. She figured he had a clue about the killer."

As hard as Chris had tried, the news about the increased body count had swept the town like chicken pox. Everyone was offering support and solutions in about an equal ratio. Miss Harmonia Mae Switzer had offered sanctuary. Harlan had offered salvation. Shawntell Malone, the hairdresser at the S and J Salon, had offered to read Chris's crystals. From all reports, the geological karma was not good.

"Thanks, guys. I'll get on down there."

Victor gave a jerky nod of his head, his eyes once again down. "Do you like gladioli, Chris? Do you think Mother would like them?"

"I think she'd love them," Chris assured him with her best smile. Actually she thought his mother was about five years past caring in the least what kind of flowers Victor brought her. Phyllis Hellerman was a box of ashes behind a marble wall down at Pleasant Grove, nothing more. And gladioli, as far as Chris was concerned, were the most hideous creations in the flower world, conceived for the specific purpose of weighting down the air in funeral homes everywhere. Chris hated gladioli.

Actually, she hated funeral homes. Ashes to ashes and amniotic fluid to formaldehyde. Complicated rituals invented to disguise the bald terror of death's inevitability. Futility versus fantasy. And since gladioli seemed designed to mask the stench of death with the cloying perfume of pretense, she guessed it made sense she had no time for them.

"The pink ones," she said, knowing that that was what Victor had already bought, and knowing that all that mattered was that he felt better for it.

His smile was radiant. "Yes. I thought so, too . . . Chris?"

She'd been all set to turn back inside to get her shoes. "Yes?"

Victor blushed again, shrank a little. Lester gave a curious huffing sound and turned to her. "He wants to say that if you need anything . . . well, we're here for you."

Funny the things that made a person want to cry. Instead, Chris opened the door and deposited a kiss on both human and wooden heads. "Thanks, you two. I appreciate it."

That was all Victor could take. Without another word, he scurried back to his house.

✦ ✦ ✦

There were times Chris was tempted to buy Trey a ventriloquist's dummy of his own. It might help him get past that tendency to whine and just let loose.

"Sergeant Lawson threatened me," he complained.

Pinned to her chair by a thirty-pound calico, Chris drowned her sorrows in a cup of highly caffeinated coffee and watched Eloise make up peach and cinnamon silk bouquets for the Pritchard wedding. "She considers that foreplay, Trey."

He wasn't amused. "Well, it's not as if I don't have anything else to do. I got stuck with most of Marianne's workload when she went on maternity leave, ya know. I'm getting an ulcer."

"You wouldn't be a real editor without one." The cat stretched and fell off onto the floor with a solid thunk. Chris grinned. There were some things she depended on more than others, constants by which she could fix her star. Sue's common sense, Dinah's tart wit, Trey's overreacting.

It never failed to amaze her how effectively he used the tactic. After all, it was the author's God-given right to moan and groan, not the editor's. This was an aberration in the natural order of things.

Chris had been both blessed and cursed by a variety of editors in her career. She'd had a visionary and an illiterate, a storm trooper and a space ranger with a taste for S and M. And, of course, Wanda the Comma Commando from Hell. For all Trey's annoyingly effective dependence on the higher vocal register to get his point across, he was a hell of an editor. Chris couldn't think of a time his insights into her work had been wrong. He had a penchant for the twisted and dark in fiction that was as strong as hers, and he thoroughly enjoyed the verbal skirmishes they had over manuscripts. He kept Chris on her toes, and editors who could do that were a rare species these days.

"So, what is it you so desperately needed me for?" she asked. "I was going to call in this week as usual."

"The letter," he said, and suddenly Chris's smile died.

"What letter?"

It seemed that he could actually be compelled by something other than his workload. Chris could hear his chair squeak as he pulled closer to his desk. She heard the shuffling of paper. She heard him stretch out his dramatic pause and knew she should have never opened the door to Victor.

"We got it a couple of weeks ago," Trey said. "The mailroom by mistake put it in the pile we were forwarding to you. I just got hold of it."

Chris suddenly didn't have any patience. "Hold of what?"

"Did you go through your correspondence?" he asked. "That sergeant told you to go through yours, too, didn't she?"

"Trey," she threatened. "What letter?"

She had gone through her correspondence. Well, at least the majority of it, all as unremarkable as she'd remembered it. Nothing even to share with the chief, which had sent his mood tumbling a couple of notches. Chris had actually thought that maybe it would all go away again. Well, she'd hoped it would.

"You want me to read it to you?" he asked.

With what felt like superhuman effort, Chris kept her temper. She was still stale from last night, jittery with old adrenaline and new uncertainties, her hard-earned optimism eroded by phantoms and fears. She was still feeling invaded by the thought that someone out there had attempted to reach past her anonymity and touch her. And Trey wanted to play game show host.

Her silence must have been sufficiently intimidating.

"It says," Trey informed her portentously, "that somebody's been sending you letters you're not paying attention to."

"Word for word," Chris insisted, the cats forgotten, Eloise no more than a shuffle at the back of her mind.

Trey offered a beat of his own silence in chastisement.

" 'Dear Editor,' " he finally intoned dramatically. " 'You'd better have some words with her. She's not listening to me, no matter how hard I try. And soon—' " There was another microscopic pause, evidence of Trey's theatre training. His timing was impeccable. " '—it will be too late.' " Pause, breath for effect. "What do you think it means?"

Chris mentally reviewed what she'd already read from her files, a small mountain of typed and handwritten notes, letters, cards from people who had found some humor, some justice, some . . . something in her work. She didn't have to review any phone messages, because until the moment she'd called Sergeant Lawson, all C. J. Turner's contact with the outside world had come through the mailroom of the publishing house or through Dinah.

She tried to remember anything that might have connected with the words. Something niggled, something vague and distant. But Chris didn't trust her memory, so she pulled over her scratch pad again.

"Tell me about the letter," she insisted.

"I just did."

She uncapped her favorite pen. "No, I mean the mechanics. What kind of paper? Is it handwritten or typed?" And, the most important of all, the one that curled like a feral thing in her stomach. "What's the postmark?"

"Chris," Trey admonished. "This isn't one of your books."

"No, it isn't," she agreed. "It's more important than that. Now, stop screwing around and tell me."

"I don't know," he whined again, crinkling at the paper that had probably suffered from the fingerprints of at least a hundred people by now. If it had been sitting in the mailroom that long, God knows what all it had been contaminated with. "It's regular paper. Cheap, like a person gets at the drugstore. Typed. Maybe a computer."

She lifted her head. "Computer?"

Chris could almost hear him nodding. "A good dot matrix, maybe. Anyway, it's not an old hunt-and-peck job. It's really neat."

"Where was it posted, Trey?"

That was the question that seemed to yank him right through the reality door. With no more than a moment's hesitation, he lost his whine and actually sounded hushed.

"You mean, where does your fan from hell actually live?"

Fan from hell. One person. No more coincidence, no possibility of hyperactive imaginations. If Trey was right, if this was really about the murders, someone was trying to talk directly to her.

Someone had been talking, and she hadn't heard.

Chris took a slow, unsteady breath, trying very

hard to quell the sudden nausea. "Well, where's he mailing his letters?"

She heard the faint rustling again and another of Trey's Pinteresque silences.

"You're not going to like it."

"I don't like it already."

"It was mailed from St. Louis."

Chris took another slow breath and silently let it out, her gaze firmly fixed on the still pristine paper beneath her pen, her hand trembling. "Well, at least we know he doesn't have to go far to fulfill his fantasies."

Chris was beginning to lose her sense of humor. She was already two weeks late on starting her next book, she had another contract to worry about, a steady increase in reruns of the nightmare of the damned that prevented slumber parties and kept her bed from being over-used, and Sergeant Lawson was overdue to show up at her door. And now Chris was wading through letters that only served to heighten her eternal sense of inadequacy and fraudulence, looking for the kind of clue Livvy would have spotted in thirty seconds.

She was going to have to use this in a book. The author of pretend crime-solving exposed as a sham. It was humiliating.

It was decidedly unnerving.

"Chris?"

She'd left the door wide when she'd gotten home, the first day she'd been able to let the spring in through the screens. It was sacred tradition with her, that first time she could open up, invite in the easy waltz time of town life, the occasional car, the bright chatter of schoolchildren like passing flocks of excited birds, the chiming of church bells and slamming of neighboring doors.

The world was turning, unfolding itself slowly to the sunlight of spring, and Chris worshiped it. She could smell the rich perfume of humus, could taste the fresh life in the breeze. Opening her door was always a major feast day on her private liturgical calendar. This year, when she needed it the most, she'd lost it in the tumble of multicolored rectangles on her coffee table and the whispers of suspicion in an anonymous letter a thousand miles away.

And the first visitor to her open door was here on business.

"Come on in, Chief."

The hinges squealed and boots clacked on her hardwood floor. Chris still didn't look up. She was searching for secret meanings to the words, "I've read all your books."

"Sue said you had a new problem."

She tossed that note away and reached for another. "A new problem, the same problem. I thought maybe you'd be better at this than me."

"Than I."

Startled, Chris looked up to see the kind of deadpan expression on his face that betrayed the instinctive response.

"Fine," she retorted sourly. "On top of everything else, I get the only police chief in the States with a degree in English grammar."

"No degree. A grade school run by the Sisters of Perpetual Punishment. They had short tempers and big rulers."

Chris grimaced. "Is that why Pentecostals can't diagram a sentence like the Catholics can? Okay, I thought you'd be better at this than I. Happy?"

His reaction was characteristically small. "Depends on what I'm better at."

Chris motioned to the two piles of stationery. "Finding clues."

MacNamara pulled off his cap and ran a hand through his hair. "I thought you'd done that."

"I thought I had, too. The publishing house got a rather cryptic letter that might just sound like somebody trying for the longest time to get my attention about something important."

She handed over the message she'd finally gotten Trey to repeat slowly enough for her to copy down. The script was just a bit shaky, the letters small, as if by printing them closely she could keep the import of the news from Eloise. It would have been just as easy to sneak a tank through the mail.

Mac took a minute to read the note, absently stroking his upper lip. His brows gathered together, and Chris felt worse.

"Her," he said.

"What?"

He looked up. "The letter says 'her.' The writer knows you're a woman."

"Is that a problem?"

"I didn't know you were a woman. How did he?"

Chris got to her feet, ostensibly to refill her coffee cup. "My initials, probably. Most of the early women mystery and suspense writers used initials instead of their names because it was thought that women didn't sell as well. Anyone familiar with the genre knows that."

"Or he could know you."

Chris stopped, coffeepot in hand, ready to pour. "You're not making me feel any better, Chief."

"I'm not paid to overlook any of the angles. Where's the letter now?"

With an effort, Chris went on pouring. She even poured a cup for him. "I told my editor to enclose the letter and envelope in a plastic baggie and keep it with him until somebody told him what to do with it. I tried to call Sergeant Lawson, but she wasn't there."

He nodded, still stroking that upper lip. It must have been a great mustache. "We'll work something out. When's she supposed to show up?"

Chris's footsteps echoed all the way up to the rafters as she returned with the cups. Her pace always increased when she was upset, her heels hitting the floor with a distinctive clack. Right now they ricocheted like an AK-47. "About two hours ago. I guess she got caught up at work or something."

He accepted his mug of coffee and took a moment to consider the pile of letters before him. "Don't you throw anything away?"

"I should at least get a thank you," she protested. "If there is something going on, think of how much tougher it would be to track down without this stuff."

MacNamara gave her a considered look, still not moving to take advantage of the coffee. "I'm afraid 'if' just isn't an operative word anymore." He gave the paper in his hand a brief wave. "I have a feeling about this."

Chris had actually managed to swallow a good, hot mouthful of coffee. With MacNamara's words, it stuck right in the back of her throat. "I don't suppose those feelings of yours are ever wrong."

That actually won her a measured smile. "Could be worse. You could really be psychic."

"Don't count anything out yet. I could find out I'm the killer and I'm writing myself these notes."

She wanted a laugh out of that. She was expecting it from the wrong person.

"Have you found anything in the letters that might mean something?" he asked.

"If I had," she countered just a bit testily, "I'd be holding them out to you right now."

He nodded and set his coffee cup down on the table beside the bigger pile of cards. "Well, then, let's get started."

Mac was amazed at the things people told a perfect stranger in a letter. Dreams, frustrations, family crises. He'd been through about half his pile, and he felt as if he'd been caught peeping through suburban windows.

He'd expected fan mail to be about books. About the skill of an author, the theme of a work. These were about loneliness and connection, and not a little about obsession. And Chris Jackson considered them perfectly normal.

"People feel they can talk to me," she explained when he mentioned it. "They think they know me somehow."

"But to tell you about their divorces?"

"I got those after the *Fury* book. There's a lot of anger out there I didn't know about."

Mac shook his head, amazed. Disconcerted. He knew how screwed up the world was. Hell, he'd earned a postgraduate degree in it. The bad guys were taking over, and on a good day all you could hope to do was stem the tide. But somehow, he'd always depended on the normal people to be out there balancing the scales a little.

Maybe he didn't see them, maybe he'd never participated, but he'd believed in them like his mother did the Trinity. But if these letters were any indication, if people were so distanced and disconnected that they had no one but an anonymous author to tell their problems to, the scales were a little lower on the negative side than he'd thought.

Somewhere out there, there had to be normal, healthy people who had regular jobs, paid their bills, and managed to stay married until natural death they did part. He guessed they just didn't write letters like these.

"All your mail's like this?" he asked.

They were seated across from each other on the facing couches, the mail piled on a brass-and-glass table between them, cups half empty and the ashtray half full. Mac thought he saw a couple of pillow feathers in the crease of the chintz couch cushion, but it wasn't something he would ask about.

Chris Jackson, her long legs tucked up under her in a curiously defensive position, gave off a little shrug. "You probably have an intense pile," she allowed, glancing up briefly from the letter she was holding.

Mac saw her gaze skitter away, the way a perp's does when he's hiding a stash just on the other side of a door, or his partner's waiting in the dark with a sawed-off to save him. Furtive, guilty, the sure sign of concealment.

"Problems?"

Her head snapped back so fast, her hair swung a little. Her quick grin was sheepish and amazingly shy. "No. I was just . . . thinking."

Without another word, she bent back to her task. Mac watched her a moment longer, a pretty, bright-eyed woman with mahogany hair and a set of legs that would have provoked a riot in the squad room back home. A square face, the kind that makes determination look good, and eyes the color of old whiskey. Mac knew why he was alone. He wondered why she was.

And what it was she was hiding back up in that loft of hers.

"Do you know Billy Trumbel?" he asked suddenly.

That set her back again. "Pardon?"

Mac lit another cigarette and picked up a white envelope addressed in purple ink. "Billy Rae Trumbel. I think he's a high school junior. Parents run the Sleep Well. Do you know him?"

Mac didn't have to look up to hear her smile. "You mean the founding member of Junior Sociopaths of America? Sure. What'd he set fire to now?"

Mac took the time to savor the harsh sear of unfiltered smoke in his lungs before answering. "Fire, huh? I'll keep an eye out."

Those sharp eyes were on him now, and Mac knew she was trying to figure out what the hell he was up to.

"So, what am I now?" she asked. "The impartial sounding board for local impressions?"

"I didn't figure you'd mind that much," he said, lifting the envelope in his hand. "After all, I *am* helping you find your mad killer."

"Please don't call him *my* mad killer. I claim no ownership whatsoever. I'd rather not even be mentioned in the same breath as he."

Mac set the envelope back down, the letter inside nothing more than a request for back titles. "I'm also helping your grammar."

"Don't push it."

Mac allowed a grin and thought how rusty that felt. He was still going to have to face that dismal, empty house tonight. He was cooling down a case of beer to shave off the sharper corners of disillusionment and jacking up on nicotine to survive the sapping monotony. But he'd be eternally grateful to anyone who could give him a reason to get up in the morning.

His next candidate for the ghoul hall of fame was a pink envelope with flowers and a "Save the Dolphins" stamp on the back. He hadn't seen anything like it since his kid sister had written him in Nam.

"It's tough bringing your big-city suspicions to a small town."

Mac looked up, distracted and surprised. "What?"

It was her turn to grin, a small, wry thing that betrayed those ghosts. "I said, it's tough adjusting your view of the world to Pyrite. It seems so outrageous to be quite that suspicious here."

Mac considered her a moment. "You weren't by any chance a cop, too, were you?"

"Cops aren't the only ones privileged enough to see humanity at its finest."

He took another drag and blew the smoke away from her. "You don't see things quite the way the town thinks you do, do you?"

Chris finished stuffing a birthday card back into its envelope and tossed it on the negative pile. "That's my little secret."

"You have a lot of those."

She faced him then, and Mac got a glimpse of her quiet defiance. "Doesn't everybody?"

Not much to argue with there. Mac made a strategic retreat and picked up a new envelope. She did the same.

Another white one, typed this time. Careful, precise spacing, the address situated as perfectly on the front as a painting on a museum wall. Mac absently fingered the carefully positioned "Love" stamp.

"Well," Chris said, sipping at her coffee as she read. "I think your instincts are right on the mark about Billy Rae. But then, I think people are much too trusting with Weird Allen over at the ShopMart, and that L. J. Watson is probably running numbers out of his basement."

Mac looked up, just a little distracted. "I hope you don't expect me to do anything about it."

"Arrest the man who recommended you? Not when the prosecuting attorney's his sister's nephew, I don't." Her smile grew very irreverent, and she reached over to take another sip of coffee. "I just thought you'd want to know to avoid L. J.'s on Tuesday afternoons so you don't catch him. On the other hand, I thought you might like to keep a closer eye on Allen."

Mac conceded both points with a short nod, taking another drag on his cigarette. He'd seen Allen and come to the same conclusions. Definitely overdue for an arraignment for weenie wagging. The kind of disenfranchised person he used to see in video arcades back in Chicago. Already well known at the station, because he was always there asking to join the auxiliary police. Just the kind of help Mac needed.

"Something else you might want to remember," Chris was saying, her gaze flicking over the note in her hand. "If you like your privacy. In a small town, it's hard to keep a secret. Paulie Twill, who does the trash, is also Luella Simpson's nephew. He just loves telling 'what I found in the cans today' stories."

She never looked up, but she didn't need to. Mac thought of the pile of aluminum that had been collecting outside his house for the last week, and bit back an oath. Maybe a small town hadn't been the answer. He'd been used to his anonymity, just one apartment in ten, in one building out of thousands across Chicago. He'd never had to worry about being given an evaluation on what Paulie the trash king pulled out of his driveway.

Mac crushed his cigarette out in the lumpy ashtray, wondering just what else the author with the sharp eyes had seen from that balcony of hers. "You perform this service for everybody who's new to town?"

Her enigmatic little smile nudged again at Mac's instincts. "Once a social worker . . ."

"How long did you beat the streets?" he asked.

For some reason, he held off opening the envelope in his hands. It intrigued him in ways he couldn't explain. Gut ways that couldn't be set out in a report. His attention had already moved to it, so that he didn't hear the funny little silence across from him. He was pulling out the thin piece of paper that lay nestled in the envelope.

"Oh," she finally said, "not that long. I guess I wasn't made of stern enough stuff."

The folds in the letter were as sharp as the crease in his uniform slacks. The note, short and succinct, was perfectly centered on the cheap paper, the words innocuous and vague. A shiver of prescience snaked down his back.

Already knowing what he'd see, he turned the envelope back over. "St. Louis."

"Yeah," she agreed. "I already told you. I worked my way through St. Louis University there."

Mac looked up, disoriented by the answer to a question he hadn't asked. He gave the envelope a little wave in Chris's direction. "That letter at the publishers," he clarified. "It was postmarked from St. Louis, right?"

Chris went very still, so still that Mac couldn't even see her breathe. He had the fleeting impression of a very small animal, caught in a sudden light and seeking protection in silence. "Yeah." There was dread in her voice.

All he could do was nod. Computer printing, probably a twenty-four-pin dot matrix. Cheap, clean paper. Careful, ambiguous words that tickled his instincts like the sight of a gym bag being carried down a street in Cabrini Green. He had an answer she didn't want, and fought the rush of exhilaration.

" 'Dear C. J.,' " he read without prompting, instinctively holding the letter by thumb and finger, even though any real evidence had long since been forfeit. " 'I just wanted you to know. I recognize what you're doing. I want you to know what I'm doing, because we're so much the same. Answer soon.' It's signed J. C."

Her dismissal was too quick, too nonchalant, and too definite. "It's somebody who wants me to read his manuscript. I get those letters all the time."

"I don't think so. Does the name J. C. ring any bells?"

She scowled. "Yeah, but I doubt he'd bother to write letters. I hear he goes in more for Sermons on the Mount."

The clock ticked in plodding monotone. Outside some girls were jumping rope, their shrill voices dissonant on the rhyming song. A car pulled to a stop and a door slammed.

"Do you go up to St. Louis?"

"Sure."

Her voice was calm, so carefully measured she could have been talking about carpet colors. Mac looked up to see the fallacy of her composure in those telltale eyes of hers. Fleeting, deep, harshly constrained, the terror betrayed her.

"Does anybody up there know who you really are?"

She merely shook her head. Mac wondered just what lay beneath that brittle control of hers. "What about the people you worked with at DFS? Would they know?"

She shook her head again. "Nobody ever knew I wrote until I moved here. It was . . . mine."

Oddly enough, he understood. Maybe if he'd had something of his own, he wouldn't have needed the force so badly. Maybe he wouldn't have lost so much when he'd left.

Instinctively he leaned forward, not close enough to touch, because that might have spooked her. Close enough to offer support, to insinuate understanding. He'd been a champ at Good Cop-Bad Cop. He knew just how to play the role to get his best results, and he knew that to get anything out of this iconoclastic, insightful, enigmatic woman, he was going to have to play it to perfection. Because what this letter told him was that without Chris Jackson, their killer had no reason for his actions. Without her, they also wouldn't have any kind of window into his reasoning at all.

"You knew this was where we were heading," he said simply, hands out just a little, posture very still.

She shook her head, her eyes a little wider, with a funny sheen to them. "I want it all to be a mistake."

"It isn't. Lawson's right, and you know it. And I think there are other letters like this one in that pile."

"I didn't even notice it," she protested, her voice just a little ragged. "It just looked like another letter asking for help getting published." She was picking at her shirt now, a childish gesture on a woman who only moments ago was so completely in control. "I get them all the time."

Mac shook his head, his instincts pointing dead-on at the envelope in his hands. "When was that last guy killed?"

"I, uh, don't know."

"Three weeks ago," a voice said.

Both of them turned to find a new player at the door. Short, stocky, untidy in a too-careful kind of way. Brown and hazel, unremarkable, unmemorable. Mac disliked her on sight.

Sergeant Lawson. Mac might not have been able to immediately place the voice, now gravelly with the cold or whatever had her wiping at her nose with a wad of Kleenex and clearing her throat. But there was no mistaking that attitude.

"Robert Weaver died three weeks ago," she said,

opening the screen door without invitation and stepping into the living room. Her gaze never left Chris's
as the author climbed to her feet.

Mac followed, lifting the envelope for her to see.
"In that case, Sergeant, I think we may have a suspect. And I think he knows you're after him."

✦ *Chapter 6* ✦

THE SKY WAS a robin's-egg blue, impossibly high and clean, it's only adornment a tattered scarf of clouds at its shoulders. Along the winding hill roads south of Pyrite, the trees were just beginning to carry the first blush of green, and the world smelled like fresh dirt and old leaves. Chris felt as if she could see forever through the sharp spring air as she geared down on her motorcycle and pulled back on the throttle.

She couldn't accelerate fast enough. There wasn't enough wind slicing at her cheeks, not enough howl to the engine, or enough shudder through the handlebars to fight. She needed the contest right now, leaning into sharp curves and popping through the gears with her foot as the bike skimmed the asphalt, roaring up over blind rises and then hauling in on the brakes when she misjudged a turn. She needed the silence of the mountains and the emptiness of the afternoon, when everybody else was at work and the tourists hadn't yet begun to infiltrate the Ozarks to finger the lace tablecloth tattered from dogwoods and redbuds.

She needed to escape.

Elise Lawson terrified her. Not just her brusque attitude, her competent, professional air that told Chris plenty about just how far she'd take this investigation. Not just her appetite for the three nearly identical letters Mac had already come up with to add to her growing evidence file.

Her unrestrained delight.

She wasn't like Mac, smelling the scent of a good hunt, or like many of the other cops Chris had known, intrigued by a tough puzzle. She was like Harlan standing up to shout down the librarian at the town council meetings. Elise Lawson saw something in this case that even Mac didn't seem to get, something personal that sat sourly on Chris's stomach.

Chris had met cops like that before, usually burnouts who'd stumbled so far into the muck they had to shovel that they couldn't smell it anymore. Hot dogs with attitude who forgot where the line was, and often crossed it without thought, their only interest what could benefit them, their enjoyment salacious.

But Lawson was too young for that. She was brand new to homicide, working the Crimes Against Persons unit from St. Louis County straight out of a stint on patrol in affluent West County. She was also probably looking for a way to compare dick sizes with all the male detectives around her, and Chris knew with a sinking feeling of fatality that this was going to be it.

Chris focused on the silvery tumble of a stream as it paralleled the road. She opened her mouth wide and sucked in great lungsful of clean, crisp air. She did her best to clear her mind of everything but the power of the motorcycle beneath her, the sway and swoop of flying along the back roads on two wheels, the millisecond reflexes needed to skirt the edges on a 350-cc bike.

She still saw the pictures. Black-and-whites, color, the tints as lurid as a tabloid, the positions stiff and unnatural, like Lester left without a hand up his back, the settings as clinical as an operating room. The eyes open. All the eyes open, and somehow looking right at her.

What have you done now?

Instinctively she squeezed her eyes shut. She almost missed a curve and opened a new doorway into somebody's barn. Damn Lawson for finding her. Damn her for goading MacNamara into joining the hunt. Goddamn her soul to all the fires of hell for exhibiting those pictures to Chris like her personal accomplishments.

"Just take a look at this," she'd insisted, flipping open the first file folder right there on Chris's kitchen table. "Tell me if this isn't a damn good approximation of the crime scene in *Hell Hath No Fury*."

Not an approximation. Not even as dissimilar as a copy. Chris had only been able to stare, open-mouthed, struck silent by the sight of that mutilated, bloated body where it lay half in the bed, one arm sliding down to the floor, the other thrown across the blackly glistening stomach.

His eyes, flat and opaque, had been wide open. Surprised, as if he couldn't imagine finding himself in such a condition. As if the last person he'd expected to see on the other end of that knife was the one wielding it.

Just as he'd been in *Hell Hath No Fury*.

Not almost. Not close.

Exactly.

Every person reading a book comes away with a slightly different picture. Even with detailed description, a reader brings his own prejudices and preferences to a book. Maybe someone else reading *Hell Hath no Fury* would have positioned the victim a little to the right, or moved his hand up another notch toward his heart, where it could have stemmed just a little of the blood that had coursed from him. Where it might have deflected the knife maybe once in its furious descent. They might have given his hair a little more red or his once-handsome eyes a darker shade of blue.

But Chris, who had written the book, who had sat for hours over the exact description of the victim, of the gruesome ballet choreographed in that nondescript bedroom, of the blood splash patterns and lividity markings, had a very vivid image of what that death scene would have looked like.

And she'd looked right down on a picture—on ten pictures, each shot from a different angle—of it.

And another set of pictures from *Too Late the Hero* and *That Scottish Play*. Perfect in every detail. Accurate enough that for just a flash of a moment Chris wondered if she'd really conceived her works or lived them. Had she really only seen these crimes in her imagination?

Just a couple of miles beyond where Rita Louise Filmore catered to every trucker and biker in the county in her double-wide, Eleven Mile Road topped the north side of Wilbur Mountain and afforded a nice view of the valley beneath. Beer cans littered the grass from necking marathons when the high school kids pretended that the lights spread out below them were really the valley seen from Mullholland Drive, and pockmarked No Hunting signs decorated the trees. Chris pulled to a stop and let the bike idle beneath her. Her heart was hammering against her chest, her palms sweaty, her temples throbbing from the vise of small spaces.

She'd deliberately bought her house because it was so high, so wide, so very open. And yet, as Lawson had moved closer, her eyes trapping Chris's with her own sense of triumph, her ambition as sharp as splintered glass and her curiosity savage, even Chris's own house had become too small. Chris had ended up throwing them both out and running like hell before she'd stopped breathing completely.

She couldn't handle this. She couldn't live with the burden of what this person with the meticulous letters and perfect, gruesome vision was doing to her, and she had no way to protect herself from it.

All Chris had wanted with her writing was to finally be able to get beyond the guilt. To finally find some peace from the whisperings and reflexes of the past. Always being chased from town to town by the specter of her own failings.

Even here, though, she wasn't safe.

She looked down at the scatter of buildings below her. The Rock of Ages Baptist Church with its steeple in the shape of her doodlings, sharp and surgical, as if God could be divined by compass and protractor. The service station with its misplaced arch, and the county courthouse in its island of trees. Cracked sidewalks and weed-filled lots, modest houses brightened with siding that surrounded the square like diminishing planets in orbit around a dying sun, and farther out in its own untidy cluster of rusted trailers and disassembled autos, the land of Oz, its dismal poverty camouflaged even now by the fog of tree limbs.

It wasn't much. Not a tidy town by any means, or pretty in a conventional way. More like an unkempt favorite aunt, comfortable and easygoing. Crippled with unemployment, spiced with pockets of vicious ignorance and gentled with the small-town concern that had already brought four neighbors and the Methodist minister to her door with offerings of food in her time of distress, Pyrite didn't merit so much as a mention in Missouri's travel brochures.

But it had become as much of a home as she'd ever had. And now, because of something she'd done, she was going to lose it. She was going to lose everything. And there was nothing she could do about it but help it happen, because she couldn't run away from those pictures.

She couldn't allow this person to keep killing in her name.

Chris had been alone most of her life. She had never felt more alone than she did at that moment, when she so needed to tell someone just how much this thing frightened her. There was no one, though, who would understand. No one who had any experience of what madness felt like when whispered in a person's ear. So, as always, she would face it by herself.

Righting the bike, she kicked it into gear and eased on back down the road toward town.

"I've had it. I'm leaving home."

Chris looked up from where she was closing her garage door, and her mood slid straight from desperate to despairing. She didn't need this right now. Not when she couldn't really concentrate on it.

She straightened and pocketed her key in her fuschia leather jacket. "What's wrong, Shel?"

Shelly's smile was fragile, at once brassy and immeasurably vulnerable. Chris wanted to pull the girl into her arms, and knew she'd never let her. So she started walking toward the kitchen door, figuring that Shelly would follow. She did.

"Wrong?" Shelly laughed as she hefted her purse onto one shoulder with shaking hands. "Nothing's wrong. My father treats me like a piece of dirt, my mother won't do anything about it, and my boyfriend has just told me he's tired of me."

"And?"

They both stopped as Chris worked the key in the back lock.

"And what? Isn't that enough?"

Chris just smiled. "No. I want a really good reason."

For a moment the two of them stood there in the dappled sunlight, the breeze picking at their hair, the Milton kids skipping across the small yard on their way home from school.

Finally Shelly dipped her head, hands in jacket pockets, hair swinging forward to mask the tears Chris knew were swelling in those woman-child eyes that were going to get her into such trouble some day.

"I'm flunking," she admitted, not looking up, her voice as tight as dried leather.

It was Chris's turn to shove her hands into pockets. She took a long, considering look at the solid, white, square expanse of her house that could hold such silence inside. She thought of the space that had been lost there this afternoon, of the clean, empty, solitary lines, her own gladioli bought to mask the stench of misery. She sighed.

Chris wasn't good at this. Another one of her secrets. She'd been trained to atone, not to care. No matter how much she wanted to, she wasn't familiar enough with getting close to people to ever be comfortable with it. She knew all the catchphrases and platitudes that were supposed to work in a situation like this, but she tended to trip over them like a blind man on barbed wire.

She wanted to help. She knew just what the judge was going to do when he found out about Shelly's grades. She also knew that Shelly was dead serious about her threat, and she couldn't say she blamed her. Chris knew just how Shelly felt. But she also knew just what she was asking for.

The chief and the detective were supposed to meet her back at the city hall at one. They were going to have to wait. Chris had other problems to sort out first, and they weren't going to be much easier.

Briefly closing her eyes, Chris did her best to complete her most important mental exercise. Slamming one door, opening another, keeping everything in its place.

Only suddenly there were a couple of doors that were getting difficult to close.

"Let's take a walk," she suggested, turning away from the house.

It took Shelly a moment to follow, but she did, the two of them looking uncannily alike, even though they bore no physical resemblance as they headed down the sidewalk toward city hall.

"I've got to get out of here," Shelly insisted, the hush of her voice betraying the real need no one would ever expect from her.

Chris automatically shook her head. "No," she said. "You don't. We'll figure something else out, if you want, but you're not leaving Pyrite."

"Why?" Shelly demanded. "So the judge can break my other arm?"

"Chris Jackson, have you found Jesus yet?"

Chris didn't even bother to look over. "It wasn't my day to watch him, Harlan."

That actually got a surprised giggle out of Shelly. "Chris, that's terrible."

Chris smiled smugly at the sound of sputtering protest from the pressboard-and-stained-plexiglass doorway of the Old Tyme Faith in Jesus Church. "Oh, what would Harlan have left to do if I actually joined the fold and became a good Christian?"

"How do you keep fighting him?"

"Easy," she admitted with that same sly smile. "Just say no."

They'd slowed, just shy of the closed Phillips 66 station. Weeds and trash littered the lot, and the board-ed-up windows sported the latest in high school graf-fiti. Bold obscenities that had to be expressed in the anonymity of darkness.

Shelly examined her shoes as she walked, her voice suddenly smaller. "Maybe I could just stay with you for the rest of the year."

Chris didn't even have to think about that. "No, honey, you can't."

Shelly stopped again, the distress on her face like an open wound. She'd obviously been waiting for that option to be proposed all along.

Chris could have kicked herself. She'd seen this one coming a mile away. She'd half been planning for it, figuring that hers was the kind of refuge Shelly would take to. Two weeks ago she would have suggested it herself. Two weeks ago, the dreams hadn't returned.

There simply wasn't any way she could have a second person in her house all the time. The only way she prevented the nightmares was not to sleep at all, and she simply couldn't do that for an indefinite period of time, especially while she was fighting a shadow that committed murder. She couldn't stay up, and she couldn't expose her nightmares to anyone else. Especially Shelly.

"Don't you want me?" the girl asked.

Chris fought against a sigh of frustration. She didn't need to be backed into a corner from two separate directions at once.

"Well, afternoon, ladies," a new, booming voice interrupted. "How are you today?"

Both of them turned to greet Ray Sullins, the town mayor and real-estate maven. Fair, fat, and forty, he had the backbone of an oil slick and played small-town politics like a first-chair violinist. Ray, word had it, was tickled to death the town might have a murder attached to it. Nothing sold like sensation.

"Hi there, Ray," Chris greeted him, her hand on Shelly's elbow as they deliberately kept walking by. Neither of them needed to get into a session with Ray.

"Mr. Mayor," Shelly echoed, that little grin flickering at the corners of her mouth again as she let Chris shepherd her past.

"Saw that little policewoman from up St. Louis

way," Ray announced loudly enough that anybody in the laundromat across the street could have heard him. "Real dynamo, isn't she?"

Chris just nodded. "That's where we're headed now."

"Well, you need anything, you let me know. Can't have our very own author facing all this alone."

Chris almost laughed. If it were up to Ray, she'd be a mention in the town's yearly calendar under civic improvements. Her picture right there under the new drive-in window at the Pizza Hut. If Chris hadn't had so many friends in town who voted, he would have been on the phone to the *Enquirer* four days ago.

"You didn't answer me," Shelly insisted when they'd made it out of earshot.

"That's right," Chris countered, letting go of the girl now that they were in the clear. "I figured you didn't want your dad's poker partner to know."

"Well?"

She was doing her best not to be stopped by the other townspeople who nodded in passing. "It's not you, Shelly," she insisted. "Please believe me. It's me."

"Then what am I going to do? I'm not going back."

Chris pulled out a smile she hoped looked a lot heartier than she felt and turned Shelly back in the direction of city hall. "I have an appointment with the chief," she said. "I thought we'd talk to Sue while we're there."

"The chief." Shelly immediately sighed with all the melodrama of a teenage girl. "Maybe he'd like to have me over."

*Lately, his dreams had begun to seem more
real than his life. Vivid dreams, the colors super-
saturated so that the sky looked like old stained
glass and the grass shuddering tides of peridots.
Hot, horrific dreams starring his wife and her
lover, clenched together in that winking, gleaming grass.*

*In his dreams, he crept up through the blades
of grass to see the heave of their bodies, to smell
the chlorine-sharp stench of sex.*

*He grew in his dreams, Alice in his wonder-
land. The genie let loose from the bottle. The terrible swift sword of retribution. . . .*

"Quite a book, isn't it?"

Mac looked up from his copy of *Too Late the Hero*
to find Luella Simpson poised in front of him, weight
on one hip, order pad in one hand, coffee pot in the
other. The skinny waitress with dyed black hair and
denim and spandex wardrobe used the pot to point
at the book in his hands.

"Not really lunchtime reading, ya ask me," she
continued with a grimace that threatened to crack the
top two layers of makeup on her face. "Too . . .
oogie."

Mac set the book down on the chipped Formica
table at his booth. Before him lay the remains of the
blue plate special, a fan of catfish bones and a little
pool of catsup still holding onto a lone french fry.
Luella was busy topping off the cooling coffee in his
mug.

"You didn't like it?" he asked, still trying to decide
exactly how he felt about C. J. Turner's work.

Luella brightened immediately. "Oh, sure. Missed

my bowling league night and two dates to finish it. Same as the others. Makes you wonder, though, how a girl who grew up in a convent school could come up with some of that stuff."

"Convent school?" Mac closed the book over a marker, his attention completely on the black-haired waitress. "I thought she was raised in foster homes."

"She was. Orphaned at four, from what she said. When she was livin' in Los Angeles, though, the family who had her had some money, sent her to one of these live-in places."

"California? I thought she was raised in the Midwest."

This time he got a shake of the head. "Nah. She moved here for college, what she said. Doesn't have a lot of nice things to say for the coast."

Mac wasn't sure why Luella's story niggled at him. Not because he thought he knew so much about Chris Jackson. All he knew so far was that she wrote books that made the hair stand up on the back of his neck, lived in a place that looked like a garage sale for eccentrics, and slept even less than he did. And that her psychic professor saw things in her dreams that kept her awake, too.

Mac believed in intuition. He had it. He'd earned it, soaking up thousands of miles of street time, watching even more people, smart people, dumb people, guilty and innocent people, on the run or standing at a quivering stop at the edge of a police .38. Mac knew people, and he just didn't know how to read Chris Jackson.

She was a woman of contrasts. Intensely private, but with a finger in every pie in town. Able to alienate the local fundamentalists enough that their pastor had vowed holy vengeance more than once about some slight or another, but still able to convince them to join the town in keeping her secret. Sharp as a narc on undercover, and as fey as a creature from the old Irish tales his mother had fed him with his bedtime snacks.

"Thought that lady detective was here already," Luella said, picking up Mac's empty plate.

Mac checked his watch. He'd seen Chris whip around the corner on that outlandish vintage Harley of hers about five minutes ago, so they should be about ready to dive back into those files. He found himself looking forward to it more than anything since he'd come to in the Neurosurgical ICU at Michael Reese.

"She's getting a room over at Harmonia Switzer's," he said.

The perfectly painted black arc of one of Luella's eyebrows raised several notches. "Instead of the Sleep Well?"

"She didn't want to stay over by the highway. Hates the noise."

"Wait'll she gets a load of Harmonia's organ music."

Mac fought a grin. "No, I think it's gonna be the monkey that's gonna drive her out."

Luella laughed out loud as she sashayed back to the counter, and Mac was left to get his things together. He couldn't believe it. He was conspiring just like the rest of the town, punishing the person who didn't belong. And another cop, at that. He should know better. It didn't make him like Elise Lawson any more.

If it were up to him, he'd grab all the records

she'd brought and send her off on a wild goose chase while he worked the case himself. He could smell something really bizarre in this one. Something hot, like the time he'd managed to nail down a murder-one rap on a guy who'd killed three separate women to make it look like a serial killer had chopped up his wife. There were layers to this, currents that he hadn't even tested yet.

He wanted to get Chris Jackson back on those pictures, wanted to spend more time on those notes she'd gotten, and dig into the reasons she wrote her books. He had his own theories after reading the first three, but he wanted to hear it from her. Somehow that figured into why three people had been killed in her name. He wanted to sit down and do a real interrogation of Chris Jackson and find out just how much of the truth she'd told him.

The first thing you learned in the real world was that everybody lies. Big lies, little lies, evasions of the truth, half-truths. When you're questioning five people about a murder, every one of them will lie about something. It's just a matter of finding out what they're lying about, and who's telling the smallest lies.

Everybody lies. Mac wanted to know what Chris Jackson's lies were.

He wanted answers. Suspects. A case.

He wanted to belong again.

God, he missed Chicago. Getting to his feet, he pulled out his pack of cigarettes and lit one up as he left. He knew his hands were shaking again, but it didn't matter.

✦   ✦   ✦

"Just how long have you had a motorcycle?"

Chris reached the doorway into Mac's office and turned to walk the other way. "Since I was about eighteen." She flashed Mac an irreverent grin where he sat tilted back in his chair. "I don't like seatbelts."

She wondered why they couldn't do this out by the courthouse under the trees. Maybe along the Watson trail up in the mountains. The rooms in the city hall were just too close, especially the small corner reserved for the police. Since the dispatcher was over at the sheriff's office, the only space they needed was for a common room with all the latest in official bulletins, county and city ordinances, and lascivious calendars, and the chief's little office.

He'd changed the office old L. J. had kept. Instead of a twelve-by-sixteen picture of L. J.'s horse Tony on the K-Mart-paneled wall, there was a collection of diplomas, obviously to reassure the town that their new chief knew his business. FBI training, Alcohol, Tobacco, and Firearms camp, bachelor's in law enforcement, and several medals for sharpshooting.

Nothing about his medals of valor, Chris noted, or his commendations from the Chicago police, which she'd heard about from L. J. An efficient display rather than a self-serving one.

In the bookcases that now sported many of the same forensic and judicial tomes that graced Chris's shelves, L. J.'s bowling trophies had been replaced by collections of pictures, the varying resemblances betraying relationships, the comfortable poses implying closeness. Mac's desk was as orderly as his uniform and his coatrack carried a Cubs cap along with his uniform cap and rain poncho. He'd even added a tape deck to the radio system. At the moment, Joe

Cocker was inviting some sweet young thing to leave her hat on.

It made Chris smile as she paced the tile room, her heels clicking in time to the funky, bluesy beat. Her hips even took on that saucy sway that had always gone with it in her mind. "That's what I always wanted to do."

"What?"

Chris turned, surprised. Evidently she'd taken to thinking out loud. Her smile was abashed, but she kept on moving, still in rhythm with the raucous music.

"Sing backup for Joe Cocker."

"You sing?" Mac asked from where he was seated in his office, his chair tilted back, his posture relaxed. Chris had noticed, though, that his hands had that funny tremor to them again, and that there had been a couple of cigarettes in the Windy City ashtray on his desk when she'd shown up.

She laughed. "God, no. But I could sure strut when I was fifteen. I figured I could get by."

"Was that when you were out in L. A.?" he asked.

Chris stumbled to a halt, suddenly, irrationally afraid. She refused to look at him, knowing that if she did, he'd know. Embarrassed more than unnerved. Instead, she examined the aerial map that took up the wall behind Sue's desk.

"Luella said you lived out there," he elaborated from behind her.

"Yep," she admitted, her voice as carefully passive as his as she headed off on another tour of the front room.

"She said you didn't like it."

"Not much."

It wasn't that Chris couldn't discuss Los Angeles. She didn't want to. She didn't want to really have to relive anything that had brought her to her life in Pyrite, any of the mistakes she'd made, the sins she'd committed, the absurdities she'd survived. Those were things best locked away behind their separate doors, building blocks in her life that belonged deep underground, story after story beneath the one she now inhabited.

Mac must have been a hell of a detective. It didn't take him a heartbeat to catch on.

"You want to come in and sit down?" he asked easily, still not moving, except to pick up a big paperweight with a tarantula caught inside a bubble of Plexiglas.

Chris just shook her head. "Not till I have to, thanks. I'm not overly fond of small spaces."

She stopped at the front window to look out across at Eloise checking the window display at the How Do. The little woman moved like a small bird, in fits and starts, her hands patting at the silk flowers like favored children, then dipping to chastise a cat or sweeping up to pat at her hair. Born and bred in Pyrite, her expectations limited by the horizon, her transgressions meager, her conscience clear. Chris envied her.

"Is that why you decided to go riding?" Mac asked. "Your house too small?"

Chris had been concentrating so hard on Eloise that the sound of Mac's voice startled her. She didn't bother to turn. "I had to have a little time to deal with those pictures."

Behind her, there was silence. She was glad that Sue had taken Shelly out for pizza, that the rest of the city hall denizens wouldn't show up until one for afternoon hours. She needed to show a calm face to them about this, and so far she wasn't really managing it.

"I thought they were a little too close for comfort, too," Mac finally said, his voice still perfectly calm. Chris wondered if he'd moved at all yet, or whether he was still just watching her with those deceptive gray eyes of his, that horrible, fat spider suspended between his hands.

She shook her head, wondering why she was giving this man more than she'd ever given anybody. Wondering what there was in his demeanor, in his background that should elicit such trust.

"Not a little too close. Picture perfect." She laughed then, a sharp, brittle sound that betrayed the hot turmoil in her chest. "This really is a personal thing, isn't it?"

Again, a measured silence, as if he wouldn't think to ask her an unconsidered question. "Any ideas why?"

That brought her around from the window. "No," she insisted, her voice more strident than she'd intended. With an effort, she backed down. "The letters are ambiguous and anonymous. I can't think of anyone I've ever met who could possibly want to do this."

Still not quite the truth. This was the portion of the truth she could give now. The truth she thought would suffice. Because, of course, the truth was, she couldn't *remember* anyone who would want to do that. But she couldn't remember a lot.

"How 'bout any other kind of contact? Phone calls? That kind of thing?"

"Nothing. I've had a lot of hang-ups on the answering machine recently, but that could be anything."

Mac righted his chair. "Nothing said?"

Chris shook her head, but his careful response incited a new disquiet in her. Was this something else she'd deliberately ignored, like the letters? Was the killer trying another way to get hold of her? It more than crossed her mind to just rip the whole damn phone from the wall and give it back to Ma Bell.

She rubbed at the weariness in her eyes. "I don't know. Maybe I shouldn't be surprised Lawson called."

"But you still don't have any idea who could be doing it."

She shook her head, picking at the hem of her brightly colored blouse.

"Do me a favor, if you will," he suggested diffidently, as if it really weren't that important. "When you go home, try and think of all the people you've known well, especially anyone who might know you have a pseudonym. Here, St. Louis, wherever you've lived in the last few years. I know it probably won't amount to anything. This character is probably just a fruitball needing to get his rocks off to your prose, but it can't hurt. Will you do that for me?"

Chris kept pacing, names and dates and places already curling past her imaginary viewfinder like the credits on a film. Each one more innocuous than the next. Safe, quiet people she'd deliberately chosen to help defray the isolation. To begin building the confidence that could eventually lead her to this spot.

Chris knew that she'd only give him part of what

he wanted. Because she could only manage part of it, even now.

"Another thing you might want to think about is what you were doing sixteen months ago. Usually a pattern like this is set off by something important to the perp. A disappointment, a trauma, that kind of thing. If it had to do with you, you might remember."

Chris refused to turn her answering grin to him. It was wry and dark. "Like not answering mail, or writing a book someone swears they've already written and I stole from their attic?"

"That happened?"

"A couple of times. But those same people also accused four other authors."

"I'd like to know anyway."

She nodded again, wishing for respite, for at least the small relief of finding out that whoever this was had never touched her. Had never shaken hands and smiled and sat down to a meal with her.

Let it be some stranger with disconnected problems, who had never relied on her or been disappointed by her, so she didn't have to bear the weight of that, too.

She walked back by the front window just in time to see her possibility of respite end. Climbing out of her Chevy sedan was Sergeant Lawson. Instinctively Chris straightened, ran a quick hand through her hair and resettled her attitude into calm consideration before having to face the detective.

"It looks like show time," she said.

Behind her, Mac's chair scraped back as he stood to join her. "You'll do fine," he encouraged her.

"No I won't," she disagreed, then turned a wry grin on him. "But I'm not going to let her know that."

He still had that thing in his hands, cradled gently,

as if the venom inside could still reach him if he weren't careful. His attention was on the detective as she pulled her briefcase from the car. "Well, I hope she got some answers while she was out."

Chris turned to see that the tremor had stopped. His hands were perfectly still, his expression quiet. And she, she thought, had stopped moving. Had pulled her own protection back over her.

"Answers?" she asked. "I thought she was going to find someplace to stay."

He turned to Chris, then, and she saw how delicately he thought he needed to approach her. It was just a hint, just a smell of caution on him, but Chris caught it and was almost amused all over again.

"She was also going to try and get a name from the post office box on the return address on your letters."

The amusement almost died stillborn. They were back to business. Settling down to the task of peeling away the layers of protection between her and the venom that she held between her hands.

The bell over the city hall door sounded just as cheery as the one at the How Do. It made Chris's teeth grate.

Mac made an attempt at greetings. Lawson never gave him a chance. Spinning right to Chris, she leveled her flat brown gaze and delivered her challenge.

"I have a name on the post office box," she announced, her feet planted squarely beneath her in shoes that didn't match her suit, her voice gravelly and her eyes red-rimmed with the allergies she'd brought with her.

Chris wasn't sure how to answer. Lawson looked as if she expected congratulations. Chris figured she'd leave that to Mac. She was having trouble enough staying inside walls that were beginning to make her sweat. She was having trouble keeping her place when Lawson came so close she made Chris's stomach heave.

The smell. It was the smell Lawson carried with her. Chris hadn't even identified it until just now. Pine cleaner. Chris had often heard that the sense of smell was the most primal, inciting raw emotion even beyond memory. Chris smelled pine cleaner and fought the urge to vomit. To run. To cower in a corner where she'd be safe. Chris was sure it was just a faint trace, but it seemed like a miasma, and the memories it culled were of hours on her knees, the smell of old cooking grease, the words of Revelations, the ache of exhausted shoulders and holy vengeance.

"And?" Mac prodded.

And. And what? With an effort, Chris pulled herself back to the present. Not grease and mold, but fresh coffee and old cigars. Lawson's feral eyes glued to Chris like lasers. Mac poised for intervention.

He didn't look excited. Maybe Lawson pissed him off, too. Maybe he didn't like a policewoman with no fashion sense. Chris couldn't pull her attention away from Lawson long enough to find out.

Lawson never acknowledged him. Clearing her throat for the fiftieth time since showing up that morning, she directed herself to Chris as if it were just the two of them involved. "The box is at the Brentwood post office in St. Louis County. 63144. You know the area?"

Chris nodded, hating the suspense, hating the bearer of bad news. "That's where most of *That Scottish Play* is set."

Lawson nodded back, so briskly that her mussy brown hair bobbed. "Does the name Jacqueline Christ mean anything to you?"

Chris fought hard to hold still. She struggled to breathe as the room tilted before her.

God, what kind of joke was this?

Lawson didn't miss an inflection. "You know her," she stated immediately.

Chris opened her mouth. She closed it. She broke through her own paralysis to try an offhand gesture. "Yeah," she admitted, waving an ineffectual hand and then shoving both hands into her pants' pockets. "I do."

Mac turned to her then, his own attention sharp. "Who is she?"

Chris could only manage a shrug, desperate to pull some sense out of this. "Me."

✦ Chapter 7 ✦

THE BELL TINKLED merrily behind Sergeant Lawson. Nobody saw Sue walk in on the frozen tableau.

"What?" Mac was asking.

Chris was still trying to breathe. That protective bubble of Plexiglas had just grown smaller. Or maybe the beast had grown larger, eating up the air between herself and it. Chris could feel its breath on her again, could hear that silky whisper of terror. There was so much to keep track of, so many doors that needed to stay shut in order to protect her. Door after door, all set in an intricate design to provide protection, to open up space. It was the only way she'd managed.

The only way she'd survived.

Sue never even got out her greeting before she, too, came to an uncertain halt, all of them now within five feet of Chris. Chris was beginning to sweat, desperate to move. She remained perfectly still.

"What do you mean, you're Jacqueline Christ?" Lawson asked carefully.

That brought Sue's head snapping right around. "What?" she demanded even more forcefully than Mac.

Chris dredged up a self-effacing grin as she direct-ed her gaze to the stain an old thunderstorm had left on the indoor-outdoor carpeting by Mac's office.

"It's another pseudonym I use," she admitted in a small voice.

"Pseudonym?" Mac countered. "You mean other books?"

"You're Jacqueline Christ?" Sue asked almost shril-ly, her sensible green eyes huge with astonishment, her purse hitting the floor with a flat thud. "Jacqueline Christ!"

Chris did, finally, face her friend. "That phone booth does get crowded sometimes."

"More mysteries?" Mac asked.

Chris shook her head. "Romance."

That brought on another shocked silence.

"Oh, God," he moaned. "Now I have to read romances?"

Sue turned on him like a mother defending her young. "Just so you know, Jacqueline Christ is the best in the business. She's written fifty-three books."

His face crumbled. "Fifty-three?"

Sue afforded him no more than a glare before she swung her attention back on Chris, the news sinking in with force. "You *really* are Jacqueline Christ?"

"I'd really appreciate it if you don't say anything," Chris said. "My mail's intense enough as it is."

That brought another heartfelt groan from Mac. "I imagine you saved all that, too."

She nodded.

He damn near dropped his head in defeat. "Then we'll have to go through it."

"Why hide it?" Lawson asked, finally coming to life.

Everybody turned on her, almost surprised that she was still in the room. She'd never even had the chance to put down her purse or briefcase, standing stiff and alert as a bird dog on the scent.

"It's just easier to keep everything separate that way," Chris admitted. "I need . . . I need to compartmentalize things to be able to manage what I do."

Lawson finally moved, her actions brisk and impersonal. "It's not important. What's important is how the killer found out. Who knows?"

"Of *course* it's important," Sue retorted, then retreated when everybody else turned on her in consternation. "But I bet I could talk to Chris about that later . . . after I go through the mail." And with that, she spun around, picked up her purse, and stalked into the mayor's office.

"Who knows?" Lawson asked Chris again, pulling out her notes along with a Kleenex to blow her nose. "Damn allergies," she muttered to herself. She had a wedding ring on her left hand, an old fashioned Claddagh ring with hands wrapped around a tiny gold heart. Chris wondered at who some people married.

She decided it was time for some coffee. Actually, she wanted a drink, but she didn't drink, so coffee was going to have to be her best substitute, unless Mac wanted to teach her how to smoke right on the spot.

"My agent," she said, her back to both of them as she hefted the pot and poured. She knew what it was going to taste like. She swore Sue filtered it through Tom's baseball socks. It didn't matter. It was strong enough to creosote railroad ties, and that was what she needed at that moment.

"And his name?"

"Her name," Chris countered, taking a slug straight up. "Dinah Martin."

"That's right," Lawson mused, pulling out a chair and perching on it. "Your agent's a woman. Our killer seems to be a woman, too."

Chris almost spit coffee on her. "Well, it's not Dinah," she said with a bark of laughter. "She'd never see any reason to resort to knives. She does enough damage with her tongue."

Lawson was bent over her notes, checking something. "She has a rap sheet," she announced.

Chris waved her coffee cup in objection. "Not for murder."

"For what?" Mac asked, following Chris's example and heading for the coffeepot. She saw him pat his pocket for his cigarettes, saw his forehead wrinkle in frustration at not finding any.

"It's nothing," Chris insisted, trying to read over Lawson's shoulder.

Lawson snapped her files shut. "Theft."

"Shoplifting." Chris turned to Mac for support. "She has a little problem."

His scowl was deeper, coffeepot poised over his official Alcohol, Tobacco and Firearms coffee mug. "A little problem?"

"She's seeking treatment."

"She's a kleptomaniac," the detective announced dryly.

Mac was hardly impressed. "Unless she's been stealing swords and bathtubs, I don't think she's involved. Anybody else know about your other pseudonym?" he asked Chris, his voice gentling noticeably. "Anybody at all?"

She didn't even have to think about it. "Nobody but the people at Rapture Press," she insisted. "Jacqueline has been well-known for a lot longer than C. J. I didn't want the town treating me like some of the people in the industry have been treated, so I kind of . . . well, protected them from the truth. I'd rather not have to spend my time defending my craft, or my privacy."

"Well, somebody else has figured it out," Lawson stated. "Some woman with access to the Brentwood post office . . . I don't suppose *you've* been up there recently."

Chris's answer was automatic. "Well, sure. Just a few weeks ago. I'm up there all the time researching . . ." Which was just about when it dawned on her exactly what the detective was implying.

It took an effort to keep from hurling her coffee at the woman. "What the hell do you mean?"

Chris didn't even notice that Mac had taken to leaning against the wall by the map, or that his full attention was on her flushed face.

It didn't seem to bother Lawson to face Chris with her suspicions. "When was the last time?" she asked.

Chris's jaw dropped. "You think *I've* been killing these people?"

Lawson challenged her with unsmiling confidence. "I think it's too early to rule you out. When were you up there last?"

Chris found herself looking to Mac for support. He considered her evenly, his expression passive. It didn't help.

"Three weeks ago," Chris said.

"And where did you stay?"

"I usually stay at the Ritz in Clayton. It's a little treat I give myself."

Lawson took another swipe at her nose and cleared her gravelly throat. "What about this time?"

"The Ritz. I told you."

"And the time before that? When were you there?"

"I don't know," Chris said. "I'd have to look. Since I set the mystery series in St. Louis County, I go up every time I start a new book. Research into a different municipality."

"Which one did you do this time?"

"Marlborough and Clayton."

Over ninety municipalities within the boundaries of St. Louis County, not to mention the unincorporated area, with enough geographic space and demographic range to keep Livvy Beckworth and Detective Stephens busy for years to come. At least, Chris hoped so.

"The three murders were in the same order as the books, right?" Mac asked, sipping at his coffee.

Lawson sneezed and nodded. "First three."

"And what about the next two?" he asked. "Anything on those yet?"

Lawson fiddled with her pen for a minute. "Not that I've heard."

Chris walked back to the coffeemaker, her cup already empty, her belly churning. "Well, one's the death by oleander poisoning in Ladue, and the other's suicide by shotgun in Fergusson."

"And the one you're working on now?"

Chris looked up, unsettled all over again, somehow sure she was asking for trouble by inviting these two people into her imagination. "Um, this one . . . I'm not sure yet. Knife again, I think."

Lawson's head came up. "You think?" she asked. "You don't know?"

A shrug, as if that were the most expansive Chris could allow herself to be. The room was too small for more, her chest too tight. "The book dictates it, and I'm only getting started." The day she wrote a book about the good detective here, she thought acidly, she'd have to pick a particularly nasty way for her to go. Death by fondue, maybe.

"Did you see anyone when you were in St. Louis?" Lawson asked.

Chris took another good slug of coffee, masking her fear with its fire. "Why?"

It took Lawson a minute to answer. She just sat where she was, her ballpoint pen clutched in white-knuckled hands, her head bent. Chris saw the swirls of her hair, still flattened a little from sleep, and thought of hospital patients.

"What day exactly were you there?" the detective asked finally.

"The twenty-fifth through the twenty-ninth."

Lawson nodded to herself. "Mr. Weaver was murdered in Affton, less than eight miles from where you were staying, on the twenty-seventh."

Chris wasn't sure how that was supposed to make her feel. She thought of the well-appointed hotel room, of the cold, spare afternoons walking the tidy, prosperous little bedroom community of Marlborough, supported by its speed traps and comfortable, middle-class taxes. A quiet, predictable kind of white-collar enclave where murder just didn't happen. Which, of course, in this book, it hadn't.

She thought of Affton, three books and a tax base away. Blue collar, its major thoroughfares lined with

small businesses and cemeteries, its politics conserva-
tive, its denizens older, and its decor row upon row
of tidy, uninspiring brick homes with neatly tended
yards.

She'd driven those streets so long ago, walked
through the subdivisions where sweetgum trees had
rained down their spiky fruit on well-loved little
yards and garage sales had snarled traffic every
Wednesday. She'd spent hours and days in the stores,
the bars, the bowling alleys watching the people,
looking for likely couples to star in her book.

The "Watsons" had been classic Affton residents,
white, middle-aged, blue collar, their entertainment
the ballgames in the summer, the television in the
winter, and the local bar all times in between, the
frustrations mounting along with the bills and the
realization that the American dream wasn't everything
they'd been promised.

Chris had really related to Mrs. Watson, caught by
her husband's violent disappointment, trapped by her
upbringing, a prisoner of that hot, crowded little
house behind the bowling alley. She'd been angry for
her, desperate with her, knowing that terrible vise of
futility. The night Mrs. Watson had actually figuratively given the Mister his with that horrific butcher
knife, spattering blood around her American Colonial
bedroom with its J. C. Penney paintings and the
knickknacks collected from years of vacations to Hot
Springs and Silver Dollar City, Chris had been more
than glad to be the proverbial hand to free the little
woman who'd existed only in her mind.

She'd really enjoyed doing the surly bastard in.

And she'd been back, no more than a few miles
away, when the real Mr. Weaver had struggled and

screamed and begged as his life had seeped away into the brown and gold bedspread. Chris knew she should ask what time it had happened. She should ask what time they'd all happened. It was important.

She didn't.

She sipped at her coffee as if the detective's news didn't unnerve her. She fought the clutch of nausea at the thought that someone out there was affected enough by her murders to emulate them. To emulate, in his mind, her.

Chris ended up back at the window, where she could see all the way down the street and wondered if the murderer had been as careful in his research as she had.

"I visited one of the women I used to work with," she finally said. "Drove around and walked around to get the feel of the streets. Did some business and some research on the occupations and personality types I wanted to portray. Ate out a few times and got a lot of carry-out from a nearby Chinese restaurant. That's the way I usually do it when I'm up there."

"And at night?" Lawson asked. "Did you see anybody at night?"

Chris knew Lawson wanted her to react. She wasn't about to give her the satisfaction, even though she'd just had her own questions answered. If the book were really being copied, Mr. Weaver would have died somewhere near one in the morning. All the victims would have. "I write at night," she said. "And that's almost impossible to do if I have company."

Lawson challenged her in silence, her non-specific accusation even more offensive. She didn't really suspect Chris. She just wanted Chris to think so to see Chris squirm.

"Then again," Chris added, just as deliberately, "that could have been the weekend I was entertaining the St. Louis Cardinals. One at a time." She paused, her voice chilling. "Except the batboy, of course. He had school the next day."

"So," Mac offered quietly behind her in his best defusing tone of voice, "we're looking for someone who knows both of Chris's pseudonyms . . . you don't have any others you'd like to get off your chest, do you?"

Chris retreated with a wry smile. "Do you count the alias I use for the phone sex line I run?"

Chris could almost see the minimal betrayal of amusement he'd allow. He'd evidently finally found his cigarettes, too. Either that or he was just playing with matches. Chris heard a rasping, and then caught the sharp whiff of sulfur. Either way, it smelled better than the pine cleaner scent on the detective.

"Then we're looking for someone who knows Chris's two pseudonyms. Someone intelligent enough to have gotten away with this three times without being caught."

"Or," Lawson countered, "someone who's pretty angry that they haven't been noticed yet."

Chris felt that one right in her chest. She turned away from her window to see that Mac took the news with a raised eyebrow and a considering look her way.

"Good point," he admitted. "He's sending letters. That means he either really hates her, or really loves her, and wants her to get the message."

It was getting hard to breathe again. "I'll send a letter right away."

It seemed, though, that she'd been left behind.

"Someone with access to St. Louis," Mac was saying. "Brentwood in particular."

Lawson gave Chris another of those pointed looks. "With St. Louis being TWA's hub, no real trick there."

"It's not Dinah," Chris insisted.

"Is it you?" Lawson countered.

Chris turned from the window then and challenged her face to face. "No." She wondered if she sounded certain enough. She couldn't tell by the expression on Lawson's face. The only two expressions the woman wore well seemed to be disbelief and ravenous curiosity. She was trying on the former now, and it pissed Chris off.

It would have pissed her off a whole lot more if she were certain about anything in this situation.

"So," she countered to them both, "you're telling me we're looking for someone who lives anywhere in the country, who figured out who I am, might be a woman, is somehow fixated enough on the Livvy Beckworth books that she—or he—wants to make them into participational art, and is probably figuring out how to get hold of an oleander bush in St. Louis."

"You want to give me one good reason why you keep qualifying this perp as a possible man?" Lawson demanded. "Even with a woman's name on that box?"

"That name doesn't mean anything," Chris insisted. "It doesn't take all that much to dress up, or even have somebody else go in and get your mail from a post office box for you. Heck, I've wandered around here in disguise and nobody's caught me. Why should it be so hard to get away with it in a metropolitan area of two million?"

"Here?" Mac demanded. "When? Not when I was here."

Chris gave him another grin. "You helped me across the street the other day. Seems to me, I remember planting a big kiss on your cheek."

That very cheek turned a commensurate shade of pink. His eyes grew in confounded silence.

"You see what you expect to see," she told him. "Even cops. It's an amazingly easy process, once you know the tricks."

"And you know the tricks."

"That Scottish Play."

"So we really haven't gotten anywhere," he countered blackly, taking a long pull from a slightly crumpled-looking cigarette. "Except that the perp knows your secrets."

"Not all of them," Chris countered.

"Like you said," Lawson challenged. "Don't assume anything."

Chris knew exactly how that should make her feel. It made her feel like crawling under the table and hiding.

The sunset that evening was breathtaking, the kind that only happens on the edge of spring. Clear, crisp, the breeze faint and the sky brilliant in jewel tones of peacock and crimson. It conjured up images of magic and power. Pyrrhic death, rebirth. Chris had her head buried in her hands and missed the whole thing.

"Well, you knew it was bound to come out sooner or later."

Chris rubbed at her eyes with the heel of her hands and sighed, the phone receiver making her ear go numb. "I know," she conceded. "I was just hoping for later."

"Oh, for heaven's sakes," Dinah said. "It's not like the FBI just discovered you hiding Jimmy Hoffa under your bed. Live with it, girl. You're famous."

"No," Chris countered carefully, too tired and fought over to be polite. "Jacqueline is famous. I'm just a normal person."

She got another telling snort for that one. "Sweetheart, you haven't been normal a day in your life."

Chris closed her eyes and pictured Dinah at her desk in New York, a black lacquered affair done in what Chris called the surgical precision school of decorating. One pencil sketch, black and white, on a white wall, one huge urn with a few six-foot feathers in it, one black leather chair. It was Dinah's firm belief that the only one who should feel comfortable in her office was she herself. That in contrast to Chris's garage-sale school of decoration, stuffed animals and flea market castoffs, clothes the color of stained glass, and books that went from slapstick to horror. A good balance, if ever there was one.

"Well," Chris said dryly, "if you'd like to put your money in the pool for who the crazy is, the betting is still wide open. You and I are even in the running."

Chris could imagine her agent shaking that dark head of hers. On the phone Dinah sounded about six feet tall with lacquered blonde hair, red nails and the posture of an S.S. officer. In person, she was chubby and brunette. Which was why she considered her phone demeanor and office furniture so important.

"It amuses me to wonder what that poor hick cop is thinking right this minute," Dinah said. "After all, *I* can hardly keep up with you. I can't possibly imagine he is."

"He's not a hick. He's not even a he. And you don't need to make it sound like I'm Walter Mitty. I'm just a poor working girl trying to make a living."

"Don't be absurd. You're a workaholic trying to drop me into an early grave, with at least three separate identities to uphold. There are days I swear you're probably screwing the President on the weekends just to get variety."

Chris managed a laugh. "I couldn't think of it. Weekends are our busiest times at the How Do."

That got her a heartfelt groan. "Please. My quaint quotient is quite high enough. Just promise me you won't spring any new surprises without telling me first . . . you know, Broadway plays, astronaut training, clown school."

"I promise. And try not to be disappointed, but you already know all there is to know."

"That's good, dear. It should be that way. After all, it's an agent's God-given duty to have enough on her clients to hold over them in times of negotiation."

"Then be glad and rejoice, Dinah. You know more about me than any living soul on earth."

The truth, she thought not for the first time. Certainly something that the powerful, often ruthless agent could easily hurt her with if she didn't have such a strict code of ethics. If she didn't have a notorious weak spot for her first client.

It was, after all, Dinah who held the strings to

each of Chris's different lives, who could most easily expose her. Dinah who understood in her own way just what Chris's privacy meant to her.

Dinah had been there at the beginning, when Chris had dipped that first toe into the world of publishing. Still caught in the morass of the St. Louis social service system, still finishing her third degree at night, still running.

Who was she kidding? She was still running. She was just able to do it with more comfort. On her own terms. As long as Dinah kept her confidence and Sergeant Lawson kept her distance.

As long as whatever was going on stopped short of her real secrets.

Chris didn't get any work done that night. She didn't even manage to stay in the house, pulled outside by the fresh throb of insects, by the fading fingers of sunset and the promise of space.

It was a weeknight, so the town was quiet. A few cars crawled along the streets, fewer pedestrians strolled the sidewalks. Only about half the streetlights were working, checkerboarding the streets in light and humming faintly as Chris passed.

Quiet. Pyrite was so quiet on nights like this, even when the kids cruised in their rebuilt cars or the Tip A Few exploded into broken glass and curses. Chris had spent too many years in places where the lights had been harsh and the noise reverberated off walls like a physical blow. She'd worked in bars where the music had battered her, where the clientele had reached out with fat, sweaty hands and pushed her back into the darkness. She'd lived in places where the cacophony of the streets had beaten her down like a fist. Like a hundred fists, folding her in, pummeling at her, squeezing her dry until she grew smaller and smaller inside, afraid one day she'd disappear altogether.

Yeah, she thought. She'd lived in L. A. She'd survived it, and then St. Louis, by keeping her eyes focused on the future and dreaming of places like Pyrite.

"What are you doing out this time of night?" Sue asked when she answered her door.

Sue and Tom lived in a cute blue-and-white frame Victorian house three blocks over. Their yard was overrun with toys, their floors littered with schoolwork, and their lives disarrayed with children. It was the only place Chris could think of where she enjoyed the noise so much.

Still dressed for city hall in her denim skirt and Oxford shirt, Sue pushed the screen door open and invited Chris inside.

"I didn't get to talk to you before," Chris demurred, glad as ever to leave the dark behind.

Picking up a pot of dying philodendron on the way by, Sue led Chris into the kitchen. "I was wondering when we'd get around to this."

Terry, her oldest, was in the huge gingham and pine kitchen doing dishes. Bobby, the second, was tormenting Ellen, Chris's godchild, with a whiffle ball bat in the living room. Chris almost closed her eyes to just soak in the tide of normality in this house.

"Aunt Ch-is!" Ellen squealed, hurtling at her like a linesman.

Chris swept the little girl up into her arms and buried her face in the cloud of silky blonde hair. She sated herself on the smell of baby shampoo and crayons, the cascade of delighted giggles, the warm softness of a wriggling body. She fought the old familiar ache and squeezed the little girl until both of them were giggling.

"Found it!" Ellen crowed, dipping into Chris's shirt pocket and coming away with treasure. Tootsie Rolls, Chris's traditional offering, always two or three tucked away somewhere for the finding. In insecure moments, she wondered if she were rigging her hugs. Bribing her affections. It didn't matter. She needed those headlong embraces.

Prize won, Ellen headed back into the fray with her brother, who got his own piece of candy, and the two women got down to business.

"Where's Tom?"

"Billy Detwieler's appendix. What's up?"

Chris accepted her twelfth cup of coffee that day and pulled up a chair at the battered picnic table the Clarksons used for dinner and homework.

"Two things. Did you get to talk to Shelly?"

Sue's pragmatic features folded a little. "She's a tough kid, isn't she?"

Chris sipped at her coffee and lifted a wary glance toward Terry.

Sue never bothered reacting. "Terry, I'll finish. Get your homework."

There was the requisite protest, but Terry, a carbon copy of her mom, headed on upstairs and left the two women alone.

"I wanted to be able to take her, Sue," Chris protested.

Sue picked a beer out of the fridge and settled herself down across the table with a knowing shake of her head. "You took that girl in full time, the judge would have you up on charges of kidnapping in a New York minute. Don't worry about it."

"I just didn't know what else to do," Chris insisted. "You know what would happen to her if she really did take out of here."

Sue didn't, of course. Not really. But Sue had all the best instincts of a good mother. "I thought it might be nice for Harmonia Mae to have someone help her out in that big B-and-B of hers. She's getting too old to keep up, and Mr. Lincoln needs somebody to play with."

Harmonia Mae. Why hadn't Chris thought of that? The very image of Victorian propriety, the town's grande dame would not only give Shelly the stability she needed, but would never in her life think of expressing the more sloppy affections that would send Shelly running in the opposite direction. And Bobby Lee would have less luck on her doorstep than the judge's. The perfect solution, if they could get Shelly to see sense.

Sue answered the question even before it was asked, wrapping a grin around the mouth of her beer bottle. "Shelly whined and bitched like a three year old," she admitted, "but she seems to get a kick out of sharing quarters with the monkey." Another sip. "I think she doesn't really mind the idea that she's at information central with all the murder stuff going on, either, with Sergeant Lawson staying there."

Chris took a contemplative sip of coffee. "I'll have to ask Shelly to give me fair warning if Lawson gets her hands on an arrest warrant."

"You think she suspects you?"

"I think she's having too much fun suspecting everyone on the planet to single me out. She did really enjoy the fact that the post office box where my strange letters are coming from was in a name only I know."

That, more than anything, got a reaction out of her friend. Sue darned near slammed the beer bottle on the scarred pine table. "Which brings us, I hope, to the second reason for your visit."

"If you mean apologies," Chris retorted as easily as she could, "you're not getting any."

Sue shrugged. "I wasn't really expecting one. An explanation might help, though. I've been reading you since I got married. Imagine my surprise at finding out you've been hiding under the eaves almost all the while."

"It was the only way I could manage," Chris protested. "My books are so different—"

Sue gave a heartfelt nod. "If anybody but you had told me that C. J. Turner and Jacqueline Christ were the same person, I would have accused them of smoking the books instead of reading them. I mean, Jacqueline is so bright and reaffirming, so—"

"Optimistic?"

"Yes, damn it," Sue agreed with an emphatic nod. "Optimistic. I can't really say as much for C. J."

"C. J.'s reflecting on a completely different side of life."

Chris wasn't sure if it was her tone of voice, or maybe the fact that Sue had never understood quite all that Chris was protecting before. Whatever it was, with Chris's words, Sue came up short, her quick blue eyes just shy of amused.

"You really do think of them as separate persons, don't you?"

Chris took a second to study the chipped

stoneware mug between her hands. Comfortable, warm, worn. "Different bits of the same person," she conceded. "I just like to keep them farther apart so that they can comment on each other sometimes."

"Don't you ever get lost in them?"

The truth? Chris didn't know. She knew where the parts of her had been born, knew how they'd been separated into their equals, knew how they had set upon their various and disparate journeys. She knew, most days, how to keep them in recognizable order. But she didn't really know, after all, what happened when she dreamed. She had an imperfect memory that held secrets even she couldn't dig out.

So, in the end, she gave Sue what would make her comfortable, and saved the rest for Victor's keen night ears. "Only when I'm in the middle of a really good book."

She was walking back home when she heard them. Footsteps. Stealthy, slow, their faint scraping all but swallowed in the rustle of wind in the trees. Twice she turned around. Twice they vanished, chimeras of her imagination, whispers from her conscience.

She stopped beneath a street light by the Axminsters'. Listened. She heard the growl of traffic out on the highway, the discordant notes of a piano from the Miller house. She smelled the thick perfume of newly turned earth. Normal, quiet things. Pyrite sounds and smells.

It didn't ease the sudden staccato of her heart. Didn't quell the clammy frisson of dislocation.

Memory.

Something niggled at her. Something dark and

slithery. Something dangerous.

Chris stood stock still for almost five minutes trying to wrench it free. Knowing already that it was futile. She walked on.

She thought the footsteps followed.

Once she even tried to double back, sure she could catch someone only a few feet back. Maybe Weird Allen, getting bold, or Bobby Lee, thinking to scare her for standing up for Shelly. Maybe anybody. Anything but specters loosed from a suddenly shaky subconscious. Chris hid alongside the Swinsons' latticed porch, peering through the faint milk of street lamps, discerning shapes from the shadows, inventing attention where there was none.

Nothing. Not even a breeze to ruffle through the trees.

Chris was stepping back out of hiding when the headlights swung toward her. A cruiser, heading toward her from the direction of Sue's house. Loping across the lawn, Chris flagged it down.

JayCee rolled down his window. "What are you doin' out this late?" There was a bag of pork rinds on the other seat.

Chris took a quick look over her shoulder. "JayCee, did you see anybody up the street there? Maybe on one of the lawns or something?"

JayCee actually turned around to look, his thick neck straining against the light blue shirt collar. "Nope. Nothin' out here but me and you."

Chris was sure that was what she wanted to hear. She thought. She nodded, wishing his answer made her feel better. "Nobody at all."

JayCee squinted at her, as if trying to decide if she were working on all cylinders. "What's the matter?"

Chris wished it could have been anybody but JayCee. "Oh, I thought I heard something. I guess I thought Weird Allen was following me home or something."

JayCee laughed. "Nah, old Weird Allen's at the church with his mama. Every Wednesday night, like clockwork. He's too busy havin' Harlan show him the road to heaven to be followin' you around."

Chris must have allowed an opinion to escape into her expression.

JayCee laughed again, waving off Chris's objection. "Ah, old Allen's harmless. He's just . . . weird. You want me to drive you on home?"

"No, thanks."

JayCee gave her one more wave before heading on down the street. Chris followed in the same direction, not feeling any better. After ten minutes of shivering in the dark, she finally had to admit that what she was hearing was the wind following her, not a pursuer. It was the dark, just like always. For a minute there, though, walking faster and faster toward the bright lights inside her house, she imagined one of her own creations had come to haunt her.

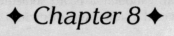

✦ *Chapter 8* ✦

"BRENTWOOD DOESN'T REMEMBER who rented the box?"

Taking a second to blow her nose, Lawson once again shook her head. "It's one of the personnel training centers. I doubt they'd notice Madonna walking in to rent a box, unless she lived in the neighborhood."

Mac doodled on his scratch pad, wishing he could turn on his tape player. It helped him think. Put things into perspective. The night before instead of adding to the recycling problem, he'd made a list of people and places to check. He was going over them now with the good detective.

"There's some kind of control on the box, though?" he asked, rubbing at his lip as he thought. "If Chris writes that reply today, we want to see who picks it up."

"We?" Lawson echoed.

Mac looked up to find a certain amount of outrage in her mud-brown eyes. Fence pissing, he decided. The fine art of protecting turf. "Nobody in St. Louis believes you about the murders, do they?"

That damn near brought her to her feet. She was parked on the other side of the table, her notes spread out amid folders of pictures and interview records and call sheets, her arms folded around them as if cushioning them from his interloping eyes.

"They're more interested in clearing cases than solving them," she intoned self-righteously.

No huge revelation there. It was the way Homicide worked the world over. The way crime stats worked. The headaches were big enough without looking for trouble. If you could clear off five or even ten open cases with one confession, you considered yourself a happy man and a step closer, with the help of God and whatever steam you had in the current administration, to promotion.

Mac reigned in his temper. God preserve him from people trying to prove themselves.

"What I'm saying, Lawson," he tried again, "is that crime isn't quite so rampant down this way. I have some extra time to help out if you want."

"Chief?"

Mac left his consideration of the Sergeant and turned to where John McIvey was leaning in his door. Short, skinny, and black as mahogany, John had announced himself as the token on the force, a local kid who'd scored honors on field and in class, and then after service and college, returned home. John was a good enough cop that nobody gave him trouble about his color more than once. One of Mac's first official functions had been elevating him to sergeant.

"Yeah, John."

The officer only afforded Lawson a fleeting glimpse before getting down to business. "You might

let the sheriff know when he sits down with the
highway patrol to map out their marijuana searches.
There might just be a new patch of it in the works
back up behind Oz up County Road Y. Word is
there's gonna be a good acre of it."

Mac nodded and made notes on his duty pad. One
of the first revelations about working in rural
Missouri, was that it was to marijuana what the
mountains of Colombia were to coffee. The climate,
not to mention the thick underbrush that prevented
easy access by inconvenient law enforcement officials, was quite conducive to its clandestine cultiva-
tion. A quarter-acre of marijuana, growing to some
twelve feet in height in this neck of the woods and
so thick you couldn't hack through it without help,
could net a street haul of damn near four million dollars. Wouldn't hurt to spread the good will among all
the forces in the area.

"I'll let 'em know, John. Thanks. How'd the range
go today?"

That brought the young man up with a grudging
grin. "Curtis did fine, JayCee failed again, and Buster
wants another chance when the weather's better."

Mac all but sighed. Typical of small-town budgets
and traditions, the police were handed a gun upon
completion of a quick course in safety, and then
never expected to practice with it again. Most of
them couldn't hit anything unless it was big, brown,
and had antlers, and then it was a toss-up. Another
one of the changes the town wasn't so sure about.
Mac was. He had the steel plate to show for what
happened to a cop caught napping. He didn't need
dead officers, too.

"No reprieve, John. Tell Buster when he can guarantee the bad guys won't go out in the rain, I won't make him go out either."

John chuckled. "One more thing. Allen brought in another application. He even bought his own handcuffs this time."

Mac groaned. Of all the problems he'd inherited from L. J. Watson, Allen Robertson was going to be the most problematic. Just how many ways was he supposed to tell the wannabe that the last thing in the world Mac needed right now was to give someone with the nickname of Weird Allen a license to peek in other people's windows?

"Lose it for a couple of days," Mac suggested. "And keep an eye on those handcuffs."

John chuckled all the way back out the front door.

"You really think you can help me?" Lawson demanded. "You have your hands full here with Barney Fife and company."

Which was why he so enjoyed working with Lawson.

"I'm getting pretty damn tired of this shit," he snapped. "You may have the murders going on up there, but I have the intended victim right here. Now, unless you figure out how to play nice, you're gonna be up to your asshole in excuses and short one murderer. I can protect Chris. I'm not so sure I give a rat's fart I want to keep you from the wolves. Got it?"

Lawson's eyebrows elevated. "Chris?" she demanded. "Oh, really. Is that how it's going to be?"

That brought Mac right to his feet. "Call me next time you're in town, Lawson. Or when that oleander poisoning case shows up, because it will. You know it and I know it. And you're not going to have a single, sorry son of a bitch to help you with it."

Lawson came right up with him, her defiance dissolving. "I'm sorry," she said, suddenly repentant. "Really. It's just that this all means so much to me."

Mac wasn't ready to give ground. "To me, too. I'm not wild about bad guys doin' a number on one of my townspeople."

She nodded, hand out, suddenly smaller, uncertain. "I know. I mean it. I'm really sorry." She offered a smile then, a beseeching look that offset some of her plainness. "The only way I get an inch up there is to march right up assholes with cleats on."

It took Mac a few minutes, but he reclaimed his patience and turned back to the files. "Have you checked your known crazies up there?"

She nodded. "The ones I've been able to get to have alibis."

"Did you see any of the scenes in person?"

"Yeah."

"Anything you might take to be a signature?"

"I thought the murder itself was a signature."

"Anything at all that doesn't fit?"

Lawson thought about it for a moment. "Weaver's wife swears the victim's high school ring is missing."

"Nothing else."

"That's why nobody bought the intruder angle. The only room in the house that has a plastic cover out of place is the bedroom."

"Any artifacts missing from other victims?" Mac asked, trying hard to call up the memory that bit about the ring had nudged.

"Deborah McClain's wedding ring."

"Rings, rings . . ." Mac mused a moment. Suddenly

his head came up. "Trophies. This clown's taking trophies."

FBI in-service on serial killers. Mac remembered a stuffy classroom at the Circle Campus that smelled like old socks and creaky heating systems, a nondescript-looking suit at the front with a pointer and a cavalcade of murder shots that looked like the Hall of Fame from Hell. Serial killers tended to take something from the scene, some kind of memorabilia, be it actual or photographed, to relive the high of the crime later.

"Look for a missing ring from the actor," Mac suggested, the adrenaline tickling at him. "Look for somebody who showed up at each scene beforehand, maybe after, during the investigation. Whoever this guy is, he's comfortable enough to take his time with his work. That means he's done his homework. He might have even gotten to know his victims so well ahead of time that they let him in, which would explain the fact that there's no sign of forced entry in each situation."

"Chief?"

Mac looked up again, this time to find Sue, her expression making him think of pop quizzes and unexpected in-laws. "You're supposed to be over at the school for that meeting with the tourism committee."

Worse than in-laws. One of the nastiest tortures inflicted on police chiefs of any kind. Political gladhanding. Meaningless wastes of perfectly good evenings spent listening to the likes of Ray Sullins wax eloquent on how, if the rest of the town would just listen to him, their businesses would prosper. It occurred to Mac, not for the first time, that he should send a letter of commiseration to the big chief back in Chicago.

Lawson was already pulling her things together.

"I need to get going anyway . . ."

Mac battled an urge to curse. He wanted to stay at this table and work out puzzles. Instead, he was doing the grip-and-grin circuit again. Facts of life.

"Is there anything else I can get hold of for you?" he asked.

She had all the folders refilled, all that tantalizing information tucked away again. "You really want to, I'm going to let you at all those romance letters," she said with a sly grin. "I'm going to spend some more time here getting more information on Ms. Jackson. Might help figure this thing out a little when I get back." She looked up, and Mac thought he caught a glint of avarice in her eyes. "I know you haven't been here long. That old bat in the mausoleum told me. Got any idea who can give me info on your famous author?"

Mac motioned toward the other room, where the clatter of computer keys could be heard. "Sue. She and Chris are pretty tight. Be real careful around here, though. Damn near the whole town considers Chris Jackson a local treasure."

Lawson's smile wasn't pleasant. "In that case, I'll just have to talk to the Reverend Sweetwater. Maybe Judge Axminster."

Mac raised an eyebrow. "You do your homework."

"Yes," she agreed with a final swipe of the Kleenex. "I do." She flashed another smile, this one belated, as if she'd just been reminded of her manners. "Thanks, Chief. I appreciate the help."

She held out a hand.

Mac hadn't realized how tense he'd gotten. Her words eased the strain across his shoulders and the tension in his jaw. "I might be able to give you some new ideas if I kept some of the information," he said.

That brought her to another standstill. She wasn't even supposed to have those files so far away from home. Copying them would be a mortal sin in any supervisor's bible, and both of them knew it. Even so, Mac was offering more than anybody else had.

She brightened again, this time a little less measured as she retrieved her hand. "I need to run by the drugstore real quick for something. Do you mind if I"—gesturing to the open files on her desk—"leave these here?"

Mac's grin was probably carnivorous. "No problem," he assured her. "They'll be right here when you get back."

As the bell jangled over the front door, Mac leaned out from his office. "Sue, let Mayor Sullins know I'm going to be a little late."

After carefully copying every scrap of paper on that desk and handing the originals back to the departing sergeant, Mac itched to wade around in them and pull out a few universal truths. Unfortunately, after the tourism committee he was headed off by a surprise delegation from the Safe Parks Forum, a visit by the mayor to discuss the cost of Mac's new fitness regimen, and a call from John to check out some vandalism that Mary Ellen Easterby just knew was the stirrings of a satanic cult.

By the time he was safely alone in his office once more, it was almost dinnertime, there was a storm brewing that would probably take out the electricity, and a pile of romance books sat on his desk with a note from Sue to read them before talking to her the next morning.

Mac turned one over, and then another. They looked pretty much alike, all with white covers, with the word Rapture swirled across the top in gold, and a picture of two space mannequins with perfect anatomy in a clinch that would have demanded a Jaws of Life to break up and a chiropractor to treat. Not exactly his type of fiction. Not even his kind of picture.

Jacqueline Christ, he noted from the short bio inside, did indeed have several degrees, and lived in upstate New York. A good place to set a romance writer, he assumed.

Jason Kilpatrick had no use for women.

Oh, that was a promising start. Mac fought a superior smirk and read the next line. And the next. By the time the lights went out an hour and a half later, he was halfway through the book.

Chris went through the Jacqueline Christ letters alone in her office. This pile was a much bigger one, stretching back almost eight years. Cards, letters, notes, mostly handwritten, many eloquent, all sincere. Somehow more personal than the mystery letters, much more elemental. Even more disquieting to Chris, who still felt she did a disservice to these women, who tended to look to the author of dynamic, capable women as some kind of role model. As if she were somehow an expert, simply because she had a good imagination.

Outside her greenhouse, the sky had taken on a metallic hue. The trees in Mary Willoughby's yard had begun to dance, and Chris could hear the wind tuning up. Another storm was brewing. It was the time of year for it, when two seasons tumbled over each other in sweaty, furious combat until summer finally won out sometime late in May.

Clouds folded and climbed into the western sky, and the late afternoon shuddered with distant lightning. As long as they hit during the day, Chris loved storms. She could sit by the hour up here and watch them assault the hills, titanic armies of gray that hammered at the land with breath and light and roaring fury. She pulled her chair up to the big windows so she could see how the normal, everyday world around her took on different substance within the shuddering incandescence of lightning.

It was as if she could see through substance for split seconds and discover the elemental forces that still lived within. Spirits and demons and gods only the Indians and mad Celts could see anymore. Not tamed by civilization or driven out by religion, but trapped, set free only with the whipping wind and otherworldly light civilization feared.

A letter in her hand, Chris stood up to watch as the dusk rushed in on ragged clouds. She grinned, the exultation filling her, the music better than heavy metal for purging obstinate ghosts. It was day and night, the best of times when the darkness couldn't hurt her, when the world could fly completely apart and take her along. When she saw things that weren't there.

Her smile died. Blinking in surprise, Chris stepped closer to her windows. A shadow among the trees.

Movement. For just the briefest of moments, Chris thought she'd caught a sidhe, set loose by the swirling electricity, caught on the wrong side of the veil. Then she cursed and stepped right up to the edge of the balcony. She couldn't discern much, but it looked like a person standing at the edge of Mary's yard, staring up at her window.

Weird Allen. She just knew it, knew that slouching posture anywhere. It was the last thing she needed, having him watching in her back window while she worked.

Then, she wasn't so sure. Familiar, yes, but not necessarily Allen. Triggering the taste of memory again. Old, rancid memory that wouldn't gel into voices or pictures. Frustrating, frightening. Unreal as her fantasies, unsettling as her dreams.

She turned, not sure whether to try and get downstairs to chase it off, to call the police and let them know she had a prowler.

Because she suddenly wasn't sure, she took one more look out.

He was gone.

The rain descended, hard slanting sheets of it, blurring the edges of reality, cloaking the town in dim silver. Dissolving her visitor like a magician's cape, until Chris couldn't tell whether she'd imagined what she'd seen or not. She shivered, wondering whether the town had taken to keeping watch on her, or whether she should really worry about the shadow figure. Or whether she was finally simply suffering from sleep deprivation.

Again she thought to call the police. She knew, though, she had nothing to tell them. Worse, she couldn't tell them what she was afraid of. That the phantom out there on her lawn hadn't been real at all.

The storm broke over her house with all the fury of a four year old in a tantrum. Wind moaned at the windows and lightning shattered the sky into ragged pieces. But Chris couldn't watch it anymore. She couldn't do more than focus her eyes on the high, white walls of her house. Clean walls. Bright walls. Open walls that protected her rather than caged her in. Her heart was finally beginning to slow, the bright wash of space easing the instinctive terror of the unknown. Five minutes later, the lights went out.

Lawson came visiting in the dark.

Chris had lit as many candles as she could without setting off the smoke alarms, and was safely ensconced in her rocking chair trying her best to work at a laptop. It wasn't an easy thing to do, considering the fact that Chris had to spend most of her time making sure that the shadows that writhed and stretched along her walls weren't alive. That the storm that had blown out daylight hadn't also blown in something she didn't want.

It made her furious. She'd been so happy. Not perfect, God knows, but content. Productive, protected, actually close enough to normality to taste it like the first hint of spring on the air.

She'd been sleeping almost dream free, channeling all that old confusion and ambivalence into something positive. She'd been able to do something she hadn't in all the years she'd fought so hard to go one on one with the world. She'd made a difference.

And now it was threatening to unravel right

around her. Now, some jerk with a vivid imagination and a need to connect was tormenting her in ways he couldn't even imagine.

After all, who could know? Who could realize just what fueled the works of both C. J. Turner and Jacqueline Christ.

Even as the candles flickered and the light undulated around her, Chris bent over the coffee table to create the dreams of a new murderer.

He didn't believe the blood was real. There was too much of it, washing over the room like a warm, blackened wave. He didn't want to look at the blood. He couldn't help it. It was only right after all. She should have to pay for betraying him. For offering him up to the highest bidder, when all he wanted was peace . . .

The knock was sharp and sudden. It so startled Chris she damn near tumbled right off the rocker.

Maybe if she ignored it, it would stop. Maybe it wasn't any more real than the phantom in her window.

Maybe it wasn't real, but it repeated itself. Louder this time and more insistent.

Chris didn't even want to get to her feet. Damn, she hated this. "Yes?"

"It's Sergeant Lawson."

Her shoulders slumped. "Shit." She hated that even more. Maybe she could sneak out the back. Maybe she could get hold of Victor and Lester to do a show for the good sergeant. For the first time since she'd moved in, Chris regretted the fact that she didn't have a phone. She'd be on the phone right now to MacNamara demanding he get this pit bull off her neck.

"It's still raining out here, Ms. Jackson," the sergeant let her—and undoubtedly everyone on the block—know.

Chris didn't have the energy to remind the good woman that she was standing beneath a porch over-hang. She shut down the computer screen and climbed to her feet.

"Don't you have regular hours?" Chris demanded when she caught sight of the detective on the other side of the screen door.

It was hard to see out there. This entire end of town was without electricity, the only light the pale reflection in the clouds. Standing out there beyond the flickering reach of candlelight, Lawson was a shadow.

Unaccountably, the sight of her gave Chris the creeps. If Lawson had wanted to re-create Chris's nightmares on purpose, she couldn't have done a better job of it.

"I only got a couple of days down here," Lawson informed her. "Can I come in?"

Chris heaved a sigh of capitulation and pushed open the door. Then she turned away and headed back toward what light she had. She didn't need any more nightmares than the ones that came as standard equipment, thanks.

"Who did you feel like accusing tonight?" she asked.

Behind her, Lawson stayed by the door. "I wanted to apologize for my behavior earlier."

That was a surprise enough to bring Chris back

around again. Again she was plagued by that unsettled feeling. The room was too shadowy, too indistinct. It gave Lawson an otherworldly look, half
formed, half felt. Chris fought the urge to find distance. Lawson was smiling, and somehow that was
worse.

"I'm afraid I've been treating you like the suspect
instead of the victim," the detective said. "I'm
sorry."

Chris tried to shove her hands into her pants'
pockets and then realized she had none. She settled
for crossing her arms. "Thank you." She knew she
should say something else. Lawson was waiting for it.
Something kept her quiet, though. Watching. She
didn't trust sudden conversions unless there was a
donkey and a bolt of lightning involved.

Lawson took to looking around the room. "Quite a
place."

"I like it."

The little woman nodded, all browns and grays
like a field mouse. With a nose like a ferret.

Chris fought a nervous smile. She was going to
have to be a little more charitable. After all, this was
the woman who was going to solve the case and let
her get back to her life.

"I just have a few questions before I go back to St.
Louis," Lawson said, wandering over to run a hand
along the sofaback table. "If you don't mind."

Chris followed and resettled the upturned edge on
the lace runner. "I guess not."

Lawson nodded, heading for the dining room
table, part of an old oak set that Chris had found up
in Soulard in St. Louis. Lawson really seemed to like
the blue-and-pink glazed sugar and creamer set. She

balanced them in her hands, rearranged them. Patted them.

"You don't have any idea who it is committing these murders?" she asked, moving on to the book-cases at the corner.

Chris straightened up her table. "No. I already told you that."

"How about theories?"

Lawson was at the pictures now, framed shots of the Ozarks Chris had taken over the last five years. People, buildings, landscapes cluttered with no more than cattle and fencing. Soothing, nurturing reminders of the recognizable passing of seasons. Reassurance, certainty.

"I don't have any theories," Chris answered, her gaze on her things as the sergeant fondled them.

Lawson looked back at her, eyes shadowed, the yellow flicker of a hundred candles licking her face. "Don't you?" she asked. "They're your books."

"No," Chris said definitely. "I don't."

For just a moment, Lawson held her gaze. Threw out a challenge in silence Chris could have heard even in her sleep. Then the detective nodded and walked on, over to the teapots. "It just seems that the person committing these murders is pretty intent on copying them exactly. I mean—" she turned, a pot in her hand, "exactly."

Chris resettled her photos and brushed a bit of dust from the mahogany sideboard before following.

"Why do you think that is?" Lawson asked.

Chris was quick growing tired of the game. She did her own challenging. "I think you probably have a theory of your own that you're just dying to tell me, Sergeant. Why don't you get it off your chest so I can have my things back?"

It wasn't going to happen yet, though. Lawson's attention was caught again. Setting down the Wedgewood teapot, she headed for the wall to the right of the stove.

"I recognize this," she said, reaching up.

Chris caught the direction of her intentions just seconds too late. Before Chris could intercept her, Lawson was standing at her wall, hands up to a rather garishly painted little ceramic bust in its special niche.

"It's the Edgar Award," the woman said, reaching up to pluck the hapless little man from his shelf. "I didn't know you got one."

"Last year," Chris answered, arriving on the scene. This time she didn't bother with tact. She plucked her statuette back before Lawson could protest. When Lawson looked up, surprised, Chris did her best to smile past the irritation. "He doesn't leave his shelf."

"Protective?"

"Superstitious." Gently she set the award back in its place and faced the sergeant. The sergeant was on her way again.

"I talked to the Reverend Sweetwater this evening," she was saying as she made a run back around to the cases on the other wall.

Chris sighed in frustration and followed. "Oh, Harlan and I are old friends."

Lawson turned on her, a hand-blown vase in her hands. "Harlan thinks you're evil. Are you evil, Ms. Jackson?"

That brought Chris to a sick halt. Lawson had no idea what she was asking. From Harlan, Chris could take questions like that. Here in the night with the light a tenuous, undependable thing, she couldn't quite camouflage herself in bravado.

"He thinks somebody's been killing people to prove I'm evil?"

"No. He thinks you're doing the killing because you're evil."

Chris didn't move, neither to protect her vase nor her reputation. She simply stood rooted there, fury and shame flooding her.

"I thought I was the victim," she challenged through clenched teeth, knowing now what game the detective was playing. Hating her for it.

"I'm sure you are. It's just that you yourself said how close the murders were to the books, and that intrigues me. It makes me wonder just what the murderer is trying to say." Turning, she set the vase back down, perfectly in place, and returned her attention to Chris. "And why you haven't figured it out yet."

As if in comment on the detective's musings, the lights chose that moment to flicker back on. Both of the women blinked at the sudden glare, looked upward in verification. Each returned her attention to the other.

Chris felt the ground solidify beneath her feet. She felt her strength return, as if she'd just witnessed the first solar eclipse and survived back into the sunlight.

"Give me some time," she offered. "After all, I only found out about this. Personally, though? I think it's somebody out there on the fringes of society. Somebody who thinks this will be a way to get his name on the news."

"Don't you at least feel responsible?"

That did it. Lawson was the very last person on earth with whom Chris wanted to discuss culpability and guilt.

"No more responsible than Jodie Foster should have felt for John Hinkley. Now, if there isn't anything else, Sergeant Lawson, I have some work to do."

Lawson flashed a funny smile and lifted her hands in an almost perfect imitation of Peter Falk doing Columbo. "Sure, sure. I just wanted to talk with you before I left. I'm due back tomorrow."

Chris forbore advising the detective not to let the door hit her in the ass on the way out. "Well, good luck," she said instead. "I hope you find out who's doing it."

Already turned toward the front door, Lawson stopped. "You do?" she asked.

Chris forgot again that she had no pockets to hide her hands in. Nothing to keep her from decking the officious woman. "Amazingly enough," she retorted dryly, crossing her arms again.

Lawson nodded as if she didn't hear the sarcasm. "Well, don't worry," she assured Chris as if the exchange were entirely legitimate. "I will."

But before she left, she reserved one last telling look that told Chris exactly where she'd like the blame to lay. Chris shut the door behind her, latched it, closed the blinds, and looked around for something to break against a wall.

In the end she didn't, of course. She settled into her rocker and eased back into the mind of a murderer.

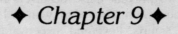

✦ Chapter 9 ✦

"JUST WHAT ARE you going to do about it, Chief?"

Mac held onto his temper just about as tightly as he held onto his screen door. "Reverend Sweetwater, I'm not exactly sure what you want me to do."

Standing there out on the sagging gray porch, his silver hair a little skewed in the breeze, his face florid with excitement, the reverend took a big enough breath to recite Deuteronomy and clutched his Good Book to his ample chest. "It's quite simple," he announced loudly for the benefit of his few followers scattered out on the lawn behind him in pastel dresses and grim-looking gray suits. "These comic books are offensive. They're an outrage to every true Christian in the town. Don't you realize what they represent? Satan, Chief MacNamara. The dark master himself, reaching out to innocent children through this trash," he insisted in that booming, pulpit voice. "As evidenced by the new and irrefutable evidence that our children are dabbling with the dark side. I'm talking, of course, about the designs being painted on the Easterby barn. Now, I know I can count on

179

you to help me uphold the Christian values of this community to prevent these deceivers from further disrupting our youth. They're truly an evil thing."

"They're Smurfs, Reverend Sweetwater. Irritating, yes. I'd even go so far as to say nauseating. I couldn't, on the other hand, say illegal. And until the Supreme Court says that ShopMart can't have them on the shelves, it's my job to leave them there. Besides, I didn't see a single Smurf on the Easterby's siding."

"What's legal and what's moral seem to be two different things, then, don't they?" the reverend lectured in his most didactic tone, sending two or three heads to nodding in chorus behind him. "Well, with the Lord's help, morality will prevail. We'll boycott! We'll picket! We'll—"

"Harlan."

Both men turned to see Chris Jackson loping up the walk, dressed today in an electric blue-, green- and purple-striped oversized T-shirt and black stretch pants. In her hand was a pile of books. She greeted the flock in passing, but they stiffened in outrage.

"I found Jesus," she announced, hopping up the steps to the porch. "He's over at the ShopMart going through the magazine section."

Mac damn near ducked. He'd never met anybody with such a knack for lobbing in missiles. And she knew just how to hit her target.

"Better hurry," she warned, eyes bright and mischievous in the face of the minister's livid red countenance. "I thought I saw Him moving toward the comics."

Mac was still safe on the other side of the screen door, watching the proceedings like a tennis match when Sweetwater leveled an accusing finger at the woman. "I've been praying, Chris Jackson. Praying hard that the Lord will see his way to taking care of you, just like a viper in the grass. Do you truly believe that you can withstand the will of the Lord?" Several amens were heard to waft from the grass. "Do you think He would not hear our prayers to defend His children against your . . . against that . . ."

She didn't mind in the least helping. "Trash? Pornography? Obscenity?"

"The devil knows his own kind."

"Considering the fact that that puts me right up on your list with James Joyce and J. D. Salinger, I'm flattered. Thank you, Harlan."

"You will not heed my warning, will you, Chris Jackson?" he threatened, his fury real, his hand trembling as he pointed her out. "I tell you these murders are an indictment on you. A real and timely judgment. The Lord hears us, and you are being punished."

"Reverend," Mac interceded gently. "I'd appreciate it if when you threaten one of the townspeople, you don't do it on my front porch. I'm not in the mood to go to the station today."

Even through the screen Mac could feel the throb of the reverend's frustration, the fury he felt for the woman challenging him. Mac had to give Chris points for having the guts to stay that close. Especially since he could tell she wasn't in the least misguided about Sweetwater's affections.

"I don't mind locking horns with you, Harlan," Chris said simply. "Figuratively speaking, of course. But lay off Luella Travers."

That stiffened Sweetwater's spine in outrage. Mac

could tell that the good minister didn't see the steel reflected in Chris Jackson's cool amber eyes.

"You'd just stand by when a Christian woman jeopardizes her immortal soul by sinning before God and her brethren? 'If the eye offends,' Chris Jackson—"

"It's not that she's living with a man that bothers you," Chris snapped. "It's that she's living with a black man. So don't quote Scripture to me, you old hypocrite."

"Beware who you consort with, Chief," the minister warned, now a dusky color, his Bible quivering in his hands.

"With whom you consort," Chris interjected.

They both turned on her.

"Never end a sentence in a preposition, Harlan. It irritates the chief."

That did it. Harlan Sweetwater swept off the porch like the wrath of God, and Chris turned a suspiciously innocent smile on Mac.

"I'm doing more business on my day off than when I'm at the station," Mac complained agreeably, still not opening the door. "You want to file a complaint, too?"

"You *do* wear something besides a uniform," she observed with that same wry consideration. "I was beginning to wonder."

Mac took a cursory look down at the old police academy T-shirt and jeans he'd thrown on when the reverend had first laid on the doorbell. He was still in his bare feet. "I'm off duty," he informed her. "As in, I shouldn't have to be solving any problems."

She lifted the armload of books. "I brought you a present."

Mac made sure all the church members got off his

lawn without incident and pushed open the screen door. "Too late. Sue was way ahead of you."

Chris accepted the invitation and stepped inside. "You already have Jacqueline's books?"

"I already read Jacqueline's books. And I have some questions."

Her grin was as bright as a child's. "Yes," she averred, "people *can* get into those positions without the aid of hydraulics."

Mac just scowled at her and turned to lead the way back into the kitchen where he'd been working. "What do you have against Sweetwater?" he asked over his shoulder. "Besides his being a general pain in the ass."

Chris surveyed the room without pretense. "He's a small-minded, petty, domineering, self-centered bigot who wants women back in the kitchen, blacks in another county, and children in the dark ages. Besides, that, I'm sure he's just a prince."

"You always that open-minded?"

Mac wasn't sure whether she realized how much her eyes gave away. There was real pain there. "Only since I had to spend more of my formative years on my knees than in school," she said. "It tends to give you a whole different perspective of the world."

Before he got a chance to follow up, though, she'd swung off in another direction completely, pulling to a sudden stop halfway across the floor.

"Well, hell, no wonder your grammar's so good."

Without so much as an apology or explanation, Chris walked up to the bookshelves that lined either side of the fireplace and began scanning titles.

"You actually *read* this stuff?"

Mac pulled a hand through his hair and rubbed

instinctively at the scar. "I actually read that stuff."

She had her head tilted back, which would have brought her about to Balzac and Flaubert. "Why?"

"Sister Mary Ignatius Loyola," he allowed, not bothering to scan the titles that took up his shelves like old friends. When Chris turned on him for the rest of the explanation, he obliged with a grin. "We called her Sister Spike. She was about six feet, and had hands like Michael Jordan. And she figured that kids in detention shouldn't waste their time on four-hundred-word essays on why they should behave, since that wasn't going to make them behave any better anyway. She had us read the classics." He shrugged, a bit uncomfortable. "I guess it stuck."

Chris just shook her head. "These yours?"

She'd picked up the picture of the twins.

"Kevin and Kate. They live with their mother in Phoenix."

"Just can't find a good place within commuting distance of Chicago anymore, can you?"

"They'll be spending the summer with me."

Another nod, and she put the picture back down. "What did you think of the books?"

Mac felt the tension escape from his chest. It wasn't that he didn't want to talk about his children. He still called them three nights a week, much to the delight of Ma Bell. They were looking forward to seeing him again, had flooded the hospital room with crayon-and-glue-constructed cards. It wasn't enough, though. It hadn't been in Chicago when he'd seen them every other weekend. Having them in Phoenix was hell. So he did what he could do and looked forward to the end of school, and thanked Chris Jackson's perception for not prying.

He tried another run for the kitchen. This time she followed.

"They weren't what I expected," he admitted, opening the refrigerator. "Beer?"

"Almost anything but. Tea or soda?"

After a foray into the pantry, Mac came up with a single can of soda. With that and a beer for Mac, they eventually migrated toward the kitchen table where his cigarettes and the manila envelopes already waited.

"You don't drink?"

"Is that a problem?" Chris countered, making a turn around the room before folding those long legs beneath a chair.

Popping the tab on his beer, Mac shook his head. "I just won't waste time asking in the future. . . . Do you want to see the basement and garage while you're here?"

Chris grinned. "Insatiable curiosity. Bane of cats, teenage girls, and writers of all ilk. Just hit me with a rolled-up newspaper if I get out of hand . . . and no, I don't drink. I'm stupid enough sober. It doesn't bear thinking about drunk."

Explanation enough for Mac. He pulled over the ashtray, but put off lighting up for a bit. After a minute or two more, Chris settled into the chair across from him and popped the tab on her soda.

"Actually," she said with a brightness that suddenly seemed just a shade brittle, "I don't have any business going through your things. I spent all last evening slapping Lawson's hands for fondling everything in my house but the chandelier. She really is a pain in the butt, isn't she?"

Mac heard text and subtext, and deliberately eased

his posture into listening mode. He didn't have to encourage her at all.

"Did she tell you that she would love for me to be the murderer?" Chris asked.

"It'd certainly make headlines up in her neck of the woods."

"I'm sure I'm also easier to find than the random nutcase with a library card, too. She's going home today?"

"Yeah."

Chris sipped at her soda. "Good. She gives me the creeps."

"How?"

A shrug. A glance that skittered away. "I don't know. Like she knows more than I do and won't tell me. There were a couple of moments last night when I could have sworn she had me on a videotape of one of the murders."

"She's just hungry."

"I know that. I just wish she'd turn those cute little sharkey eyes in somebody else's direction."

"You didn't kill anybody, did you?"

It was a joke. A throwaway line. Mac could have sworn she stiffened.

"Not that I remember."

He wished he could say why that sounded so important. Frontal assaults weren't going to work today, though. It was time to start finessing a little.

"I'm glad you stopped by," he admitted. "I got hold of some stuff from Lawson, and it's gotten me to thinking."

The change was instantaneous. Minute, barely perceptible, but definite all the same. Chris pulled a rather doleful face. "And here I thought we were going to wax eloquent about the immense talent of Jacqueline Christ, and how her work has opened up new vistas for you."

Mac was caught with a hand already in the envelope. When he faced her accusation, he saw the challenge of humor and retreated.

"All right," he conceded. "Let's start there."

"With the romances?" she asked. "You don't think those have anything to do with it, do you? I went through my mail with a fine-tooth comb, and I couldn't find anything more aggressive than a lady who was upset that none of my heroines have been black-haired virgins."

"I'm not to the point of specifics yet. I'm just interested in some background. What do you consider your themes to be?"

That knocked her straight into silence. "Themes?" she finally countered. "What themes?"

"Why do you write?" he asked.

That brought her back up off the chair.

"You need another look at the dining room?" he asked dryly.

She glared at him. "There isn't another policeman in the world who would ask me what the hell my themes are."

"I'm just curious," he said diffidently, holding his place against her agitation, intrigued by it.

"I write romance," she stated baldly, daring him to contradict her, "because it's the closest thing to sex I get. Same for mysteries. You can't imagine how many times I've done away with Harlan, not to mention any number of Cooters."

Mac finally took a minute to light up, giving her the figurative room she seemed to need. "I've read all five mysteries," he acknowledged, dropping the match in the ashtray. "They're all pretty different, but there are certain . . . themes, images that run through all of them."

Chris was walking again, pacing off the corners and peering out the window. "I know that."

"Dreams, for instance. You and Hawthorne like that idea that reality is expressed in dreams a whole lot."

That brought her to a halt across the table, a small smile giving her away. "All that Jungian shit. Yeah, I know. I think it's an intriguing notion. Nothing like the subconscious for control and illumination."

Mac ostensibly turned his attention on the papers before him. "And there's the concept of evil. Lots of guilt and redemption, too."

She focused on her soda can. "Use what you know. First lesson in writing."

"All those Sundays on your knees, huh?"

"And Tuesdays and Fridays and whatever day I happened to transgress in between."

Mac lifted his attention back to her. "The sisters in the convent school?"

He caught that brief hesitation, that betrayal of something she didn't want him to know.

"Among others," was all she'd say.

Everybody lied, he couldn't help but think again.

"Why mysteries?" he asked, letting the deception go for now. "Why not fantasies or science fiction or an exposé of the social service system?"

"Because murder is the ultimate decision," she said, slowing to a stop, her hands splayed across the back of the plastic-and-chrome chair, her nails sharp slashes of red against the dingy white. "The real showdown of all that good and evil, grace and instincts stuff . . . why."

"Why?"

Chris took off again, turning away while she talked. "Why do people murder."

Mac couldn't help a short bark of disbelief. "What do you mean, why do people murder? They murder for sport, for spare change, for a break from the monotony."

"I'm not talking about gangs or psychopaths. I'm talking about normal people, raised with all those good, solid values, lots of religion, middle-class America at its finest."

"And your theory?"

That took her a minute. Mac was happy to wait. She reached down to pick up her soda for another long drink and spent a second looking off into space, obviously consulting with some other voice, maybe C. J.'s, maybe one even older.

"I think," Chris admitted finally, her tone just a little too tight to be offhand, "that any one of us is perfectly capable of it. That we just need a good push in the right direction, and all that wonderful training goes right down the toilet. The better the people, the bigger the shove, that's all."

"And our friend?" Mac asked. "Why do you think he's killing?"

Finally she faced him, and Mac saw the truth in her eyes. Fear, loathing, anger. A big, deep hole right in the middle of all her confidence that most people had never seen. "I don't know," she said, and sounded lost.

The hair on the back of Mac's neck stirred. There were currents to Chris's discussion he hadn't even considered. Subtext that was completely foreign to him, and he had no idea how to go for it.

It was there, right in front of him, in her eyes. The darkness, the street eyes, wary, knowing, ultimately as bleak as death. For a moment unguarded. There for him to just pluck out if he just knew what to use.

"Why do you write romance?" he asked, not sure why.

She didn't even look at him. Again she was inside; again he got a peek at a place he wasn't sure many people saw. "Same reason."

"What? Why men and women get together?"

She shrugged, a vulnerable gesture that betrayed more than her words. "Why people love each other."

For a second Mac couldn't even breathe. He sat perfectly still, stunned at the desolation behind that bright facade of hers. Faintly ashamed at the rituals he'd carried out at kitchen tables like this one. He'd had the core eaten out of him over the years. He had the feeling Chris Jackson had never been allowed to grow one.

"And why do you think they do?" he asked finally, cautiously, a hunter approaching its prey.

Standing there, a bright bird with sharp, snapping eyes and the gall of a con man, she told him. "I don't know."

He wasn't sure how long it was before the phone rang. Probably seconds. It seemed like a frustrating eternity. Inside that drab little kitchen, the silence throbbed. Mac sat perfectly still, the smoke tickling at his nostrils as it curled up from the ashtray. He could hear birds rustling out under the eaves. He could smell tobacco and the brisk tang of soap. He could almost see the shimmer of tension on Chris Jackson, as if she waged a silent battle within herself, let loose by incautious words.

He caught the whisper of indecision, that split-second breach in defenses that could presage confession or the explosion of violence. A catch in the wind, a hitch in sound that betrayed vulnerability, a window into revelation that was so tenuous that even reaching for it pushed it closed.

Mac had the sense that she was about to reach a decision, and it stroked his instincts and set them humming like the strings of a harp. Humming, warning, goading. There was something Chris needed to tell him. Some confession she wanted to make, and it balanced on that moment like a child at the edge of a high roof.

It was the shrill of the bell that shattered it.

Chris jerked to life like a fireman caught napping by the alarm, her eyes wide and wary, her posture promising flight. Mac managed to stay in place, his features passive, as if he hadn't just trespassed into an area to which she never would have knowingly allowed him admission. With deliberate movements he picked up his cigarette and stood for the phone, taking a long, cleansing drag to burn away the quick frustration.

Behind him, she turned back to the window.

"Chief? It's Marsha."

Mac reached around for the rest of his beer while he still had the chance. "What's up, Marsha?" He didn't suppose he could hope it was just the Reverend Sweetwater down there raising hell again.

"JayCee just called in. Looks like he's found himself a body. He wants you to come look."

Mac rubbed the warming can against his temple and bit back several oaths. "Where?"

"In the old Phillips station. JayCee tends to head off behind there to relieve himself. You know how small that boy's bladder is. Well, he says he smelled somethin' godawful, and went sniffin' around. Sniffed as far as the door of the station and won't go any farther. He thinks it's Cooter Taylor."

"Cooter? Which one?"

There was a pause. "Well, he didn't say. Not that it makes much difference. They're all of a kind. Bound to end up rottin' someplace sooner or later, ya know?"

"Yeah, I know."

Mac sneaked another peek over to where Chris was sipping at her soda and trying to look as if she wasn't eavesdropping, and took a quick drag from his cigarette. "I'm on my way. Call Doc Clarkson, have him meet me over there, and Sam Milligan. He's the coroner, isn't he? And call JayCee back. Tell him not to touch a thing. Not anything. And to make sure he keeps everybody else out of there, too. You hear?" God, he was even beginning to talk like a small-town police chief.

"Sure thing. You want Heilerman's standin' by?"

"Might as well. It won't matter how slow they go this time."

He got a chuckle for that as the dispatcher hung up. Mac downed the rest of his beer in one gulp.

"I was joking," Chris protested.

He looked over to see that all pretense of disinterest had vanished. "About Cooter," she explained. "Which one died?"

Mac noticed that all defenses were securely back

in place. She was once again sharp and certain, her expression avid.

Everybody lies, he thought, that old litany of homicide. Small lies, big lies, stupid lies. It was time for Mac to make a call and find out about Chris Jackson's.

"JayCee didn't take the time to find out."

"They all look pretty much alike anyway," Chris assured him. "Can I come?"

That brought Mac to a halt. "To a murder scene?"

Her grin was at once brash and coy. "Research. I don't get to attend crime scenes down here like the guys in the big cities do."

"Chris—"

"L. J. always let me tag along. I don't get in the way, and I have never once compromised a crime scene." She lifted her gaze to the heavens and recited, as if from the Good Book itself. "'The best place for your hands at a crime scene is in your pockets.'"

Damn it if Mac didn't want to grin at her. "You don't have any pockets."

"I keep mine behind my back. Like this." She showed him, looking for all the world like an English schoolgirl instead of an impending pain in the ass. "I am the consummate professional," she assured him with a glint that really did make him laugh.

"No wonder you piss Harlan off." He scowled and scooped up his cigarettes as he headed out the kitchen door. When Chris followed right along, he didn't say a word.

It was Cooter, all right. Senior rather than any of the juniors, who began to show up within moments of Mac's arrival, each and every one of them meaner, dirtier, and more stupid than the next. Their father lay sprawled in a prone position in the corner of the old Phillips bay, a grotesque, bloated black thing that had already been visited by vermin.

"JayCee," Mac snapped with his first eyeball check through the grimy window JayCee had uncovered beneath the boards. "Go in my trunk and pull out my black bag. Get out the Vicks VapoRub."

JayCee wasn't the only one to stare at him.

Mac backed up from the window with a sour smile. "He's gonna be a popper," he warned. "You're gonna want to shove something up your nose before you walk in there."

JayCee didn't need any more encouragement than that. Within the space of two minutes, the beefy patrolman was back with the bag that held Mac's old homicide paraphernalia. Latex gloves, Vicks, rolling tape measure, extra Polaroid, yellow legal pads, tweezers, evidence bags.

"I bet you'd be great fun on a date," Chris quipped as she took a peek inside.

"This isn't my date gear," he retorted, the adrenaline of the job already shooting through him. "There aren't any handcuffs."

He got a round of nervous chuckles for that from the assembled crew, JayCee, John, and the Heilerman team. Mac could see the neighbors starting to venture out from nearby houses, and one or two patrons of the TrainWreck were standing at the door. He wasn't going to have long before he had a three-ring circus on his hands.

"OK," he announced, dipping his fingers into the jar and dabbing a sizable dose beneath each nostril.

Anointing yourself with the holy oil of homicide, his old Irish sergeant had always said at the door of a crime scene before making a sign of the cross over his crew like the presiding bishop. "JayCee, you keep every person who's about to show up out of here. John, come on in with me. And you," he said, almost accusingly to Chris, who had just taken her own helping, "stay out of the way."

She lifted her hands in protest. "I'm a mouse."

Mac shot her a scowl and slipped on his gloves. John followed suit, and they bent to the task of prying the door open.

The stench rolled out of the fetid, closed room like a livid green wall and sent everybody to gagging. Measuring his breaths carefully so that he got as little of the smell of rot as possible past the menthol, Mac stepped in, his eyes already tearing.

Motioning to the drag marks, the traces of old blood on the floor that didn't show up on Cooter's back, he began his notes. "Victim a white male Caucasian, approximately sixty, two hundred pounds. Found in prone position, unbound . . . he was moved in here. Probably killed somewhere else. Whatever happened, it happened face-on."

John's voice was quiet, hushed, as if afraid to desecrate the dead somehow. "Probably a fight over the marijuana."

Mac briefly turned away from where he was cataloging position and decomposition. "Your information on that field?"

John nodded. "Word around here is that Cooter controlled most of it. Enterprising old son of a bitch for being such a waste of protoplasm. And he controlled with more than an iron hand. I have the feeling somebody finally objected."

"One of his kids, you think?"

John shrugged. "He had all of Oz pretty much under his thumb."

"Jesus . . . oh, Jesus."

Mac swung around at the intrusion. "Damn it, you said you could handle it."

Chris was standing in the doorway, white and shaking and wide-eyed. Mac had the feeling that given half a chance she'd toss her cookies right into ground zero.

She didn't move at his challenge. She just shook her head. "Jesus."

"Harlan's going to be happy you finally found him," Mac snapped. "Now, get the hell out of here."

She lifted her eyes to him, and what he saw sent sudden shivers down his back. "He was moved here, wasn't he?" she asked faintly. "Shot out in the marijuana field and dumped here for somebody else to find."

"Shot?" Mac echoed, stepping away from the body. "How do you know?"

She looked desolate. "Because that's the way I wrote it."

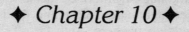

✦ *Chapter 10* ✦

CHRIS WAS GOING to be sick. She'd felt a sense of unreality with the pictures. A sickening outrage. This was different. This was live theater. Rancid, sweltering, even in the mild spring air, obscene in ways that she couldn't even name.

"What do you mean you wrote it?" Mac was demanding, his face too near, the walls too close, the scene unreal and disorienting.

Chris gulped, the tide of menthol in her nose not enough. "In a book," she said, trying her best to focus through sudden tears. "It's called *Family Business.*"

She couldn't take her eyes off Cooter, off the fingers with their dirty fingernails and crude blue crosses splayed out on the concrete, the greasy plaid shirt he'd been wearing when he'd walked out of jail. She couldn't swallow past the nausea that churned in her. She wasn't even standing close, only in the doorway, and yet it was overpowering, as if this closed off, shadowy, silent room had been waiting just for her. As if her punishments had come to grisly life.

I'm sorry, Mama. I'm sorry, I'm sorry, I'm sorry.

Other scenes suddenly rode in on the miasma,

superimposed themselves on the thick, oily light. Shadows and lines, half-formed memories she'd only seen in her nightmares. Sickening thuds, dizzying panic, hands everywhere. And, far off, a figure. A shadow, standing. Patient and inexorable as time, uncertain as memory. Always there, waiting. Familiar, like the shadow under the tree. Soothing, terrifying, faceless. Sucking the air out of her, the life out of her . . .

Mac closed a hand on her wrist and yanked her farther inside. Chris instinctively flinched away, so close to crying out that she shook with the effort of control.

"What are you talking about?" he asked, letting go.

She shuddered, arms wrapped tight around her waist to protect herself, to hold herself away and safe. Fighting to shake off terrors nobody else could see. With a bitten-off curse, Mac turned on John.

"Secure the scene and don't touch a damn thing. I'll be right back. And get somebody to find out if Lawson's still in town."

He was dragging her out the door when they ran into Tom Clarkson coming the other way.

"Whoa," Tom protested, wheeling back into the grim sunlight. "You want me to tell you he's dead? He's dead. Can I go home now?"

"Tell me how," Mac snapped and dragged Chris right on past, out to the side of the station away from the gathering crowd where broken bottles of Old Crow and Sweet Rosie O'Grady littered the cracked asphalt.

"I've read all your books," he said without preamble. "This wasn't one of them. And you said the one you're working on is going to be knives.

Did you change your mind, or what?"

Chris bent over, hands on thighs, her back against the greasy, chipping wall, willing her stomach to stay settled, forcing the nightmare back into the darkness. There was an old condom at her feet, cigarette butts, a torn, stained section of poster from Harlan's latest revival. "No," she answered, closing her eyes. "Nothing's changed."

"Then what the hell are you talking about?"

Slowly she straightened and faced Mac, the vivid images and almost-forgotten instincts fading just enough to let her through. "It didn't occur to me to mention *Family Business*. It isn't due to come out until November."

That brought him right to attention. "What?"

She made a vague motion, suddenly too spent to offer more. "It's still in the editing process in New York. I mean, how could anybody copy it if it isn't even out yet?"

Mac looked toward the front of the station, to where the coroner's car had just pulled up alongside the latest Cootermobile. "They could if they'd seen it in New York."

Chris's reaction was immediate. "No."

When he turned back to her, his expression was implacable as Judgment. "We're going to need to go over that list of people," he said. "Especially the ones you work with who might know about the book. We're going to have to check them."

"It's not them," she insisted desperately, terrified for them, for herself. "It can't be."

"And everybody here," he mused, almost to himself, "who could have access to your house."

When Chris followed his gaze this time, she saw

Weird Allen standing right at the front of the crowd, his usually blank features avid.

He's been following me, she almost said. Even opened her mouth to do it. The words died stillborn. Suddenly Chris wasn't sure that that shadow under the tree in Mary Willoughby's yard had really been there after all.

She looked hard at him shouldering his way clear of the rest of the crowd, hands in work pants' pockets, his shirt just a little grimy, his hair just a little greasy, close-set eyes the color of old urine. A vague sense of vulgarity followed him like a distasteful smell.

Chris wanted it to be him. She wanted to be able to give the phantom a name. A recognizable form that could be supervised and cautioned and, if necessary, threatened. She couldn't quite do it, and the world shifted just a little more.

"Chief?"

They both turned to greet Tom as he walked over, stripping off gloves and wiping the sheen of perspiration from his upper lip with his forearm. "We rolled him a little. Easy answer. Small-caliber gunshot wound to the chest. Two of them. He looked pissed."

"How long?"

Tom shrugged, his posture still betraying the effort of facing that room. "Can't say right now. It's been cool, so longer. When did you let him out of jail?"

"Five days ago."

Tom nodded. "I'd guess he had another day after that. I'll bet nobody's seen him for a while."

Mac took a look at the assembled Cooters. "Looks like I get to take a trip down the yellow brick road."

"Ding dong. You want me for anything else?"

That brought his attention right back. "Yeah, will you take Chris home for me?"

Tom's answering grin was at once sympathetic and faintly superior, the kind those in the loop gave to greenhorns. "Reality a lot smellier than fiction, Chris?"

Chris launched herself away from the wall and hoped her wobbly legs would carry the day. "I'm not sure anymore, Tom," was all she said. She liked Tom a whole lot. Except now. Maybe she could see her way to decorating the seat of his new Cadillac for that one.

"Think Sue'd mind having her at your house?" Mac asked.

Chris brought her head up. "Think Chris might have an opinion about it?"

She almost got a grudging grin out of him. "Just until I check out your house."

"I can check my house out myself. Thanks, Mac, but I hate having someone holding my hand when I barf."

Tom nodded commiseration. "And Sue is the champion hand-holder."

"Humor me, then," Mac suggested in a voice that implied it wasn't a suggestion at all. "Just until I get some calls made . . . and talk to a few people. I'll meet you at the Clarksons' as soon as I'm finished here."

It took every ounce of willpower in her, but she straightened to her full height, which put her just a few inches shy of Mac's. Wiping her hands on her pants, Chris drew the shakiest breath she'd ever managed and faced him down. "No."

The good chief of police had a look on his face that betrayed the fact that very few people had ever

gotten away with saying that word to him in his professional capacity. "I guess I didn't make myself clear.
Your friend has hit town. That means that you're in
some danger yourself."

"You made yourself perfectly clear," Chris obliged,
her tones just as steely. "And although I disagree with
you, I appreciate the concern. But I'm either going to
my house, or I'm staying right here."

"Here?" This time he sounded as if she were insin-
uating herself into a locker room of unclad athletes.

Chris glared at him. "My books," she reminded
him. "My killer. I might be able to help."

"In the condition you're in?"

That damn near cleared Chris's head completely.
"In the *what* I'm in?"

"I'm sure I have better things to do," Tom demurred.
"I'll be at home if he manages to change your mind,
Chris."

"He won't."

"He will," Mac echoed decisively.

"Have I thrown up?" she demanded, not even
noticing Tom's sad headshaking as he walked to his
car. She directed her attention instead to where
JayCee was rather spectacularly decorating the parking lot with the blue plate special of the day. "Have I
contaminated the scene?"

"That's not the point."

She didn't know what else to do. What else to say.
So Chris told him the truth. "It's my fault, Mac. At
least let me do something to make up for it."

Chris could see her words' impact on him. Saw the
instinctive denial, the classic soothing responses take
shape. He never got a chance to make use of them.
They'd run out of time with their crime scene.

"Chief MacNamara?"

Mac hesitated, obviously taken aback by Chris's words, frustrated at the intrusion. Chris thought it couldn't have been better timed. She didn't want commiseration or consideration. She wanted expiation, and she knew the only way to do it.

Finally Mac spun on his heel. "Yes, sir."

Sam Milligan followed much the same procedure Tom had as he approached. A neat, gray-haired businessman with well-connected poker-playing pals, Sam had been coroner long enough to know where most of the bodies, both corporal and figurative, were buried. "Body's goin' over to Puckett General. Tom'll do the autopsy tonight. I'd say that unless that boy in there shot himself twice in the chest, threw away the gun, and then dragged himself in there to die, we have a homicide on our hands. You got any problem with that?"

"Other than wishing he'd done it in Iron County? No."

Sam smiled, a friendly, unpretentious smile, and nodded to Chris. "Liked your last book. When's the next one comin' out?"

"Seems it already has," Mac said. He motioned toward the building. "Looks like we might have a copycat murder on our hands."

Sam took a glance back over his shoulder to where the crowd was getting restless and JayCee was trying to reassert his authority after providing a moment of entertainment, and then looked back with a whistle. "Well, what do you know?"

She ended up staying. Through the measurements and the pictures, the struggle to get the body into

the bag without exploding, and the interrogation of
the other Cooters on the scene. She rode along
when they all caravaned up the road to inform
Cooter's wife and two daughters, one of whom was
grossly pregnant at fifteen with, no doubt, another
Cooter.

The trailer that had housed Cooter and the missus,
the two girls, and two pasty, whey-faced toddlers,
was rusted and bastardized bits and pieces of other
trailers, of trucks and sheds added on for space, plastic over the windows, and every old appliance that
had ever died littering the yard like ancient elephant
bones.

Chris saw the impact of Cooter's death strike the
women, not the way she'd imagined, with cries of
freedom, but with sullen silences, as if this were just
another misery to be balanced on top of all the other
miseries in their lives.

You can't bring me anything new, Chris could
almost hear his wife say, even though her eyes were
still puffy and discolored from where Cooter had evidently made good his promise to beat her for calling
the police the night of the fight. You can't hurt me
anymore. The reason Chris had left social work was
that she understood why freedom was just as terrifying as prison.

Chris told Mac where the murder site would be.
John directed them from the information he'd
received, back through the brambles and blackberry
bushes and early poison ivy. They found the blood-
stain there at the edge of the new marijuana patch.
The faint traces of drag marks back to the dirt road,
where Chris supposed the tire tracks had been erased
by the rain. Mac and John conferred and measured

and photographed, and Chris watched in silence.

And while she watched, something else managed to worm its way through the miasma of Cooter's murder. Something only Chris seemed to notice.

It wasn't the Cooters or the Cooters' women. It wasn't her book or the mystery murderer. It was Mac.

Mac, who had been completely at ease at a grisly murder scene, who had handled the various Cooters with tact and patience, who had delegated all the various tasks and quietly exerted his own authority when the sheriff had shown up to take his share of the action.

He'd been the first to step from his car when they'd reached the trailer. As Chris had climbed out, she'd seen him settle his navy blue cap on his head, wincing a little and giving a passing touch to the scar at his temple.

And then he'd waited.

Waited for the boys to untangle themselves from their vehicles and fight off the six or so mongrels that bounded forward at their approach. Waited, his hands with that funny tremor, even hooked to his belt, as the Cooters had stepped up the iron grate steps, pulled the door open, and bent a little to step inside.

And standing there, at the other side of the police cruiser, silent and watchful, Chris had seen his hand instinctively go for his gun when the door had opened. She'd seen him sweat.

All the time they searched for the weapon they knew they wouldn't find, while they measured distance and took photos and nudged the freshly turned earth for spent casings, Chris saw the police chief struggle to maintain his composure. She thought of that scar, of that tremor, of the short time he'd been in town, and she wondered.

They never did catch up to Lawson. By the time Mac finally dropped Chris off, they'd collected the autopsy results, a .38-caliber bullet, evidence bags with clothing and nail scrapings and hair samples to be held for the lab in Cape Girardeau. They had no idea at all, though, who had managed to shoot Cooter Taylor point-blank in the chest and then drop him off at the edge of town without anyone noticing.

The sun had already set by the time Mac pulled the cruiser up in front of Chris's house. The streetlights were on, and down toward the high school, cars were wheeling in and out of Main Street in a never-ending round of cruising the drag. It was Saturday night, and the teens were enjoying age-old mating rituals. The only ritual Chris was enjoying was the anticipation of her high, white, empty walls. Like a cloister away from the real world.

Chris took a considering look at her rumpled, limp T-shirt with its gaudy stripes. Chris Jackson, cloistered nun. That'd be one for the books.

She saw the note when she stepped up to unlock the door. Taped with a Band-Aid, since Sue was probably out of tape, it read: "I hear you don't like my bathroom. I'm insulted. Stop by for lasagna." No signature necessary. It was classic Sue Clarkson, Empathy Through Pragmatism. It worked. For the first time all day, Chris felt better. Well, since she wasn't going to get over to the Clarksons' tonight, she knew Sue would be over in the morning. Chris would just make some coffee cake for them both.

Better than trying to sleep after the day she'd had.

"What's this?"

Mac had just stepped up beside her when he came to a shuddering halt like a bomb defuser with a trip wire in sight. His attention had been snagged by something on her step. Chris took her own look and smiled.

"It's sweet," she insisted, and bent to pick up the single pink sweetheart rose that lay across her doorstep. "It's from Victor."

"And Lester!" came a high, reedy voice in the night.

Chris fought a chuckle as she straightened, the rose in her hand. "Thank you, you two. It's beautiful!"

Again the voice through an open second-story window, this time deeper, more recognizable. "You're welcome, li'l darlin'."

Mac was not in the least amused. "Does he do this all the time?" he asked.

Chris ignored his scowl as she unlocked her front door. "What's the matter? Don't any of your friends leave you little presents?"

Instead of answering, he reached around for his gun. "Let me go in first."

Chris stopped dead in her tracks, her hand already on the doorknob. She hadn't really thought about it. Somebody invading her house. Threatening her. She turned to find that Mac was deadly serious, and pulled her hand back to wait.

Mac took her place. Reached out for the door, gun in hand, expression steely. Tensed, silent. Sweating. Hesitating, there on the threshold before pushing the door open onto the darkness.

Chris saw him drag in an uneven breath. She heard her own pulse begin to thud in dread and realized that she was seeing it again.

Suddenly Chris saw all the way down to that final layer Mac protected with his starched shirts and measured speech. She realized just how terrible that wound he'd suffered had been. Farther down than pride, deeper than self-esteem. As devastating an injury as a man could suffer and still force himself awake in the morning. And yet, Mac did.

He edged her around behind him with his hand, and took another careful breath. Crouching down, so that his head was about half the height it should have been, he pushed the door open. Chris waited, watched. Held her breath with his as he moved and wished like hell she could somehow make it easier for him.

Mac paused, straightened, eased on into the house. Catching the screen door with her own backside, Chris followed.

She felt it the minute she stepped inside. A shiver of prescience, a whisper of dread. She almost came to a dead stop right there in the doorway. There was something in her house.

"Oh, shit," she whispered, and sensed Mac's head coming around, his hand already on the light switch.

Again he hesitated, terrible seconds of indecision that pushed Chris back against the wall. When the lights suddenly flipped on, she squinted in surprise.

"What the hell . . ." Mac sputtered, coiling back into a shooter's crouch, the gun swinging up in his hands.

"I knew you'd have to come home soon, Chris Jackson. I knew it."

Chris was stunned into silence by the woman rising from her sofa.

"Mrs. Axminster?"

Mac stepped in past Chris and scanned the room, his gun still held out before him. Chris couldn't seem to move, her attention on the small, plump, motherly looking woman in the stained housedress who stood before her. In her house. Right in the middle of her living room, as if it were the bus station.

"How did you get in here?" she finally demanded.

That brought Mrs. Axminster up short, her expression hovering between guilt and defiance, like a teenager caught out after curfew. Another woman with misery piled on her head. A self-perpetuating victim who'd never once considered leaving the judge, even to save her children. Chris wondered how she'd react if they'd brought her the news that her husband was dead.

"The door was open when I got here," she said, settling on defiance and advancing, not even noticing the man to her left who had his gun trained on her.

"Not the front door."

"The kitchen door. You think I want everybody knowing my business? You think the judge is happy the whole town already knows about Shelly?"

Her features had been pretty once. Over the years they'd been deadened, the careful lack of emotion meant to protect her from retribution stealing the individuality from mouth and cheeks and eyes. The colors had bled from the painting, leaving nothing but indistinguishable grays. Chris could have felt sorry for the judge's wife if she hadn't consigned her own daughter to her same fate.

She still couldn't believe it. She'd expected Shelly

to explode. She'd never even considered that her mother might do it.

"Who do you think you are?" the little woman demanded suddenly, as if resuming some conversation interrupted only a moment ago, her voice shrill and almost otherworldly. "God? You think you got the right to just meddle in other people's lives if you want?"

Mac had circled behind the woman and watched her with his police eyes, his balance on the balls of his feet so he could move fast. Chris saw him at the corner of her own field of vision and felt better for his presence. She'd never seen Mrs. Axminster like this before. She'd never once heard anything but courtesies from her at all.

"My life has been hell since you've moved to this town," Mrs. Axminster persisted, a bit of spittle flying with her words, her eyes hot. Chris held perfectly still before her. "You come into my house and think you know everything . . . know . . ." Tears welled, old, thick tears that traced familiar pathways. Mrs. Axminster didn't even notice them. "That girl's nothin' but trash, no matter what we've tried to do for her, and you're pushing her into it. *Pushing* her . . . and her daddy . . ."

"What do you want me to do?" Chris asked as gently as she could, knowing there was no answer that would be acceptable. "I couldn't let her run away. That's where she was headed."

But Mrs. Axminster wasn't listening anymore. She was staring, the spittle still caught on the corner of her lower lip, her eyes betraying her. "We tried to tell the girl you were no good, but she wouldn't listen," she said. "No, no she wouldn't. She has to now. Your judgment's on you, and it's your fault. It's been your fault every time . . . the reverend's right. He's always been right about you . . . about me . . ."

"Do you want me to take you home, Mrs. Axminster?" Chris asked, the acid in her chest suddenly suffocating her.

Mac finally straightened, holstering his gun with a shaking hand. "I think I'd rather do that," he said.

Those tormented brown eyes flickered with recognition. "He'll be mad."

Chris knew which he she was referring to. "No, he won't. The chief'll think of something, won't you, Chief?"

Mac's expression was enigmatic as he stepped quietly forward. "Yes, ma'am. Now, come on."

His hand was gentle on the woman's arm, just enough pressure to get her into motion. Mrs. Axminster didn't acknowledge him or so much as look at Chris again as they walked together back into the night.

"And lock all the doors this time," Mac suggested dryly as Chris helped him settle the little woman into his front seat.

"I did," she said. When his gaze flicked back at her in alarm, she admitted the truth. "I think."

She did for certain this time, though, checking every lock, every window, wondering how she could have forgotten last time. And then, the exhaustion overtaking her, she sank onto her couch and let her home soothe her.

Just like chanting a mantra, Chris catalogued her small collection of securities, overstuffed furniture and wind chimes, music and sculptures. Teapots and teddy bears. Not people. Not yet, although she'd been hoping to finally graduate to that. Artificial life, handpicked and nurtured like inanimate children. As carefully arranged as standing stones at a holy site. Settling and safe, with no psychoses to impose on her, no traumas that she couldn't ease, or demands she couldn't meet. No demands at all.

Tonight, though, her things were different. Disturbed by Mrs. Axminster's intrusion. Infinitesimally changed, so that it was like looking at a familiar picture through a different lens.

Unsettled by the thought, Chris got back to her feet. Suddenly she needed to make sure everything was still untouched.

She ran upstairs, to where her desk sat in front of the great expanse of greenhouse glass, and checked her papers. Files and notes and lists of things to research. Personal memos that weren't supposed to be shared with anyone else.

She swung around for her bedroom to find the covers just as rumpled as when she'd left, the pillow limp and misshapen on the floor as if it had suffered a great injury. Nothing had been moved. Nothing affected in a tangible way that Chris could put a finger on. Even so . . . different.

Or was it just her? Was she imagining Mrs. Axminster running her stubby fingers over her secrets and leaving traces of stale madness behind? Did she envision the resulting guilt sitting on all of her possessions as solidly as it sat on her shoulders?

Slowly Chris sank onto her bed beneath the skylight and the stars. She willed the quiet of her high, open walls to surround her. Shoved and pushed and grunted with every ounce of mental energy to close the door on Shelly's family and Mac's history, at least for a minute. Tried to relax enough to maybe get some rest.

But for the first time in the years she'd lived here, it wasn't enough. Her world had shifted imperceptibly. Her security, built up step by step, minute by minute, had been breached. Her certainty, so hard won, was threatened.

Her haven, where she could be safe, wasn't safe anymore.

This time when she left, Chris made sure she locked the doors behind her. She knew she couldn't stay in the house right now. She might as well make use of the time she had before Mac could start the wheels rolling and call New York. She had some home numbers in case of emergency. And if this wasn't an emergency, she didn't know what was.

Mac didn't need to come up with an explanation after all. The judge was out when he showed up at the house with Mrs. Axminster, and her two other girls took her in like a dirty secret. Mac lingered a minute on the front porch of the solid, square brick house with its lawn ornaments and miniature windmill, figuring he should do more. Certain the judge's wife needed it.

There was all kinds of trouble in this household. Mac had the feeling he was going to get a call here one day real soon, and he couldn't think of a single way to prevent it. One of the nicer things about being a detective. Preventive medicine in law enforcement was virtually nonexistent anymore. Watching the inevitable happen ate away at you after awhile, the frustrations collecting like sins until everything was stained. But if you were a detective, you just saw the broken shards. You never got a chance to see the whole and miss it.

Mac climbed wearily into his car and made it all the way back to the station. The doors were locked, the lights off. Curtis was on, which meant he was taking his turn on the drag. Mac opened the door to his office, threw his hat to the coatrack, slipped off his gun, and pulled off his uniform shirt, which was beginning to smell like sour sweat. Then he walked into the bathroom and vomited up every bite of food he'd taken all day long.

Even with the help of B. B. King and J & B, it took twenty minutes in the john and another ninety in his dark, locked office, for the shakes to settle.

It had been as bad as he'd expected. Worse. Every inch of the way, all day long whenever he'd walked into a strange room, whenever he'd had to pull his gun, he'd seen it. Double barrel, black as death. Pointed straight at his face. A vision that just wouldn't give a man enough room to handle the streets of Chicago.

By the time the B. B. King tape ran out Mac could at least function well enough to get back to business. Flipping on the lights, he doused himself with water and shrugged into another T-shirt. It was time to call St. Louis. He had as much as he needed to make Lawson a happy woman. In exchange, she was going to coordinate real information instead of copies.

"What do you mean she's gone?" Mac demanded ten minutes later when he finally got a detective named Garavaglia instead of a half-asleep dispatcher.

"She's been suspended for a couple of weeks," he said in a very satisfied voice. Lawson must have been an absolute joy to work with. "Of course, if you see her, you might want to give her a little warning. The brass up here is pissin' fire. Seems she and couple of open homicide files left the department right after the lieutenant gave her the good news Wednesday."

"She was here Thursday working on a case."

"That crap again? Goddamn, she just doesn't give up, does she?"

"What was she suspended for?"

He got a bark of laughter, and pictured a guy like his old partner, beefy and sanguine. A player. "Not understanding chain of command."

Mac almost winced. He could just see it. Impatient, self-righteous Sergeant Lawson, so convinced that her superiors couldn't see the shit on their own noses that she jumped a few levels in the food chain. Probably made her case like the Nazi SS at Nuremberg, too. It would not have been a pretty sight.

"Well, Garavaglia, I hate to tell you this," Mac said dolefully, "but I have bad news."

"She's screwing the county supervisor and just got herself promoted to captain?"

"She was right."

Garavaglia would have been happier with the first answer. "What?"

"That far-out, ridiculous theory she had about some wacko playing *'Me and My Shadow'* with C. J. Turner? She nailed it in one."

"Bullshit."

"We had a murder down here today that the author herself identifies as an admirable copy of her work. Work, by the way, that has yet to be seen by the public eye. She also identified pictures of the other murders with the same amazement. The wacko, evidently, has an eye for detail. I'm surprised Lawson hasn't been up to gloat about it. I sure thought that was where she was going when she left."

Silence. Mac could hear his counterpart struggling to come to grips with the inconceivable, that pain in the royal ass Lawson could possibly have one right.

"Son of a duck-fucking bitch," he finally breathed.

And Mac, who had been too long away from the smell of fifty-year-old linoleum, eighty-year-old dust, and age-old sin, smiled. "Exactly."

At two A.M. the next morning, Chris woke shaking and sweating. Her heart hammered. Her T-shirt was soaked with sweat. The lights flickered briefly, and it seemed a dim shadow drifted across the room.

But that wasn't what terrified her into dry sobs or sent her stumbling down the stairs. It wasn't even the nightmare. She'd been awakened by the sound of a baby crying.

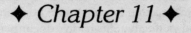

✦ *Chapter 11* ✦

"YOU LOOK LIKE HELL."

Chris didn't even bother to move as Sue opened the door and stepped inside. "I had a little trouble sleeping last night."

"It looks like it, honey . . ." Sue got as far as the foyer before coming to a dead stop. "Chris?"

Chris turned after her and considered the state of her house. She wasn't surprised that Sue felt it necessary to stop. Sue had been in her house enough times to know how carefully she kept it, how even though the floor of her living room looked like a secondhand shop, every item had its particular place, and woe unto any person who tried to move it. There were no places left this morning. She'd upended the entire house.

Sue turned on her, real fear in her big blue eyes. "Honey? What happened? Are you all right?"

Chris just rubbed at her temples and smiled. "I'll explain over coffee. I have some streusel. Interested?"

It took Sue a moment to answer. "Sure."

They proceeded past piles of CDs, nests of cushions, towers of stereo equipment, and at least one shattered ceramic ashtray on their way through to the kitchen. Chris could tell by the set of Sue's shoulders that it wasn't making her any more comfortable. Chris understood perfectly. She hadn't unearthed anything, anything at all that would have explained the noise. Nothing more than a few dust bunnies and a 1898 silver dollar that had somehow found its way beneath her couch.

"Tom said that Cooter's murder really upset you," Sue said as gently as possible as the two of them sat down in a kitchen that looked like a tornado had swept through and fulfilled the familiar rituals of morning coffee. Chris poured and Sue cut and passed around the coffee cake. Neither of them looked over to the counter where every one of Chris's glasses, cups, and plates rested in uneven piles, like modernistic sculpture, on the white counters.

"It's another copycat murder," Chris admitted, her attention on the swirl of cream she'd added to her coffee.

That brought Sue to an upright position. "And Tom didn't tell me?" She immediately blushed at her less than altruistic reaction.

"Don't get out the superglue yet," Chris advised. "He didn't know, either. From what I gathered, that information was classified."

Handily mollified, Sue considered the situation over her first sip of coffee. "But how could that have been a copycat?" she demanded. "I've read all the C. J. Turner books, and not one mentioned a bloated body in a garage. I would have remembered."

So Chris told her. In plain, unemotional words. In clinical detail. Even Sue came close to blanching.

"It's my fault," Chris said in defeat. "Somehow I set

this in motion without even knowing about it, and now he's dead."

"Chris, how can you say that?" Sue leaned over, hand on Chris's arm.

"Because," Chris admitted. "I think it's true."

I've created it, she wanted to say. Molded it like a golem out of the clay of my own guilt. Out of the lies I've lived.

"Well, I wouldn't waste my sympathies on Cooter Taylor." Sue sniffed. "For whatever reason it happened, you know he got what he deserved."

A popular idea, evidently. Chris hadn't had to make the coffee cake after all. One had appeared on her doorstep that morning, still warm and moist, with an attached note that simply said, "Thank you. Cooter received his just punishment."

As if Chris had been the instigator. The town's avenger. She wondered if that meant she would also be responsible for her own judgment, since both Harlan and Louise Axminster had decided she deserved it. She could go into business. Write a book about the person you would most like to see punished. Any particular style of execution? Lethal injection too tame for you? How about shotguns or slow poison? We're running a special on Colombian neckties today . . .

"Mac's putting a protective guard on you, isn't he?" Sue asked, her pragmatism winning out. "After all, whoever this is has shown up here . . . God, that's enough to make you want to buy a gun and lock the doors." She shook her head, unnerved. "Here." She said it with that same kind of amazement every upstanding, average neighbor used when crime hits the neighborhood. Anywhere but here. We're safe from all that here.

"I don't know," Chris answered truthfully.

"Why don't you come stay with us?"

Chris almost gave herself away by answering too fast, too loudly. Instead, she hid behind another long sip of coffee.

"No," she finally said, as if she'd really been considering it. "I'm far enough behind on my deadline as it is. I'd never get any work done on the book if I stayed with you guys." She smiled. "I'd end up playing Chutes and Ladders with Ellen all night. But thanks."

Chris knew Sue wasn't happy with her answer. The little blond would probably find a thousand excuses to stop by, or have Tom stop by, or have Curtis, JayCee, and Buddy in their patrol cars, just to make sure Chris was safe. It helped ease just a little of the isolation. It didn't do a thing for the disorientation, the minutes that ticked inexorably away like heartbeats toward death, back to the dark from which Chris's dreams had finally begun to escape.

The doorbell chimed. A hand restraining Chris from getting up, Sue took over the chore. "You aren't really still working on a book, are you?" she asked over her shoulder as she picked her way through the mess in the living room. "Can't you talk your editor, or whoever, into holding it until this is all over?"

"I might try as soon as I find somebody," Chris allowed.

"Find somebody?"

She rubbed a little at the headache that had taken up residence behind her eyes. "They all seem to have been out of town this weekend."

Chris heard the exchanged greeting, heard the

staccato of shoes across her floor, and looked up, her headache suddenly worse.

Shelly was red-faced and trembling. "What did she do?"

Behind her, Sue slowed to a stop in the doorway to the kitchen. Sunlight poured down on the three of them, gilding hair and brightening eyes. A beautiful day, bestowing health and sensuality. A special gift from God, illumination and warmth. An odd sensation considering the three women so blessed were discussing madness and death.

"What did she do?" Shelly demanded, her voice a jagged slice of disdain and shame.

Chris fought the urge to walk out on both of them. "I should have talked to her, Shel. It was my fault."

"*Talked* to her?" the girl countered shrilly, all angles and motion. "Talked to her? Why? So she could tell me that it's an ungrateful child who turns away from her family? That I didn't get anything I didn't ask for? So she could tell you to your face exactly what she thinks of you?"

"I found out," Chris admitted.

That made Shelly laugh again, that strange, harsh laugh that sounded like crows over a dead body. "Not in a pig's eye, you didn't. She was drunk last night. Wait until you catch a load of her sober."

Chris climbed to her feet, too worn out to finesse her way around this one. "Shelly, you're still not my daughter," she said.

The girl stiffened, stilled, her hands clenched as tightly as her jaw. Chris saw tears glint against emotions she'd only suspected in the girl, seething whirlpools of loss and betrayal and pain. Chris braced herself, buffeted by that hostile silence.

"Well, we sure know that," Shelly accused. "Don't we?"

And without another word, she turned on her heel and slammed back out the front door.

Five minutes later, Mac walked in.

"We need to get some work done, Chris. I need that list of people you think might have something against you."

Chris just looked at him. "Alphabetically or chronologically?"

Mac was not happy with the looks of her. He'd expected her to be a little washed out after trudging through that nightmare the day before. Maybe a little drawn around the eyes. She looked as if she'd just survived Chernobyl. Pale as death, and almost as quiet, when he'd arrived. Picking at things and losing the train of conversation.

And her house . . .

At first look, Mac had been sure she'd had an intruder in the night, even though he'd had Curtis parked out front almost all night long. He'd seen neater prison riots.

But nothing was destroyed—except that worthless little hunk of ceramic she used for an ashtray—and nothing missing. Except, initially, her objectivity.

"You want to tell me what this is all about?" he asked, settling in at the pine kitchen table with his back to the wall so he could watch house and yard at once. It gave a person a great sense of space, an illusion of control. Too bad he couldn't enjoy it.

Chris fiddled with her coffee cup. "I, uh, had a little trouble with finding a surprise guest in the house last night."

Mac took a cursory look around. "So you decided to put everything out for the Rock of Ages rummage sale?"

He almost got a ghost of a grin. To his right, Sue watched with hawk eyes, not in the least shy about her concern.

"I figured I could keep busy today putting everything away," Chris retorted quietly, still not looking at him, still making him very nervous.

"I thought you wanted to help solve murders."

Her gaze flickered and lit. Lifted. Mac caught that same hint of indecision, that dark shudder of something private. There wasn't a chance in hell she'd unload in front of Sue, though. He was going to have to be patient.

"What can I do?"

Mac pushed the pile of folders he'd brought closer to the center of the table. "Go over the murders with me. Go over possible suspects. We need to come up with something."

For some reason, that made her look like she wanted to cry. Mac waited, not at all sure what was going on, experienced enough to know how to wait it out. Chris climbed to her feet, still picking at the royal purple-and-yellow sweatshirt she wore, the hand that held onto her coffee mug trembling.

"Can we do it someplace else?" she asked finally.

Mac scooped up his files and followed her. "No problem."

He really wouldn't have minded basking a little in all that sunlight, watching the new leaves on the trees outside or the birds dipping and swooping around the feeders. Keeping half an eye on the town from Chris's back window.

He wasn't going to get any kind of coherent answers from her here, though, either about the murders or the reason she'd found it necessary to pile all her worldly belongings in one big heap in the middle of the floor. And the other answers he needed were going to have to wait on his call to Chicago.

"How 'bout city hall?" he asked, pulling out his keys. "Nobody's there on the weekends."

Nobody except Weird Allen.

Mac saw him when they pulled into the parking lot, standing over by the back windows, his hands in his jeans' pockets, his attention on the street. Mac caught the glint of something silver on the back of Allen's belt and realized it was the handcuffs. Just what he needed to deal with right now.

"Chief . . ."

"Allen."

Mac kept his hand on Chris's arm and felt her stiffen at Allen's approach. She was spooking real easily this morning, he thought in passing. Not that she didn't have reason. Allen would have been spooky enough even without his own restraint devices.

"Considerin' what's been goin' on," the young man began in his curiously high voice, "I thought I'd help with surveillance around town . . . you know, when the patrollin' officer is unavailable."

Mac didn't turn away from where he was unlocking the city hall door. "And did you see anything, Allen?"

"Yes sir, I did. I observed Victor and Lester committing a 10-65 last night."

That brought Mac to an uncertain halt. "He committed a mad dog?"

Allen did his best to bluster. "No, sir, of course not. He was trespassing."

"Where?"

Allen swung his attention toward Chris in a way that let Mac know just how he'd discovered his information. "Miss Jackson's place of residence, sir. The subject . . . subjects were sitting out on the sidewalk at approximately oh-three-hundred hours."

Mac didn't want to betray the fact that he was intrigued. The last thing he needed to do was encourage Allen. On the other hand, he wondered why he hadn't heard about it from Curtis.

"He . . . they were helping to keep an eye on Miss Jackson," Mac explained. "I think it would be advisable for you to hold off town watching for a little while, Allen. I'd hate for somebody to mistake you for the murderer."

"I'm perfectly capable, sir—"

Mac didn't have any patience left. With an upraised hand, he cut the man off. "Allen. I have to get in and work on this with Miss Jackson. Now, I'd appreciate it if you'd head on home . . . and ditch the handcuffs."

"Weird Allen with handcuffs," Chris moaned a couple of minutes later as they were turning on lights and heading for Mac's office. "Now, there's a scary thought."

"What *was* Victor doing outside your house this morning?"

Chris busied herself starting a new pot of coffee. Mac could see the fine tremor in her hands. "Victor worries about me," she said in an offhand voice. "He also seems to find it quite romantic to pine from afar."

"Would he kill for you?"

That spun her right around, her eyes stark, her face as pale as he'd seen it. "Victor?" she demanded. "Don't be silly. He doesn't have the guts to stand up to his mother, and she's been dead for five years. Just how well do you think he's going to do against Cooter?"

Mac threw off an easy shrug. "I once had a ninety-pound woman rip her two-hundred-pound boyfriend's throat out with her bare hands when voices told her he was possessed."

"Well, what about old Allen?" Chris challenged. "From what I've read about serial killers over the years, they tend to be real knowledgeable about the law. Some of them impersonated police to get information on the murder investigations."

Mac put a David Sanborne tape into the player and turned it on. Then he closed the blinds against the rest of the town and pulled out his notes. "We're going to consider Allen. And Victor, and your agent who likes to wear things home with the price tags still on them, and your romance editor who doesn't know you write mysteries."

Chris was still out in the front room where the coffeemaker was making noises like a choking retriever. "Couldn't it just be some crazy person who thinks he knows me?"

Mac looked at her through the doorway, all angles and funny grace, like a wading bird caught in a trap. He wanted to tell her it was going to be all right. He wanted to call Danny back in Chicago and tell him to stop the trace he was doing on the life and times of Chris Jackson. He wanted, most of all, to know who was doing this to her and why, and what there was about her that was making it so much worse.

"It could be," he admitted. "That's St. Louis's problem. Ours is to make sure you don't open the door on a familiar face and end up in a body bag."

Still she hesitated, caught between the dread of something big and the frustration of what she was going to have to do to people who trusted her. Age-old dilemmas, Mac thought to himself as he sat himself down, the dark threnody of a saxophone wrapping around his shoulders. Somebody had to be offered up all the time. The answers were never the ones you wanted, even for somebody as objective as a cop.

But the answers were all that mattered. Even if that long, quirky bird might never find its way back to the water.

Mac picked up his paperweight and began to balance it in his hands.

"Let's go over the list," Chris finally said, sagging just a little and turning to pour them both some coffee.

Mac uncapped his pen and set to work.

"That's it?" he asked some time later as he looked down at the notes he'd made. "Eight people from your stint in St. Louis, four people each from the publishing houses, your agent, and the townspeople. Doesn't seem like much."

"You'll need to talk to the publishing house to find out who's actually handled the manuscript," Chris said. "Those are only the people I deal with."

He was nodding, thinking. "And none of them

have ever expressed a working knowledge of the St. Louis area?"

Her grin was wry. "When I sent the first book in, I had to explain to the copy editor that the arch here wasn't just another McDonald's. In the east, St. Louis is looked upon as that green wrinkly area under the left wing of the plane on the way to the other coast. Most of them couldn't put it on the correct side of the Mississippi."

"You didn't work with anybody else in St. Louis?"

"Sure. But these are the only ones I hung around with. Anybody else was just a passing acquaintance."

Mac looked up at her, relieved that away from her house she'd seemed to relocate a little of her spark. It made him wonder just what she'd been looking for the night before. "That doesn't mean one of them couldn't be the killer," he suggested.

She nodded her concession. "It means I can't give you anything helpful. I worked at least three jobs at a time to pay for school, and I took classes with about sixteen thousand other people. But the only people I really got to know were at DFS."

Mac conceded the point in return. "Boyfriends?" he asked. "Ex-spouses? Anything like that?"

He'd almost expected to get a flash of anger on that one. Instead he got a grin. "The first two names in St. Louis," Chris admitted. "The first one's a cop and the second one's a C.P.A."

"You do like variety. Did you leave on good terms?"

"The best. They both found women who wanted to settle down and I sent flatware."

"So you've never been married?"

"Not even unhappily."

"How about any of your foster families growing up?" Mac asked, still not content with the length of that list for the years it should have covered.

There went her humor again. "They don't even know I'm alive," she said simply, coldly. "There wouldn't be any connection."

"You're sure."

This time, Chris looked at him, and Mac saw the ashes of a childhood. "I'm sure."

He just nodded and made his own mental note to have Danny check on it once he got something. "OK," he said. "Nobody else you want to add to the list?"

He'd said it casually enough, leaning back in his chair with his attention ostensibly on the tarantula Kevin had sent him from Phoenix. Big, ugly, hairy thing. The truth caught suspended in a protective bubble of careful and not-so-careful lies. Mac waited, listening to Chris's stillness, smelling her indecision. Holding his breath for a breakthrough.

Instead, she shook her head. "Those are the only ones I can remember. Now, what do we do?"

Mac shrugged, disappointed again. "Focus on the people who might have somehow had access to this latest book." He looked hard at her, assessing, challenging. Nailing her in place. "I need an honest answer. Is there any name on that list that sounds more promising than another?"

She froze, eyes on the paperwork, body perfectly still. Mac could see the instinctive defenses charge in. Saw her struggle with them to give him an answer. Wondered just what was way at the back of those brittle brown eyes.

Finally, though, she had the guts to face him. "There's something," she admitted. "A feeling."

He made it a point not to move. "Yeah?"

She let out a very small sigh. Then she shook her head. "I don't know how to explain it. Something . . . something about this is real familiar. Personal. It's not just somebody making a point to the world. They're making it specifically to me."

"What point?"

Her eyes grew even larger, bright as if she were actually fighting tears. "I don't know. I just . . . I think somehow I've heard the person tell me what they're trying to say in person. I just don't know who. I don't know when."

"A face?" he asked. "Anything? Man or woman?"

Chris shook her head again, her motion more agitated. "I don't know. I don't have the world's best memory, and it's just not helping me right now."

"But it's someone you know."

"More than that," she countered. "It's someone who knows me."

That was when Mac let himself sit forward, when he allowed Chris to see his attention. "Which means we can lop off a few names from the list and concentrate on the rest."

"How?"

He considered the pile of folders. "God, what I'd give for a computer link. To get anything this way, we're going to have to wait for Lawson or call Cape and use theirs. And I hate doing that. By the time I get off the phone everybody in town'll know who we suspect."

"What computers?" Chris asked, the change of

direction reflecting in her mannerisms. "VICAP, NCIC, MULES, that kind of thing?"

Mac nodded. "It was a hell of a lot easier back in Chicago. All I needed was the time and a couple of warm bodies."

He didn't even notice the sly expression creep across her face. "I can help."

Mac looked up, surprised to see interest in her eyes. "What?"

She motioned to the pile of information between them. "The computers. VICAP, NCIC, MULES, LETS, all the law enforcement networks. And a lot of others, like credit check places. I can tap into them from my computer at home."

This time it was Mac who was surprised into silence. "I hope you know that's completely illegal."

Chris grinned like a kid caught swimming in the wrong pool. "I figure you won't rat on me as long as we can get the information. I learned how to do it a couple of months ago. Amazing what a couple of mai tais'll do for a computer hacker."

"A book, no doubt."

"The one I'm working on now. Of course, I won't divulge state secrets, but do you know how easy it is to find out anything you want to know about someone just from his social security number?"

"Yes," Mac said. "I do."

"If I can get the portable, I can modem from your phone here," she said, then proffered a smile that was just shy of assured. "If you don't mind."

Mac didn't mind in the least. But he didn't get the chance to take her up on her offer. Once again, the phone interrupted.

First Mac cursed. Then he picked up the receiver.

"MacNamara," he snapped.

"Halleluia, somebody's home. This is Garavaglia, St. Louis County Police. Chief?"

Mac straightened his chair, already recognizing the clipped tones of his caller. Something was happening.

"You got me. What's up?"

There was a small sound, a short grunt of frustration. "What's up is we can't seem to find our sergeant. She never surfaced here after visiting you. When did you say she left?"

Mac was already pulling over his scratch pad. "Friday."

There was a short silence on the other end of the line. "Yeah, that's what I was afraid of. Husband hasn't heard from her. Nobody's seen her. We already had the highway patrol check along Highway 55 all the way to Cape, and they've come up dry. She told some people here she was maybe thinking of driving down 21. Can you do some checking on your end? Chevy Cavalier four-door, license KRT-226."

"Yeah. I'll get the word out."

"You sure she left?" Garavaglia demanded. "She's not sneakin' around down there someplace trying to catch something?"

"Not that I know of. There are plenty of places to hide back up in the hills, but if she'd been talking to anybody, I'd know it. I'll check, though."

"Appreciate it. I'll be comin' on down your way tomorrow to talk to you, but till then, we're at a high rock wall without a rope. And all hell's breakin' loose."

Mac tapped at the files on his desk. "Some of the information panning out?"

"Yeah." Garavaglia couldn't have sounded more disgusted. "You were right about that rump rustler over in Webster. Missing his promise ring from his housemate. It didn't turn up at the time, because nobody knew he was wearing it. Nobody bothered to get worried until probate went through and they started splitting up the proceeds. Which means, you and Lawson were right. You missin' a ring from your DB down there?"

"He didn't wear 'em," Mac said, scribbling away. "I have the family checking for items he might have been carrying with him. Keys, mementos, good-luck charms, that kind of thing."

There was a long sigh. "Well, son, looks like we got a real Mr. Stranger Danger on our hands. Cap's tryin' to keep a lid on things up here, but we got a major cluster fuck brewin', especially with two suspects ready to go to trial. And that stupid bitch took every one of those case files with her. We got nothin' but air and a chief lookin' to relieve his indigestion in the worst way."

Mac considered the untidy pile of manila and Xerox paper on his desk. "Well, I might be able to help a little there, too."

He could hear the percussion of a detective bureau on the other end of that line, footsteps, voices, computers, radios. He could almost smell the burnt-away coffee in the pot and the raw scratch of disinfectant. It made him crave a cigarette like sex.

"I hear you have the author down there," Garavaglia was saying.

"Yep."

"I'll need to talk to her."

"As long as you're nicer than the last one."

The answering oath was succinct and heartfelt. "Six fuckin' months till retirement. Six months . . ."

It took Mac five minutes to put out the APB for the Chevy sedan Sergeant Lawson had been driving. When he was finished, he looked up to find Chris checking the files on the McClain case.

"Do we *have* to find her?" she asked without looking up.

Mac grinned. "Her chief wants to yell at her."

Chris positively beamed. "Oh, in that case . . ."

"What are you looking for?"

"I was checking dates. The first three murders happened just about the time of year the books said they did."

"And?"

Chris tapped at the brand-new, original file on Cooter. "The victim in *Family Business* died in a fully grown stand of marijuana."

Mac was on the verge of getting to his feet. That brought him right back into his chair again. "Late summer."

She nodded. "Does that mean something?"

"Yeah. I just don't know what." He was going to have to talk to Danny again, brainstorm about the kind of killers they just didn't see in Pyrite on a given day. Maybe call up some markers from the FBI. There was something here, he knew it. Mac just couldn't put his finger on it. Only a few months away from the real streets, and his instincts were getting rusty.

In the end, he flipped all the files closed. "I need to go over to Harmonia's."

"Can I come along?"

Mac looked up just in time to see a flicker of something in her eyes, a splinter of fear that seemed oddly out of place.

"Yeah, I don't care." I don't really want you out of my sight, he thought. Mac didn't like the idea of her being in that house alone, especially a house she'd just ripped apart with her bare hands. Much better she tag along after him, where he could baby-sit her without her realizing it.

It wasn't much of a drive. Harmonia Mae Switzer still lived on the site where she and about four generations of Switzers before her had been born. A big, ugly brick Victorian house that had grown up around a series of successively bigger frame homes. The Switzers had been the mine owners and the only Confederates to return unscathed in body and reputation to Pyrite. Staunch members of the DAR and the DCA, organizers and major donors to the Puckett County Museum and major benefactors of everything from hospital wings to town morals and standards, the Switzers had always been a town force. Now, there was only Harmonia Mae left, and her grand, sprawling house and land had to share a road with the Mobile Home Hall of Fame.

Harmonia answered the door in dress, heels, and pearls. The town joke was that she'd never had children because she couldn't figure out how to give birth without taking her girdle off.

"Yes?"

Mac instinctively straightened, cap in hand. Miss Switzer put him in mind of every nun who'd ever laid a ruler across his knuckles. Ramrod straight, iron gray hair, ample bosom, no-nonsense attitude. Which was why he'd stopped by his house on the way here and retrieved his uniform for the visit.

"I'm Chief of Police MacNamara, Mizz Switzer," he introduced himself. "I need to talk to you for a moment."

They ended up having iced tea and saying hello to the monkey.

"Of course, my dear brother Edwin brought him back from Burma with him from the war." The old woman smiled fondly at the beady-eyed pet. "I named him Mr. Lincoln because of the obvious resemblance."

Mac kept an eye on the animal, certain he was going to bite and even more certain that he didn't want Mr. Lincoln's teeth in his arm any more than he'd wanted Cooter's. "And you say you haven't seen Sergeant Lawson since Friday?"

Harmonia Mae immediately stiffened. "Unpleasant young woman. Never had a civil word for anyone. I was relieved to see her go. I don't believe we will have room for her when she returns, either."

"Did she leave anything behind?"

Like homicide files.

"Certainly not. Unless Shelly missed it when she cleaned. The girl does need some discipline in those matters."

"How's she doing otherwise?" Chris asked from the other side of Mr. Lincoln, her tea untasted in her hands.

Harmonia turned sharp eyes on her. "I was, of course, happy to take the child in . . . unlike some of the people in town who expressed interest in her welfare. And although her father the judge is, of course, a dear friend, it is quite understandable when one child becomes a bit . . . out of hand, that maybe alternate living situations should be considered."

Mac wasn't sure whether the old woman expected thanks or praise. He'd heard all about the Shelly Axminster situation, and thought the resolution creative.

"If I could look at Sergeant Lawson's room," he suggested diffidently when Chris didn't even manage an answer.

It took Harmonia a minute to break off her silent remonstrances and gather herself to her feet. "Of course, Chief."

"Old bat."

Mac smiled. "Seems like Shelly was pretty set on moving in with you."

Alongside him, Chris sighed. "Yeah, I know."

They were in the cruiser, headed past the colored lights and pink flamingos of the Hall of Fame. Tommy Blue, who ran it, was standing out front hosing down the asphalt as if it would improve the chances of those flocks of tourists he'd been expecting. Mac wasn't sure, but he bet that an acre lot with fifteen half restored old mobile homes with Astroturf lawns and cement lawn animals wasn't going to be the biggest draw in the county. But hell, what did he know? As Tommy had been quick to point out, Mac wasn't even from Missouri.

"We need some more answers before that next detective gets down here."

Chris turned towards him with sick surprise on her face. "The next what?"

"Name's Garavaglia. He says he's six months away from retirement, and he got handed the case. He'll be down in a couple of days. I thought we could get a jump start on him this time."

She groaned, her head dropping back on the seat with a thud. "I don't want to play anymore."

"Not even if it means this all stops?"

"It's not going to stop," she retorted, head coming back up, eyes snapping fire. "It's going to go on and on, with one detective after another picking at me like crows at a road kill. Who do I know? Who's mad at me? Who have I pissed off and liked and made love to and maybe, just maybe convinced to murder? I thought Lawson was bad, but she was just the first round, wasn't she?"

"If you'd rather, we'll get her back."

Chris snorted rather unkindly. "Yeah, my life's suddenly full of happy choices, isn't it?"

"How 'bout picking up that computer?" Mac countered. "At least we can try and have some answers before the next wave comes barreling through from St. Louis."

"Excellent idea." Her voice was hearty. Her hands were clenched in her lap.

"Dispatch to Chief MacNamara."

Mac picked up the mike and keyed it. "This is MacNamara. Go ahead dispatch."

"Sheriff Tipett wants you to reach him on Tac 2."

"Acknowledged." He flipped channels and keyed again as he pulled up to the stoplight by the courthouse. "Sheriff?"

"Chief MacNamara? That you?"

"Whatchya need?"

"I think you'd better meet me on Highway K by the forty-mile marker."

"You got something?"

"Yes sir, I sure do. I think you'd better see for yourself."

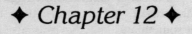

✦ *Chapter 12* ✦

CHRIS COULD SMELL it the minute she stepped out of the car. Caught there in the still afternoon air, heavier than the sunlight and the fresh pine and moss. Wet smoke. Scorched metal. Destruction.

Eldon waited for them right by the mile marker, there at the crook of the road that crested Miller's Mountain, about ten miles north of town. A beautiful spot to drive through in the summer, the road was cut through a private camp, heavily wooded and steep. Isolated, the back way into town from Highway 21.

"What did you find?" Mac asked, slipping on his hat as he approached.

Chris followed, her eyes already drawn to the deep gully at the side of the road where Miller's Stream dug its way though old granite and limestone.

The sheriff tipped back his hat and hooked thumbs into his belt. "Think I found your girl. She looks to have taken a zig when she shoulda zagged."

The three of them stood there a moment, their attention all focused in the same direction.

At first, it looked like an old boulder. Dark, crum-

240

pled, misshapen. Shoved in amidst the other boulders that dotted the Missouri landscape. This one, though, was metal. It had fallen and burned so thoroughly that the only things identifying it as a car were the tires. The grass surrounding it was blackened and scarred, a few of the overhanging tree limbs charred.

"She in there?"

"Oh, yeah. Looks like a marshmallow left on the stick too long. Know what I mean?"

"Yeah, I know what you mean. I'm surprised nobody saw the fire."

Tipett shrugged, his belly straining against uniform shirt and belt. "Only thing I can figure is that Wilbur Carter called in about seein' a UFO landing up this way a few nights ago. But Wilbur's always callin' in about UFOs. Maybe this time what he saw was a car burnin'."

Mac started picking his way down the hillside. Tipett followed, and Chris trailed behind, hanging onto saplings and skidding down the new grass in her tennis shoes. The stench rose in her nostrils, thick, sharp, heavy. A smell you carried around with you for a long time. A fitting introduction to the sight inside that car.

"Not much left," Mac commented, leaning toward the shattered side window.

Chris fought a lurch of nausea. Not anything that spoke of memories or nightmares or confusion. Good old-fashioned physiological response to a horrifying sight.

"I hope she had bad teeth," Tipett was saying. "It's gonna be a bitch IDin' her."

"She's got her ring," Chris managed.

Both men turned. "What?"

She pointed to where the thing that looked like an old spider rested against the crushed steering wheel. "Her wedding ring."

Mac's head swiveled to look, and then back to Chris again, a new respect in his eyes. "You're right. It might help an identification. I'll have to call St. Louis."

"I'll tell 'em," Tipett offered, lifting off his hat to wipe at his forehead. "I figure they'd like for me to ask 'em for help with the autopsy anyway. It's a cinch Doc Clarkson ain't gonna wanna go pokin' in there if he don't have to."

Mac nodded absently, gingerly picking his way around the steep ground on which the car rested. "You called a wrecker yet?"

"On his way."

"I don't suppose those files survived the fire," Mac mused, peering into the car from the other side.

Chris eased her backside down on the damp grass and looked up into the lace of the new leaves. She didn't really need to watch him sharing space with a human briquette. Especially when she'd been talking to that briquette no more than a couple of days ago.

She tried to decide how she felt. Lawson had been a pain in the ass, going after Chris like a terrier with a bone in its teeth. She'd been unpleasant and unpopular, and determined to make Chris one of the rungs on her personal career ladder.

Even so, Chris should feel some kind of grief. Lawson had been married. She'd left behind at least one person to mourn for her, at least some good she'd accomplished with her work, which was more than Chris would have taken with her if she'd been the one reduced to an unrecognizable hunk of carbon. Lawson had talked with Chris, walked through her house, made some kind of impact on her life that should have at least left a hole.

And yet, all Chris could feel was an awful relief.

Not that somebody else wouldn't come with the questions. Chris would probably have to end up telling Mac the rest of the truth sooner or later anyway. But this was different. It was primal. It had something to do with the intensity of Lawson's eyes when she'd turned her subtle accusations on Chris in the shadows. It had to do with those troubling flashes of memory and dislocation.

Mac had compassion. He would bring it to bear when he found out about her. When Chris thought of Lawson she didn't see compassion. She saw hunger.

"Mind if I pop the trunk?" Mac was asking.

Tipett never moved. "Be my guest."

The sound of metal screeching against metal was enough to send a person diving for cover. Chris turned her attention to the violets that dotted the grass at her feet. Reaching out, she stroked them with a finger and fought the instinctive guilt at her feelings. The shame of venality. Maybe she was evil, just like they said. Maybe there were things locked away she still didn't have access to that would explain the discrepancies she'd found, the uncertainties. The terrible suspicions she couldn't share even with Mac yet.

She didn't even see Mac return to her side of the car. "You're not going to throw up on me or anything, are you?" he asked.

She shot him a glare. "Don't patronize me, Mac-Namara."

"Then what's wrong?"

"Besides the fact that I'm sharing a lovely spring

afternoon with a corpse who came to town just to see me?"

That brought him to a halt, an eyebrow lifting. "So it's your fault?"

She knew he'd never really understand. "Why not? She sure thought the other ones were."

So that was what it was going to come down to. Not loss or grief. Guilt. It figured.

Tipett actually laughed. "Little girl, you got nothin' to do with the fact that this lady drove like a bat outta hell. Just be glad she didn't take a school bus out with her."

Chris lifted her head then and offered them both a small smile. "Well, at least I didn't write this one."

Chris had another gift waiting for her when she got home. A ham casserole this time, placed inside her screen door with no note. But Chris didn't need a note. Every potluck dinner the Methodist church had ever thrown had been graced by a ham casserole from Luella Travers. This time the gift made Chris smile.

"You sure have an interesting front step," Mac observed dryly. "You never know what's gonna show up there."

Balancing the baking dish in the curve of her arm, Chris unlocked the front door. "You should drop by when Harlan's been in the neighborhood," she retorted. "There's enough reading material to stock a library."

Once again, Mac stepped inside first. Once again, his actions were robbed of ease by hesitation. Chris waited in silence until he motioned her in.

She shuddered to a halt just inside the doorway.

The house was back in order. Everything in its place, every surface cleaned, and the bears all back with their legs in the air. Chris didn't even notice.

Disinfectant. She could smell it where it had no right to be. Not just pine cleaner, with its accompanying flashes of penitence and punishment. The harsh singe of chemicals. As distant as memories, as familiar as her last nightmare. Even as faintly as she could smell it, it upended her.

"Chris?"

Her stomach, which she'd just been thinking about filling, heaved. The blood drained from her face. Shadows shifted, whispered, threatened. Daylight dimmed and briefly, terribly, memory took hold by the frail thread of a scent.

Chris fought to hold onto reality. She clutched at the dish in her hands until the aluminum foil rattled around her fingers. She opened her mouth, seeking air and only came up with that awful chemical smell.

"Someone's been here."

Mac picked a note from the top of the jukebox. "Yeah. Sue. She cleaned up while you were gone."

But Chris shook her head. "No. Somebody else. Can't you smell it?"

"Smell what?"

"Disinfectant." Anything but that. Anything.

Mac tested the air. "I don't know. Why?"

"I never use disinfectant," she insisted, still not looking over at him, still trying to overcome the instinctive terror the old smell provoked. "I hate that smell. Somebody else has done it."

Mac lifted the note, his expression bemused. "Sue."

Chris wanted to argue. She wanted to say Sue would never do that to her, but, of course, Sue didn't know about Chris's aversion. Nobody did.

It was possible. She'd call Sue and find out. She'd hear her laugh and say, well, yes, since I was in the neighborhood I thought I'd terrorize a few dust bunnies, and feel better for it. Saner. Chris sucked in an uneven breath, trying her damnedest to feel saner right now.

"I hate that smell," she said again and threw open every window she came to on her way out to the kitchen.

She could still sense that stale aftertaste of invasion in her house. Displacement, disturbance, as if the very molecules in the air had been subtly rearranged until they carried a faint charge to them. Nothing had been taken, nothing disturbed. Even so, she felt something there, like a breath being held in a darkened room. It seemed somehow to intensify the smell of the cleaning liquid.

"Are you sure you're all right?" Mac asked after helping her check the rooms just to be sure.

Chris pulled herself up short. She'd done everything but rifle through her book boxes and toss the mattress. She was going to have to be a little more careful, regain a little control.

She found herself wanting Mac to stay. Wanting anybody to stay, just to stave off the inevitable. They could get out a deck of cards, run down to the Clarksons' and borrow the Monopoly board. Play jazz and discuss the town's problems. Anything but being left alone in that empty, echoing room with company no one but she could feel, waiting for the hallucinations to begin again.

"No," she demurred. "I'm fine. I think I'm just a little tired."

Mac took another look around from where he stood by the couch. "Well, you sure have reason to be. Probably wouldn't be a bad idea to knock off early tonight and get some sleep."

Just the thought threatened to bring up what little was in Chris's stomach. She shoved her hands into her pockets and fought to stay still. "What about the computer?"

"I'll meet you first thing in the morning."

"You sure?"

He nodded.

"In that case, I'm probably gonna head on over to the How Do and try and call my agent again. Anything you want me to tell her?"

"Ask her what she was doing Wednesday night."

Chris's answer was just a little too shrill. "She did not kill Cooter. She would have had to risk chipping a nail."

Mac's expression was carefully bland. "All the same, it'd save time if she got her alibis all in order."

Her alibis. All their alibis. Even Chris's. It didn't even bear thinking about.

Chris thought Mac would leave then. He didn't. He stood right where he was by the jukebox, rubbing at the upper lip, eyes pensive, posture careful.

"I'm going to have somebody watching the house," he told her, hitching that restless hand on his belt. "I've already asked Ray for overtime for the men. We're coordinating with Eldon and the highway patrol to start searching for suspects. I'd rather you didn't stay here alone."

"No," Chris managed. "I, uh, don't think I'd be very good company right now. Besides, you don't have to worry. The author never died in one of my books."

Mac took a step forward. "Remember what we said about this character. It's someone who either really loves C. J. Turner or really hates her. That could apply to Chris Jackson, too, if he knows who you are. Which means that all bets are off, as far as I'm concerned. I think somebody else should stay with you."

"Like who?" she demanded. "Shelly? Sue? Maybe Weird Allen? I have problems enough, Mac. Don't make it worse."

"Do you want me to stay?"

That brought her damn near to a dead halt. Chris recognized the offer for what it was. Mac was concerned. He was responsible in his own jurisdictional way. His offer included no real subtext, not so much as a sexual innuendo in sight. It was probably just a way to get into her computer. Even so, she knew just how good an idea that one was. "In this town?" she countered.

"I thought they considered you to be Virginia Woolf."

She waved him off, by turns tickled, frustrated, and dismayed by his offer. It had been a while since Chris had even considered a "dalliance" as Harmonia Mae preferred to call it. She certainly couldn't see it happening with a cop who had bigger scars than she, especially when she was battling the worst nightmares she'd had since her fifteenth birthday. The last few weeks had just proved how untenable an idea like that would be. Still, Chris couldn't help the instinctive regret. In another life, she might not have minded trying her hand for someone like Al MacNamara.

"Not all the townsfolk believe that," she retorted. "And they sure don't see you as Oscar Wilde. Shit, Mac. You'd have Harlan on the doorstep in fifteen seconds flat. And right after him, you'd have the Reverend Mr. Rayford and L. J."

She saw it, then. Not so much in Mac's next words, or the impatience of his movements as he rubbed instinctively at the scar that couldn't easily be forgotten or overlooked. She saw it in the flash of something way back in his eyes. Conflicting emotions, a fleeting betrayal that he should have never allowed. Frustration, anger, fear. All the subtext she could want. Shut back off as ruthlessly as weakness. Surprising him even more than it did her. Sparking, astonishingly enough, a like emotion in her.

Damn it. Damn him. She hadn't been paying attention. He hadn't either, obviously.

Chris wheeled around on her heel and headed out toward the kitchen. "I appreciate the offer," she said over her shoulder, furious that suddenly she should be the one with the shakes. "But I just can't write with somebody looking over my shoulder."

She should have been surprised to hear the clack of footsteps following. She wasn't. It just made her feel even wearier.

"I don't think you understand," Mac said, his voice all business again. "You said it yourself. This wacko has a very special message for you. And he went out of his way to deliver it right to your doorstep."

Chris reached the refrigerator and yanked it open. An automatic response after too many years of being hungry. Looking for all your answers beneath that little cold light bulb.

"Cooter's been dead for four days," she insisted.

"And his was the only murder to take place outside St. Louis County. By now, whoever it is is probably at a nursery in Ellisville looking at shrubs."

She thought Mac would at least give her room. He didn't. He reached right over and grabbed her by the arm.

"Here," he insisted, his eyes now as hard as Judgment as he turned her back around to face him. "Right here. The murders were in order until Cooter. Suddenly we have a book being acted out that hasn't even seen the light of day yet, which means that unless either you or your shadow really are psychic, it's somebody you know. Somebody you probably know real well. Somebody who's starting to get unpredictable enough to start killing cops."

"Killing . . ."

"There weren't any skid marks up there, Chris. Not a mark on any of the trees along the side of the road, which should have happened if she'd been fighting that turn and missed."

She'd known. Somehow, even soaking herself in Eldon's assurances, Chris had distrusted simple bad luck and worse timing. Even so, it wasn't something she wanted to face just yet.

"Even if she'd been sideswiped or something, there'd be marks."

Mac deliberately shook his head. "I'll bet you your next royalty check that right after they identify that body they're gonna tell us that she was already dead when that car caught on fire. Come on, Chris. You're the suspense writer. Think it out."

"She still had her wedding ring on," she argued. "I thought this character collected souvenirs."

"All the other murders had to do with your books.

This one has to do with self-preservation. And it's telling me that we're dealing with a whole new ballgame just at the minute we landed back on square one."

"We're not at square one," Chris insisted. "We have a better idea of who's doing it. We know that it has to be somebody who had a hell of a lot of access to St. Louis. That can't be everybody on the list."

"It's an hour and a half away," Mac retorted, leaning closer. Forcing her a step back with his frustration. "Not that much of a stretch to pull out after dark and be home well before breakfast. There are flights to New York all the goddamn time."

Still Chris fought him. "Those people were stalked. The murders were carefully planned. It would have taken a lot more time than a couple of hours after the Letterman show to do that."

Mac never gave an inch. "Victor's in St. Louis every other day to audition for something," he argued. "The judge spends two days a week up there as part of his law practice. Allen worked up there until six weeks ago. And those are just the people I'd already thought to check."

Chris couldn't come up with any other arguments. She couldn't imagine how they were possibly going to get to the truth of the matter before it was, truly, too late. "I'm helping you every way I can," she protested, hands out. "What else do you want me to do?"

"Be honest."

That froze her on the spot. She came so close to giving herself away. To betraying the purulence that she'd always thought she'd purged herself of, that had been bubbling free again in the last few days. To telling him the awful coincidence she'd discovered in Lawson's files.

She couldn't do it, though. Not if she wanted to get through this. Not if she wanted to believe in herself enough to make it as far as morning. One nightmare at a time, thank you.

She retreated to the near-empty shelves of her refrigerator. "I am honest."

"You didn't tell me that your editor is gay."

Chris swung on him. "All you had to do was ask him yourself. He'd be more than glad to tell you. And what the hell does sexual preference have to do with anything?"

"Maybe nothing. Maybe everything. Some of the most notorious serial killers have been homosexual."

"Men terrified of their homosexual tendencies," Chris corrected. "Trey has had a steady relationship for ten years."

"And you know him well enough to swear he doesn't have any problems with his homosexuality."

She shook her head, knowing that Trey couldn't be the killer. Knowing that nobody could.

Knowing at the same time that somebody certainly could. That somebody was.

"Homosexual serial killings all follow a pretty similar pattern," she said. "And this isn't it."

"This isn't any of it," Mac insisted. "We're talking about a crafty, intelligent wacko with a mission here, and right now you're the only one who can give us any insights into why. And you're going to have to do it tomorrow for the guy coming down from St. Louis."

"Then I'll do it tomorrow."

Chris didn't even have to turn to see how frustrat-

ed Mac was. He gave himself away without a word.
They stood that way for a long time, the two of them
facing the open refrigerator as it clicked on to com-
pensate for the chill lost to Chris's indecision. Both of
them rigid, each battling his own frustration.

Chris held her breath against the next assault. She
fought the urge to run. Instead, she deliberately
leaned forward and plucked an old peach from the
shelf, as if that had been what she'd meant to do all
along.

Behind her, Mac did his own reorganizing. She
could sense it in the deliberate easing of tension. In
the careful cadence of his breathing, as if he were
bleeding off his frustration through a safety valve.

"Would you tell me one thing?" he asked, his voice
deceptively gentle.

Chris closed the door and turned back to find him
once again worrying at that scar, his eyes suddenly
weary.

"Only if it has nothing to do with how I research
my romance novels," she retorted as easily as she
could with her own suspicions weighing on her.

He almost managed a smile. "Did you ever think
of what might have happened eighteen months ago
that was unusual?"

Chris lifted the peach in her hand in invitation.
Mac shook his head. She took a bite and finally gave
in to her need to move, heading back to the living
room. Mac followed at his own pace.

"I made *The New York Times* best-seller list for the
first time," she offered, resettling a pair of brass Art
Deco candlesticks on the other end of her sofaback
table and straightening an edge of lace on the runner.
She noticed that the Edgar Award still sat quietly on

its special niche by the dime-store Indian that had occupied her dorm in college. It seemed that everybody knew better than to touch the little statuette. Everybody but Lawson, of course. But Lawson wouldn't be bothering Mr. Poe again.

Mac stopped beside her, not poised to leave just yet. "*New York Times*, huh? Is that when the stories really started on the famous reclusive author?"

She nodded, brushing at imaginary dust on the table.

"Anything else? Anything closer to home?"

That brought her head back up. Chris had been thinking about this a lot lately. "It was almost two years ago that I first tried to have the judge arrested for abusing Shelly."

Mac's eyebrows did a quick slide north. "I bet that was popular."

She snorted. "Old L. J. Watson himself came to the house and explained the facts of life to me. I didn't make the same mistake twice."

"Anything else?"

She sighed. "Victor's engagement to Suzy Gliddel was called off. Sue lost her last baby, and Harlan and I went a couple rounds at the town council meeting on which books in the school library were obscene."

"You're not making this any easier."

"Imagine how thrilled I am. I'd really rather not have any more bodies on my conscience."

Again, briefly, that harsh frustration flashed across his features. Chris almost flinched from it. She held her place, munching on the already-sour peach and desperately wishing there were some way to avoid what was sure to happen. Knowing what she had to look forward to.

"No more books, right?" Mac asked.

"No more books."

"Do you have a copy of the one Cooter starred in?"

Chris shook her head. "I'll print one out for you."

He paused. Took a second to look up to where the office still bore the ravages of her search. "How's the security on your computer?" he asked.

Chris turned to give a considering look to the workstation at the back of the house. Right now it was camouflaged by towers of books and Spy Shop boxes. "Security?"

"Do you use code words for files? That kind of thing?"

"No. It never seemed necessary."

Mac's expression eased just a hair back into concern. "It might be now."

Chris turned again. Thought about the unsettled feeling she'd been having. The questions, the suspicions.

"As in, somebody could easily get into my house and boot up the book?"

"As in."

The first thing Chris did after closing the door on Mac was yank out the air freshener. She usually didn't use it, preferring the natural scent of potpourri. But chemicals demanded like chemicals and she still smelled that disinfectant. She sprayed the rooms as if warding off an infestation of roaches. She straightened and she dusted what had already been dusted. She shut the blinds and turned on the music, Buckwheat Zydeco this time, and tried to drown out the old voices; all the while plagued by the gnawing suspicion that someone was looking over her shoulder. Someone was whispering in her ear, trying to make her see something she was missing.

What was behind this? What was it someone was trying to tell her?

The questions were too dangerous. Too difficult. There were acres of lost memory and miles of carefully erected defenses to get through in order to reach that one.

After all, she'd spent the last seven years trying to get to the same kind of answers. And she could only approach them in careful increments, like rappelling off a high cliff, inch by inch, letting out the lifeline as she swung deeper and deeper into the darkness.

What they were asking her to do was free-fall, and she simply couldn't do it.

Maybe if she came at it from another angle, she'd get through it OK. Maybe if she just used the skills she'd learned over the years, providing alibis, evidence, clues. Maybe the material evidence would be enough. After all, the very last thing the police really gave a good goddamn about was motive anyway. All they wanted was the smoking gun.

Positive action. It had been what had gotten her this far. It would get her through the rest. Pulling over a yellow pad, Chris uncapped her favorite fountain pen and tried her damnedest to come up with an objective list of her own.

It was all falling apart. Her peace, her stability. Her sanity. She had escaped to a cloister, a safe, secure place far away from the world, and it had been breached. Her dreams hadn't just returned, they'd begun to take over.

Briefly she squeezed her eyes shut. She was so tired. So overwhelmed. It wasn't a matter of hypothesis anymore. Conjecture. It was survival. And suddenly Chris, who had survived so much, simply didn't know whether she had the strength anymore to do it all over again.

Her friends. Her family, as close as she'd ever in her life come to one. And one of them was hiding something this hideous from her in daylight and acting it out at night. Someone seething with rancor or madness. Or both. She had to know. She had to protect herself.

She had to make sure she couldn't see the murderer in anyone else for the simple reason that she should have been looking to herself.

Al MacNamara had Eric Clapton on his stereo. He had all the lights off except the floor lamp by the old leather wingback he'd rescued from the ashes of his marriage, and a scotch on the rocks on the table with a half-eaten TV dinner. Kafka lay open and unread on the footstool. Mac was on the phone, his attention completely on his caller.

"What do you mean she's not C. J. Turner?" he demanded, drink, book, and blues forgotten.

"I mean," his brother informed him from Chicago, "that she's not even Chris Jackson."

✦ Chapter 13 ✦

MAC THOUGHT HE had him. "Jacqueline Christ," he said, picking his drink back up.

"What?"

"Her name," he said. "I bet you found out she's Jacqueline Christ."

"God, she's somebody else, too? Who is this chick, Sybil?"

The drink stopped halfway to Mac's mouth. "Don't fuck with me, Danny. I've had a bad day."

"So have I," his younger brother retorted. "I spent all of Sunday dinner listening to your mother wonder why you haven't called her."

Mac pressed the cold glass against his temple. "Not now," he warned.

"If you wanted to run away from home, why didn't you just join the circus like everybody else? At least people'd know where to find you."

Mac pulled in a calming breath. It was getting very dark outside. His windows were open to the quiet town, the breeze picking at the limp gauze curtains by the front door. Mac fought the urge to yell, knowing that would only encourage Danny toward higher levels of recalcitrance.

It was what made Danny Danny. What pissed off the brass and made Danny such a good cop.

"What," Mac demanded, "is her name?"

"Your mother?" his brother countered easily. "Mary Rose. You might remember better if you talked to her once in a while."

"Danny . . ."

Even Danny understood the import of that tone of voice.

"Christian Evensong."

Mac was caught short by the sudden capitulation. "What?"

Danny laughed, a rasp like sandpaper on wood. "Yeah, no shit. That's a real beaut, isn't it? My parents named me that, I'd change it, too. Shit, I'd probably sue."

"So she's using an alias?"

"No. She had it changed legally . . . wouldn't you?"

"When?"

"Uh . . . seventy-seven."

Mac was leaning forward now, his drink all but forgotten, his mind on overtime. She must have been pretty young. Eighteen at the most. "Where?"

"Where what?"

"Where did she get it changed?"

"Oh. Uh, Jefferson City, Missouri. Since that time she's gotten a GED, a bachelors' in science, social service, and English lit—hey, you two could bore each other to tears, couldn't you—with a psychology minor, which means she's a liberal, candy-assed fruitcake with a good vocabulary, huh? No outstanding loans, two credit cards without big balances, no wants or warrants, record as clean as your long-distance bill. She's lily white in every way, pard."

A mystery wrapped in an enigma, Mac thought, even more intrigued than ever. Furious at her duplicity, intrigued by her secrecy. What could have been so bad that she'd locked it away behind a legal decision? Why hadn't she admitted it to him when he'd asked?

Just who the hell was Chris Jackson anyway?

"Mac?"

"Yeah, I'm here."

"A thank you might be nice. Especially since I had to actually break bread with MacElheny to get her to cough up the computer time."

"You're a prince."

"That's what I keep telling you."

"Anything else?"

"Yeah. Are you please going to call Mom so I don't have to suffer through another pot roast dinner like tonight? I'm not exactly sure why, but she worries about you."

Mac wasn't paying attention enough anymore to be irritated. "She's just afraid you're going to be the only one left to carry on the MacNamara name."

"Just for that, I won't pass on your best to Loose Lips Livingston. She'll be so sorry."

They abused each other for ten minutes, finally making Mac smile and promise to call his mother the minute he got off the phone with the twins. Right after he made a few other phone calls.

"You coming home soon?" Danny asked.

"When the kids come in. I'll have a weekend, at least."

"That's not what I mean."

Mac fought to hold onto his humor. He knew how hard it had been for Danny to watch his brother walk away from the force. There was nothing Mac could do about it. Danny had never had to face the twin barrels of a sawed-off just before it exploded in his face. He'd never puked just over the thought of opening a strange door.

"And give up all these perks? Don't be ridiculous."

There was a small silence, and Mac knew that Danny was doing his best to finally keep his opinions to himself. That, after everything else, did make Mac smile.

"I'll talk to you soon," he promised.

"Yeah," his brother countered. "When you need something else."

"Keep digging," he commanded.

"I've missed you, too."

"I know. Oh, by the way, did you get a DOB and place of birth on her?"

"Sure. Springfield."

Mac had just been about to set his drink down to pick up a pen, ready to write down a California zip code. "Illinois?" he demanded, halted once again.

"No. Missouri. Right down by you somewhere, isn't it?"

Mac finally set his drink down. But he didn't pick up the pen. He simply sat staring out the front window into the spring dusk. "Thanks." He didn't remember saying good-bye before he hung up.

Dinah wasn't there. Chris hung up before the second beep and dragged in a quick breath of frustration. Nothing all weekend. Chris wished like hell the agent would learn to be a little more dependable, especially when she was on the shortening list of suspects in a multiple homicide. Chris wished she could talk to her, could use the agent's brash pragmatism as a balm for her escalating anxiety. She needed something to settle her back down again. Not just Sue's sanity, but the sharp edge of Dinah's tongue to shave off those suspicions and fears that had been growing like bad fungus.

Well, it would just serve Dinah right. The next time Chris talked to her, it would be recorded for posterity, whether Dinah wanted it to be or not.

It was the next thing on her list of things to do. Unzipping her gym bag, Chris pulled out a black box with attendant wires and hooked it up to the phone. A recorder that would not only take calls but would save the time and date they were made. This way she'd maybe be able to catch any surprises and find out when they were being sent. She would have preferred to have the call identifier that could have located the phone number of anyone phoning in, but the local phone system wasn't wired for it.

Chris had pulled out all that equipment she'd hoarded over successive books. Recorders, directional mikes, hidden cameras, bugs, lock picks, binoculars, and night goggles. She wasn't exactly sure what she was going to use them all for yet. She hadn't even managed to convince herself that she would need to resort to less than legal intervention, much less set up a plan.

After all, what was she going to do? Wiretap Harlan? Wear a body mike around the judge? Break into Weird Allen's house while he was down at the video shop and see if he had a new collection of rings he couldn't explain?

Chris's stomach churned just with the idea of betraying her friends, her neighbors like that. Spying on them. Suspecting them.

But she didn't have a choice. Not anymore.

That was why she was going to do some clandestine research on her computer. Why she'd already rigged her own house for sound. No matter who it was doing these things, she had to know.

If only Dinah would call.

She woke to the darkness.

At first, she thought she was still trapped in the dream. Then she smelled something.

Flowers. Gladioli.

Chris opened her eyes. Closed them again. Fought the panic that exploded in her.

She couldn't see.

Chris bolted upright and cracked her knee against her desk. She stumbled back and sent her chair tumbling, the noise ricocheting in her head like a gunshot. Disorientation cleared. Terror didn't.

The shop. She'd fallen asleep in her office rather than face that sense of prescience back at the house. She'd fallen asleep with all the lights on, just as she always did. Only they were off now.

Her heart slammed into her ribs. The reflexive screams choked her. "No, Mama, no," she muttered instinctively, her voice small and tight. Pleading. "Please don't . . ."

And then she felt it. Something close, indistinct,

like the first ripple in a pool of water. The invisible shudder of another presence.

Someone had been here. Or was still here with her. Chris didn't wait. She couldn't fight in the darkness, couldn't so much as think. She ran.

Her hands were out, but she couldn't see them. She knew where the door to the front room was, the door that was never closed, but she couldn't find it. She tripped over the coffeemaker and sent it crashing to the floor. She fought for the light. Reaching, stumbling, sweating. Suddenly eight years old again and shattered by the feel of the darkness against her eyes.

The wall. Chris flinched at the unyielding feel of it, too well remembered. Too primally feared. Memory overriding sense and threatening to send her back into the corner. Any corner. Just away. Just safe from the darkness, from the faint, awful scent of a pursuer straight out of her nightmares.

She could smell her own sweat. She could hear the rasp of her breathing, as harsh in the black silence as a saw on fresh wood. She could see a vague form, way at the back of her memory, the watching figure. Waiting. Knowing.

She fought for calm. She was losing fast.

The office door that was never closed was closed. Chris grabbed for the handle and pulled. She didn't even think anymore of the wall switch. It was too late for that. She didn't have to see the walls to feel them, all the old phobias piling one on top of the other until she couldn't breathe. She just had to escape.

Throwing the door open, she ran. There had never been a straight path to the doorway. Chris made one, upending wreathes and sending an entire shelf of azaleas toppling into the silk flower arrangements. She never noticed. Her eyes were locked into the spill of light from the street lamp outside. Her hands were reaching for it. Her lungs were bursting with the need to scream. She didn't even see the shadow waiting there at her front door.

She wasn't paying attention to anything but the salvation of that light, the promise of all the space of a spring night. She opened the door and ran right into something solid.

That was when she finally gave in to the scream.

"Holy shit, settle down."

Hands clamped around her arms. Chris drew breath to scream again, and ended up with one of those hands over her mouth.

"It's me," Mac informed her briskly. "MacNamara. Scream again and I'm gonna lose my job."

For a minute, instinct overrode sanity and Chris fought.

"Chris, hey . . ."

It was still dark outside, the world composing itself in shadows and shapes. Chris heard the first train of the early morning rumble through at the edge of town and felt the damp air on her sweaty face. Reality crept back over the ragged glass of terror. She shuddered and went quiet.

Carefully Mac took his hand away. He didn't let go of her arm. Chris did her best not to flinch away, knowing damn well he was all that kept her upright.

"I've been knocking for ten minutes," Mac explained. "I figured you must have fallen asleep. I was just about to go on in." He bent a little closer to peer at her. "You're not just glad to see me, are you?"

Chris's giggle sounded just a little too hysterical for her as she shook her head. An explanation for what had awakened her. Still nothing for what she'd felt in that office.

"The lights . . ." she managed, her voice scratching like a badly drawn bow. "They went off. I . . . I think someone was in there."

Mac didn't bother with remonstrances about safety and staying where she was. He simply shoved her far enough out of the way for safety and reached around to pull the Glock .40 from the back of his shorts.

"Watch her," he said, crouching on his way into the store.

"Glad to," another male voice answered.

Chris managed to straighten and wipe her hands against her pants legs. "Who the hell are you?" she demanded. He was short, stocky, bald, with a beaut of a shiner beginning to show even under the street lamp. "And what the hell are you two doing at my shop at this hour of the night?"

His smile was as irrepressible as a child's. "Dick Franklin," he introduced himself easily. "And I believe I was on my way to be booked for breaking and entering."

"Breaking and entering? Where?"

"Your house. I'm a free-lance reporter from St. Louis."

That was all she needed. Chris didn't even bother to groan. She simply sank down right there on the sidewalk and put her head into her hands.

Luckily for him, Franklin had the sense to keep his thoughts to himself.

Mac returned no more than three minutes later. "In the mood to redecorate in there?" was all he said.

Chris never lifted her head. She was shaking so badly she wouldn't have been able to stand right then if she'd wanted to.

"I find azaleas pretentious," she retorted, eyes wide open, her field of vision limited to shoes and shadows. It didn't help. It didn't matter. She couldn't move. That feeling of eyes in the darkness wouldn't go away. She knew Mac had been unsuccessful. Even so, there had been something. It gnawed at her like a rat.

"Nobody in there but the phone tap," he said. "When did that arrive?"

She struggled for a calming breath and at least a semblance of control. "Tonight. Why were you in the neighborhood?"

Chris half expected Mac to inform her it was time to buck up and attempt to get her on her feet so she could get on home. Much to her everlasting astonishment, he did neither. He resettled his gun and joined her on the pavement. She wasn't sure what the reporter did.

"I told you," Mac said. "I came to visit you."

Chris didn't move. "In your underwear."

She imagined that he looked down at the torn T-shirt and running shorts he was wearing. From her position, she could now see a length of hairy leg and battered running shoes. It made her want to laugh. But then, if she did, she wasn't going to stop.

"I was having some trouble sleeping," he admitted. "Went down to the office to check up on some stuff when the B-and-E call came in."

Chris motioned limply. "Him."

"Him."

"Too bad I had to miss it. I have a Beretta that would have been perfect for him."

That earned her a small pause. "You have a gun?"

Then she did chuckle. She even managed to keep it fairly sane. "L. J. left out a whole lot in your orientation, didn't he? He's the one who taught me to use it. Don't worry, I only keep it as a research tool. There wasn't anybody inside the shop just now, was there?"

"Not when I got there. Why did you think somebody was there?"

She shuddered, even though the night was fairly warm. "I felt something when I woke up . . . at least I think I did. And the lights were off. I never would have done that."

Another pause. Beyond Chris's field of vision a car scrunched to a sudden stop and a door opened. A pair of hard-soled shoes hurried across the street. Chris figured that Curtis had finally decided to make an appearance. She wondered where he'd been napping when the chief had gotten the call.

"Tell you what," Mac offered. "Why don't I let Curtis take care of Mr. Franklin here, and you and I can go someplace and talk."

Chris squeezed her eyes shut, her stomach lurching with something she couldn't put a name to yet. Something she didn't want to face. "Kozy Kitchen isn't open yet."

"We'll think of something."

She just nodded, her head still in her folded arms.

"Chris?" Curtis greeted them all, pulling to a stop at the edge of the sidewalk. "That you? What happened?"

"Anything to that call?" Mac asked.

"Aw, it was another prank. Probably Billy Rae Trumbell again. She OK, chief?"

"She's fine, Curtis," Chris assured him dryly without moving. "She's just paying obeisance to the ancient concrete gods in thanks for front doors."

Curtis shuffled just a little bit before he offered a slightly bemused, "You attendin' the service too, Chief?"

"A person should never pray alone," Mac retorted easily from where he still sat. "Why don't you escort the prisoner on in, Curtis? I'll be there in a while to talk to him."

It took Curtis a minute to sort things out, but in the end Chris and Mac were left to sit out on the sidewalk in front of her store as the night began to pale toward morning.

"This probably isn't a good idea," Chris said, finally lifting her head. Then she saw why Mac was still sitting with his back to the store window, his arms atop his knees, and realized that she really hadn't been the only one wishing her gods were porcelain instead of concrete.

"You want to go back in?" he asked wiping at his forehead with a shaking hand.

"No."

"Home?"

"No."

He nodded. "Good. I'm not in the mood for a walk yet, anyway."

Chris actually managed a dismal laugh. "I do know the feeling. How'd you know I was here?"

"Curtis. He's been spending a lot of time parked in front of your house. He saw you come over earlier."

"You really have been keeping an eye on me."

"Ray would never forgive me if we let our

world-famous author get murdered just as the public's about to find out where she is."

Chris wasn't sure she didn't want to just let her
head sink right back down again. "Didn't take very
long, did it?"

"It was bound to happen. It's going to get worse,
too."

She leaned back against the front window so that
her view was of the stars, still sharp in the dry air.
Hundreds of them, shimmering and silent.
Magnificent. Twinkle, twinkle little star . . . Her wish
would have been to go back just two weeks. To have
anticipated this, headed it off. To, for once in her life,
have been able to step cleanly away from what she
was. What she'd been.

"It's about to hit the fan," she said. "Isn't it?"

"From every possible direction." Somehow Mac
had also managed to stuff a pack of cigarettes into
the waistband of his shorts. He pulled them out now
and lit one, not bothering to hide his shakes from
her.

"In fact," he said, blowing the first lungful straight
up in the air, "it already has."

Chris looked over to find that something new had
taken hold in his expression. Something hard and
careful, something that put her in mind of an inter-
rogator rather than a protector. She knew what he
was going to say even before he did. It made her feel
so very tired.

"I thought we were going to be honest with each
other," he accused without noticeable inflection.

"We tried," she admitted miserably, wishing she
had a cigarette to hide behind. Wishing she had more
than just a name to disappear into. Wondering

whether a man who had spent his life comfortably
situated within a constant code of right and wrong
could really comprehend hers.

"Your name isn't Chris Jackson."

"No," she admitted, turning her attention to the
windows of the old Jameson house across the street.
"It's not."

"Why?"

She instinctively curled just a little tighter. "I
changed it legally."

"I know."

The light was gathering just a little, pearling the
glass in the windows behind which the Masons,
who'd lived across from the How Do for ten years,
fought every Friday night like clockwork. The town
had long since tuned them out, knowing better than
to interfere.

"How would you like to go through life with a
name like Christian Charity Evensong?" Chris asked.

Mac took his last drag and crushed the cigarette
out on the sidewalk. "Why lie about it?"

She looked over at him then, and saw that, unlike
her, he was back in complete control. Eyes calm and
quiet, waiting. Hands still. Posture relaxed. She felt a
brief flash of resentment that his injuries had been so
much smaller than hers.

"Same reason I let them all figure I'm a lesbian, I
guess," she said as evenly as she could. "It's just easier that way."

"It's easier to make up a series of convoluted lies
about being a foster child in L. A. than to admit that
your mother's still alive in Springfield?"

That hit her like a mallet. Even knowing that it
was coming. Knowing that it had to come, consider-

ing the kind of cop Mac was. Even so, Chris had fashioned her entire adult life knowing that any story was better than hers. And now he was going to want it. And with that awful sense of watchful silence still plaguing her, with the walls closing in from every angle, she knew she was going to have to tell him.

At least what he wanted to hear.

"I wasn't a foster child," she admitted. "I was in L. A."

"Doing what?"

She was almost able to smell the streets again, different streets, ragged, garish streets littered in dreams and spent reality. "Whatever it took to get by."

"How old were you?"

"Sixteen."

There was a tiny pause. Chris refused to look away from where the windows across the street were beginning to reflect, just a little, like an old television that had just been turned off and hadn't quite lost its glow yet. She couldn't bear to see any reaction on Mac's face. Distaste, disappointment. Worst of all, pity. She'd run screaming if she saw pity.

"And you really returned to Missouri when you were eighteen?"

"The rest of the story is true. I did get my degrees. Worked at bars and hospitals and cleaning services to get enough money. I did my time with DFS and flunked out when I couldn't deal any better with my clients' problems than I could with my own."

"No nuns."

"No nuns."

"No foster families?"

"Mine was bad enough. I didn't want to end up in something worse."

"Your mother was the one who had you on your knees?"

Chris did her best to stay where she was. It was the price she had to pay, after all. The lies had been collecting for years, balanced like the china she'd piled on her counter, ready to tumble with the slightest nudge. Well, Mac was nudging. And once Mr. Franklin really got going, he was probably going to give it all a big shove.

Chris should just tell Mac what it had been like. Should paint the picture of those dismal, dingy rooms that had never seen forgiveness or heard laughter. The heavy reek of pine cleaner and submission that clung to the air like old frying grease, the darker, mustier hint of rot that lay beneath. She couldn't. She couldn't tell anyone and keep from breaking something in fury.

"Chris?"

Chris wouldn't look away from the stars, the same ones she counted from her bed at night when she was trying to sleep. "I know I should have said something sooner," she said. "I just . . . I've been trying to get past it all for so long."

All of it. Every sordid, sorry secret that kept a person running for fifteen years. Every moment sweated out in the darkness.

"She made a prayer box," she found herself saying, choking on her own memories, the ones she couldn't forget no matter how hard she tried. "Fashioned from a little storage closet. About three by two, just big enough for a child to kneel on the hardwood floor with the door closed and the lights out as punishment." And beg for forgiveness. Promise never to do it again, even not knowing what the sin was that had precipitated this round in the box, with the terrors of Revelations filtering through the flimsy pressboard door along with the assurances that devils came out in the dark to bite children's feet and wrestle their souls to hell where the light would never return.

Well, the devils had come and taken her, and she'd been trying to live with it ever since.

"The day I walked out, my parents told me I was dead to them. I haven't heard from them since, nor have I wanted to." Chris shook her head. "I spent a lot of time in that box."

Trembling hard, Chris kept facing the sky, the clean, sterile sky, folded rigidly into herself where she couldn't be hurt. Even so, Mac reached over and wrapped an arm around her shoulder and she let him.

He didn't say a word, either in support or judgment. He didn't ask for more, which Chris appreciated, because she couldn't give it. Not another word, another picture. Even the ones he was going to need if he was to really understand the enigma of Chris Jackson. The most important ones. Right now, though, he bridged the distance between them in the chilly morning hours and let her rest her head on his shoulder. And Chris, unused to accepting comfort, for once did.

She didn't even hear the hurried footsteps. Neither, it seemed, did Mac.

"Chris? Chief? What are you two doing here?"

Chris felt Mac jerk to attention alongside her. She damn near came right off the pavement.

Mac recovered first. "What are *you* doing here, Victor?"

"And Lester."

"And Lester," Chris and Mac chorused together.

The pair stopped just feet away, a little out of breath, a little hyped up. "Oh, just checking on what's been going on. We saw the fracas at Chris's house. When Chris didn't come back, we thought we'd make sure everything was all right."

"It's fine," Chris offered as nonchalantly as possible, considering the fact that Mac's arm was still around her shoulder. "The chief and I were just discussing things before going home. Weren't we, Chief?"

Mac nodded. He didn't, however, relax.

"Oh," Lester retorted in a nasty voice. "Does this mean we don't have a new rumor for the town?"

"Lester," Victor admonished. "That's hardly appropriate."

"Neither is sitting on the street at dawn in your underwear," Lester assured him.

"I'm fine, Victor and Lester," Chris offered quickly, knowing how quickly the dummy could get out of hand. "I'll probably be home after I go to the jail and press charges against the reporter."

Chris could have sworn both faces lit up. "Reporter?" Victor asked, his voice childish with delight. "I'd be happy to bring him lunch, Chief. I could entertain him with a dramatic reading from *A Tale of Two Cities.*"

No real question of who'd play Carton, Chris thought dryly.

"He's a crime reporter," Chris said blithely. "Probably wouldn't know *A Tale of Two Cities* if it came out in the comics."

"Oh." Pause. Chris could have sworn Lester was

giving her an assessing look. Just what she needed on top of everything else. "As long as you're OK."

"I'm OK."

"Then we'll be going on down to visit Mother, since we're out anyway."

By way of the jail. Poor Mr. Franklin. He was going to pay in ways he'd never imagined for breaking into her house.

Chris was still watching the odd little duo head on down the street when Mac spoke next to her.

"I don't remember his being up when I was over there," he said.

Chris turned to consider him. "Victor? He sees a lot when you don't . . ." Her voice trailed off when she caught sight of Mac's expression. Stomach sinking all over again, Chris turned to consider Victor's departing back. "No," she insisted. "It can't be Victor."

"Yes, it can," Mac said simply. "It can be any one of a number of people who know you very well."

And she'd just been thinking how Victor always managed to make her feel better. It seemed that Mac wasn't going to be finished until he took back all the peace she'd accumulated and left her back in the darkness.

The darkness.

The reaction was immediate. Automatic. Chris knew Mac could feel her tense up all over again, and would figure it was because she was upset about his accusation.

He'd be wrong.

She was reacting to another accusation. An old accusation she hadn't heard in almost fifteen years.

Without realizing it, Chris turned to look down the street to where the granite facade of the Missouri

Farm Bank disappeared into the early morning gloom. She didn't know whether it was the feeling of being watched or the old story about the box, but her memory had coughed something up.

Something unnerving.

Something that would explain the silent intruders and feral smells and vague itches of recognition.

Something that she'd kept hidden away for so long she thought she'd forgotten it.

"Are you ready to go?" Mac asked, not making any move to go.

No, she thought. I don't want to take another step. I don't want to open that particular wound back up and look inside.

"Yeah," she said, her gaze still down the street, her legs suddenly as unsteady as her resolve. "Let's go see who knows me quite that well."

✦ Chapter 14 ✦

"WHERE HAVE YOU BEEN?"

The line to New York crackled faintly. Chris could hear the buzz of sirens outside fifteen-storied windows and pictured the chaotic state of the office.

"What do you mean, where have I been?" Trey demanded, his voice as querulous as the siren.

Chris settled herself more deeply into her chair. "I'm sorry. It's just that a lot's been going on here. I've been trying to reach you."

"A lot's been going on here," he retorted edgily. "And it seems the police have also been trying to reach me. I've been hoping you just wanted me to have a new life experience by being a suspect in a bunch of murders."

"Not me," she protested, even though the weekend had sorely eroded her confidence. "The police. They can't figure out any other reason *Family Business* would be acted out."

"Chris, I don't have time to get to theater here," he said blackly. "I'm certainly not going to provide it for your little town."

Chris took to doodling again, this time concentrat-

278

ing on tracing concentric circles. Slow, smooth, soothing lines that belied the frayed, desperate state of her patience. Soft blue patterns to offset Trey's uncharacteristic surliness and Chris's incomprehensible suspicions.

"It's just that you've been gone from work so much lately," she said quietly. "They wanted to know dates and times . . . just to be sure."

"Yeah, right."

Chris expected more from him. She hoped for answers without having to betray herself with the questions. Trey wasn't cooperating. He merely waited while Chris drew and ignored the exchange out at the desk between Eloise and somebody wanting roses.

Chris hadn't slept much in almost a week. She was sore and stretched and jumpy, seeing things that weren't there, knowing full well that she was going to have to walk over to the bank and face something she hadn't in fifteen years. Expecting that she was going to be called over to the police station any time now when the St. Louis cop showed up. She wasn't sure which unnerved her more. By now, though, it was a moot point. All terror tasted the same after awhile.

"Trey?"

"I've been missing work because of Phillip," he blurted out ungracefully. Chris could hear the ragged edge of grief in his voice and caught herself just shy of begging him not to burden her even more. "He died Friday."

Chris dropped her head into her hands. "Oh, Trey. I'm sorry."

"He had AIDS. The police can come check with

anybody at the hospice. I haven't been in St. Louis butchering brewery workers. I've been sitting with him."

She didn't know what else to say. She wasn't close enough to him to offer real solace. She hadn't known Phillip to be able to reflect on his worth or loss, couldn't call on a God to comfort or redeem. As usual, she battled that flash of guilt. Instinctive, searing, unproductive as hell. In the end, all she was able to give him was another, "I'm sorry."

"You might want to let Dinah know," he said. "I haven't been able to get hold of her."

"You pressing charges?"

Chris nodded. "You bet your ass I am."

Mac turned to the reporter. "I know you wouldn't think of leaving town until the judge can see you around two. He's not real fond of people breaking and entering in this county."

"I thought the lady was in some kind of danger, Sheriff," Franklin said. "Just doing my civic duty."

"Chief," Mac corrected him, leaning back in his chair. "The sheriff's down the block."

Franklin's irrepressible grin reappeared. "Well, while I'm here . . ."

Mac just shook his head. "I don't think you're going to find a whole lot of cooperative people."

The reporter consulted the battered little notebook he'd pulled from his jacket pocket. "How about a Reverend Sweetwater?"

Both Chris and Mac turned on him in unison. "Harlan?"

Franklin beamed like a kid. "Yeah, that's him.

Know where I can find him? He's the one who dropped the story."

"Harlan?" Chris demanded, her voice just a little too shrill for Mac's taste. Her whole demeanor just a little too frazzled. "Harlan called you?"

Franklin didn't seem to know how to look apologetic. "Said something about the real story on C. J. Turner." His mouth quirked. "Any comment?"

Chris came right to her feet. Mac intercepted her just shy of impact. "Old Tyme Faith in Jesus Church," he instructed calmly, a hand on Chris's arm and a determined eye on the reporter. "I'd go there right now if I were you."

Franklin held out for one more try. "You'll be around later?" he asked Chris.

Chris made another try for him. Franklin escaped by inches.

"You can't really be surprised," Mac offered diffidently once the door had closed again. "You have been asking for it."

That brought her to rigid attention. "Of course I've been asking for it," she snapped, pulling out of his grip. "You think I should stand by while that pompous son of an egg-sucking, maggot-ridden, pox-infested bitch does his best to do over the town in his image?"

"I get the idea."

She was shaking and wild-eyed. So far removed from the cool, composed woman he'd tried to shoot that first night that Mac found himself upshifting from concern to real worry. A serial murderer on your ass would be enough to give anybody an off day, but this was working on levels so deep she couldn't even share them. Levels only hinted at with that little story about her mother. Mac really hoped he could get this all cleared up before it broke her right into little pieces.

"You want to sit down?"

Chris paced a little more. "Actually, I wondered if you might want to swing by my place."

Mac saw Sue, out in the front room, lift her head a fraction of an inch. Probably thought she was sneaky or something.

Chris waved an aimless hand. "I wasn't sure you really wanted to let the entire city know about your computer activities. Maybe we could grab the modem and computer and go to your house."

Mac didn't even need to think about it. She was strung so tight she was humming like a high wire. Definitely not in any shape right now to go the distance with a lifer like Garavaglia. He'd eat her up and spit her out. Climbing to his feet, Mac grabbed his hat.

"Sue, I'm on the radio," he announced, pulling it out of his desk and clipping it to his belt. A reassuring pat to the holster, and he was ready to go.

"What if that policeman gets here from St. Louis?" Sue asked over her shoulder as the two approached her. Mac and she exchanged brief, telling glances he hoped Chris didn't see.

"Send him over to Harmonia Mae's."

That even got a chuckle out of Chris. "He's not going to thank you for that."

"I thought I'd start a tradition."

"You thought you'd figure a way to keep outside police from coming back."

Mac flashed her an unrepentant grin, relieved at her irreverence. "Those big city jocks just got no business down here, ya know?"

Outside on the streets of Pyrite, spring had official-ly arrived. Trees were in full bud. The storms that had swept through had turned shoots into flowers. Grass had taken on a decidedly green tint, and the air was warm and moist. The breeze was fresh, push-ing high, white clouds before it. Mac sucked in an appreciative breath. He couldn't get enough of the country smells. Even the ones from Oz.

"Looks like a good day to go fishing," he mused, thumbs hooked into belt as he matched Chris's quick pace along the sidewalk.

She looked over, still distracted. "You fish?"

"Well, I always thought I'd like to when I got the chance."

"I always thought I'd go horseback riding."

They walked on, settling their rhythms into the rhythms of the town, nodding hellos to people they passed, answering questions, deflecting curiosity. Mac noticed that the camps were beginning to be drawn to either side of Chris. Luella stepped out of the Kozy Kitchen to ask if Chris was all right after having an intruder in the shop the night before. One of Harlan's flock made a sniffing remark about people getting so far above themselves they thought no one would notice them sitting out at all hours drunk on the side-walk. Chris soothed Luella and ignored the little lady in the flowered polyester. She walked a little faster, though, her heels clicking like castanets. Her hands were shoved deep into her jeans and her head was bent a little.

"Mac?"

"Yeah?"

She was addressing the sidewalk. Too uncom-fortable, obviously, to face him with her question.

Mac listened very carefully. It took her a minute to continue.

"You know how I was up in St. Louis when Mr. Weaver was murdered?"

"Yeah."

She walked deliberately, missing the questioning looks of the librarian as she passed by without an answer to her hail.

Finally Chris lifted her head. "I was in St. Louis every time somebody was murdered."

Mac damn near stumbled to a dead halt. He needed a cigarette. He needed an interrogation room and a lot of silence to play this right. Instead he had Main Street and witnesses. He opted for discretion. "And?"

Chris shot him a startled look. "And?" she echoed. "*And* isn't that an amazing coincidence? *And* aren't there a few questions you have to ask me?"

"Yeah. When did you find out?"

"Yesterday. It's easy enough to verify. I stayed at the Ritz most of the times on my American Express card. I did a lot of research—"

"Chris . . ."

"Dinah was there—"

That did bring him to a stop. "What?"

She faltered to a halt a couple of steps on. He'd obviously reacted to the wrong piece of information. She blinked like somebody'd just awakened her from a nap. "Pardon?"

"Dinah?" he asked, trying not to sound too interested. "What was she doing in St. Louis with you?"

Chris shrugged. "I'm not a huge fan of big cities. Dinah would rather have her toenails removed with a hedge clipper than visit rural America. St. Louis was always a good compromise. We meet up there when I go for research."

"Three times in the last two years?"

"Jacqueline is negotiating for reprint rights."

Mac could feel his palms begin to itch. "She knows your books pretty well."

Somehow that was what brought Chris around. Her eyes widened. Her mouth dropped. Her face lost a lot of its color as she took in Mac's implications. "It can't be Dinah," she whispered, shaken.

"Would you feel better if it's you?"

Then, just as suddenly, she was on her way again, hands stuffed in pockets, attention solidly on the sidewalk. Damn, Mac wished they'd already made it to her house before all this started coming down.

"Why did you want me to know?" Mac asked, eye out to intercept any other interruptions.

Chris gave her head a brusque shake. "You'd have found out. I thought I'd save you the time."

And? he thought. This time he just waited. They were half a block from Chris's house and only had to make it past the Marshall place before he had privacy and isolation in which to conduct a real interview.

"And . . ." she continued on a half sigh. "I know the books pretty well, too."

Mac gave her a little breathing room. "Yeah."

She turned to him, and he realized how very fragile she was right now. Friable as paper-thin skin, all that brass and defiance dangerously eroded by the past few days. Mac literally held his breath, afraid of losing more than just the truth.

"Do you think there really was somebody in my store last night?" she asked.

Mac wanted to stop again. He wanted suddenly to

blow off the investigation and just reassure her that everything was going to be all right.

"You want to talk about it?" he asked, his steps slowing no more than a few feet from her front door.

Her expression didn't ease any. Her eyes were large and dark and unsettling. Her posture betrayed the pressures building up in her. For the first time Mac actually thought to wonder whether Chris had reason to suspect herself of the crimes.

"It's why . . ." she looked away, sought space. Mac gave it. "I just can't tell this stuff to Sue. She wouldn't understand."

Mac should have been amazed that she'd think to come to him first. He wasn't. They were both fish just a little out of water here. Survivors. They understood each other in ways none of the people raised and nurtured in the safe, known world here would understand.

"Harmonia should be able to keep Garavaglia busy for a while," was his answer.

She dug up a slightly battered smile, and pulled her house keys out of her pocket. And turned to find Shelly sitting on the doorstep.

Shit. Goddamn fucking lousy timing. Mac saw the situation sized up in the girl's eyes even before she'd climbed to her feet and knew he wasn't going to get within ten fucking feet of the truth this morning.

Chris headed right for her. "Shelly, what's wrong? Why aren't you in school?"

Mac knew Shelly was here to bring disaster to Chris. Even so, the girl managed to smooth down her black miniskirt and settle right into posture for him, hips out, head up, hair back. Eyes as brittle as frozen metal, only the kind of kid she'd attract would never notice.

"Hi, Chief," she cooed, twisting a little on her high-heeled boots. "Haven't seen you in a while."

Reining in his irritation, Mac pulled his own pose, the one he'd copied right from L. J. Hands on hips, eyebrows gathered, head forward. The "man in charge" pose. He didn't need there to be any chance of Shelly's getting the wrong impression.

"Shelly." Another thing he'd learned from L. J. More than one word was superfluous at any given time.

Chris barely waited out the little display. It seemed she could see through that facade even in the condition she was in. "Honey?"

Shelly swung her attention Chris's way. Mac was sure she was trying to look judgmental as hell. She only looked lost. "I have a pass," she insisted sharply. "I'm . . . Tracy and I, anyway . . ." Her head dropped and she shuddered. "Have you seen my mom?" she asked, her voice small.

Chris gave Mac a quick look before turning back to Shelly. "No, Shel. I haven't. What happened?"

"She just kinda wasn't there this morning. Tracy said she's been screamin' a lot about you last couple of days. I was afraid . . ." Her admission died in an uncomfortable little shrug.

Mac was already unhooking the radio mike from his collar.

Shelly came right to attention. "Oh, no," she begged. "Don't . . ."

"Judge is up in St. Louis today," Mac said. "Right?"

She nodded.

"We'll keep it real quiet. Just John and me."

Shelly couldn't decide who she wanted to look at.

She finally settled on Chris. "I'm sorry," she said miserably. "She has no right."

Chris took hold of the girl's hand. "Don't worry, sugar. It'll be okay."

It only took John a couple of minutes to roll to a stop alongside them. Mac ushered Shelly into the car as he filled John in. A couple minutes and a plan later, John was shifting the car into gear.

"Oh, by the way," John said, idling a moment longer.

Mac was already turned back to the sidewalk where Chris waited, arms wrapped around herself like protective armor. He paused to hear John out.

"All the Cooters finally went through their daddy's things. Seems he did have something that's missing, and they want it back. For the sentimental value, no doubt."

"No doubt. What is it?"

"A vintage silver dollar. 1898, I think."

"That's it, then," Mac acknowledged with a nod of satisfaction. "We've officially been visited by the angel of death. Thanks, John."

John waved and took off. When Mac turned back to check with Chris, she was no longer on the sidewalk. Her door was open, and Mac could hear her hurried footsteps on the hardwood floor.

Now really curious, he followed.

"You planning on tossing the place again?" he asked placidly from the open doorway.

She was raking through every teapot on the counter. At this rate, it would take her all week to get through the lot. She never gave any indication that she knew he was there.

A nasty chill slithered down Mac's neck.

"Chris?" he tried again, pulling open the screen door and stepping inside. "What's the matter?"

Still it took her a minute to react. When she did, Mac saw real desperation in her eyes. He stepped farther in and shut the big door behind him.

"What's going on?"

She took one more look into the teapot she held, a fat, garish caricature of Queen Victoria. Whatever she was looking for didn't seem to be residing in the queen's head, though.

She was shaking and pale, and Mac was afraid for her.

"I thought . . ." She gave a little laugh. "I thought for sure I put it here."

"What?"

She considered him as if she were a dog about to get kicked. Then she shook her head. "I'm not sure anymore."

Mac took a couple steps closer, only to make her shy away. Nothing major. She didn't exactly run screaming for the kitchen. She straightened, her grip tightening on the poor queen's ears. Defensive, frightened. Teetering on some edge Mac couldn't see.

"You want to tell me what's wrong?"

That provoked another small laugh. Another small, frustrated shake of the head, the kind Mac had seen in confused old people found wandering the streets. He held his place, fought the urge to reach out to her. Reined in his impatience.

"Nothing," she finally said, not looking at him. "Nothing." With shaking hands, she found the royal tiara and fitted it into the hole on the royal hair.

Mac knew better. He wanted to stay and find out

what the hell was going on. He wanted to find out just what was dragging her right to the edge of the precipice.

Abruptly, Chris looked up. Smiled. Still shaking, all but throttling the ceramic monarch in her hands, she did her best to flash him an attitude of nonchalance. "John's gonna need your help," she said.

Mac was amazed. He was about half an inch from throttling her himself. "I don't think I should go anyplace."

"I'm not going to stack the furniture in the living room," she promised. "Louise hasn't ever disappeared before. I think she might be in real trouble."

Mac lifted his cap and finally gave into temptation to rub at the old scar. It didn't ease the sudden throbbing that always preceded disaster like achy knees predicting the rain. "You think she could be our killer?"

Chris settled the little queen back on her table. She slumped a bit. "Anything's possible."

"Yeah," Mac agreed, relieved to at least have her considering her surroundings with a wary eye. "It is. Would you mind starting the search for me while I'm gone?"

Chris looked up, surprised.

"I am not computer friendly. Especially when it takes any kind of creativity."

At least he got a smile out of her for that. He really wasn't sure about leaving her right now.

"Where do you want me to start?"

"Your friend Dinah," he said, ignoring her start of protest. "Victor, Weird Allen . . . Louise Axminster, I guess. Get printouts of anything you find."

"My editor was with a sick friend," she said. "He has a hospital full of alibis."

"Good. One less name to check. Oh, and see if you can find any history of mental illness on any of them. Any unexplained disappearances."

She started again. Obviously hadn't remembered that she'd been the one to tell him that she'd misplaced her agent for the last few days. Mac knew it wasn't making her feel any better. He didn't care. Rather she suspect everyone than confide in the wrong person.

"I'll call . . ." He stopped, chagrined. "No, I guess I won't."

Chris managed a grin. "If you'd like, bring Garavaglia by here when he shows up. I promise to hide the printouts so he doesn't find out we're conducting illicit investigations."

Mac shook his head. "You're probably a bad influence on me."

"I also have plenty of surveillance equipment gathering dust if you want."

"Don't tempt me." Resettling his cap, Mac shot her a conspiratorial smile. "I'll try and give you some kind of warning before we descend."

Garavaglia wouldn't be in the least happy. Rule one of control in interrogation is keep it on your own turf. That put the advantage on the home court. Mac had never had a problem siding with a fellow officer before this. He must have been getting too much of that small-town air in his lungs.

She couldn't find it. Teapot after teapot ended up on her table until it looked like she was having a close-out sale. Her hands were shaking and her stomach churned. She knew she'd seen it. Held it in her hands, a scarred, dull silver piece that had winked up at her when she'd moved the couch.

A 1898 silver piece.

Chris spent another half hour looking for it, even when she knew that she'd put it right inside Queen Victoria.

At least she thought she had. She wasn't so sure anymore. She wasn't so sure of anything.

She had to get over to the bank. She had to walk calmly in, present Hattie McDermott with her safe deposit key, chat about the weather and the sales of the last book, and then closet herself away with her past.

Her past.

Chris clutched the plump queen to her chest, as if she could forcibly hold in the terror, shore up the certainty.

She would have told Mac. Would have admitted that she had held Cooter's good luck charm in her hand—had thought she'd held it—if not for what had finally begun to come clear the night before.

The pattern. The unnervingly familiar series of events that only she had seen.

The answer.

It was waiting for her in the safe deposit box in the bank. It had been waiting there, in banks like it, since the day she'd walked away from Springfield with nothing more to her name than her clothes and the fifty-eight dollars she'd saved up working at Burger King. Crumpled, smudged looseleaf papers filled with erratic words, terrifying images, terrible conclusions.

She couldn't face them.

She had to.

She had to go back into that cramped, untidy handwriting, because it might explain some of what had been happening. What shouldn't have been happening, because it was impossible.

Impossible.

Because no one had seen the words on those pages but her.

It hadn't occurred to her at first. After all, only books were coming true, and she'd never thought of it as a book. Only murders had been taking place, and there had never been a murder in this story. Not exactly.

But there had been a villain.

There had been things misplaced, phantom footsteps, half-seen images at the edge of perception, sounds and smells no one else perceived. There had been a stalking figure.

If she was right, though, then the rest of her reality wasn't. If, indeed, the words she'd written so long ago were coming true, she couldn't trust anything else she'd seen or heard. Because the villain of the piece was Christian Charity Evensong. And the figure stalking her was her own conscience.

✦ Chapter 15 ✦

"WHEN WE GO in," Mac suggested, pulling the car to a stop and killing the engine, "be gentle. She's really had the fuzzy end of this lollipop."

"You mean she's had to deal with Lawson?" Garavaglia retorted, pulling a huge unlit cigar from his mouth and scratching his chin with it. "I'd be a little fucked up, too, I had to sit on interrogation with that dickhead."

Mac took a look over at the gray-haired tower of humanity next to him and felt right at home. Harmonia Mae had damn near fainted on the spot when she'd caught sight of the good detective. "Lawson really had a way with her."

They both climbed out of the car. Mac could see the shocks lift by inches when Garavaglia popped out.

"They're treatin' her like Joan of Fucking Arc up at HQ," Garavaglia groused. "She probably pissed the perp off so bad he just couldn't stand her anymore. Pumped a couple of slugs in her and rolled her off a cliff. Can't really say the idea didn't appeal to me when I heard about it."

Mac settled his cap on his head and hoped that Victor and Lester Presley had given Chris enough notice. He hoped she was in the right frame of mind for the visit. "Check with the lab at Cape," he suggested. "I'll bet you get a match on the gun that did Taylor. They definitely ID'd her?" he asked.

"Oh, yeah. She had crappy teeth and a coupla old broken bones. Turned into a real easy ID, once we had her records."

Mac nodded, unsure why he didn't feel better about it.

"The lab didn't find traces of the files in the car?"

"*Nada*. The question is whether they were in there at all." Garavaglia lifted the second set of copies under his arm. "I'm glad she left you something. Although I have to say I'm surprised as shit. That woman was as territorial as a she-wolf."

Alongside him, Mac stepped up to the screen door and knocked. Chris was already there waiting for them, smiling.

"Afternoon, gentlemen."

Upon stepping into the high foyer, Garavaglia leaned his head way back and stared up at the ring of furry legs over his head. "Well, fuck my duck and call him Albert."

Chris was in her black jumpsuit, tucked into the shadows behind Victor's house. It was Monday evening, which would put Victor about three hymns into the Rock of Ages evangelical services. A perfect time for a little B-and-E. Chris's hands shook as she pulled the oblong little leather case from her pocket and popped it open to reveal her picks. She hoped

Lester hadn't decided to stay home alone tonight. She'd hate to be caught.

Behind her a tree hissed in the wind. She wiped the sudden sheen of sweat from her forehead. God, she hated the dark.

Three pins. Easy. Victor's grandparents had probably had the old locks installed sometime in the twenties. Simple, dependable workmanship. Sliding the rake into the bottom of the lock, she inserted one of the rake picks and began to slowly tickle the pins.

A car turned the corner on the other side of her house. Chris hugged closer to the building, her heart pounding so hard that it was making her hands shake. She was glad she had the gloves on. She was sure her palms were getting slippery. Wiping at her forehead, she decided that she hadn't had a clue back at the How Do of what it felt to really illegally break into a place. She'd been playing before, sure she'd be forgiven her silly transgressions. If anybody found her tonight, she'd not only end up in the Cooter Taylor Memorial Cell, she'd do it without any flowers from Victor.

She didn't have a choice. The afternoon had been an unproductive one. After making her pilgrimage to the bank, she'd only had time to run Louise and Weird Allen on the computer, coming up empty on both of them. No wants or warrants, no records, no problems with money or medicine that she could find.

Mac had been frustrated that she hadn't run Dinah. She couldn't. Not until she talked to her. Not until she tracked her down. Dinah hadn't been at work today, either, and people in the industry were wondering. Chris was afraid.

Garavaglia hadn't been any better, although Chris had actually ended up liking him enough to trade filthy jokes. Mac had spent most of the interview with raised eyebrows. Chris hadn't been surprised, especially after her performance earlier. But Mac didn't know how ruthlessly she could close off questions. He didn't realize that the only way she'd ever learned to cope with the impossible was to go on the offensive.

A water-stained, battered manila envelope still waited on her desk to go through. Mac still had to be told. She could only do it on her own terms. And that meant helping Garavaglia. It meant working the computer for Mac. It meant sneaking in to get information Mac wasn't privy to.

Tonight she focused her attention on Victor. Poor, sweet Victor. Chris despised herself for preferring him to be the murderer instead of Dinah.

Instead of herself.

So, when opportunity knocked, she opened the door. With a lock pick.

Success. The lock eased around. Chris made one more check of the quiet neighborhood before pulling the kitchen door open and slipping inside.

Somewhere a clock ticked. The refrigerator Victor's mother had served him Jell-o from hummed contentedly in the dim room, and one of the cats Eloise had managed to foist off onto Victor sidled up to check out the newcomer. Chris took her bearings in the familiar kitchen decorated in early fifties and headed on into unknown territory.

She knew the first floor very well. Overstuffed, drab furniture, plastic runners on the carpet, framed samplers with pithy little sayings to ensure a good life, like "Penny wise, pound foolish," and "You're never alone when you have a friend." Or a dummy, Chris thought.

The home was pure Victoriana, with glossy woodwork, a wonderful staircase that led up from the front door, and high ceilings with plaster molding. Mrs. Marshall had effectively robbed the house of its personality, though, selling off her parents' furniture and installing her own avocado-green couches with plastic doilies and original pine veneer entertainment system. Victor, being the dutiful son he was, kept everything just the way she'd left it. Chris couldn't really complain. She'd picked up one of his grandmother's chifforobes from a local antique dealer.

She felt guilty creeping up those stairs. Victor was as innocent as Abel, genetically unprepared to battle with the cynicisms and distrust of his neighbors. That was why Lester hung around. Dummies could simply say things a polite young man couldn't. Sometimes Chris wished she had something so safe to hide behind.

She didn't need to have a guidebook to tell her which room had been his parents'. She was sure it hadn't been changed since the day Heilerman's had rolled old Phyllis out.

Victor's room was the one with the biography of Charlie McCarthy and the posters of Rockefeller Center. Chris checked drawers, dreading the sight of a coin, of rings. Surreptitiously wishing for it. Instead she came up with spare dummy parts, a lot of neatly folded underwear and a Kermit the Frog piggy bank filled with pennies.

Victor's decorating taste had been arrested right around freshman year of high school, and his reading taste completely nonexistent. Chris stood in the middle of that room and realized that she learned more from Lester than she could from the items in this room.

Even so, she walked back out into the hallway and headed for the next room, checking her watch to make sure the Reverend Bobby Rayford was still exhorting the faithful.

It was such a quiet house. Dead, as if the air itself hadn't moved in thirty years. As arrested as Victor. Chris fought a shiver of distaste, and realized that she was glad she hadn't known his mother all that well. She probably would have ended up pissing her off, too.

Well, might as well get this over with. Chris had to try and get through to Dinah again. She had to do some more work on the computer.

Please let someone else be doing this, she prayed, although to whom she wasn't sure. Let me find proof someplace so I'll know for sure. Please don't let me be sliding away again.

Chris opened the next door and looked inside.

It was too dark here, even with the hall light on behind her. She couldn't see a bed or dresser, just a lot of floor space. The last thing she needed to do was flip on a light. Somebody on the block would see it and break up the evening service with a call to arms within five minutes. Chris pulled out her penlight. Flicking it on, she swung it carefully upwards.

And saw someone in front of her.

"Shit."

Her heart slammed back into overtime before she realized she was looking at herself. Her first reaction was that she'd just managed to shine her light on a mirror. Then she swung the beam a little to the left and came up with herself again. And again.

Instead of slowing, her heart sped up.

"Oh, Victor, no."

It was a shrine. One entire wall had been covered in corkboard, and that covered in photos and articles about Chris and her work. Victor even had a shot of the Edgar Award on her shelf, taken by itself so that it looked as if it sat on his. There were copies of *The New York Times* list with her book on it, dust jackets, reviews, commentaries.

And there were books.

Chris came to a second, sick halt. There weren't just C. J. Turner books on the wall. There were copies of every one of Jacqueline Christ's books there. Well-read, well-loved originals, as carefully arranged as the mysteries. And beyond that, the press on Jacqueline.

Chris stood where she was, shaken by what she saw.

She hadn't known. She'd heard Victor extol her work, defend her life-style, plead her case. She'd heard Lester excoriate any reviewer who had been less than gentle with C. J. Turner, and knew that Victor had kept her reviews. She'd even asked him for a copy when she'd lost one herself. But somehow, she hadn't seen the extent of his obsession.

She hadn't understood until she stood looking at that wall quite how lonely and afraid Victor was.

Chris hadn't cried since her eighteenth birthday. She came very close to it as she stood in Victor's house in her black clothes, with the lock picks in her pockets.

She eased back out of the house five minutes later

and slipped through her kitchen door, hoping that whoever was sitting in the squad car that sat out in the square didn't notice.

Victor. It couldn't be Victor. Even though he'd known. Even though he'd been carrying on a one-sided relationship no one knew about.

Anybody but Victor.

Not *anybody*.

Chris sat down at her computer. It was time to check on Victor's past. She booted up the system with shaking hands and waited a moment while the machine whirred and blipped, her mind skimming alternative answers, her eyes drawn again to the package at the corner of her desk. It drew her like a snake. Like the sight of a disaster. She might have her answers there. It didn't mean she wanted them.

She turned back to the computer, ready to see her menu.

She didn't.

"Oh, God . . ."

A message. One line, no signature. None needed. Chris couldn't have mistaken the meaning or the sender if she'd wanted to.

You know me, and you can't escape me.

Chris kicked over the chair in her haste to get to her feet. "Who are you?" she demanded out loud, her voice rising. "Who the hell are you?"

She didn't bother shutting down. She just ran.

The front door was closed. Chris yanked it open, thinking only that she needed to get to Mac. To show him. To demand his help. To beg for reassurance.

"Well, it's wonderful to see you, too."

Chris almost careened right into the person on her

porch. It took every last ounce of restraint in her to keep from crying out.

"Just where the hell have you been all dressed up like that?" her visitor demanded slyly.

Chris couldn't do much more than stare. "Dinah?"

✦ *Chapter 16* ✦

CHRIS WASN'T SURE just how much more she could take. Reality was shaky enough without this.

"If you showed up at my door, I'd probably invite you in," Dinah noted dryly. "But then, maybe they do things differently in this part of the galaxy . . . God knows they build their roads differently. I think I was almost sideswiped by a bear."

Chris still couldn't manage much more than an openmouthed stare. Comprehension would only bring more questions, and she didn't have the room for them.

"What the hell are you doing here?" she blurted out anyway, the doorknob still clutched tightly in hand.

Loaded down with Vuitton luggage, dressed for lunch at the Plaza, Dinah rested her weight on one hip and a surgically manicured hand on the other. "Well, kill the fatted calf, my children. There will be celebrating in Pyrex tonight."

"Pyrite," Chris countered.

"Whatever. It has man-eating mosquitos. May I please come in?"

Chris mutely moved aside. Dinah handed off a shoulder bag and an overstuffed garment bag and proceeded through with the rest. Chris looked out into the street, certain she would find something following behind. Rod Serling, maybe, or the crew from "Candid Camera."

She turned back to find her agent openmouthed herself as she took in her surroundings.

"Dinah—"

Dinah's head came down and her hand went right back on her hip. "Haven't I trained you any better? How dare you mix minimalism with country kitsch?"

"What," Chris repeated, so confused she couldn't make it past the basics, "are you *doing* here? And where have you been?"

Dinah flashed her one of her shark smiles. "I am here," she announced, "to kick off the next leg in the career of the infamous Jacqueline Christ. Where I was is my business . . . and a certain tennis pro's. Now, where do I sleep?"

Chris's reaction was automatic. "New York."

Dinah scowled at her. "I'm disappointed. I'll admit I expected a certain amount of surprise at my generous gesture. But I was hoping for at least a little delight."

"I am," Chris retorted, her voice dying uncertainly. "Delighted, I mean. And surprised . . . no, I'm stunned. Dinah, this just isn't like you."

"Don't push it. I needed a change. Now, are you going to show me around, or do I call for the concierge?"

That finally got Chris to giggle, even though the sound was sharp and desperate. Dinah, here. Now. Chris gave more than fleeting thought to wonder whether she hadn't just graduated to the big league hallucinations.

If she had, she was also hearing things. Knocks on the door. Another voice. Dinah must have heard it, too, because she turned right around to answer it.

"Wait—"

Too late. With the appropriate flourish, the little agent threw open the door to expose Mac standing in uniform out on the step.

"Well, well, things might just be looking microscopically better," Dinah greeted him. "Are you what they call local color?"

Chris shoved right past her to get the screen door open. Mac paused a second, obviously unsure that he wanted to jump right into this particular situation. Chris could hardly blame him.

Well, at least it proved that she wasn't hallucinating. Mac saw Dinah, too. She could tell by the look on his face.

Dinah stared way up at him and held out a hand as if they'd met at a cocktail party. "Dinah Martin," she said as he finally stepped in. "You are?"

Mac came right to attention. "Dinah Martin?"

Dinah didn't miss a beat. "If you insist," she conceded. "Except I think people are going to get us confused."

Chris couldn't take her eyes off her friend. Dinah was a character, but Chris couldn't say she'd ever seen her quite this . . . volatile.

"Dinah, this is Police Chief MacNamara," she finally managed. "Mac, this is my long-lost agent. Evidently she's been on the wagon train for Pyrite with a tennis pro."

Mac gave Dinah a policeman's official nod. Dinah

actually preened. In all their association, Chris had never seen the likes.

"Heard a lot about you," Mac offered noncommittally. Chris almost winced.

Dinah flashed a perfect set of teeth. "Well, I sure as hell haven't heard enough about you. Do you play tennis?"

Evidently Mac took that for a rhetorical question. Chris was glad. Although she had to admit she was relating to the tennis analogy. All of a sudden she was feeling like a ball in a hot match.

"I'm sure you had a long trip," Mac said evenly. "Which means you'll feel more like coming in to talk to me tomorrow."

"Talk?" Dinah demanded. "You want to waste time on words?"

Mac's answering smile was as perfectly worn as his uniform shirt. "I know you wouldn't be able to think of anything else until this whole thing with Chris's books is cleared up."

Dinah glanced over at Chris as if Mac weren't even standing there. "Oh, he's good."

"Could I talk to you for a minute, Chris?" Mac asked, still not quite able to take his eyes off the diminutive agent who stood between them.

Chris tried to pull her scattered thoughts together enough to answer.

Dinah never let her. "I'll just put my things away," she suggested, reaching up to pull off the bag that still hung over Chris's arm. "Wherever away is."

Chris gave a vague motion back toward the living room. "There's, uh, something in the fridge. I think. I'll be right back."

The night was cooler than the last time she'd been

out sampling it. Chris could use that right now. She stepped outside and leaned against the front wall of the building, hands up to rub at suddenly burning eyes.

"Looks like you're having a busy night," Mac mused, pulling out the ubiquitous cigarettes.

Chris groaned. "You don't know the half of it."

"Want to tell me why you're in your felony two clothes?"

She was still trying to rub away the confusion. "You did see her," she couldn't help saying. "Right?"

"What?"

Chris just shook her head. "Never mind. I'm just a little . . . overwhelmed."

"I can tell. And I thought my day was full with Garavaglia. What's she doing here?"

Chris dropped her hands and laughed. Not a very sane-sounding laugh, she realized. "Hell if I know. She just showed up on my doorstep like Dorothy back from Oz." That earned another dismal shake of the head. "She *never* comes here."

"Any ideas?"

"Not one."

Mac spent a few seconds smoking and looking in toward where they could hear Dinah moving around the house.

"Something else," Chris said while she could still pull her thoughts together.

Mac's attention returned.

She took a breath for courage. "It's Victor," she admitted. "He's known about Jacqueline Christ all along. I found out tonight, only . . . he doesn't know. He's got a goddamn shrine in that house, and I'm all over it."

Mac considered her quietly. "You're surprised?"

Chris turned on him. "Of course, I'm surprised." Her shoulders slumped. "Oh, hell, I guess not. It's just . . . spooky. Sad."

"Well, hopefully we can keep his secret."

Chris looked over, not sure she was happy with the change in his tone of voice.

"I came over to tell you that we finally tracked down Louise."

Now Chris knew she didn't like it. "She OK?"

Mac blew a cloud of smoke at a hovering swarm of insects. "Depends on your definition of OK. She's safe, she's under observation, and there's some hope she's treatable."

Chris slumped all over again. "Oh, God."

He gave her a considering look. "She'd broken into the old barbershop."

"Next to the How Do?"

"She had a knife. We haven't been able to get anything coherent out of her, but she's been screaming about you for about three solid hours now."

Chris tried to shake her head, as if denial could erase the truth. As if it could ease the splinter of guilt in her chest.

"I think," she said miserably, "I'm just going to stop trying."

Mac took another drag, his gaze still passive. "Your fault again?"

Like books stacked too high, boxes without balance, her stability was getting too precarious. She didn't have anything to say.

"You might like to know that she did have a mental history," Mac said quietly. "Judges are in a perfect position to hush things up. Evidently she's been paying real close attention to Harlan's suggestions that you suffer for your crimes."

Chris battled a flush of fury. "Well, why am I not surprised he had a hand in this?" She took a minute, rubbed a little more at gritty eyes. Tried to piece together what Mac was saying. "So, you're telling me you think you have our killer?"

A car slowed at the stop sign and rolled through, its lights washing across his chest. "Garavaglia couldn't be happier. I'd like to hear more than delusional ramblings. Evidence might be even nicer. We think whoever did Lawson has all those files. So far, we haven't seen squat."

"Could Louise have done it?"

"Sure. Crazy people fool me all the time."

"Can she work a computer?"

That brought his head around again. A moth was beating itself against the screen to get to the light inside.

"What?"

Chris sighed. Struggled for the courage to take the next step and actually show him. Because once she did, she'd have to explain.

She'd have to share what was in that manila envelope.

"Come here." When she opened the screen door, the moth followed them in.

Chris did not normally invite people up her stairs. It was a natural barrier for her. The floor was community territory, where she shared tea with Eloise's poker group and potluck with the Hospital Auxiliary. But the balcony was hers. It was where her alter egos lived, where her secrets were kept. Where she could indulge herself in the illusion of being able to look out over the world unseen and remain safe as she dissected it.

"I was on my way to get you when I ran into Dinah coming the other way," she was saying as she rounded the corner to where her desk waited by the wall of closed blinds. "This showed up when I was booting up the system to find out about Victor."

They came to a halt by the computer. Chris surreptitiously slid the envelope aside. Mac bent to consider the screen.

"What?" he asked

Then Chris looked. Reality slid a little farther off-center. "Oh, shit, no," she moaned, leaning forward, punching keys, calling up screen after screen. All of them innocuous, all of them exactly what had always been on her screen. The message had disappeared like the phantom out in her yard.

"Dinah!" she yelled, leaning over the balcony. "Did you touch my computer?"

"And chip a nail?" the response floated up from the closed bathroom door.

"I didn't see her go up the stairs," Mac offered behind her.

Chris was sweating. She couldn't believe it. She knew she'd seen it. She'd been awake. Wide awake. You just don't imagine things like that.

But she wasn't sure anymore.

"What did you want to show me?" Mac asked.

She couldn't quite face him. "It was there," she insisted out loud. "I know it was there." Even she could hear the rising desperation in her voice.

Mac took a cautious step closer. "What was there, Chris?"

wonder you appeal to middle America. You've suc-
cumbed to it."

"Don't be a shit, Dinah," Chris warned, stretching
in her chair to ease out some of the kinks from
falling asleep mid-diatribe sometime near dawn.
"Middle America is paying your grossly inflated rent."

"God bless 'em."

"Did you read the last manuscript I sent in?" Chris
asked, just as she always did. Knowing the answer.

"Of course not," Dinah intoned self-righteously. "I
never read Jacqueline. You know that."

"Might do you some good," Chris teased. "Help a
little in those tight spots with the tennis pro."

"Don't be absurd," the agent said, lifting another
square of cake by the ends of her fingernails. "The
last thing I need is help."

Leave it to Dinah. For the first time in days, Chris
was beginning to feel a little better. A little saner.

"What's so funny?" Dinah demanded when Chris
chuckled.

"Nothing," Chris assured her, curling back into her
chair. "I've missed you."

Dinah let that faint layer of distress color her
expression again. "I've missed you, too. Next time,
we'll do New York."

Chris played a little with her coffee cup. "Do you
know that all the murders happened while we were
in St. Louis together?" she asked.

Dinah went on sipping her coffee as if they were discussing the weather. "I knew there was something more
to that city than bad weather and brain sandwiches."

"Dinah!"

"Well, what do you want me to say?"

"Don't you think it's awfully friggin' odd?" Chris

demanded. "I insisted on those times. Made sure we were there, somehow, just as a murder was committed using one of my books as a trail guide."

"Maybe you're not as unacquainted with the psychic phenomena as you thought. Who knows? I have more important things on my mind."

"More important?"

She shot Chris a sly smile. "Tell me about the chief of police."

"I did."

"You told me he reads Balzac, wants to fish, and moved to a small town for the clear air. Sounds like the Episcopalian priest in *The Quiet Man*. Where's he from?"

"Chicago."

"And?"

"And," Chris countered testily, "he's here now. As a matter of fact," she admitted, conveniently checking her watch, "he's probably just about looking for us to show up for that little chat."

Dinah waved her off. "Not till I've done something with my hair. And my nails. And my outfit."

"It's interrogation, Dinah. Not coming out."

Just then the radio on the table sputtered to life.

"Chris?"

Chris pointed to it as if in proof. Actually, she was more surprised than Dinah. She picked up the radio and keyed the mike. "Yes, Crystal."

"Hi," the girl chirped, obviously ignoring several FCC regulations. "Chief wants to know if you'd meet him in city hall in about ten minutes. And bring the computer?"

"10-4," Chris answered, producing a waterfall of giggles from the other end. "Over and out."

"Good God," Dinah growled, downing the rest of her coffee like a vodka stinger. "I *am* in Mayberry."

"Sue, what do you want me to do?"

Sue bristled. "Protect her."

Mac set down his ATF cup and rubbed at his head that hadn't stopped hurting in the last forty-eight hours. "I've had a man outside her house for the last two days, Sue. As a matter of fact, I was the man out there last night, which means I haven't had any sleep. Which means," he assured her acerbically, "that I'm just a little tired."

"But, have you *seen* her?"

The voice that answered sounded almost as tired as Mac's. "She appreciates the concern."

Sue whipped around like a shot to find Chris standing in the doorway, portable computer in hand, Cardinals cap on her head. Today she was in scarlet and black.

"A celebration?" Mac asked, seeing just what Sue meant. There was more color in the old floor tiles than in Chris's face. Her eyes looked haunted.

"Opening day of baseball," she said brightly.

She didn't convince either of them. Mac, though, knew to give her room. Sue was standing there as if she were stuck in mud, not sure whether to go forward or backward. Agitated enough that she made Chris look calm.

"So you were the one at the window with the binoculars last night, huh?" Chris demanded, stepping on in to set the portable computer case on a chair. Mac noticed that the minute she got through that door, her steps faltered badly.

He wished he could move them someplace roomier. Unfortunately, there was company everywhere else they could work. "Bird-watching," was all he said.

She brought up a laugh. "Yeah, well, you would have had more fun over at the Taylors'. Last night it was cookies and milk at my place all the way."

"I saw. She still talking?"

"Probably."

"Isn't she going to join the party here?"

"Later. She said something about a shower."

"You coming over for dinner tonight?" Sue asked.

Chris frowned in confusion.

"It's Ellen's birthday," Sue reminded her, looking, if possible, worse.

Chris's smile was apologetic. "I'm not sure if you guys are ready for Dinah," she demurred. "We spent the morning in a clinical discussion of male anatomy."

"Well, she'd clean up her act for the kids, wouldn't she?"

Chris looked a little pained. "She doesn't recognize kids. Says they're just large, rude Schnauzers with braces."

Mac wished he were back at the squad room. They could have had a great pool going on who was going to walk away from a meeting between those two. Even after meeting the agent, Mac's money was on Sue.

"Just for a little while," Sue suggested, as if she could bestow some kind of magic protection on Chris after only a few minutes in a normal house.

Chris's smile made Mac wonder if maybe it couldn't happen that way. "I'll be there," she promised.

"One more thing," Sue said, an accusing eye in Mac's direction. "Evidently Mr. Franklin has been heard. The press has pulled into town. TV, radio, newspaper. They're all on the way. The Sleep Well rented its last unit to the people from the *Globe*."

Maybe it was better coming from a friend. Mac wasn't sure. Either way, Chris slid into the chair with her computer as if somebody'd just snuck up and taken off with her knees.

"I'm sorry, honey," Sue said.

Chris just nodded.

And they were supposed to get some work done.

Amazingly enough, they did. Holed up in Mac's office with Sue playing palace guard, they fine-tuned that computer in no time at all. They didn't find out anything, not at first. The obvious stuff was negative. But Chris Jackson was nothing if not resourceful. She began to hit pay dirt after following Harlan to his fourth state.

"Who'd think it?" Mac mused, looking at Harlan's sheet.

"Me," Chris said, typing away. They were onto Dinah now, much to Chris's chagrin. "Harlan just isn't the kind of guy to wait for divine intervention. God has millennia to make a point. Harlan only has weeks."

"So he manufactures false evidence against his opponents."

"From that history from Florida, it looks like he manufactured everything about himself except his hat size."

"Including the divinity degree."

Chris actually grinned. "Means to an end, my boy. A very popular refrain among Inquisitionists throughout the centuries. What amazes me is that I didn't think of using this kind of ammunition against him before this."

"It's illegal," Mac admonished.

Chris's grin was piratical. "I'm going to hell anyway. Might as well enjoy the ride."

He was sitting on the edge of his bookcase behind her, a sheaf of papers in his hands, his attention half on those, half on the figures that scrolled out before Chris. She'd calmed noticeably since coming to the office, even with the door closed to keep her out of sight of the invading press. She was obviously happier taking action than sitting back and letting things happen. Mac just wished he could get her close enough to whatever had been going on last night to open up again.

A stalker. He'd talked to JayCee, who'd been the one she'd flagged down that first night, and Curtis, who'd sat outside the house on damn near every one of his night shifts the last few days. They hadn't seen or heard anything. Except, of course, Victor pining and Weird Allen patrolling. But both of those activities had come to a simultaneous halt.

Mac shook his head in frustration. He'd made inroads into the police here. He had a long way to go. To that end, he'd moved Curtis back to patrol and accepted the help of one of the highway patrol guys as backup.

He wondered, though. Why Chris hadn't brought her suspicions to him earlier. Why she'd incriminated herself. Why she believed she was more capable of murder than anyone around her. But then, Mac had never spent his childhood locked in a dark closet. He couldn't imagine that he would have come out of it as well as Chris had.

The phone rang and Mac picked it up. "Chief MacNamara."

"Mac?" Sue asked anxiously. "There's a Special Agent Willis from the FBI on line one for Chris."

"For Chris?"

"That's what he said. Hurry up and take it. I have another TV crew headed this way."

Mac punched the line. "This is Chief MacNamara. Can I help you?"

She'd meant to bring the accusation right back to Dinah. Confront her with it, demand explanations, justifications, at least rationalizations.

She couldn't.

Dinah had always been her rock, implacable in the rush of the publishing business. Common sense in a sea of insanity. When Chris hadn't been able to trust anybody, she'd been able to trust Dinah. So when she got home and found Dinah sound asleep on the couch, she'd just pulled a rainbow afghan over her and headed on upstairs.

Embezzlement. It was such an ugly word. A crime committed by mousy bank tellers and shady mob figures. Not by your own agent. Not by your friend.

Chris knew Dinah had her problems. Chris had supported her, helped her, even walked her into treatment the time she'd been caught red-handed in the lingerie section of Bloomingdale's with a pocket full of bras.

"She came from an alcoholic family," Chris had explained to Mac after the call from Special Agent

Willis. "Terrible uncertainty. They never knew from one meal to the next where the food was going to come from. It left terrible scars. She's been trying to get her parents' attention since she was five. Just about as long as she's tried to protect her future."

Was she trying to get Chris's attention now, or making sure she had a next meal? It broke Chris's heart.

Evidently Dinah hadn't been with a tennis pro of any kind. She'd been avoiding the federal officials who had shown up in her office the week before with questions raised by another client. Chris hoped like hell Dinah had appeared on her doorstep to admit to Chris what had been going on, rather than just to escape to a place she figured the police wouldn't know about. Chris had to give Dinah the chance to make the admission. So she'd begged Mac not to confront Dinah until she did.

And then she didn't.

Instead, as if in punishment for having to send her friend back to New York to face the FBI, Chris finally climbed her stairs and sat down with the manila envelope.

Chris Jackson had a juvenile record. Or rather, Christian Charity Evensong did. Mac was amazed. He wouldn't have been so surprised if he'd found one in California. In fact, after what she'd said, he'd almost expected it. But she'd been clean in California. Her record was from Springfield, Missouri.

Word had come after Mac had gotten off the phone with the New York police about Dinah Martin. An acquaintance of Mac's from FBI school now worked Juvey out of Jefferson City. He'd gotten in touch with a buddy down in Springfield who'd worked the area for years.

The records had been closed, of course. Slate wiped clean on the eighteenth birthday, whatever the crime was. Privacy for the sake of the child. The old cop had remembered the name, though. Mac's friend had called with the news, said he'd try to dig up something more. Mac thanked him and hung up. Then he simply sat there in his quiet office, the staff long gone, the traffic outside picking up, the highway patrol cruising his streets to supplement the staff dealing with all the extra people in town.

A Juvey file. And something worthwhile enough that a cop remembered it after more than fifteen years. Big lies and little lies.

Mac was rubbing at the side of his head again. It was time to get a beer. To get a couple of beers. Then, since he'd given in to Chris's pleas not to question Dinah until she'd had a chance, he'd take the first shift outside Chris's window. Tomorrow he'd ask the tough questions.

She must have fallen asleep. Chris woke in the corner, curled against the wall by her desk. Her T-shirt was soaking wet and her limbs were shaking. It was morning.

"Oh, damn . . ." She lifted a hand to swipe at her hair. She hoped to God she hadn't made any noise last night. "Dinah?"

Her voice was tentative. Afraid. She prayed she hadn't been found out. She wished she could remember what happened.

The last thing she remembered had been writing. Funneling the terror and pain and fury she'd discovered in those crumpled old papers into fiction, just as she'd done all these years. She must have finally given into the sleeplessness and dropped off over the computer.

"Dinah!" she yelled a little louder, climbing unsteadily to her feet. Still in her lurid scarlet and black. Stale and sweaty and shaking. Ashamed. Frightened.

It had been the pages. The terrible images churned up by those haphazard words. The trauma of going back and then comparing it to the present. Chris would have to take it all to Mac this morning. She'd have to explain and hope he understood. She'd have to pray there was another explanation for what was happening.

Still shaking and unsteady, Chris turned to climb down the stairs. "Damn it, Dinah, are you up?"

Another problem to handle. Deftly sidetracked the night before between Ellen's party—at which Dinah had behaved admirably and Chris had barely survived—and a one-person toast with champagne to the new contracts. Dinah had finally dozed off before Chris had worked up the nerve to confront her, and Chris had escaped upstairs.

Escaped.

She laughed bitterly. Not exactly the word she'd use.

"Dinah?"

She reached the bottom of the stairs. Looked first in the kitchen to find it empty, the blinds still closed. Which meant Dinah was still out. Dinah despised having the blinds closed. Or coffee not constantly percolating, the sound as soothing to her as a mother's bruit to a fetus.

Chris turned into the main room. The couch was still open. Tumbled.

Strange.

Chris came to a halt, wondering what had happened to her afghan. The colors were all wrong. All dark, as if a bucket of paint had been dropped on them.

Something crawled into her stomach. Something vile.

She whispered now. "Dinah?"

Whispered and crept, like a child. Terrified of what she'd find. Suddenly knowing and still not believing.

Dinah was there. She was there, but her arm hung over the end of the bed. Her hair was strewn out like black seaweed. Her peach satin gown was drenched.

Drenched. Glistening and thick and black.

Chris heard the first buzz of flies and gagged. "Dinah?"

Now a plea.

She stumbled toward the radio.

Elvis Jones heard the screams for help from the dispatch radio all the way back to the last jail cell where he slept.

✦ Chapter 17 ✦

MAC BROKE THE door in to find Chris trying to do CPR. One look at the scene should have told anyone how useless that would be. She was pumping, though, breathing into wherever the mouth had been and yelling as if with just her own will she could force life back into the stiff, mutilated figure that hung off the edge of her foldout couch.

He made it over to her in three steps. "Chris, stop," he commanded, pulling her away. "There's nothing you can do."

She struggled to get free, her eyes wild, her hands and clothes thick with old blood. "No! Damn it, I did this to her!"

Which was just about when the first reporter elected to show up.

From that moment, it was a madhouse. Mac didn't have nearly enough men to control the scene. Ray Sullins pulled up hoping to be interviewed, and Weird Allen almost got into a fistfight with a sound man from CNN. Neighbors gathered and traffic stopped to see what all the commotion was for. Inside, the air was thick with the distinctive stench of disaster, and Chris was curled up into a chair out in the kitchen, her hands clenched in her lap, her head down, ignoring Victor's attempts to get her attention through the window.

Mac had seen some ugly ones in his time. This one stood right up there. Multiple knife wounds, stabbing and slashing, mutilation at its finest. The little agent hadn't had a chance.

And Mac couldn't figure out how the hell it could have happened.

He'd been sitting out front until two watching the two of them talking on the couch. He'd been relieved by JayCee, who swore he hadn't left his post until he heard the screaming. He hadn't seen or heard a thing.

"The lights were on all goddamn night long," Mac insisted, one eye on Chris, another on John, who was doing measurements for him. "How the hell couldn't you see anything?"

JayCee was beginning to sweat beneath his chief's scrutiny. "Nobody came in or out of that house," he retorted. "Not nobody. I'd swear it."

Mac swung his arm around behind him to indicate the level of mayhem. "I suppose the serial killer fairies snuck in from under the floorboards and then disappeared again while you watched. Maybe sprinkled some fairy dust on you so you couldn't see 'em slashing their way through a hundred pounds of person."

"Doc Clarkson just pulled up," Curtis announced from the door, still in his sweatsuit. "And Reverend Sweetwater."

"Oh, shit," Mac said, now truly pissed. "That's the last thing I need."

"Don't worry," John advised from where he was poising the Polaroid. "He'll be too busy performing for the minicams to bother you."

"They deserve each other. I want a time of death!" he yelled to Tom as the doctor stepped into the door.

"Shit, shit, shit," Tom breathed, faltering to a halt, truly overwhelmed. "I'm gonna have to find me a quieter county."

"And see to Chris."

Tom's head snapped up. "Where?"

Mac motioned. "Kitchen."

He turned to check on her again, to see her climbing to unsteady legs. "Mac?"

It was impossible that she was upright. She looked paler than the corpse on her couch. Her eyes were sunken and bleak, her hands trembling. Mac had cleaned off her face at the kitchen sink. Had washed her hands as she stood there shaking and silent. But her clothes were still stiff and muddy with blood. She still clasped her hands together as if forcibly holding herself together.

Mac stepped over tape and fingerprint equipment to get to her. "Go sit down, damn it. You're not helping a thing."

She shook her head, her expression dazed. "I have to . . . show you something."

Something more? he wanted to ask. He followed her anyway. Slowly, holding onto the bannister like a lifeline, she climbed up the stairs.

Mac heard the humming before they reached her work area. The computer was still on. Evidently she'd been working on it. He wondered how, considering what was in her living room.

"I fell asleep," she explained as if she'd heard him.

Down below, Tom looked up at the sound of her voice and frowned. "I was working last night after Dinah fell asleep. A new . . ."

Mac didn't want to hear the rest. He bent to read the screen.

> . . . *so bad it was difficult to recognize the victim as human. Blood saturated the sheets, the cushions, the floor. Blood, a dark, thick tide of it . . .*

He didn't need to read anymore.

"I think I did it," Chris whispered, stricken. Ashen and shaking. "I think I must have killed her."

It only got worse. Much, much worse. Mac couldn't convince Chris that she hadn't murdered her agent, and he couldn't find a reasonable explanation for how someone else could have done it. He wanted to take her away someplace where they could talk, where he could get to the core of things without interruption or interference. Instead, he had to deal with the mayor and the press and every two-bit official this side of Farmington, all vying for their chance at sensation. He had to try and glean information from a hopelessly contaminated scene.

"John, do me a favor," Mac asked as he guided Chris back down the stairs. "Take Chris on over to the sheriff's office. City hall's already overrun with people. I need some prime time with her."

"She under arrest, Mac?"

"She damn well better be," Judge Edward Lee Axminster III said from where he'd taken up a position by the grandfather clock.

Mac didn't need him on his case, either. Axminster was here for revenge, pure and simple. And if Mac didn't step very carefully, give up some of the little points to the local power boss, the judge was going to get just that. And then Chris would be left to the wolves, which meant they'd never find out what was going on.

"I'll read her her rights," Mac conceded, turning to a dazed Chris.

John brought out the cuffs. Chris took one look at them and backed away as if she'd seen a copperhead. "No," she begged in a horribly small voice. "Please, I can't . . . don't . . ."

"Chris, I have to," John protested.

Still reciting the too-familiar words, Mac waved them away. ". . . do you understand these rights as I've read them to you?"

Her eyes were still focused on John as he reclipped his cuffs.

"Chris?"

She started. Gave a jerky nod. "Yes."

"I'll be over as soon as I can. Till then, Elvis'll keep an eye on you."

She wasn't listening again. "There's a . . . an envelope," she said, her head down so the judge couldn't hear from where he was busy destroying the integrity of Mac's crime scene. "Of Christian's. You bring it," she said. "Nobody but you."

Mac nodded, not having the slightest clue what she was talking about. "It'll be OK," he promised.

She looked over to where they'd finally covered the body with a tarp. "No, it won't," she disagreed and followed as John ushered her out the back door to try and escape all the lights and film.

It took Mac another fifteen minutes to resecure the scene. Five more to find the envelope he thought she meant. An old battered thing with the carefully printed name of Christian Charity Evensong on it.

He was heading back down the stairs when his radio crackled to life.

"Chief!"

It was Marsha and she sounded desperate.

Mac damn near dropped the envelope to get to his radio. Everybody in the room could hear the terrible high screams in the background.

"What the hell's going on?" he demanded of the dispatcher.

John came on, breathless. "Elvis was trying to get her into a cell . . . Chief, you'd better get down here."

The screaming went on and on.

"Tom!" Mac yelled, vaulting the last four stairs and running for the door. Bag in hand, Tom was right behind him.

Chris opened her eyes to a bright, pastel room where the sunshine splashed across yellow walls. It took two more hours for her to be able to pull together any kind of coherent thought.

Her brain was cotton wool. Her mouth was parchment, and she could feel the cool slime of drool on her cheek.

Drugs. They'd sedated her.

Panic threatened. Who'd sedated her? Where was she?

Who came back first. *Why* took a little longer.

She ran her tongue around cracked lips and shifted her limbs. There was going to be a bruise on her thigh. A big one. She wondered why. Her memory of the jail was fractured, drifting. Difficult to pull together.

Elvis. She'd told him not to put her in there. Anywhere but in those terrible little black holes. Anywhere but back in the dark. She wondered if they'd used IV Valium to settle her down. Still the drug of choice for a quick, painless nap. As out of control as she'd been, they'd probably needed about fifty of Thorazine, too. Maybe Haldol. She wasn't sure. Her tongue was thick, her mouth brackish with the aftertaste of chemicals.

She'd begged them not to, to just get her out in the open where she could get a breath. She'd pleaded and wept. But no one understood. They didn't realize that the drugs terrified her even more than the dark. That the reason she'd never had a drink was because it sucked the control from her, just like the drugs. Uppers and downers and psychotropics. Crowd control on a trolley.

She blinked a few times, trying to pull the room into focus, trying to pull her memory back.

"Chris?"

She turned her head to find good old dependable Sue sitting next to the bed. Chris tried to smile for her, wondered how long she'd been sitting there, thinking that she must have heard Sue's breathing and mistaken it for the wind or the ghost of Christian Evensong come back to haunt her.

"Hi."

Sue's expression was the same one she'd worn the day Tommy had fractured his skull on a bike. "How do you feel, sugar?"

Chris tried to lift her hand to wave away the gravity of the situation. "Stupid," she managed, although it came out closer to schtupid, and her hand never even twitched in the right direction.

Trust Sue to react with outrage. "Stupid?" she demanded hotly. "After what's happened to you? How dare you?"

Chris's smile felt more natural. "Thanks," she muttered carefully. "I needed that."

Sue was surprised into a sheepish grin.

"Am I at Puckett?"

"They thought it would be better for you. I tried to take you home, but they couldn't keep a . . ." Sue's voice faltered. Her eyes drifted.

"Guard," Chris said for her. "They couldn't keep a guard on me."

Sue nodded, ashamed.

"It's OK, honey. I'm a murder suspect. They do things like that for murder suspects."

"Oh, bullshit!" Sue retorted.

Chris decided it was time to sit up. She twitched a little without much noticeable success. With, however, effects. She winced. "Those damn ringbolts," she groused, and remembered. She'd cracked her hip on one when she'd wrestled with Elvis. "I have to apologize."

"For what?" Sue demanded, leaning forward in her chair as if getting poised to jump once more to Chris's defense.

It was Chris's turn to look sheepish. "For slugging Elvis. He didn't deserve that."

Sue grinned. "He only lost one tooth. You can't even tell the difference."

"Yeah, but he needs every one he has."

She was still feeling flat, empty. No emotions, none of the upheaval she sensed she should be experiencing. Her head was finally starting to clear, though. Like mist lifting, tendrils of confusion uncurled from pertinent facts. From memories. Like just what had brought her to be sedated at the jail in the first place.

She looked down at her hands, as if still expecting to see blood.

Sue understood without a word. "I'm so sorry, honey."

But Chris didn't hear her. She couldn't hear anything but the sudden buzz in her ears. A flash of terror swept away the rest of those deadening mists. Something had just crashed through the protective barrier of sedation.

Her wrists. Restraints. They'd tied her to the bed.

She didn't need to test them. She did anyway, pulling her arms up. Jerking to a stop only inches above the bed.

Suddenly she couldn't breathe.

"Chris?"

"Get these off," she begged, not able to look away. She bolted upright and came to another shuddering halt. A posey. They'd completely tied her down.

Sue was on her feet. "I can't," she protested, eyes wide. "I would, but they said it was for your protection."

"Get . . . them . . . off!" Chris panted, yanking with each word. Shaking the bed, sweating, panicking like a horse in a fire.

It was all coming back. All of it, every torture, every terrible penance she'd paid for her sins. She was paying for them again, and she wasn't going to survive it this time.

"Sue," she ordered, desperately trying to keep still, to keep her voice sane. "Get Tom here. Mac. I need . . . to talk to them."

"But Chris . . ."

Chris impaled her with a hard, level look that took every ounce of crumbling will. "Please, Sue. You don't know how important it is."

Mac made it there in five minutes. By the time he shoved open the door, Chris was drenched and shaking. Jaw clenched against the overwhelming urge to scream, to scrape her wrists raw in an attempt at escape. To gnaw at the cloth with her teeth if she had to. But if she did that, they'd never let her out. They'd make the mistake of thinking she needed more of the same to be controlled. Drugs and restraint. Age-old answers, palliative measures. Topped only by electric shock therapy in the hopes that the patient would simply forget that she had a problem and not need either of the former to control.

"Please," she rasped, not even able to look at him when he walked in. "Get me out."

"Give me your scissors," he barked to the nurse who'd followed him in.

The brisk little woman balked. "I don't think—"

His hand shot out. "Give me the goddamn scissors!"

Chris wasn't really sure whether he cut or just ripped, but within seconds, she was free. She came off the bed as if she were spring loaded, trailing the straps on the heavy cloth restraint jacket and sending the nurse stumbling back in alarm. The woman would have been down the hall for help if Mac hadn't slammed a hand against the door to keep it closed.

"I have a gun," he reminded the nurse gently. "She's not going to go far."

With fumbling hands, Chris ripped her way out of the posey and threw it to the floor. She made it to the window before the dizziness hit. Waves of it, swarming over her and stealing her balance. She grabbed the sill and closed her eyes, forcing herself to stay upright. Feeling the cool tile against her bare feet and the warm sun against her face. Then she finally managed her first good breath since waking up.

"Better?" Mac asked.

She just nodded.

Mac let go of the door. "You can go now," he told the nurse. "She'll be just fine."

"Don't count on it," the nurse warned, heading out anyway.

Chris laughed, the sound shrill against the sibilant hush of the closing door. "She's right, ya know. Most people who acted like I did would have gone right for your throat."

"Most people aren't that afraid of being closed in," he said. "I'm sorry. I didn't know they'd restrained you. I should have made it clear to John that I only wanted you in interrogation."

Chris gulped in some more air. Some more room. As soon as she could tell up from down she was going to start pacing. "They didn't know." Another breath, as if she could suck in control from the air itself. "Poor Sue. I think I scared her."

"She's OK. I told her to wait outside for Tom."

Chris nodded, closed her eyes. Fought her own body for control.

Mac waited for her, let her open her eyes out to the sun and just enjoy the sight of that open sky. She was still flashing back to that awful, small darkness. The smell of sour sweat and urine, old terror and thick fury. Terrible futility. It would be a precious long time before her heart slowed back down.

"You want to tell me about your stint on Fantasy Island?" he finally asked, his voice just as even as if he'd been asking about dinner preferences.

Chris straightened, her hands on the sun-warmed metal of the windowsill, her memory still fragmented. "How'd you know?" she asked.

"Deductive reasoning. Most people in a panic don't scream out recommended dosages for antipsychotics at the top of their lungs."

Another memory, Mac's hands. Tight, secure. His voice, always quiet, strong, steady.

"Oh, God," she moaned, closing her eyes in humiliation. "I tried to bite you, too."

She shot a careful look over her shoulder to see an edge of humor in his eyes. "Under different circumstances, it might have been an interesting tactic."

Chris wanted to giggle. She wanted to crawl away in shame. "Into bondage, huh, MacNamara? Well, I'm not."

"Obviously."

She finally took a look down, just to make sure it was there, and saw loose blue cotton and knees. "Jesus, I hate these things," she breathed in disgust, fingering the patient gown with a hand that trembled like an old woman's. Then her dismally slow brain filled in the rest of the pertinent information about patient gowns. "And keep your eyes off my back-side."

She could hear the grin in his voice. "But it's so cute."

"Yeah," she countered, turning toward him, hands still on the sill. "My fantasies are all about drooling drugged-out psychotics, too." Just to make sure, she took a swipe at her chin to make sure it was dry. Humiliation and terror, her favorite memories.

That sapped a little of the light in Mac's eyes. "We're gonna have to get down to business some-time," he reminded her.

It took her fifteen minutes more to be able to pull thoughts together in a reasonable pattern. The staff left Mac alone with her, obviously figuring to either trust his aim or just scrape him off the floor after she got finished with him. Chris knew she was coming back on line when she began to pace again.

"What's going to happen?" she asked, feet padding against linoleum.

Mac never moved from where he was leaning against the door. Contrary to every hospital policy, he was smoking.

"You need a lawyer."

"Should you be the one advising me of this?"

"Nope."

"Okay. Lawyer. What else?"

"Arraignment hearing."

That brought her to a halt. "Before the judge, right?"

Mac's smile was not pretty.

"What are my options?" she asked.

"It's up to him to set bail. There's a very real possi-bility he won't."

Another surge, a blinding wave of fear. "Meaning?"

Chris managed, even though she knew.

Mac gave her a level look. "You'd be remanded to the county jail until trial."

Chris's knees almost buckled. She saw Mac move to intercede, and waved him off. Instead, she headed back for the sunlight. "I can't," she said, knowing just how it sounded. She shook her head, looking out to where the row of tulips was blooming on the hospital walk. Vivid reds and yellows, splashes of new color, so bright you could almost touch them from here. Rebirth, resurrection. For a while there, she'd thought she'd actually made it. "I can't."

Mac took a long drag from his cigarette and blew the smoke up toward the smoke detector. "I think you'd better tell me why."

"In that case," she answered, "you'd better get a tape recorder."

Mac took a second to answer. "After you've retained a lawyer."

City hall looked like a chorus number out of *Les Miserables*. Politicians courted cameras and citizens shouldered through to offer opinions. Harlan had gathered the majority of his flock to demand protection from the Satan among them and justice for her heinous crimes, and Sue served coffee to the Chris Jackson Freedom Fighters. A third contingent demanded protection for their children from the madwoman they hadn't seen in their midst, which entertained the reporters much more than the mayor. Mac was hip deep in a headache and not seeing his way out for the forseeable future.

"My client is undergoing psychiatric evaluation,"

the lawyer was informing the judge, who'd temporarily forsaken his chambers for the spotlight. The lawyer, a sharp, savvy black woman named Brenda Fitzwalter who'd hit Pyrite at light speed from St. Louis, hadn't wasted a millisecond in town. She'd even made friends with Mr. Lincoln. Mac had taken her to Harmonia's himself, which he was sure was not going to endear him to the judge's cronies.

The judge wasn't in the least impressed with Ms. Fitzwalter's arguments. "I don't care if she's having an audience with the Pope," he informed her from behind Mac's desk, his massive silver eyebrows bristling and his attitude patronizing and officious. "She's going to appear before my court in the morning for the arraignment. And may I say, Missy, I won't tolerate any of her outbursts."

"Call me Missy one more time," Brenda Fitzwalter challenged, leaning a slim hand on the battered old desk, "and I'll be talking to the judicial review board. Do I make myself perfectly clear?"

Mac ignored them all as he gathered together his tape recording equipment and sidled around the milling bodies to get back out the door.

He should have known better. John intercepted him first.

"Just thought you might want to know," he said. "Mary Willoughby reported a weenie-wagger this morning."

Mac shifted the equipment in his arms to rub at his head. "You're kidding. When?"

"'Bout four-fifteen. She'd gotten up to go to work at the hospital and saw this guy out on her lawn playing the one-handed flute. Right in front of the picture window."

Mac sighed. "Allen?"

"She didn't see a face. However, she would remember the flute. Said it was symphony quality."

Mac let out a surprised bark of laughter. "Head over to Allen's," he said. "Get inside and talk to him . . . wait a minute. Willoughby's is right behind Chris's, isn't it?"

John nodded.

Mac wasn't sure whether he felt better or worse. "Then make sure you talk to him. He might have seen something. After that, meet me over at the hospital. I have to do an interrogation."

Mac tried another run at the crowd. This time, Sue appeared in front of him like the avenging angel. "I'm counting on you," she warned.

Mac heaved another sigh. "Count on her lawyer," he suggested. "My job is to conduct an impartial investigation."

"But you know she couldn't have done it!"

Mac stared her down on that one. "No one knows that, Sue. Find me some way somebody else could have gotten in that house without JayCee seeing them, and I'll be right at the barricades with the rest of you rebels."

Still Sue didn't move. "Come on, Mac," she pleaded, eyes wide and moist. "Tell me you don't believe what she's saying."

Mac considered the little woman before him. Loyal to a fault, pragmatic and fierce. He wanted to be able to agree with her. More than he'd ever have thought only a week ago. Shit, he'd come to Pyrite for some peace and quiet, and one gawky, opinionated, bull-headed woman had kept him awake for the last three nights. And he didn't see how the hell he was going to get to sleep any time soon.

"I don't want to," was all he was able to admit. "I don't know what else to tell you."

Sue hadn't been witness to that harrowing scene in the jail. She hadn't seen Chris Jackson screaming and spitting. She hadn't read the disjointed, rambling fifteen-year-old story on those crumpled yellow pages. But then, Mac had, and he still wanted to give Chris the benefit of the doubt. Go figure.

"God, I hate those tests," Chris admitted, munching on an apple. "They're a pain in the ass. And, considering the fact that I have a psych minor and know how to administer every one, kind of worthless."

Mac sat across the table from her in the nurse's conference room, the recorder between them and John lounging on a chair by the door leafing through *American Journal of Nursing*.

"Are you saying you skewed the results?" Mac asked.

Chris shot him a grin and hoped it didn't look quite as out of control as she felt. She was ready to explode, to run screaming down the halls. Hours of innocuous questions from the bland, passive psychiatrist ("How do you feel about that, Ms. Jackson?" "Go with that, Ms. Jackson") whose specialty was alcohol abuse, suffering every test from the Minnesota Multiple Personality to good old Rorschach, blander food, and four immobile, intractable walls had not improved her mood. Chris had lived this life once. She just couldn't do it again.

Her only victory had been convincing Tom to prevent anybody from ordering sedation for her. That would have been the last straw. The staff still tiptoed around her, and the guards, most of whom she'd researched with, had smiled uncomfortably.

And Chris had spent her time staring at the arc of the sun and washing her hands to get Dinah's blood off. To get all the blood off.

"I have a question," she said, apple in hand. She didn't see the crescents her nails made in the wine-red skin or the tremor in her hands. "You read it?" She made a vague motion to the envelope that sat alongside the recorder.

"I read it."

She overcame an urge to waste a look on John. This wasn't something she could share. Chris knew John, though. No one in town would hear from him.

They'd hear from the trial.

She fought a new surge of nausea.

"The murder happened the same way, didn't it?"

Mac was too professional to hedge the question. "As the one in the old story? It mimicked the scene the writer was doing at that moment. Yeah."

Chris nodded, the certainty crowding her throat, suffocating her. "Then I must have done it."

"Why?"

She looked up at him, not sure what to expect. Chris saw the consummate cop, the man who'd tried four times to convince her to get Brenda here for the interview, who'd brought John with him because he'd trusted John's discretion. The man who was giving her more chances than she was herself.

"Because I've kept that story locked away in safe deposit boxes since I wrote it. I'm the only one who's ever seen it."

"You're sure."

That brought her to the point of the interview. The truth she'd never shared with a soul since changing her name so long ago.

"I think so. I wrote that story as therapy when I was incarcerated in Fulton Hospital. Since then it's been locked away." She tried to flash a grin, but she knew how frightened it looked. "Kind of a personal talisman, ya know? The end and the beginning. Death and resurrection. I didn't consider it as any part of the pattern, because it wasn't a book. I'd never had it anywhere around where somebody could have seen it. But then, I found myself missing things, seeing things and . . . and hearing things. . . . And then, Dinah. Just like in that story."

"You said you didn't think anyone else had ever seen that story. You're not sure?"

Chris kept her gaze on the chipped imitation wood surface of the table. Somebody had actually scratched, "For a good time and a better enema, call 454-4444." She sucked in a deep breath to quell the fires of panic. To hold herself together long enough to admit the truth. She refused to look up for a reaction to her words.

"The treatment of choice at that time in history was drugs and electroshock therapy. Cure whatever ails you and all that. Problem was, it also destroyed short-term memory. I . . . I can only remember scattered images of my time at Fulton."

"What images?"

He was peeking into her soul now, into places Chris had never wanted anyone to see. She clutched onto that apple so tightly it began to weep juice. "Darkness, leather restraints. Voices. Constant babbling and crying. People wandering around, kind of like slow-motion bumper cars. Emotions, mostly. Fear, loneliness, confusion. A feeling of being smothered. One person."

"One person?"

She looked up then, surprised at her own words. At the words she hadn't expected to come up with. "I don't know. Someone . . . staring. Watching. Maybe a nurse. I can't really remember. I just have this vague . . . image of them, always in the periphery. I just thought of them as The Watcher. I hadn't thought about it in a long time." Chris felt herself curl in tighter and tighter, her arms wrapped around the bright blue-and-green sweatsuit they'd let her wear. "I think The Watcher was real. I'm not sure."

"What was the treatment for?" Mac asked, his voice unaccountably gentle for a cop in interrogation.

Chris wanted to cry, and she hadn't done that in fifteen years. Even when she'd seen Dinah lying on her couch. Even when she'd suspected that it was all coming back again, no matter what the doctors had said.

"Acute psychotic break," she whispered, rocking a little to ease the terrible grief in her chest. The fresh surge of guilt. "My mother said it was my judgment."

"Judgment for what?"

Chris closed her eyes and saw darkness. Even so, she kept them closed. "Becoming pregnant. I was fourteen."

"What happened?"

"I don't know. I can't remember. I can't remember anything of my pregnancy at all. The doctors said I probably never will. That after hearing how evil I was all those years, I evidently set out to prove my parents right. When I was successful, I couldn't cope with my parents' reaction, so I just denied the whole thing. Disassociated from reality. In my mind, nothing was wrong."

"And that's why you were at Fulton?" Mac asked. "For your break?"

Chris knew that John was watching her. She couldn't open her eye on either of them. "Kind of."

"Why, then, Chris?" Mac asked, his voice so calm, so low, the way Chris wished a psychiatrist's voice really sounded. "Fulton is a hospital for the criminally insane."

Chris realized that if she didn't face Mac with the answer, she'd never survive. Even if she'd done what she'd feared. Even if she really was suffering the punishment that never stopped for her sins, for her rebellion and her disobedience to God and father. Even if, in the end, she was condemned to return to Fulton.

So she opened her eyes, and she pulled her arms away, and she straightened. And fought the urge to sob. "For murdering my daughter," she said.

✦ *Chapter 18* ✦

SOMEWHERE OUTSIDE THE room, the hospital paging system was announcing the end of visiting hours. People passed by, voices and footsteps muffled and their features disguised by the smoky glass in the door. Elevators dinged and a phone rang. Inside the conference room the tape recorder whirred on uselessly. The silence was thick, harsh, echoing with old pain and older outrage. The pages of the magazine rustled as John dropped it in his lap. Chris bent over that apple in her hands as if she were praying over it, a priest about to consecrate the Host. Mac only kept his place because it was what he'd been trained so well to do.

Son of a bitch. Son of a mother-fucking bitch. No wonder Harlan set her off like a Fourth of July rocket. No wonder she adopted every stray in town. No wonder she had so much darkness at the back of those sassy eyes.

It had been a long time since Mac had had to shut down an interrogation in progress simply because he couldn't manage it. He reached over now and punched the Off button, and the tape recorder hissed to a stop.

Chris caught the movement and looked up. Mac had seen insanity. He'd seen disaster and small-minded cruelty. He couldn't ever remember getting a punch in the gut like this.

Which meant that he should be the last person conducting this interrogation. He was far too fucking involved.

He should get the hell out of here and hand this baby over to the patrol. Maybe Garavaglia; he was due back down here to coordinate information. Even John could be more impartial than Mac.

Mac pulled out his cigarettes and lit up. "I'm kinda glad I never had the pleasure of meeting your parents," he mused. His mother had called the night before, worried that she hadn't heard enough from Mac. Invoking Mother's Intuition that she knew he wasn't OK and wanting somehow to help.

Chris never eased her hold on that apple. She laughed, though, a harsh bark of sarcasm. "They had their convictions," she said. "Born again in the Lord, with a clear eye to goodness and evil, and the corporal wages of sin. They were not, evidently, as conversant with the signs of pregnancy."

Mac took a few more drags, eyes still on the top of her head, once again picturing that terrified little girl on her knees in the dark. Now seeing her cuffed and bowed as she stumbled onto a locked ward. The terrorizing of children in the name of God. Old stuff. Mac had been sent to too many homes with that kind of God-fearing parent. More than once, he'd been tempted to let them meet their Savior on the spot. He kind of hoped he'd get the pleasure of making the offer to the lovely Mrs. Evensong in person.

"And you don't remember anything of that time?" he asked.

Chris shook her head, facing him again. "Nothing. I was in the kitchen scrubbing the floor one day and waking up in hell the next."

Mac took a couple of more drags, lazily studying the table, the parking lot out the window, the new bruises along Chris's wrists where they'd had to hold her down yesterday. "Did you commit those murders?" he asked.

Chris damn near flinched from him. "What other possibility do you have?" she demanded. "JayCee didn't see anyone in my house but me."

"I'm not talking about Dinah," he said. "I'm talking about the rest. Would you have done that?"

She took a minute, dipping her head, shuddering, as if in private communication. Mac waited, the silence stretching in the room. Finally she shook her head. "I don't know," she admitted miserably. When she lifted her head, Mac saw the terrible uncertainty there, the child's confusion. "I must have."

"Why?"

"Because I had the opportunity. I knew the books. I spent an awful lot of time in St. Louis just following people, watching them, so I could get the right ones. My story from Fulton is a perfect fit with Dinah's murder, and I'm the only one who knew what was in it."

"You think."

She made a small, chopping motion, as if dismissing the idea. "The point is, whoever's doing this isn't someone I know now. It's someone I knew then. Someone who was there at Fulton. I think the chances of somebody in this town having known me there are pretty damn slim. And, even if they had, nobody but me ever saw evidence that I was being stalked. I must have been getting delusional again."

"I thought I smelled the disinfectant. Was that part of it?"

"But you didn't see the man in my yard. You didn't hear the footsteps, or the baby . . ." She choked, swallowed a little sob, her eyes widening in defense. "The baby crying at night. You never saw that silver piece."

That even brought John to attention.

"What silver piece?" Mac asked, trying to keep his voice level.

"The 1898 silver piece of Cooter's," she retorted. "I saw it when I was tearing my house apart . . . when I was trying to find out where that baby's cry came from." She squeezed her eyes shut this time, and Mac saw that she was trembling. The effort at control must have been awesome. He caught himself about to reach across to her and stopped. Not here. Not now.

"I must be . . . it must be happening again," she whispered to herself, her voice condemning and final.

"What happened to the coin?" Mac asked.

"I don't know if it was ever really there. Or maybe I took it and then put it somewhere else. I'd thought it was in the teapots . . . I couldn't find it again when I looked."

Mac spared a second to look back at John. John got the message without a word and silently stood and headed for the door. He'd go back over Chris's house with a fine-tooth comb.

"Tell me about acute psychotic breaks," Mac said

without bothering to turn the tape recorder back on.

Chris forgot her apple for that one. "Why? There's a perfectly boring psychiatrist who can fill you in on that."

"I want to hear your impressions."

She shrugged. "They explained it to me as a basic circuit overload. Too much to handle, not enough coping power, bam! you think you're a dog."

"And the prognosis?"

"You mean is it treatable? Very. Will it come back? I guess so."

"What did *they* say?"

Funny now that she was facing all this she didn't pace. She crumbled inward, like a building with the center supports taken away. "They said that if I acquired the skills to cope, it shouldn't happen again. I guess they were wrong."

Mac stubbed out his cigarette and resisted going for another. He was rubbing his upper lip, thinking fast. "Can people with acute psychotic breaks function in a day-to-day environment?"

"What?"

"You were the most surprised one around to hear about those murders. Do you really think you could commit serial murder and not even know it?"

"I killed my own child and can't remember it!" she cried shrilly. "Why should this be different?"

"Because you can't *remember* anything at all about that time before," he retorted, leaning closer. "You've been functioning just fine here."

"But my nightmares," she insisted. "At night, when I . . . when I sleep. I . . . it's like I disappear. Like I know there's something happening and I can't remember what, but it's horrible."

"Like murder?"

"Yes!"

"How many times have you had this nightmare?"

"Since this started?" she countered hotly, her eyes suddenly filled with tears. "Constantly. Every time I fall asleep. So I just don't fall asleep."

"But the town's been safe," Mac insisted. "We haven't had a rampage of murders."

"Cooter and Dinah aren't enough for you?"

"What do *you* think, Chris?" he challenged, right in her face, his voice hard, brooking no escape. "Do you think you did it? Do you think you could commit serial murder?"

"But I . . ."

He came to his feet. Towered over her. "*Do* you?"

She jumped up. "No! No, damn it, I can't see how I could possibly do it. But don't you get it yet? I can't see how I could have murdered my own child. And I did. I smothered her. The police found her in my closet, in a plastic bag, as if she were trash. They said I . . . I tried to keep it all a secret. That I killed her to protect myself."

She was sobbing now, her body shuddering with the impact of all that old poison. Finally disintegrating with the burden of all that guilt right before Mac's eyes.

He forgot to be a policeman then. Walking around the table, he pulled her into his arms and just held her. One or two faces appeared briefly at the door and then drifted away again. No one interfered. For a long time, Mac just soothed. Just listened to the tumbled words of grief and rage and guilt that spilled out, just waited through the inchoate terror that had been building right behind that smart-ass attitude all along. Just finally gave into the need to hold her again so that even for a little while, she could be safe. And then, when she began to calm, he challenged her again.

"Give me some options," he said.

"Who else could it be?" Her nose was still buried in his chest, her body beset by dying tremors. "They would have had to have known me in Fulton."

Mac smoothed her hair and looked out to the gathering dusk. "Tell me more about The Watcher."

Chris didn't need drugs to feel dazed this morning. The cacophony of the courtroom was doing it for her. She sat at the defense table next to Brenda, her hands clasped together to keep them still on the old mahogany table, her attention carefully on the bench, her attitude deceptively calm.

Behind her, she could feel the accumulated attention of the crowd that overflowed the paneled room. Camera crews, reporters, sensation seekers from five counties. Harlan and a contingent with signs about the wages of sin and the forgiveness of the Lord, and the Reverend Bobby Rayford front and center with the Freedom Fighters. Eloise and Luella and the Clarksons arrayed right behind Chris, and at least fifteen people who'd expressed their most sincere concern to her and their latent suspicions to the cameras. The Tower of Babel at its finest.

A major cluster fuck, as Garavaglia had called it yesterday afternoon. Chris couldn't have agreed more. A cluster fuck of catastrophic proportions.

The prosecuting attorney had her medical file from Fulton. Brenda had character references and two psychiatrists. The only thing saving Chris's sanity was the fact that Roger Peterson, the prosecutor, had nixed the idea of finding her mother and asking her to testify. That would have cinched Chris's reputation and case for good when it sent her screaming out into the streets.

Mac sat stiffly behind Peterson, here in official capacity. He'd testified as first witness on the scene, telling Peterson how grisly the scene was, and Brenda how he'd discovered Chris desperately trying to perform CPR. He'd produced the interview tapes in which Chris had admitted that she might have committed murder, and the tapes from the recorder Chris had hooked up in her house, which provided what might have been the sound of a door opening sometime during the night when JayCee had sworn he didn't see anything. The sounds of struggle had been brief, with no more protest than a surprised gurgle. And then the chilling sounds of metal against flesh, faint splashing, and grunts of exertion. And once again, maybe, the door. Or maybe, as Peterson offered, simply the bathroom door.

The search of Chris's house and place of business had failed to turn up the missing trophies taken from the victims. The autopsy had put the time of death at approximately 4 A.M. Description of injuries seemed to go on forever, and attract the whirring of TV cameras.

All the time, the judge presided with dignity and solemnity. It was only at recommendation time that he betrayed himself. There was no question in anyone's mind that he was going to bind Chris over for trial. It was just a matter of bail.

Chris held her breath. Sue reached up to lay a

hand on her shoulder. The crowd shuffled impatiently.

"In light of the seriousness of the crime," he said, doodling with his pen, "I am inclined to refuse bail."

Now Brenda added her hand.

Chris didn't move. She couldn't. All she could think of was the terror that awaited her in those black, cold little cells. If she stepped into one of them, she'd never see the opening of her trial.

"However," the judge went on, and let his gaze briefly flicker toward L. J. where he sat beside the reverend in the front row of the Freedom Fighters. "The court is sympathetic to the defendant's good standing in the community, and her . . . delicate situation." Meaning that L. J. had pulled his weight. L. J. hated Harlan more than he liked the judge. And Chris had put L. J. in one of her books as the good-old boy-cop on the trail of truth, which he'd never stopped being fond of. L. J. had probably reminded the judge just what Chris could do with the story of the Axminster family if she'd had a mind to.

"Therefore," the judge said with a smile that told everyone how crafty he was, "with the approval of her psychiatrist, after complete evaluation, and with the recommendation that she spend nights under observation at Puckett County, since those seem to be the hours at risk, I will set her bail at two million dollars."

A cry of outrage swept the room. One side of the room considered the amount far too large, the other far too small.

The judge had obviously figured he'd met all markers by setting bail at all, and then making it an obscene figure. He slammed down his gavel and climbed to his feet, well satisfied with himself.

Brenda turned to Chris with a big grin. "We got him," she crowed.

Chris started breathing again in faulty gasps and starts. "Oh, God." She sighed in relief. One step at a time. One day at a time. She'd held the darkness off by inches.

Sue was all set to storm the desk. "You mean it's OK?" she demanded.

Chris gave her her first real grin since two mornings ago. "It's OK." She didn't see the judge come to a sick stop not four feet away.

"You have that kind of cash handy?" Sue demanded a little more loudly.

Brenda was the one to stop that. "Maybe you'd like Geraldo to hear that," she suggested dryly.

Sue immediately shut up. She didn't stop shaking her head.

The crush of people was heading their way like high tide, so Brenda grabbed Chris's arm and led her over to where John and Mac were waiting to escort her out.

Chris took one look at the avaricious eyes on that crowd and fought the urge to run. Brenda held on tight. Sue and Tom stood right next to her, L. J. and Reverend Rayford behind her. She could do it. She could get through this.

"Gosh," she observed a little giddily as John and Mac took up position in the lead. "I've never been a phalanx before."

Mac shot her a suspicious look and then turned his attention to keeping microphones out of his face and Harlan out of his way altogether.

"Vengeance is mine, sayeth the Lord!" the minister cried like a martyr at the stake.

"Then maybe He'll be speaking to you about that degree of yours," Chris couldn't help saying, sending his skin color straight to the danger zone.

She smiled prettily, just as half a dozen cameras went off. Which kept them from seeing the way her hands shook as she shoved them into the pockets of her suit jacket.

Chris thought she'd effectively dodged everyone when they headed back around to the judge's chambers to wait out bail. It was Harlan who found them, though, his face red, his posture stiff. He was alone. Chris wasn't at all sure she could handle him in the shape she was in.

"You think I'm doing this for my own benefit?" he demanded without preamble.

Chris dragged Mac and John and Sue to a halt as she faced the preacher. "I think," she countered, "that you wouldn't know the Lord's work if it bit you in the butt."

She expected a tirade. At least a reading or two. Instead, Harlan merely shook his head. "Don't blame the Lord for what your parents did," he said simply, his voice quiet. Almost sad. "He doesn't just offer punishment, but glorious salvation. They forgot that."

And then, without another word, he walked on, and Chris was left to stare openmouthed.

Mac settled a hand on her shoulder. "Chris?"

She was stunned to realize that she was fighting tears. "I hate it when he's right."

And then, they, too, went on their way.

If Chris had thought she could sneak back out once her bail was met, she was sorely mistaken. Not one person had left in the intervening two hours. Outside in the hallway, a reporter from St. Louis was doing the intro to his piece. "The spotlight has hit this sleepy little Ozark town of Pyrite as world-famous author C. J. Turner is finally revealed—as a prime suspect in a series of grisly murders . . ."

Chris was jostled, glared at, questioned, patted, accused, and sung to. No matter how many times Brenda repeated the phrase "No comment," people still demanded a comment. Aggressively. Ob-noxious-ly. Persistently. Chris began to sweat. She kept smiling, even though she felt as if her face were on fire. She kept putting one foot in front of the other, even though her knees were dangerously weak.

She wouldn't let them see the panic. She wouldn't.

But it was getting close.

Instead, she kept her eyes on Mac's back as he cleared a path. She thought of enigmas and scars. Of gentleness in the form of challenge.

They'd just made it down the side steps to where Brenda's car was waiting when Shelly stepped out of the crowd. Ashen-faced, tear-stained, heartbreakingly uncertain.

No, Chris thought, knowing that this was what was going to make the difference. She could handle Harlan. She could handle the judge and the crowds. She couldn't handle Shelly's distress.

Chris shoved three people aside to get to her.

"I'm sorry," Shelly said, hands clasped, finally looking like the child she was. "I didn't know, Chris. I didn't know what you were going through, and I . . ."

Chris was the one who made contact. Hands on arms, gaze steady. "It's all right, Shel."

"I . . . would have helped," the girl protested. "I maybe could have . . ."

But Chris shook her head. "No, you couldn't. You think I'd put you in any kind of danger?"

She didn't hear the stutter of cameras or hear the expectant hush in the crowd.

Shelly straightened like a shot. "You didn't kill *anybody.*"

It made Chris smile. "Thanks, honey. But even so, somebody did. I'm much happier with you at Harmonia's. For now. OK?"

She nodded, relieved. "I'm just so . . . sorry."

And for the first time, it was Chris who did the hugging. "That means a lot to me, Shel." She should have done it sooner.

Shelly joined the phalanx and waited while Brenda ushered Chris into the passenger seat. As even more cameras went off, as questions were tossed out like confetti to a departing ship, Mac leaned close.

"You ready to help me find out who's doing this?"

It took Chris a second to answer. She'd just had too much turmoil. Too much revelation, until all she wanted to do was curl into a shell somewhere on an empty beach and listen to the water. She couldn't go home, she couldn't leave town.

She couldn't call Dinah for support. She couldn't call Dinah ever again.

And here, without any warning, was Mac offering help. Those damn tears she'd finally let loose yesterday threatened again, so that she had to dip her head a moment. But as Brenda climbed into the car, Chris looked back up to see that hint of smile in Al MacNamara's eyes.

"As soon as I get my nap," she promised. "We crazy people sleep a lot, you know."

"My house. I'll cook."

She nodded, fighting the awful temptation of hope. "I'll bring the computer."

Straightening up, he slapped the hood, and Brenda got them on their way. Behind her, Chris could just hear one of the reporters saying to someone, ". . . can you furnish proof she's a lesbian?"

"Do you have any evidence that doesn't fit?" Garavaglia asked.

Mac rubbed at his lip. "No. But we don't have any smoking guns, either."

Garavaglia tapped about an inch of ash from his cigar into Mac's Windy City ashtray. "I don't need any fuckin' smoking gun. I'm the circumstantial king, didn't you know that?"

Mac grunted in frustration. "Give me a couple of days," he said. "That's all I ask. I'm waitin' for a possible witness who just had to go to St. Louis for a friggin' ballgame yesterday."

"You kiddin'?" Garavaglia demanded, wiry black eyebrows dancing indignantly. "Even if I didn't care what happened to those three cases in the county, I got a cop killer. You think those Boy Scouts in Clayton are gonna give a dog fart that the prime suspect is a nice person with just a few reality problems?"

"I think we're all gonna be hip-deep in shit if she isn't the killer," Mac retorted. "Because that means we still have a real crazoid out there. And if this cat's following the game plan Chris Jackson wrote out fifteen years ago, it's not finished yet."

She didn't want to be here. She didn't think she was ever going to be able to sleep under her own roof again.

That wonderful high, open roof. That bright, white, clean expanse of air that had cushioned her for so long from the reality outside. Reality hadn't been outside, though. It had been inside. Deep inside, trapped like that spider in Mac's paperweight. Waiting to spring.

The smell of blood had been trapped in the closed-up house. It permeated the rooms, brackish and metallic, cloying, damning. Even if she was able to scrub the floor clean, throw the couches out, air out the rooms, Chris knew she'd never get that smell of blood out of the building. She'd never erase Dinah's death from the air.

"Do you want some help?" Brenda asked.

Chris shook her head. "I just need some clothes and my computer," she said, trying to breathe through her mouth. Trying so very hard to maintain some calm.

If only she could remember. Somehow that would be better. It would at least be an answer. There would be some sense of comprehension to that grisly scene they'd tried to sweep away. There was only the darkness, though, the shame and the terror and the horrible emptiness. The dislocation of oblivion.

Just like before.

"Chris?"

Both Chris and Brenda turned to the voice at the door. Victor. Alone.

"Where's Lester?" Chris asked instinctively.

Victor blushed and dipped his head. "He . . . he wasn't sure he wanted to come over."

"Why?" Chris asked, the inanity of the conversation threatening her composure even more than walking back into her house. "Does he think I'm guilty?"

Victor shot her a look of pure misery.

Chris laughed. "Oh, my God, he does," she said, the laughter building into something less than sane.

"No, Chris," he objected, stepping even closer to the screen door, his hands up against it as if he were caught in a cage. "I'm sure that's not it. He just . . . well, you know how he gets. He didn't feel he could . . . see you right now."

Chris couldn't stop laughing. Absurdly, all she could think of was that that was the first time she'd seen both of Victor's hands at once. "Oh, I know. Well, tell him thank you. He's been just about the most honest person in town."

"I couldn't convince him to go to court, either," Victor said. "Even after suggesting that *Hard Copy* would probably be intrigued by our Dan Quayle-and-the-banana routine."

Chris laughed even harder. "It's a great . . . bit, too," she gasped ungracefully. She turned to include Brenda in the conversation. "Lester does a wonderful Ted Koppel." Brenda wasn't nearly as amused as Chris.

"We'll be there for you, Chris," Victor promised. "You know that."

Chris managed to gulp to a stop. "I know. It means a lot to me to know you're watching the house while I'm not here."

Brenda couldn't even wait for Victor to open his

own door before asking. "Who's Lester?" she demanded. "His brother?"

Chris broke out laughing again. "His dummy."

She was halfway up the stairs to get her clothes before Brenda managed a bemused, "What?"

Weird Allen returned from his trip to St. Louis at two that afternoon. At two ten, Mac and John knocked on his front door.

Allen lived in the house his grandparents had first bought, a small, single-story frame home that sported clematis and rose of Sharon bushes. The outside of the house was neat and tidy and well-kept, since Allen's mother loved to garden.

The inside was different.

"I thought you'd come to tell me about my application," Allen whined when Mac asked him about Mary Willoughby's allegations.

Allen was sitting on an old tweed couch in a torn T-shirt and saggy jeans. The house smelled musty and closed off, as unkempt as its occupant. Mac noticed a magazine corner peeking from beneath the cushion on which Allen sat and the torn out ad with the picture of a young girl in a swimsuit Allen shoved in a drawer as Mac opened the screen door.

"Shopping, huh?" Mac asked with an offhand gesture.

Allen couldn't seem to keep his hands still. "Uh, yes. My cousin's birthday. Chief, I told you I wasn't in Mrs. Willoughby's yard. I mean, if I want to have fun, I don't need to do it alone, ya know?"

He flashed Mac one of those between-us-guys smiles, which on him looked as thin as the paint on his walls.

"Yeah," Mac agreed. "That's what I figured. But ya know, we have to check these things out. And, since it was in proximity to the murder scene, I was kind of hoping for a corroborating witness. You know, help me and I'd help you."

"I'd help if I could," Allen protested, and for the first time sounded absolutely sincere. "Jeez, I wasn't even on patrol that night. I was . . . I guess I was tired."

Mac nodded and joined John by the front door. "Well, thanks anyway. Appreciate the help."

Allen stepped forward. "About my application . . ."

Mac raised a hand. "Let me get through this three-ring circus first, Allen. OK?"

"Yeah. Sure, Chief."

John waited to speak until he and Mac had almost reached his cruiser. "Now, maybe he has a magic formula I don't know about, but I don't see that man having the kind of equipment that's noticed in the dark."

Mac nodded. "Definitely minor leagues. On the other hand, when we get back, I want you to get a search warrant for that house. And an arrest warrant."

John shot him a look. "You saw it too, huh?"

"You're not going to find anything," Chris sighed, head in hands.

Mac just kept on tapping at computer keys. "Have you had any more visitations from your phantom?"

She didn't want to answer. She didn't really want to move. "This house is a pit. Can't you get the judge to paint it?"

"You didn't answer me."

"No. No, I haven't had the feeling of being followed. Except by the entire staff of the *Enquirer.*"

"And if the story—what did you call it?"

"*Stalking the Beast.*"

"If *Stalking the Beast* is coming true, it's not over yet, is it?"

Another sigh. Depressurization of the tension in her chest. Defense against the palpable passing of each minute, each second until the sun went down. Until her own beasts were let loose again. "No," she answered. "It's not."

It should have been another beautiful day. Spring was exploding throughout the Ozarks. Chris should have at least had that to hold on to. But the weather had closed in, the sky heavy with an unbroken layer of clouds that trapped humidity like a pot lid. The day was warm and thick and as uninspiring as Mac's ceiling. Oppressive. Chris felt the weight of it right on her shoulders.

"You said the story was therapeutic," Mac offered.

Chris nodded, her movements jerky and quick.

"And the protagonist's conscience stalks her because of some evil she's done that she hasn't paid for."

A smile, grim and small. "Guilt and redemption again. The heroine redeems herself in the end by offering herself up to save someone else."

"So, you have guilt, redemption, and sacrifice," Mac countered absently, attention on the screen. "Are you sure you aren't Catholic?"

He almost got another smile out of her. Almost.

She was curled up in his couch, trying her damnedest to focus on the mundane, the active. The positive. Anything but the realization that Dinah was really dead. That she'd never sit across a table from her agent again and be reduced to tears by Dinah's outrageous outlook on life. The funeral was in three days. Chris wasn't going to be allowed to go. The grief would simply pile up in silence where she'd kept everything else all these years.

"Do you really think that Ray is going to allow all this extra manpower searching out every deserted building in the county just because you have a 'feeling' that my phantom really exists?"

"He already did. You're much more profitable to him absolved than convicted."

Chris did grin this time, her humor thin. "It's nice to have friends." At least, for the time being, she felt safe. She felt as if she weren't a threat. The press didn't dare cross the chief, and the town didn't mind that she was sitting in a room with a man with a gun. Besides, it made for great conversation.

Chris rubbed at her eyes and fought the urge to run buck naked into the street, just to give everybody something else to talk about.

"Do you really think Allen is a pedophile?" she asked.

"I'll put money on it."

"When do we find out?"

"John's serving the search warrant about now. I sure do wish I could find someone with a big dick, though."

That did manage to catch Chris's attention. "Something you want to tell me, Chief?"

He allowed a small grin as he punched up a new screen. "Police business. Have you heard about anybody in town with a reputation for being better endowed than average?"

"Sure. Victor. Why?"

That brought him around from the screen. "Victor?" he demanded, incredulous. "How the hell do you know?"

She grinned. "Suzy Gliddel. His fiancée. She complained to me once that it was a dead waste that Victor had such a promising appliance when he wouldn't plug it in. It's one of the reasons they broke up. Victor just didn't seem destined to participatory sports. Why?"

Mac was smiling. "You said he showed up today without Lester?"

"Yeah. Boy, did he look funny. Again I ask. Why?"

"I think I know why he did."

She got no more out of him than that. After having been acquainted with Mac even this long, Chris didn't figure she would. She turned back to considering the mottled gray of the ceiling and Mac turned back to the computer.

"Holy shit," he breathed no more than three minutes later.

Chris looked over. "What?"

"What years were you at Fulton?" he asked.

"Nineteen seventy-four and -five."

He looked over at her, and she sat straight up. She'd never seen Mac so surprised. "So was Sue Clarkson."

✦ *Chapter 19* ✦

"WHAT ARE YOU talking about?"

Mac motioned to the screen he'd been studying. "Her work history. She was a secretary there in seventy-four."

Chris came right to her feet. "So what?"

Mac simply watched her where he sat. "So, isn't that kind of a coincidence?"

Chris was already on the move. Her chest simply didn't have the room for more surprises. She couldn't breathe as it was. And Sue couldn't have murdered anyone. Sue was normal. Sue was sanity. Sue had children and a husband, for God's sake.

"Come on," she challenged. "You can't think Sue's the one. Hell, I *will* admit I killed all those people before I believe Sue had anything to do with it. I'll admit I committed the goddamn Lindbergh kidnapping if you want." She stopped right in front of him, agitated and angry. "Not her."

Mac never flinched from her. "At least we can talk to her. Find out if she has any ideas."

Tears again. Hot, frustrated tears. He was trying to take everything from her now. She'd lost Dinah. Lost her silence, her isolation, her security. He wanted to rob her of her reality as well.

"Do you want to come along?" Mac asked.

Chris straightened. "You bet your ass I do."

He was shutting off the computer as she walked over to pick up her purse. Overstuffed, as usual. Overbalanced. When she reached to pick it off the table, the whole thing upended and rained down everything from checkbooks to aspirin to miniature screwdrivers. And one other thing.

She saw it bounce. Heard the little clink, caught the metallic glint as the light flashed from it. Saw the dull glow of scarred metal.

"I'm not picking all that up," Mac said without looking up from where he was working.

Chris couldn't answer. She couldn't take her eyes from the circle of silver that was spinning like a top on the hardwood floor. Mesmerizing. Terrifying. Damning.

"Jesus," she whispered, hands to mouth. "Oh, Jesus."

Mac immediately turned around to see.

"Oh, Jesus is right," he agreed as he bent to pick up Cooter Taylor's 1898 silver dollar from the floor.

"You were supposed to search her house!" Mac was yelling.

John faced off with him, nose to chest. "I did!"

Mac waved the evidence bag with the coin at him. "Then explain this to me. Tell me how the fuck it ended up in a purse that's locked in a house behind police tape for three days."

"I don't know, all right? What else do you want me to say? But I went through that purse. I went through every drawer and cabinet. I damn near ripped apart the bears."

"You two are giving me a headache," Chris complained quietly from where she was stretched out on the couch, inside Ray's office, trying her damnedest to come up with her own answers. "There's nothing to argue about. I must simply be craftier than either of you thought."

That actually brought them to a halt, still in face-off position, right outside the door to the mayor's office. City hall was closed for the day, the door locked against people with press passes and the evening shift still out serving the search warrant on Allen. There was another major scandal brewing, about how local parents allowed their young daughters to visit Allen alone in his home. How their pictures were now ending up in his very private albums.

Allen hadn't been stalking Chris. He'd been stalking children. Chris would have been much happier with it the other way around.

Her head hurt. Her chest was on fire. Her stomach was trying to bring up the lasagna she'd managed to force down at Mac's. Just when things had started looking minimally better. Bail and help to prove she wasn't really crazy. The silver of that coin had burned her hand like fire.

Maybe it *was* someone else, Chris thought, watching the play of shadow on the mayor's newly painted ceiling. Maybe she wasn't the monster.

Maybe if she hadn't lived through nineteen seventy-four and nineteen seventy-five, she'd be more inclined to believe it.

"Am I going to have to come out there and break

it up?" she demanded toward the open doorway, closing her eyes instead of jumping to her feet.

"Not unless you want to scare off Victor in the process," Mac suggested. "He's at the corner right now. If he knows you're here, he'll close up tighter than a virgin on a blind date."

"Does he have Lester with him?"

"Yeah."

"What about Sue?"

"I'm going to talk to her next."

"After Victor fingers her, huh?"

Chris massaged her eyes, desperate for silence, for distance. For peace.

No, not peace. Answers. Finally and truly and irrevocably. Pictures, sounds, smells, whole and telling. Good news or bad. Innocence or guilt, Chris wanted her memory back. She wanted to be able to call up her life and not have it skip around like a badly spliced video. She wanted to know whether she'd just learned to close those doors too well, whether she really had murdered and then forgotten, just as she had so long ago. Or whether, maybe, this time it was someone else's nightmare. Someone who wanted to share their delusions with her.

She was so tired. So goddamn weary of all that guilt bearing down on her.

Out in the front room, the doorbell tinkled. Chris cringed farther into the soft Naugahyde of Ray's couch.

"Chief? You wanted to see us?"

"I'm glad you brought . . . came along, Lester," Mac answered quietly.

Chris kept her eyes closed. She measured her breathing, focusing on water, on sunlight, on the springtime that was exploding outside Ray's window rather than the revelations she knew were due out in that front room.

"Sit down, Victor. I'm really stumped about something, and I think you can help me."

There was a small pause.

"John's just leaving," Mac offered. The bell tinkled again, and Victor finally moved.

"Is it about Chris?" the young man asked anxiously as he scraped and rustled into position right out by Sue's desk. "Is she all right?"

"She's fine."

She's not. She's ready to cash it in.

"She said that you wouldn't see her today, Lester. Can you tell me why?"

"Where is she?" Victor asked.

Deep, easy breathing. Calming. Quieting. Escaping anyplace but here. Anytime but now.

"She's asleep," Mac said evenly. "Lester?"

"Is that what you said, you little jerk?" Lester demanded. "That I didn't want to see her?"

"Well, I . . ."

"And I suppose she thinks *I'm* the traitor now. Fine, I can take it. I can live with the mistrust. I'm sure there are some other ventriloquists out there who'd just love to work with hot property like me."

"Lester, please . . ."

"He didn't want her to know. Can't blame him really. How would it look, with him bein' the first life-loyal member of her fan club, and he spends his Friday nights outside her window yankin' ole Willie the one-eyed wonder in her honor."

"Lester!"

Sinking, settling, swirling, distancing herself from the turmoil that was building out there. The revelations that would change everything even more. That would undo the world strand by insidious strand.

Away from the guilt of the pathetic disdain in a dummy's voice.

I'm sorry, sorry, sorry . . .

Mac wished he were surprised. He wished he could have spared the gentle young man the discomfort of revelation. Victor was ready to crumble into tiny bits of distress. Lester was the storyteller now, the accuser and confessor of crimes committed mostly in Victor's mind.

"And nobody's ever seen you do it?" Mac asked quietly, wishing he could turn an eye in to where Chris was curled up on the couch on the other side of the paneled wall. Victor couldn't even lift his head, his face scarlet and small.

"It's pretty easy," Lester admitted, those bright blue dummy eyes somehow feral. "Sneak out his back door and take advantage of that deep shadow in the big oak behind the houses. He prefers the back window to the front, since he'd rather his devotion be anonymous. No one has ever seen him back there."

How did I get here? It's so dark. So dingy and smelly and hot. What's going on?

Oh, God, I know. I know where I am. I know where they're taking me. What's going to happen.

I'm so afraid . . . don't make them take me, Mama.

Don't make them do it again. I'm sorry. I didn't mean it. I'll repent. I'll do penance on my knees in the dark for the rest of my life. Just don't let them take me back there and strap me down. Don't let them hurt me again . . . Please, Mama, please . . .

"And the night Chris's agent was murdered. You tried to go to the window, like always."

"*He* tried. He never takes me. I guess he figures dummies don't have the same *needs* a dweeb in a bow tie does. But I know all about it, because he can't wait to tell me when he gets home. What do you want to know?"

"You were outside Mary Willoughby's, weren't you?"

"He was. Remember? I don't get invited to *those* parties. I have no party favors to play with."

"Why not Chris's house? Why didn't you keep to your schedule?"

"Because the dragon lady was there."

"But did you . . . . did he see anything?"

She hears them. Gurgles, cries, awful despairing sobs that echo around the high walls and embed themselves into the shadows. People shuffling along the hallways. Faceless, nameless, hunched over and blank, their drool drying on their clothes.

One person. Here, waiting. Right by the edge of her bed.

"*Who are you?*"

Waiting. But she can't remember. Not her own name, not where she is, not even the reason the side of her cheek is all wet. She drifts in some vague bath of distress, and her head hurts. Her jaw hurts.

"Come here. Closer."

The panic curls in, a wave lifting far out at sea, deceptively small in the vast expanse of water. A swell without definition, without focus. Approaching. Rising.

"If the right eye offends . . ."

I'm sorry, sorry, sorry, sorry . . .

"Victor, tell me what you saw at Chris's house that night."

"He would have come to tell you sooner. He really would have. It's just, he couldn't tell Chris. Not about what he'd been doing. Not about why he'd been standing out there under the trees. I mean, what would someone like her say about that? How would she feel about Victor after knowing? . . . Does she have to know?"

"One of you has to tell me what you saw out there first. Then I can let you know whether or not Chris has to find out."

"Well, I really didn't see anything. I mean, I waited until JayCee left to . . . well, you know, relieve himself. He does that a lot, doesn't he?"

"JayCee left?"

"Oh, yes. Well, not *left*, really. Just stepped around behind the Detweillers' shrubbery to the side where nobody would see him. Several times. Must be all that coffee he drinks. Then I slid out . . . back by the corner of Chris's house, it's easy to hide. It's so dark there, and the bushes offer some cover."

"Nobody was there?"

"Not that I saw. But it's easy to hide. I do it . . . I, uh, well, anyway, I was turned toward the Willoughby's house when I thought I heard a door close. I thought Chris had seen me and come out. But she didn't. I guess I just heard that person closing the blinds."

"She'd closed the blinds? Who?"

"The agent, I imagine. I couldn't see well. But it wasn't Chris."

It's the dream. The hospital halls, half in shadow as the night shift takes over. Decorated in drab institutional colors and partitioned by the geometrics of grillwork on the windows. Awash in the sighs and moans and mutters of medicated sleep. Steeped in half-felt rage, half-remembered terrors, half-realized dreams. A hell even Dante couldn't have envisioned.

And she has been consigned there. Judged, sentenced, cast down with the muttering, half-mad goats while the sheep share the love of the Lord. A fourteen year-old without visitors or mourners. A lost cause with a curable disease.

This time she knew it. She knew she was dreaming, that the terror and shame and revulsion were old news, that the doors—at least this time—swung open for her in the end.

She knew that the shadows were just shadows and the ache in her jaw was from clenching down on the airway when she convulsed from the electroshock therapy.

She knew that there really was someone standing at the bottom of her bed. That that person had been standing there all along. That that person had a familiar face, a familiar voice.

She just had to look into it and see.
"Please. Come closer."

Sue didn't waste a minute on Mac when she walked in.

"Victor?" she asked, kneeling down in front of him. "Are you all right?"

Victor refused to look at her. "I'll be fine," he assured her, although Mac wasn't so sure. "May I go now?"

"The blinds were closed," Mac said yet again. "Front and back for at least ten minutes."

Victor nodded, curling even farther into himself. "I've told you the whole story five times. I . . . I can't anymore. Please."

"I know, Victor. I just wanted to make sure. JayCee didn't do anything during that time."

A shake of the head. "He was eating his breakfast in his cruiser. I'm not sure he really noticed."

"And you didn't see anybody you didn't know hanging around Chris's house before that."

"Just the police and the reporters."

"And the reporters liked to slink around the back of the house?"

"I ran off a couple."

Mac pushed himself away from the edge of the desk. "Thank you both, then," he acknowledged, reaching over to help them up. Even the dummy looked vaguely ashamed now that Sue had joined them. "You don't know how much you've helped Chris. If you think of anything else, anything at all that you didn't remember this time, let me know, OK?"

Victor lifted those distressed Bambi eyes at Mac,

and Mac knew he was going to give in. "I appreciate your coming forward, Victor. I'm sure JayCee will be happy to testify about those blinds. The only other thing I may need is to have you identify just which reporters you chased off."

Victor slumped noticeably. Nodding mutely, he turned for the door.

"Now," Mac said, heading to refill his coffee cup as Sue regained her feet. "You want to tell me all about Fulton State Hospital?"

"The blinds were closed?" Sue echoed instead, turning on him. "You mean JayCee missed something after all?"

Mac scowled at her. "A subject he and I are going to discuss at length in about ten minutes. Right now, though, I want to talk about your work history."

Sue didn't get the chance to answer. Just then, Chris appeared in the doorway to Ray's office.

"There's no need to," she said quietly. "I remembered."

Mac swung around, not sure what he was expecting to see.

"Remembered?" Sue asked, stepping up to her friend. "Remembered what?"

But Chris didn't even seem to see her. Her gaze was riveted on Mac. She was haggard, her face tear-streaked, her eyes sunken and dark. She held onto the door by white-knuckled hands, and her knees had a tremor in them. Even so, her voice was quiet and calm. Controlled.

Mac didn't say a word.

"The watcher was real," she said, and he saw the brief tumble of every horror she'd faced in those haunted eyes of hers. "Another patient. Somebody who . . . who was always there when I woke up from the electroshock treatment. Who waited by the door when I went in."

Mac watched her, gauging her to the split second, knowing just how close she was to crumbling into a little pile on the floor. Frustrated as hell that he couldn't simply walk over and physically help her slog past this.

She wouldn't have accepted a strong arm right now anyway, well-intended or not. So he waited again and marveled at his patience.

"I know who it was," Chris said simply.

Still Mac held his place, held the damn coffee mug, held his silence, not needing to spook her. Desperate to know the identity, to find out once and for all whether he'd finally made the biggest mistake of his long, sorry career by trusting her.

"Who?" Mac asked.

Chris never let go of the door frame. She never acknowledged the hand Sue laid on her arm, or the frank distress in the other woman's eyes. Her words were for Mac alone, because she knew he was the one she needed to convince. And when she gave him the name, she gave it without inflection.

"It can't be," he retorted, his anticipation dying. "You know that better than anyone."

Chris shook her head. "She was there. Kind of like a shadow, always at the periphery. She must have read my story . . . maybe I told it to her, I don't know." Chris took a deep, shuddering breath, and Mac could see fresh tears glitter in her eyes. "Could she be the killer?" she asked.

"Chris . . ."

When Harmonia Mae Switzer entered a room, people knew it. She blew into the hall just then like an explosion.

"Where is she?" the woman demanded in her best DAR voice, the door still jangling behind her, the traffic outside growling angry counterpoint.

All three people turned on her. "Where is who?" Mac demanded.

But Harmonia Mae only had eyes for Chris. "I have a houseful of guests, and that senseless little chit simply disappears just as she's supposed to start supper. Said she was going to help you."

Chris straightened like a shot. Mac felt the punch of inevitability in his gut. There was no question in his mind, now. Somehow, Chris had been right.

"Where'd she go?" he demanded, slamming down his coffee cup on his way to the radio.

"Well, I'm sure I don't know. After receiving that phone call, she simply grabbed her purse and ran out. Said something about Chris being in terrible trouble, and she had to intervene."

"There should have been a patrol car outside your house, Mizz Switzer," he protested. "Did you see it when you left?"

"Still right there," she said, brow crinkling a little in confusion. "Nobody in it, though."

"Fuck," Mac snapped, keying the mike. He never heard Harmonia's gasp of outrage or Sue's questions. "One-Baker-Five, this is Chief MacNamara on Tac Two, do you read?"

Silence. Static.

"Curtis," Mac snapped into the mike, "where the hell are you?"

"Chief," another voice spoke up. "This is John. I'm two blocks away. Want me to look?"

"Yeah. I'm putting an APB out on Shelly Axminster, too. She's missing, and I want her found."

"10-4."

"Dispatch?"

"Here, Chief."

"I want the sheriff and the highway patrol captain on this channel in three minutes. We're starting a search for Shelly Axminster. And put an APB out for . . ."

He turned to find Chris at his elbow, hand at mouth, eyes huge. "You're sure?" he demanded.

She nodded.

He turned back to his mike. "Sergeant Elise Lawson."

✦ *Chapter 20* ✦

"CHIEF, I DON'T think . . ."

"I don't remember asking you to think," Mac snapped at the dispatcher, sharp as his creases and thinking at light speed. "Just do what I said. I want an APB out on the woman who calls herself Elise Lawson. Everybody around here's seen her. Caucasian female, five foot two inches, brown hair, hazel eyes, no scars. She may have Shelly Axminster. She's definitely armed and dangerous."

"But how can that be?" Sue demanded. "She's dead. They identified her."

"They identified Elise Lawson," Mac said. "My guess is that she was dead before whoever we met ever hit town. The person we met must have known who Lawson was. Maybe followed her from St. Louis and then ambushed her where she wouldn't be seen. Borrow the car and wedding ring for a couple of days and then send it all off the side of the road so that it looks like Elise Lawson just missed a corner on the way home."

"I had a murderer under my eaves?" Harmonia demanded in a tone that grated like ground glass.

She promptly plopped into Sue's chair.

Chris felt Sue's gaze on her. She should have answered the hundred questions she knew were whirling around in her friend's head. Should have demanded some answers of her own. She couldn't quite get that far.

The dream still had hold of her, the shame and terror and lost, helpless panic churning in her like old acid. The sights and sounds still kept her prisoner. Dingy green walls, scuffed linoleum floors, the smell of urine and old sweat and industrial-strength disinfectant. Cries and moans and murmurs, the symphony of madness. Harsh lighting and no privacy and limp mattresses being turned to chase away the cockroaches. Endless, numbing hours of nothing.

And The Watcher. The vague, discomforting face of familiarity caught at the edge of her consciousness, expression always expectant, always waiting. Like a dog. Like a sentence, waiting to be imposed for crimes rendered.

Chris had been able to put features on that face. She still couldn't come up with a motive. She simply couldn't remember enough about that other person, about her time at Fulton at all, to be able to understand why someone from fifteen years ago would seek Chris out after all this time and act out her books. Chris couldn't think what she possibly could have done to the other person to warrant this kind of retribution.

"What can you tell me about her?"

Chris started back to attention with Mac's question. He was standing back in front of her again, completely in police mode, his features stern, his jaw tight, his finger working that upper lip.

Chris did her best to dredge up active thought. To slam all those pictures behind a heavy door, to push them far enough away that they couldn't hurt her, couldn't distract her.

Cards.

Chris shook her head. She had no idea where the thought came from. Playing cards, with color pictures of the national parks on the back. Yosemite had been on the jokers.

"All I can remember," she said, rubbing at her aching head with a hand that refused to steady, "was that she would wait for me. She had long hair then, stringy brown, and glasses. They were standard issue, with black rims and tape at the bridge where she'd broken them . . ." She lifted her head, memory sliding into a stumbling gear. ". . . throwing them at one of the techs. She hated him. Used to try and bite him."

"But she never bit you?"

"I don't know. All I can remember is her standing at the edge of my bed . . . and, oh, yeah. Her allergies. She couldn't stand the smell of pine cleaner. It made her . . ."

Mac nodded, already ahead of her. "Sneeze constantly and talk like a frog. She may be nuts, but she's smart as hell. She did a great job of disguising her voice. Anything else?"

"Cards. I just remembered something about cards."

Mac didn't exactly lean closer. Chris felt his attention focus in, though, laser sharp. "Her name," he prodded gently. "Do you remember her name?"

Chris tried. She ran names past her personal viewfinder, looking for matches; she considered that old face, those blank, staring features pocked with acne and Band-Aids, and searched for inspiration. There was nothing, though. Only the frustrating gap of missing memory chips. Brain cells permanently scrambled by successive jolts of electricity.

She was so tired. So sore and frightened and confused. Picked apart and left lying out in the leaves like the Scarecrow, without a clue as to how to put herself back together again. With no choice but to pick herself back up and wade into the fray before something happened to Shelly.

> *. . . A sacrifice for the sake of your soul. A lamb for the slaughter with my knives if you don't offer yourself up instead. Penance, repentance, an eye for a like eye. A life for a life . . .*

It was a story she simply couldn't allow to come true.

"I know how you can find out," she managed, at least giving into the luxury of closing her eyes. "My Edgar Award. Shelf to the right of the fireplace. Dust it for prints."

Mac didn't even thank her. He simply turned back to the radio and barked out orders.

Shelly. Oh, God, it wasn't fair. It couldn't be like this. No matter what the story had said, no matter how this all had to turn out. Chris couldn't let Shelly suffer for her, too.

"Honey?"

Chris opened her eyes again to find that Sue stood before her with a cup of coffee in her hand.

"Come on, drink up. It's gonna be a long evening, and you don't look very good already."

Chris wanted to cry again. She wanted to beg

Sue's forgiveness for even, for a moment, wanting to suspect her. Hoping that it could even be Sue, who had never flagged in her support of Chris in all this, rather than herself. Rather than have that monster still alive inside her.

She should be relieved. There was a chance she hadn't really killed those people. That the madness she'd been sinking into had been someone else's.

It was still her fault.

Even if Elise—or whoever she was—was the murderer, she was doing it for Chris. To Chris. To get Chris's attention and give Chris some kind of message, to maybe pay her back for something she'd done years ago that she had no memory of.

Judgment is never escaped, her mother had always said. Maybe, somehow, it was true. Maybe she'd run to Los Angeles in the hopes that she'd outdistance not only what she'd suffered, what she'd done to her child, but whatever she'd done to this nameless, vague person.

Only she hadn't escaped anything. It had all been waiting for her back in Missouri, years later, lifetimes later. Chris accepted the cup into both hands and did her best to smile. "I guess you don't have anything to say about keeping secrets anymore," she accused gently.

Sue actually blushed. Dipped her head, just the way Victor did when he was confronted. "What was I supposed to say when I found out?" she demanded. "Oh, Chris, you and I have something in common? Remember the good old days?" She lifted those huge, babydoll eyes, and Chris saw the fresh tears of distress. "I didn't know what to say. I never worked on the halls. I was a secretary in medical records, and I hated every second I was there. I couldn't . . . couldn't get those case histories out of my mind, all those sad, sad stories."

"They were crazy people," Chris protested, self-protection long since found in sarcasm, "not crime victims."

Sue stared at her, outraged. "You were fourteen years old when you were hospitalized," she said in that mother's tone. Defending the defenseless, as always. "That's not exactly hardened criminal country."

Chris sipped at her coffee, the hot liquid scalding the pain that was already waiting in her chest. "But I was paying for my crimes."

"You were being treated. Just like everybody else. And don't forget, I saw all those case histories. Hundreds of them. And what I always felt was that they *were* the victims. Innocents unable to cope somehow with the madness around them."

Chris did smile now with genuine gratitude for her friend. "I wish I could have known you then," she admitted.

Sue smiled back, sincere and earnest. "Me, too."

"Curtis is missing, too," Mac announced as he stepped back out of his office.

Both women turned to him, their smiles discordant in the tense room.

"Inconsiderate of him," Harmonia intoned from where she was perched on the couch.

No one else paid any attention to her.

"She just wanted Shelly," Chris assured Mac. "It's a personal thing now. Curtis's safe somewhere. Try the hospital. Maybe the filling station."

"Why?"

She shrugged, uncomfortable with intuition. "I

don't know. It just seems right. What to do you want me to do?"

"Stay right here. As soon as I get to the scene I'm sending John back for you."

Chris almost dropped her coffee cup. "Don't be ridiculous. I'm not sitting here while she has Shelly. You know the way the story goes."

Mac nodded, completely in control. "Yeah, I do. You die. I'm not real interested in seeing that happen."

"You'd rather offer up Shelly?"

"I'd rather have everybody walk away intact. Now, I've been on the horn with Eldon and the highway patrol. We have the chopper and the dogs. Where should we look?"

Chris tried to think. She did her best to pull that story back up, the harsh, disjointed flood of guilt and desperation. The charred core of despair from which she'd spun her tale of salvation and resurrection. The path of her own redemption, the metaphoric act of her death at the hands of her conscience.

Except now, it could well be the very real thing.

"I think . . ." She paced, mug clenched, Mac and Sue forgotten as Chris forced up images and concepts she'd sublimated and displaced so well she'd become a best-selling author. "I'm not sure. It should be Fulton, or my house in Springfield. Back to a place where she . . . where I'd be most afraid. Where I'd been captured and cornered, and have to come back to face my truths . . ." She closed her eyes, clenched her courage to her and finished, knowing that neither of them would understand the weight of her words. "Back to the darkness."

"Fulton?" Mac countered. "You think she'd try and get there?"

When Chris opened her eyes, it was to find herself back at the front window, looking out onto her town, onto the simple, neat streets and familiar faces.

Even the town looked as weary as she, flagging beneath the clouds and dingy haze that looked like old hospital halls. The sun was setting, but that only sapped the light. There wouldn't be any reaffirmation tonight.

"Fulton's too far," Chris admitted, still looking. "She'd stay here. Maybe my house. Maybe the hospital. A nice figurative substitute."

"Then that's where we'll look."

"She's not stupid, Mac," Chris said, out to the flat, overcast sky. "She's been building her case for this moment, which means that she isn't going to give in without some kind of resolution."

She could hear Mac checking the clip in his gun. Heard him sliding shells into the shotgun he'd pulled from the gun closet. Wondered whether he was already chafing at that scar, and what it would cost him to walk into that hospital.

She wondered whether his hands had started to shake.

"I'm not stupid, either," he told her. "I'll have plenty of help. Now, you three stay here until John shows up. And keep the doors locked."

"Stay here?" Harmonia objected, jumping right to her feet. "And all those news people waiting for their meal?"

Mac stared at the woman, nonplussed. "I don't think they'll be there anymore," he offered diffidently.

Harmonia simply walked out.

Her act seemed to set off something in Mac. "Shit," he snapped, dropping his weaponry on the table and unclipping his mike. "The press. It's gonna look like a war game out there . . . John?"

John's voice came back right away. "Yeah, Chief."

"Tell Grover to get his men searching the woods north of Oz. I want every dog up there but one. And put the chopper up over Eleven Mile Road. Up by where Lawson's car went off the road."

There was a pause, a mutter of confused protest in the background. "What about me?"

"Meet me at the hospital. You and two of the state men and that dog. We'll head out from there."

"10-4."

Mac was rubbing the scar now, his movements taut and telling. "I've got to get the press away from that hospital," he said almost to himself as he reclipped his mike. "They think the search is concentrated around Oz, they may give us a little more chance to get the grounds searched before she finds out we've pegged her."

"What about me?" Chris asked, giving it one last try. "What's she going to do when you show up instead of me?"

Mac was picking his equipment back up again. "By the time we find her, John will have you out there already."

Chris turned on him one last time. "I can't be a bystander in this, Mac. You have to understand that."

Mac stopped just short of the front door. Faced her with solemn, quiet eyes that betrayed things Sue never noticed. Chris saw the apprehension there, the first betrayal of what he was going to face. Not just a madwoman, but the darkness in himself. She recognized, too, though, the new uncertainty. The fragile shoot of something growing in the midst of that desolation. It unnerved her. It also gave her the courage to step up.

"I have to know why," she said simply. "Please."

Mac didn't move. He stood before her, hands filled with radio and pump shotgun. In the distance, a siren moaned, and a car jumped the stoplight at the corner. Voices muttered outside the door. Sue waited in perfect silence.

"I promise," he said simply. "I just want to know where she is first."

Ten different tensions rose and released in her chest. Fifteen different emotions. Resolution. Answers. Sunlight after all this damn darkness. A walk through hell to get there. Chris did her best to maintain her composure in the face of his generosity.

"In that case," she offered, turning on her heel. "Don't put anybody at risk. Especially Shelly. Go into my house and get my parabolic mikes. Direction finders, body mikes. Whatever you need to find her. I'll wait right here for John."

Chris pulled her keys from the bottom of her purse and walked them over to tuck them into his shirt pocket.

"And be careful," she commanded, then did her best to grin. "I had to say it before Sue did."

With his hands full and his mind already on the search ahead of him, Mac paused long enough to bend over and give her a kiss. It wasn't much as kisses went. A simple declarative statement. For the first time in two weeks, Chris felt hope.

❖ ❖ ❖

Mac locked the city hall door behind him with a curious feeling of expectation. Anticipation. He hadn't enjoyed this kind of action since that night in Chicago. For a second before he turned for the back parking lot, Mac looked out into the waning afternoon. It was a miserable day, stale and heavy. The fresh green of spring was sapped by humidity and the sky had been soiled by pollution. He was starting to sweat just stepping out of the office. Even so, he could still smell the earth. The sweet scent of fresh-cut clover and the first perfume of flowers.

And he was looking forward to searching out that hospital. Even if his hands were shaking. Maybe things were beginning to look up after all.

"Oh, Chief, hello."

Halfway back into the police parking lot, Mac turned to find the Reverend Sweetwater at his elbow. "I'm a little busy right now, Reverend." He didn't stop moving. Sweetwater didn't seem to notice.

"I wanted to speak to you about young Allen," the minister insisted. "His mother came to me about these terrible rumors that have been circulating . . ."

The last thing Mac needed right now was a confrontation with Sweetwater. He just kept on walking, back toward the empty lot where the car sat in shadows. Overhead the highway patrol helicopter swept up toward Oz. Mac nodded instinctively, his mind already on the search. Now if only the news crews would take the bait. If only Chris understood when he used that fancy makeup kit of hers to dress somebody up in her place for the showdown.

"Chief, I don't think you appreciate what this is doing to do Allen and his family," Sweetwater insisted. "Do you know what a vicious allegation like that will do to that poor boy?"

That finally brought Mac to a halt a good fifteen feet from his car. "I'm pulling pictures of young girls out of that house, Reverend."

Sweetwater waved him off. "Then there's a perfectly good explanation somewhere. He's a faithful church member," he protested without even hearing Mac. "Everyone knows Allen. Why, his mother is an Elder. You can't just take the word of some anxious mothers and precocious girls over that of a contributing member of the community . . ."

Mac damn near missed the sound of the second helicopter when he heard Sweetwater's protest. "Word of what anxious mothers?"

"I'm sure they're just imagining things. That's what I told them when they came to me."

"When did they come to you?"

Sweetwater took a step back at the tone of Mac's voice. "Well, over . . . I mean . . . it was obviously a mistake. After all, Allen's been saved. I personally put up his bail money as a sign his Christian family believes him."

Mac counted to five to keep from hitting the minister. He wondered how long that little band of believers had been enabling Allen to practice his trade in peace. Finally there was nothing for him to do but get on with business.

"Better move out of the way," he snapped. "I'm going to be leaving now."

"But Chief . . ."

Mac shouldered past him without another word.

Sweetwater seemed to realize he'd overstayed his welcome because, with one final nod, he headed on back toward the street. Mac watched him go before opening the trunk of his unit. It would be nice if he could see some indication that the reverend felt the least bit responsible for protecting Allen. No such luck. He walked like a man without worry, safe in his convictions.

Guilt and redemption. Chris seemed to be the only one who really gave a damn about any of it.

"One-Alpha-Five to Chief MacNamara."

Mac unclipped his mike. "Yeah, John."

"Everybody's in position. You on your way?"

"I have one stop to make." He lifted an eye to that second chopper, this one from one of the television stations up in St. Louis. Good. At least he'd have a few clear minutes in the field. "Make sure everybody is ready to move on short notice. We're not interested in apprehension, just location. Got that?"

"Got it. See you in five."

"On my way."

Two satellite trucks careened around the corner without paying attention to most traffic laws. Mac didn't care. He was just relieved that they'd taken the bait, and that he could deal with Lawson, whoever she was, without having tungsten lights in his face. Reclipping his radio, he bent to drop his shotgun in the trunk.

He heard the footsteps approach and braced himself for another argument. Probably Harmonia Mae this time, crabbing about the noise.

Then, suddenly, the hairs on the back of his neck bristled.

Mac didn't even consider it. He just acted. Spinning around, he reached for his gun.

He never had a chance. Before he could even clear his holster, something blunt and heavy and cold slammed into the right side of his head. Fireworks exploded behind his eyes and the world outside tilted and dimmed. His last coherent thought before consciousness winked out in a sea of red pain was, Oh hell, not again.

"So, what do we do now?" Sue asked.

Chris kept her attention on the darkening streets. "We wait," she said, watching the street lamps flutter to life in the gray dusk. She was sweaty and stale, and the air conditioning was on. She couldn't imagine what it was like tromping out through the woods or climbing through the pipes in the subbasement of the hospital. Two helicopters roared overhead at about treetop level, and a couple of camera crews shot through town as if they were trying to beat them to the scene. Everybody wanted to be in on the action.

Everybody but her. She wanted to be somewhere else. Anywhere else. Anywhere but contemplating coming face to face with her own private nightmares. Exposing them for public consumption. Sharing them without benefit of anonymity or isolation.

"Well," Sue mused. "At least I know now why I didn't like her."

Silence settled again in the little room. Chris saw the swing of Mac's lights as he pulled out of the other end of the parking lot. She wished she could have stowed away in his car. She wished she could just open the door and walk on out after him. City hall was getting too small. Too close, with the humidity seeping through even the chug of the air-conditioning. She needed room. She needed to breathe. Something was going on. She could feel it dead center in her chest, and she couldn't do anything about it. She was stuck here in this tiny room with a baby-sitter to keep her sane.

Sane. That was a joke. She'd been tumbled around more than a surfer after a wipeout. There wasn't a chance in hell she'd come out of this whole. If she came out at all.

"What are you going to do?" Sue asked, as if privy to Chris's thoughts.

Chris never faced her. She was too busy facing the pictures she'd painted with words over fifteen years ago.

"I'm going to do whatever it takes to get Shelly out of there."

"But Mac said that if you follow the story . . . if *she* follows the story . . . that in the end, you get killed."

"It'd sure be simpler than facing all those cameras again."

Sue wouldn't have any of it. Stalking right up to Chris, she grabbed her by the arms and swung her around. "Not another word," she commanded, shaking Chris as if she were one of her own children. "You even consider doing something that stupid, and I won't let John within twenty feet of you."

Chris wanted so badly for Sue to understand. She wanted someone else to share the burden of grief and guilt and confusion. But Sue had only read those case histories. She'd never lived them. She would never quite understand the need to wash away the stain of sin. She'd never had her mother stand her in the middle of a church meeting, place her hand on her head, and proclaim to the congregation that a child who rejected the Lord was not worthy of her mother's love or forgiveness.

She'd never spent her teen years proving to the world that every horrible word her mother had ever uttered about her had been true, and then shattering because of it.

"I'm not going to be stupid," she assured her friend with every ounce of confidence she could muster. "But I am going to find out what I've done to warrant this. I want to know just what sin I'm being punished for. And that will mean talking to her. It'll mean, if I'm lucky, sitting down with her and convincing her to trade Shelly for me."

It would all come down to her own words. To a story she'd written as a way out of hell. And now, to keep her out, she had to remember it. To understand it.

. . . there, deep in the shadows, where her terror had risen to claim her, the pursuer, who had her own face, waited. Sighed with satisfaction, crouched in anticipation. Steel knife glinting in the harsh, stark light above. The knife of retribution. The instrument of sacrifice . . .

Deep in the shadows . . .

But Chris didn't think of the hospital as in the shadows. When she thought of it, she thought of sunlight. Of big windows looking out onto lawns and indirect lighting and the hush of crepe-soled shoes.

Shadows.

Darkness.

Chris ran back for the window. "Oh, shit."

But Mac was gone. Out of reach, approachable only by radio, and that would be suicidal for them all. It might already be too late already anyway.

"What?" Sue demanded as Chris whipped around and ran for Mac's office.

"It's not the hospital," Chris said, slamming into the cabinets. Rummaging through the closet. "I've got to let them know."

"Radio them," Sue suggested. "There are some extras back here."

Chris came up with one of them and hooked it over her own belt. "We can't," she disagreed, pulling a vest down off a hook. "She's been listening to everything that's been going on."

Sue looked around, obviously at a loss for answers. "How?"

Chris didn't exactly answer. She was thinking. Organizing. Praying.

No atheists in a foxhole, she thought distractedly as she tried to decide what to do. Oh, what the hell. Cover all bases, just in case.

She'd sent absolutely everyone in the wrong direction. It meant that Sandy wouldn't worry about being discovered just yet. It also meant . . .

"Sandy!"

"What?"

Chris laughed, her voice shrill, her heart suddenly slamming into her ribs. "Her name's Sandy," she admitted, amazed. "She was the same age I was. Killed both her parents because the voices told her to." She shook her head, the sudden revelations tumbling around with the implications. With the comprehensions. With the brand-new set of questions and problems. "I still don't know why she's doing this."

Chris piled all her booty on the desk and took a second to think. It didn't seem to help. She had to get close enough to find out just how Sandy had set things up. She had to get some kind of advantage. And then, she had to go in alone and face the nightmare she'd been having for the last fifteen years, just as she'd known all along she would.

Chris sucked in a steadying breath. She did her best to appear in control as she turned on her friend, who had never really had to deal with situations like this. She grabbed Sue by the arms and forced her to help.

"You need to get out to the hospital," Chris commanded. "Get to Mac. Tell him that Sandy isn't there. She's at the jail." Chris tried to take another breath, but just the word "jail" had already closed off her air. "That means she also has Marsha, maybe Elvis. And the only way she's going to let them go is to talk to me."

"You're not going there!" Sue protested.

Chris challenged her with a determination she didn't feel. "Nobody else is going to be able to get in that front door. Tell Mac I'm going to try and get Sandy back outside. Into some kind of range. Tell him. Now, get going, or we're going to be too late."

"I thought you said everybody else was safe," Sue said.

Chris shook her head, already sweating. Stomach churning. "Not at the jail. That's . . ." She could only shake her head again, words not able to convey the terrible power of those claustrophobic, suffocating cells. Beasts lived there, terrible truths, ancient evils. And Sandy, with her hypersaturated sense of reality, would be able to sense every one.

"Tell him that I'll get her out of the cell block. Tell him that."

Sue balked, her eyes wide with terror, her experience insufficient for this. "Chris . . ."

Chris knew better. "Go!" she shouted, giving the woman a good push.

She couldn't wait any longer. She wished for the time to carefully plan, to maybe concoct an act, a disguise to get her past the door. The outside world was ready to close in, though, and once it did Shelly would be forfeit. Chris had suspected that might be the case at the hospital. She knew it at the jail.

Why hadn't she understood? Why hadn't she admitted that Sandy would have chosen the door to Chris's own personal hell to act out the final chapter?

Because just the thought of stepping back over that threshold threatened to break her.

She'd have to face the dark.

She'd have to face the small, dank well of confinement.

She would have to face the demons those places awoke in her.

That was when she realized just how courageous a man Mac was. He had to face those demons every time he walked into a new situation, and yet he did it. Chris only had to do it once.

Only once.

But she knew there was only one way she could survive this at all, whether anybody died tonight or not. She had to move. She had to act, and this had given her her chance.

She waited long enough for Sue to get out. Then, before she could so much as consider what it was she was about to do, Chris went in search of her accuser.

✦ *Chapter 21* ✦

THE TOWN WAS so quiet. Chris imagined that everyone was probably watching the feeding frenzy up by Oz. She could hear the steady drone of helicopters, the sporadic whoop of sirens, the faint yap of bloodhounds. She just hoped that Sue had gotten to Mac so that he could keep everybody off her back until she got into the jail.

She'd thought she might actually catch up with him at her house when she went for the extra parabolic mike. He hadn't been there. He hadn't even stopped to pick up equipment. Maybe he'd wanted to coordinate with John first. Chris didn't wait long enough to wonder about it. Slipping inside with her spare keys, she grabbed her mike and ran.

Even with the streetlights on, the illumination was horrible. Some of them weren't working, and a couple that were flickered feebly. At any other time something to worry about. Tonight, a definite benefit. With the darkness quickly falling, maybe her tricks would work. Maybe nobody would catch her. Maybe Sandy wouldn't notice her until Chris was ready.

Chris wished she could have taken care with her

disguise. She had all the equipment necessary to pull off a professional job. A little spirit gum, some facial hair and a short wig, maybe glasses and a mole or two. Nobody looked at old men on the street, and at Chris's height, it would have been an easy identity to pull off. She'd had to settle for stuffing her hair into a fedora and wearing Mac's long raincoat instead. There was nothing for it but to hope that it would keep her unidentifable enough for the time she needed. That it would help camouflage the extras she carried with her.

The mike was a godsend. A small hand-held unit that could pick up sounds inside the sheriff's office and the jail block. That way she could pinpoint location, identify occupants. Prevent surprises. She hoped.

She was so scared. Furious with impatience, terrified of movement. Sweating and nauseated and certain that any moment Victor was going to walk up and ask what character she was pretending to be out behind the sheriff's office.

At least Eldon's wife was gone. The lights were out in the sheriff's house, the missus down at the Methodist church for a meeting.

Chris swiped at the perspiration on her forehead and set up position in the side parking lot by the jail. Safely in a tunnel of shadow, out of the range of windows, with an eye toward the front of the office at the other end to prevent surprises.

Setting the sensitivity, she tuned the mike in toward the cell block. At her hip, the radio crackled faintly with ongoing news from the hospital. News that Sandy was also privy to at the dispatcher's office not ten feet from the cells.

Breathing. Chris caught it on her first sweep, harsh and uneven, struggled for. Right by the back of the jail, echoing faintly. Inside one of the cells.

Chris's stomach fed on empty fear. It can only get so bad, she kept telling herself. Only so bad. Even so, she heard the rasp of her own breathing. She tasted bile.

Another person. Slower, steady, quiet breathing only a few feet farther on. Not deep. Careful. Awake.

Chris crept along the wall with its barbed-wire fence until she reached the sheriff's window. The lights were on, but the blinds were closed. Nothing to see, but she heard something there, too. A funny whimper and a sigh. One person or two? she wondered.

She tried very hard to hear more, but one of the helicopters roared overhead and drowned out the sound. Chris instinctively looked up to see a television logo. Held her own breath. She was sure they'd caught on somehow. She waited in agony for the spotlight to flash on, for it to pin her on her circle of asphalt like a bug in a flashlight.

They flew on, though, swooping over the next ridge and disappearing. Evidently they'd grown tired of the search or were low on gas.

Chris breathed again, took another swipe at the rivulets that had begun to trace their way down her temples. There were others snaking along the small of her back. Under her arms. She wasn't going to make this. She just couldn't face it.

Temptation whispered. Wait for Mac. He can handle everything. You're pretty sure you know where they are. Let somebody else brave those awful, empty places. Somebody who doesn't see terrors in the darkness. Who doesn't remember voices and heavy hands and formless terror.

If she did that, though, she'd never know. She'd never find out why. Sandy would give Chris her answer. She might not give someone else the chance to ask.

"We've found her," came the voice from the radio on Chris's hip.

Chris started at the sound. Certain again that she'd been heard. That somebody had read her mind and, this time, meant to answer. Holding perfectly still, she looked down for her answers.

John's voice came on, small and tinny. "Where?"

"Down in the basement. Her and Curtis. She's a little shaken up, but she's fine."

Shaken up? What did they mean? Could Chris have been wrong? Could she have just heard Elvis sleeping off a sugar jag in the back? Could there really have been a reprieve?

"This is Sheriff Tipett. Chief there?"

Chris waited through the static-filled pause. It seemed that the town waited, hushed and heavy, the air thick with anxiety, the hesitation pulsing with the wash of distant rotors. Chris was sure everyone could hear the faint conversation issuing from beneath Mac's coat. She was sure most of all that Sandy could, sitting there in the dark with her knife at Shelly's throat.

Because no matter what she heard or hoped, Chris knew somewhere deep where her instincts lived that she was still in the right place.

"Uh, not right now, Sheriff . . ." John again. "We have the Axminster girl here, though."

Chris heard her own gasp. They had Shelly?

"And the suspect?"

"Negative. We're still searching. Chief wants you to, too."

Chris couldn't breathe. She couldn't think. If they had Shelly, who did Sandy have in there? What sacrifice had she prepared with her terrible knife?

Over the parabolic mike she heard the moan. Soft, hurt, echoing just a little. She recognized it. And she knew.

Her hands shook. Fury and fear clotted in her throat until she thought she would choke. Shelly had been a decoy. Sandy had orchestrated this moment with the precision of a choreographer. All that was left was for Chris to show up.

And she had no choice but to do it.

She had to go in. Now. Alone. She had to face whatever waited in those haunted little cells. Had to face the worms of madness that squirmed in her own cells of penitence.

With cold, clammy hands Chris reached up to remove her hat. She turned for the front of the sheriff's office, the main entrance to the jail where Sandy would be. She stepped up to the platform of her own execution knowing that even a glittering knife in the darkness wouldn't be as awful as what she was about to face.

The office was empty. The coffeemaker was on, the dregs burning away at the bottom and filling the room with a thick, acrid odor. The TV was tuned to CNN, and the dispatch screen was scrolled with calls, times received, times answered. The last time was twenty minutes earlier.

The radio crackled and muttered with all the calls that were being routed to different channels among the search teams out on the mountain and at the hospital seven miles down the road. The phone rang suddenly and went on ringing, unanswered. Chris had left the front door unlatched, and it swung open a little, letting in more stifling night air.

Chris wondered if Sue had reached John instead. She wondered whether John would be able to know what to do. She hoped he'd be able to save Mac's life. She wasn't at all sure Sandy would let her do it. She wasn't sure the rest of that crowd out there would give anybody the time to do it once they realized who was waiting in the sheriff's office where the dispatcher wasn't answering her phone.

Chris could smell her. Something feral, musty, like a stalking animal waiting in a lair. Back in the jail. Beyond the barely opened door where the lights had somehow gone out. Chris fought to stay silent. Battled back the bubbling terror like a lone survivor with her arms out against a flooding tide.

Sandy waited for her back there. Sandy with the answers Chris knew she didn't want. With the judgment she couldn't avoid.

Chris turned to the sheriff's office instead. Carefully twisted the knob and pushed the door open.

Marsha and Elvis looked up with identical terror in their wide eyes. Marsha's mascara had run down her gaunt cheeks. Elvis had a little smear of blood along his neck. Chris wondered whether his or somebody else's. They were both bound and gagged. Chris lifted a finger to her lips for silence and slid a knife from the sheath at her wrist. It took three quick swipes to cut the curtain cords that bound them. It took another silent warning to keep them from going right for their gags.

Chris motioned rather than spoke. She instructed them to get the hell out and leave the rest to her. She let them know she knew where the danger was. She wasn't about to let them know what she was going to do about it.

They did their best to keep silent as they crept for the front door. Chris knew they were heard. She also knew it didn't matter. They weren't part of the ritual. At least, not yet. And by the time they got help, it would be too late to make a difference anyway.

Chris got one more piece of information from Marsha before the dispatcher fled. Mac wasn't bound. He was handcuffed. Chris would have to try and deal with it when she could.

She waited for the fading staccato of footsteps before turning back to her original goal.

It was hot in the office. Oppressive, the air old and congealed and prescient. It was so still, as if the molecules had stopped moving in anticipation of the confrontation. Chris imagined she could hear that careful breathing in the darkness, that coiled, waiting entity that for so long had lived only in her nightmares.

For just a moment, she squeezed her eyes shut. Leaned against the wall. Dropped her head and fought the overwhelming urge to run. Then with hands that shook as if she'd just discovered Dinah on her couch all over again, Chris pushed open the door into the jail.

Silence.

Empty, harsh silence. Chris reached around and flipped the switch for the overhead lights.

Nothing. She stood outlined in the doorway, her eyes trying to adjust to a blackness so deep it seemed she'd tumble right into it and never stop falling. She clutched at the rough cold stone of the wall with slippery hands and battled the terror.

"Mac?" she called quietly, her voice echoing flatly into the emptiness. Reverberating with the old echoes that waited there. The faint shrieks and moans and mutters, her own voice added to the echoes of decades. Suddenly she couldn't tell the difference anymore. She wasn't sure she knew which nightmare she was stepping into.

"Mac?" she whispered again, her voice raw as grief. "Mac, please answer me."

The voice that came out of the darkness was quiet, calm. "He's here."

Chris clutched harder, closed her eyes, opened them. Prayed for help. For . . . she didn't know what she could possibly pray for. She was at the brink of hell. It was too late to hope for redemption.

"Back in the dark," the voice continued evenly.

"No . . . please . . ."

"It's what you asked for. What you've planned ever since we walked away from that place." Such a seductive voice, sounding so reasonable, so assured. "You want to look in the dark, Christian. But you can't do it alone. You can't face the truth without me."

Whispering out of the blackness, out of the memories of madness and despair.

Chris teetered on the brink of hysteria, caught there like a wild thing between the darkness and the light. She wanted to laugh, to scream and run and fall down frothing with the insanity of it.

"There is no truth," she insisted instead, her voice louder now, edged with the steel of defiance.

"Of course there is," the voice answered as if it

were Chris's own voice. Her own conscience come back to pay a final visit, echoing through the blackness like memory through her own skull. Faint, certain, so damnably reasonable. "It's why you've written your books. Why you've asked over and over again what it is that corrupts the soul to murder. I told you once, do you remember?"

Chris physically swayed with the pull of that voice, with the growing conviction that there really wasn't someone mortal attached to it. She sucked in a harsh breath, trying desperately to retrieve her shards of reality.

In the dark.

In the close, hot dark where monsters lived.

Where the world had disappeared in blinding, flashing seizures of electricity.

"I don't . . . all I remember is the . . . the dark, the fear, the smells . . . I remember . . ."

She couldn't. She couldn't survive this. The pictures had resurrected in the darkness. The shuddering of memory, disjointed, terrifying, humiliating. Faster and faster, threatening to overtake her. The awful moments of panic here when she'd lost control. When the blackness had closed in on her like the lid of a coffin, like earth on a grave, and she'd spat and shrieked and bucked. When she'd tried to bite Mac for holding her still for the needle.

Other memories, older, clearer than ever as if the darkness were the only place to allow them, bits and moments of memories that only served to stir the maelstrom of terror in her chest.

"What? What do you remember?"

Chris closed her eyes to escape the darkness and found only more. "Crying," she whispered on a ragged breath, tears splashing against her shaking hand. "Just sitting huddled over in the corner crying."

"Do you know why?"

She shook her head, even if no one could see, her eyes still closed. "No."

"Then we're not finished."

Chris shook her head, knowing the words. Knowing the next act.

"You can't have him, Sandy."

"Then you do remember me."

"I remember you."

"I'm glad. I thought for a while you hadn't. That all you'd meant to me had been lost, even after I'd waited for so long to find you again. After I'd planned and worked, even before you found me at the Ritz."

"The Ritz?"

"Of course. That first time, when you made the best-seller list and you and your agent were celebrating, and I was your waitress. You were sent to me so I could know that you hadn't completed the lesson. So I could read your books and know what you still needed. I took that second job with the police so I could keep track of how well I was doing, but it was worth it. It was all worth it, don't you think? Don't you think I did a good job?"

"You did a good job," Chris found herself saying, and then realized she'd said that before. Often, endlessly, back in the days when darkness had ruled.

Cards. Chris saw it again. The ragged, tooth-scarred deck with the jacks missing that she and Sandy had played with because there was nothing else to do. Poker, gin, anything, just to make the time go by. Always with a price, praise for the girl with the broken glasses, reassurance for the child with pleading eyes.

"Would you like me to sacrifice him for you?" the woman who had murdered her own parents asked. The woman who as a girl had bitten her own arms and waited by Chris's bed to make sure she was all right.

"I want to see him," Chris demanded.

It was getting harder to breathe. To think. To keep it all straight in her head. The terror swirled in her, red and hot and virulent. She could taste the familiar musk of atavism on her tongue. The beast at her core waiting to leap.

"No," her conscience answered. "He's here with me."

"I have to see . . ." Chris gulped in air, losing control. "I mean, how do I know there aren't . . ."

"Monsters?" So quiet, so sure. So sane sounding in the roiling, rank darkness. "No monsters, Christian. Just people. Always has been. You just never understood that. It's why you never figured out why they locked you away."

With the last of her courage, Chris took a step in. "And you . . . did?"

"Of course. I was in because I saw the truth. I saw that people were the monsters and I killed them. You were in, of course, for the exact opposite. You couldn't kill the monsters. I've tried to illustrate that for you."

"I want . . . to see him." Cool, coarse, hand-hewn granite against her fingers. Stifling miasma of old despair and older fear in her nose. Chris did her best to approach the voices. All the voices.

Suddenly, a light speared into the blackness. A flashlight in Sandy's hands. It flickered like a poltergeist and etched shadows into her pasty face as she stepped out of one of the cells. Limp brown hair, avid eyes, small, pointed teeth. The face of madness.

She stood at the edge of the far cell, dirty and rumpled in a police uniform. Thrumming with the energy of purpose. With the adrenaline of delusion. The very vision of every nightmare Chris had ever had. The light glinted off the hunting knife in her hand.

"Why him?" Chris asked her, hands carefully at her sides, coat flapping open just a little, heart hammering.

Sandy smiled, and Chris saw what she hadn't in fifteen years. She saw the terrible, childish insanity. The vulnerable malice that fueled destruction. "You thought it would be the girl, didn't you?" She shook her head. "Couldn't be. She didn't believe you. The sacrifice had to be worthy. What more worthy than the man who'd risk his career for you?"

"He's not going to die," Chris said as certainly as she could. Eyes on Sandy, the light, any light better than the night. Her chest burned with fear; her lungs struggled for air. She balanced herself right on the edge of sanity and stepped forward.

Sandy's smile grew. "Then you're willing to die for him."

Chris nodded carefully. "Yes. Let him out."

A shake of the head. "Not until it's over. You know that."

"Then let me say good-bye. You can let me have that."

That blank face puckered a little. "It's not the way it's written."

Chris lifted her hands out to her side in supplication. "Please." It took every ounce of control in her, but she kept her eyes on Sandy rather than the small square of blackness to her right. To where she could hear Mac's breathing.

Finally Sandy swung the light. "OK."

Chris retrieved her hands. Stuffed them in the coat pockets. Drew in a few more shaky breaths. Took the necessary steps closer to that gleaming, deadly blade in order to reach Mac.

In order to step into that awful little hole where over a century of misery remained embedded in the walls.

It closed in on her. Weighted her down until she couldn't breathe at all. Whispered to her in familiar voices, in voices she'd never known, old voices, sad voices, terrible, despairing voices.

She turned into the cell and bent to where Mac was slumped against the wall.

"What did you do?" Chris demanded, seeing the blood that gleamed blackly along the side of his face. His eyes were closed, his face as pale as death.

"He kept waking up. I couldn't risk letting him go. Not before you got here."

Chris couldn't believe she could be more terrified. Mac's slack features did it. She'd been counting on him to help himself. To get himself away while she dealt with Sandy. Suddenly Chris wasn't sure he was going to make it out of this cell alive at all.

"Mac?" She lifted a hand to his forehead, to find it cold. Clammy. God, what was she going to do? He was curled up in the corner, his hands cuffed behind him, his shirt stained with his own blood and the side of his head swollen. "Mac, it's Chris. Come on . . ."

Nothing. Just that stertorous breathing. She wanted to shake him, to scream at him, that he was the only one who was going to prevent this from ending in a massacre. Sandy was primed for it, Chris could tell. She could see it in those flickering, hot eyes of hers, in the spasmatic movements of her body. Smelled it in the heat that shimmered from her. Chris's blood wasn't going to be enough. And Chris had depended on Mac to help everybody else. Especially himself.

She'd wanted answers. She didn't have time anymore.

"You've seen him . . ."

Chris whipped around, fury dimming even the terror. "You're going to have your resolution, damn it. Let me have mine!"

And then, crumpling as if it were too much for her to bear, she threw herself onto Mac's still form.

"I'm doing it for you," Sandy protested behind her. "Haven't you figured that out yet? All for you. I've been planning and working for this day ever since you wrote that first story . . . since you decided to devote yourself to understanding. How could I do anything but help?"

Chris left tears on Mac's cheek and straightened with his blood on hers. She also left behind a gun and an unlocked set of cuffs. Sandy didn't see them. Chris didn't know if what she'd managed would help. She simply couldn't leave Mac helpless like this.

She couldn't continue to play Sandy's game at the expense of his life.

Straightening, she faced that half-seen face in the echoing darkness. She saw Mac's blood on the sleeve of the coat and knew a fear that swept away delusions. He was going to die if she didn't do something. If she didn't do something fast.

"All right," she said, facing her accuser, her friend, her personal demon. "I'm here. In the dark. Don't you think it's time we got on with it?"

Sandy's face actually fell a little. "You still don't get it, do you?"

"Why?" Chris demanded stepping forward, forcing Sandy a little farther back. Away from the cell. From Mac. "Why have you done this?"

The knife lifted, deadly and long. Sharp as retribution, the light gathering and sparking against its steel. "To show you," she insisted.

"To show me what? To tell me what?"

"Why," Sandy insisted, her eyes flickering in the light like the knife. Dark eyes, black eyes with the random, deadly lightning of madness in them. "Why," she repeated, straightening, stepping carefully back over the threshold into the hallway. "Just like you asked."

"Why what?" Chris shrilled, desperate, suddenly certain that this was the most important thing. "What did I do to you to deserve this?"

"You were my friend!"

It stopped her. Deep into the cell block, where the darkness was so thorough, where the only light had been shredded by the grillwork on the high, small windows. Inches from her foe, from her nightmare, from her friend.

Cards.

No one else had played cards with Sandy. No one else had even talked to the girl, the sad, sorry girl who had spent her days trailing Chris like a puppy and her nights trying to inflict new pain on herself.

Who had killed her parents because they had so grievously assaulted her.

Chris had felt sorry for her.

Even battling her own sanity, even struggling to maintain a toehold on reality behind those terrible, high walls, she'd felt sorry for the whey-faced girl who had eviscerated her own mother.

"Why?" Chris asked, the tears welling again. "Why hurt me if I was your friend?"

Sandy took a step closer, eyes hot and anxious. "To help you know. To help you remember what you couldn't."

"I didn't want to remember!"

"You did! You did, or you wouldn't have written all those books."

"I wrote those books to get past it!" Chris cried, sobbing, hands at her chest to keep the loathing from escaping, from staining her shirt and burning her. "To finally get away from that place!"

"But you can't until you face it," Sandy insisted. "Until you face me. And you didn't even know me. You didn't even recognize the face of your own mirror."

"So you had to kill my friend?"

"You needed me to. I knew when you didn't recognize me that it wasn't just memory you wanted. It was expiation. Redemption. Cleansing."

"Why?" Chris screamed, shaking and desperate. Feeling the weight press on her again. Smelling the terrible fear that seeped from her. "Because I murdered my baby?"

"No!" Sandy screamed back. "Because your mother murdered your baby!"

Chris never heard her own strangled cry. She

never saw the knife rise. The darkness exploded on her, the madness. Shattering the night into a million fragments, pictures and sounds and smells, overwhelming her, forcing her down to her knees. To the position of supplication, of abjection.

Of sacrifice.

Chris didn't see what Sandy was doing until the knife struck home.

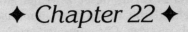

✦ Chapter 22 ✦

THE IMPACT OF the knife knocked Chris completely over. Pain exploded in her chest and took her breath. The darkness shuddered with dancing lights and agony.

Above her, Sandy shrieked. "You lied!" she accused, her voice suddenly high and terrible. "You lied, you lied, you lied! You weren't ready to die for him!"

For a second Chris couldn't even focus on the vague blur of white over her head. She was trying to get her breath back from the force of that blow. She was trying to pull sense out of the swirling madness. All her plans, her precautions had been lost in one terrible sentence.

"She didn't," Chris gasped, curling in to protect herself. Feeling the tear in the protective vest. Struggling to get her breath back.

"You lied!" Sandy screamed again, reaching down to grab Chris by the collar and yank her back up. "You said you were ready to die!'

Chris fought to regain her balance. She fought for air. She fought for reason. "Please . . . I can't . . ."

The knife struck again, lethal and swift, slicing along her arm on its descent to her stomach. The power behind the thrust was immense, the aim deflected by Kevlar. Chris grunted, struggled to get free. To get clear of that knife, to escape those terrifying eyes.

"My whole life!" Sandy screamed, shaking her again, "I've given my whole life to you, following you, learning you, disciplining my mind to work in tandem with yours so I could paint your pictures for you, so I could give you what you wanted. And you deny me?"

"Because you didn't explain!" Chris shouted with the last of her breath. She felt her feet beneath her. Struggled to get them into position to lift her out of Sandy's grasp. "I don't believe you."

Sandy pulled tighter on the collar, bunching material in her fist and cutting off Chris's air, cutting off her escape. The knife winked at her in the diffused light from the fallen flashlight.

Sandy's eyes were wild, glittering. She panted with the effort to remain in place. Her fingers curled like talons and her breath smelled like old metal, as if she'd been tasting blood. Chris fought a surge of nausea. She brought her hands up to claw at the clothing that cut off her air. She shuddered with the impact of exploding madness.

Chris had seen it before, the sudden, terrifying detonation of insanity. From silence to shrilling, screeching terror. From reason to the hurtling, howling kaleidoscope of delusion. It reverberated around her, a hot wind of dementia completely unpredictable, awesomely dangerous. It battered at her like a physical blow, like the knife thrusts. It sucked her in and spun her around, she who was no real stranger to the episode herself.

"I don't believe you," she insisted on a strangled breath, her chest on fire, her gut heaving, her black, blank memory tumbling with undefined sensations.

Sandy leaned so close Chris could smell the sweat on her, could almost taste that acrid scent of madness that clung to her like a foul wash.

"It's why you're crazy," the woman accused in a funny singsong voice. "Because you don't believe. Because you won't believe. Because you turn away from everything that is righteous and holy and have to be punished for it . . . punished . . . punished, like the fires of hell, eternal and scorching and never-relenting . . . punished . . ."

Her mother's voice. Chris heard it coming out of this madwoman's mouth, the cadence, the words, the awful, damning disdain. Chris shuddered with its impact. She sobbed with its import.

"You don't know her," she insisted brokenly, her hands hooked around her captor's. Her throat clogged with terrible sobs. "She was never there . . . she never came to see me."

"She came to judge you," Sandy insisted, shaking Chris like a rag doll. Bringing the knife so close Chris could see her own blood on it. "She came right there, close, bending down to your bed like a mother tucking in a child, when you were still so quiet, and she told you. She told you . . . she told you and I listened, and I knew . . ."

Chris tried to shake her head, even her own culpability easier to bear than this. "No, no, she wouldn't . . . not even she . . ."

"God's righteous judgment, child . . . that you

should bear the stain of your awful sin, that your pro-
fane whelp should die, that you bear the responsibility
. . . your sin . . . your judgment . . . your sin . . ." She
clutched tighter, hands like steel, eyes wild, tear-filled,
sorry and triumphant. "It's what you wanted," Sandy
whispered in her own voice. "What you wanted . . .
because you couldn't live with what she did . . ."

Chris made one more try for her throat, the world
beginning to pulsate in her ears. "No," she begged,
suddenly not sure. Suddenly terrified that she would
die in this reeking, echoing darkness with her own
mother's voice in her ears and her ghost's face the
only one she could see. "Please . . ."

The knife lifted this time. Sandy whirled Chris
around, grabbed her by the chin, lifted her head.
Chris fought. She kicked and bucked and clawed.
Struggled to get at the gun she'd hidden away, the
one she'd thought she wouldn't need. The one she
couldn't reach.

"Can't have that kind of scandal . . . good . . .
church . . . members . . ."

Chris lifted her hands to deflect the knife. She
sobbed out in desperation. She struggled against a
woman who had the strength of ten. And she lost.

She heard the howl. She thought it was Sandy's.
She closed her eyes. Waited the heartbeat for the
cold slice of the knife. She felt Sandy jerk upright.
She heard the knife descend. Felt its touch, and then,
suddenly a thudding impact.

Mac.

Chris heard something snap. She heard Sandy's
shrill howl of anguish at the interference. She heard
the feral cry from Mac when he made contact with
the woman.

The three of them slammed into the wall together. They spun away and landed on the floor. Chris saw a tumbled image of faces, heard the stunned grunts of contact. Desperately fought for air and balance and action.

Mac was ahead of her. Even as his gun clattered against the corner, he threw himself at Sandy, shoving her to the floor beneath him. His shirt soaked in blood, his face half recognized, he snarled and struggled and wrestled with the madwoman who still had the knife.

"Get it," he rasped, atop a bucking, screaming Sandy.

Chris scrambled to her feet, her chest screeching in protest. She dove for the outstretched arm and slammed it into the concrete. Sandy bucked them both off.

"Vengeance is mine!" her cry echoed from the tight walls. Her body bolted upright. Her knife hand aimed right for Chris's face.

Chris finally got hold of her own gun just as Mac tackled Sandy at the knees. "Goddamn it, stay down," he commanded, shoving his head right into her solar plexus.

Sandy grunted, went down, lost the knife. Struggled to get up. Chris scrambled across the floor for either weapon. Came up with them both. Stuffed them into the pockets of her coat.

Mac ducked his head to keep his face away from those terrible claws. Sandy was trying to scratch his eyes out. She was trying to rip his throat out with her bare hands.

"I have . . . have to . . . save her!"

"Not today," he panted. "Chris, get help."

"But Mac . . ."

"Get it!"

Chris struggled to her feet and then slid in a puddle of something. She tried to run for the door and only managed a disorganized little limp. It seemed so far away. She was having such trouble keeping it in focus suddenly, keeping her body in motion.

Behind her Sandy howled again, a high, fearsome wail of panic and fury, and Mac began to murmur to her, trying to calm her, trying to get control. Chris reached the door and pushed it all the way open. She saw the blood on her hand, all down her arm, but it didn't register. She ran for the radio.

It was too late for courtesy. "John!" she screamed into the mike. "The jail! Help!"

And then she slid again, the pool of liquid on the floor somehow following her.

Her sense of time must have been funny, because it seemed that no sooner had she screamed than the door blew open. Bodies poured through, all of them in uniforms, bristling with guns, mouths open in a dull roar of aggression.

"Help him," she begged, not understanding why she was on her knees. "He's back there . . ."

Tom. Right behind all those uniforms. Anxious and harried and in a hurry.

"Mac's . . . Mac's hurt . . ." she told him, spinning, struggling to even stay on her knees.

"So are you," he said, and suddenly she was looking up at the ceiling. Then she wasn't looking at anything, because the room and the noise and the terror eased away into blackness.

❖   ❖   ❖

Mac thought his head was going to explode. His chest hurt. His arms hurt. He couldn't see anything at all from one eye, which was probably the only thing preventing double vision.

He wasn't going to make it. He heard the thunder of footsteps out in that office and still knew it would be too late. His strength was vanishing. He was conscious by a thread, and the woman screaming and battling him was as strong as five people.

It didn't matter, though. He'd gotten Chris out of there. He'd made up at least a little for getting blindsided.

"Get some light in here!" John barked, slamming the door open on his way through. He cursed when he slid on something and righted himself against the wall. Mac couldn't afford to pull his attention away long enough to notice. "Mac?"

Lawson made another stab for his eyes. Mac was slowing down so badly that he damn near let her. And then there was a herd of men in the room. Shotguns being racked, pistols pulled. Mac felt the hands take her from him. Felt more hands pull him back and up and away. Heard the reverberating screech of the woman he'd known as Elise Lawson, now fighting off five men. Saw the sudden explosion of light into the room and blinked blearily.

"Jesus Christ!" John gasped, taking over for one of the sets of hands that held Mac up. "Somebody get the doc in here!"

"The doc's busy where he is!" Mac heard. And then he saw the blood. Everywhere, splattering the whitewashed walls like an exploded balloon. Pooling on the floor, seeping through his pants legs and along the sleeves of his shirt. An explosion of blood.

"Then get the paramedics!" John demanded, and Mac could see the fear in his sergeant's eyes. "Mac, man, lie down. You're . . ."

Mac knew perfectly well what he was. Suddenly it didn't matter. He had to get out and find out just what Tom Clarkson had meant. He had to follow the trail of blood that led out into the office.

"Lie down!" John insisted.

Mac threw off the hands and stumbled for the front. He slid on the blood and grabbed onto the wall right next to Chris's handprint. He didn't even feel the hands still on him as he tripped up into the office.

Chris was sprawled out on the floor right by the console. The brand new linoleum beneath her was stained, the stain spreading. Tom had the coat open, had the vest open, had his fingers in a hold in her neck.

"Oh, God . . ."

Hands red and glistening, Tom spared him a look. "Shit!" he snapped, "will somebody make that stupid son of a bitch lie down? And get the fuckin' paramedics in here!"

"You want Heilerman's on standby?" one of the men asked as somebody caught Mac on the way to the floor.

"No," Tom retorted, his hands full of silver clamps and his best shirt full of blood. "I don't fucking want Heilerman's. I want these people to make it!"

Mac closed his eyes for just a minute, fought a wave of nausea, battled back the darkness that threatened to overtake him. He ended up wedged against the wall, much as he had back in that black, cold little cell. This time, though, the lights were on.

The knife was being lifted from the floor by one of the sheriff's men and the bad guy was under about half a ton of law enforcement.

"She gonna be all right?" he managed to ask, blinking to stay in focus.

Tom didn't bother to look up. "Since I happen to be one of the few country doctors who interned at Cook County Hospital, I'd say yes. Knifings are my specialty." He did look up then. "And you're next."

Mac didn't have to look down to see. He could feel the fire of deep cuts. He tasted the blood on his tongue and smelled the sickly sweet, coppery bouquet of it. As familiar to a Chicago cop as car exhaust and the lake.

"You need any help?"

Tom's reaction was instantaneous. "From a *cop?*" Then he looked up and must have seen the expression in Mac's eyes. He backed right down with a smile that made Mac think of Sue. "It'll be all right," was all he'd say, sounding just like a parent.

Mac sat like a lump and didn't know how to ask for more.

He almost hadn't made it in time. Crumpled in that black, black corner, he'd been a mass of pulpy protoplasm without so much as a coherent thought. A mass of pain and nausea and confusion that only managed to move when he realized that it was Chris's voice out there come to save him. Chris who was about to offer herself up.

He almost hadn't hauled himself together in time to save her. And if that had happened, he might just as well have crawled right back into that little corner and let the lights go out again.

Thirty police in half a dozen different uniforms

milled around the room. Outside the copters thumped in syncopation, and a couple of tungsten lights flashed on. There were questions waiting. There was publicity and outrage and salacious curiosity to be salved. But for right now Mac was content to lie half-sprawled against the wall and watch Tom work his magic.

"She told me to wait," John protested, his young face crinkling into concern as he crouched in front of Mac. "That she was going to get her out of the jail."

"She tried," Mac allowed, thinking how much more pleasant it would all be if he could just pass out, too. Then he caught sight of a beefy figure in the crowd. "JayCee?"

"Yeah, Chief."

"You're fired." Everybody stopped dead in their tracks. Mac decided that he didn't have to explain. He didn't have the energy to, anyway. From the back room, the howling echoed on like a bad scene from a John Carpenter movie. "So, what do you think, Tom? Fifty of Thorazine?"

Tom grunted unhappily. "That'd be an hors d'oeuvre in there. We're talking well into three figures. That's if I don't just lose my temper completely and use a baseball bat. By the way, there are two guns here. Didn't either of you think to use one of them?"

Now was not the time to go into details. "It all happened kind of quick."

At the door, the sea parted, and the paramedic crew slid their gurney through. And stopped, obviously not sure who to head for first.

"Over here," Tom snapped, then offered Mac one more assessing look. "Is this it?" he demanded, his eyes no longer flip at all. "Is it over now?"

Mac felt the mists gather. He realized that the voices outside were no more than buzzes, and that the lights had begun to fade. He smiled. "Almost," he said, thinking of what he'd heard in there. "Almost."

And then he refused to answer any more questions at all.

✦ *Epilogue* ✦

SHE WENT TO Dinah's memorial service after all. Pale and unsteady and wearing a turtleneck dress with long sleeves to hide all the fresh stitches, Chris sat between Trey and Sue, while the magazines took shot after shot of America's latest news item. The remembrances were irreverent, the emotions heart-felt, the surprise revelations ignored. Just another chapter in the hottest story to hit news, entertainment, and literature in a decade. Before, Chris wouldn't have had the nerve to show up. Now she simply ignored the attending commotion and paid her respects to her old friend and mentor. And then, with Sue still hovering over her like a suspicious nanny, she got on the plane and came home to Pyrite.

It was supposed to be late spring. Unfortunately in Missouri there is no such season. The temperatures had a firm hold on the nineties and the flowers fared well only in the shade. The hills were thick with foliage, the helicopters busy looking for new stands of marijuana, and Truman High was gearing up for the prom. Life went on.

"Are you sure you're up for this?" Sue demanded.

Chris didn't bother to look up from where she was folding a hot-pink-and-green T-shirt for her overnighter. "I just got back from New York," she retorted.

Tired. She was tired. Too much time off her feet, too little privacy, too deep a grief. It had been nice of Dinah's family to wait on the memorial service until she'd been out of the hospital. Even so, she hadn't been out long. She still ached in funny places, still gauged the blood she needed by her easy fatigues.

It was going to get better, she knew it. For the first time she could remember, she was sleeping. Really resting without benefit of nightmares or suspicions or sudden surprises. She was able to walk back into her house without vomiting. She'd never live there again. But at least she wouldn't fear it.

And somewhere in that little dance in the darkness, she'd lost her overwhelming claustrophobia. A good thing, considering what she had in store for her today.

Not all better by any means. But working that way.

"New York's not the same as this," Sue protested, sincerely distressed. "Not the same at all."

"Even so," Chris said, "I have to be there. I have to have the closure, or it's not going to have been worth anything."

Sue threw up her hands in frustration. "I give up. Both of you teetering around like plague survivors, and you're gonna drive across the state. Go ahead. Get into a major accident. Lose all the blood this town donated for you and see if they care."

Chris couldn't help but laugh. "If we get into an

accident, *People* Magazine will come interview you
again and Ellen can sing "Tomorrow" for them," she
promised.

Sue glowered at her. "It's not funny."

"What do you mean it's not funny? It's hysterical.
Pyrite is the new norm in quaint middle-America. Ray
is being considered for a senate seat, Victor's doing
Letterman, and Harmonia Mae has been proposed to
by a miner from Alaska who thought she looked
handsome on the *Entertainment Weekly* special. And
you say that's not funny?"

"You could have died!" Sue snapped, her eyes filling, her posture frustrated. "Both of you, damn it.
You didn't see what that place looked like when they
pulled you out. You didn't have to watch Tom get
drunk after he had to helicopter the both of you out
to St. Louis rather than lose you."

"Sue . . ."

"Don't Sue me," her friend retorted, her outrage
withering into misery. "I've had a really rotten
month."

Chris just gathered her in for a big hug. "It's all
going to be OK now, though. Don't you get it?"

Sue sniffled a little. "Easy for you to say. I'm the
one having nightmares this time."

Turning back to zip up her bag, Chris shrugged
away the statement. "That's just because you're not
used to the sight of blood."

"Not when it belongs to somebody I like."

"Well, think of it this way. We're fine, the town's
back to normal . . ."

"You call the Chris Jackson addition to the Mobile
Home Hall of Fame normal?"

"I never called the Mobile Home Hall of Fame normal. But all the attention has helped the economy, Harlan's attendance is down, and Mac's staying. Even after his whole family came down to harass him into going back to Chicago."

That, at last, brought the first real smile from Sue as the two women turned to the door. "My favorite part was when his mother told him that Pyrite was just too dangerous."

"It is," Chris retorted. "That's why he likes it here so much."

He hadn't had a chance to go fishing yet. That was the reason he'd given his mother, anyway. He'd also put a down payment on a big old Victorian over on Third. Chris had been invited to meet the twins. The idea terrified her. On the other hand, since getting out of the hospital she'd been staying at Harmonia's with Shelly. After that, seven year olds should be a breeze.

"I still can't believe it," Sue mused. "I mean, how that woman planned all those years to do this to you. How she really thinks she's your conscience."

Chris reached the door first and looked outside. Shelly and Victor were on the porch arguing with Lester about agents. Across the street Mrs. Peterson was arranging a wedding dress in the window of the dry cleaners, and three of the grade school girls skipped by giggling over something. Pyrite at its finest. Blessed normality.

The town would never be the same, but it would always be Pyrite. Chris couldn't imagine living anywhere else. Except maybe, if asked, Chicago.

Even the ghosts had begun to fade a little. "I never realized how much she depended on me in there," was all Chris could say.

It had all come out, of course. Spread across headlines, discussed on talk shows, dissected in police and psychiatric quarters. The police dispatcher who just happened to be a psychotic with access to her own investigation, who had been able to terrorize a town with lessons learned in C. J. Turner books. Diguises for wandering around the country, supplies for hiding out in abandoned mine buildings for days, computers for tracking credit card addresses.

Even the necessary equipment had come from the same shop Chris used. Mikes for listening in, recorders outside open windows for strange noises, modems for tapping into computers. Copied keys and crepe-soled shoes for breaking and entering. Perfectly planned, damn near perfectly executed.

All to deliver one message.

Well, Chris had received it. Maybe not the one Sandy had intended, though.

"So," Mac had asked the night before as they'd slumped together on Harmonia's couch. "What does this do to C. J. Turner?"

Chris hadn't even had the energy to move. "C. J.'s not going anywhere. She's just changing her outlook a little."

"How so?"

She sighed, enlightenment a heavier burden than she'd imagined. "Motive. That good and evil thing. I guess I always wanted there to be good people."

"You don't think there are?"

"I'm not sure anymore. It was just all easier when I thought that evil was exceptional. It isn't. It's small and banal and ordinary. And that scares me more than before."

Mac had turned his head just a little, brows gathered. "You don't call what happened to you exceptional?"

"That wasn't the evil. The evil was done fifteen years ago. And it was done because I was different. Because I threatened a comfortable norm. I mean, think about it. I was punished because I didn't cooperate, and Allen was abetted because he did."

"Are you still going to write about murder?"

"Not in my next book," she'd admitted, closing her eyes. "I think that one's going to be about obsession."

The perfect theme for the day. Especially this day when she was going home for the first time in fifteen years.

"Did you ever figure out how she knew about that one book?" Sue asked. "The one about Cooter?"

Chris shook her head. "A definite case for *Unsolved Mysteries.*"

Said more lightly than thought. Chris still wanted to know. She probably never would. The answers were locked up behind Sandy Baker's delusions. Her disjointed explanations about two sides of one person, of melded minds and unified purpose. The perfect timing of Chris's trips had been explained by Sandy's job at the Ritz. She'd just waited for Chris to show up to put her plan into action. But there was still *Family Business*. The one book no one could explain a connection to. Chris wondered. But she didn't ask.

"Chris!" Shelly yelled, not three feet away. "Mac's here!"

Chris saw. The cruiser pulled to a stop and Mac opened the door.

"I've seen better looking mugging victims," Victor allowed.

"I've seen better looking road kills," Lester countered.

Shelly was already straightening her hair. "I don't care. I still think he's spunk."

Chris laughed. She shoved open the screen door as Mac climbed out of the cruiser in his best uniform. His face still bore the ravages of his injuries. His poor mother had taken one look at him up in the neurosurgical intensive care unit in St. Louis and gone right into Gaelic. But even with the fresh railroad tracks that matched the set on the other side of his head and the residual swelling alongside his jaw, he looked better than anything Chris had ever seen. He looked alert and alive, and there was a lot to be said for that.

There was even more to say for the fact that after this fresh assault on the old brain cells, his memory was a little sketchy, too. It gave Chris a rather companionable feeling.

"Welcome back to work," Shelly greeted him.

"He's not at work," Sue objected. "He shouldn't even be on his feet."

Mac shot Chris a scowl. "Is she always like this?"

"Get used to it," she suggested, handing off her bag to him. "She now considers you part of the family."

Mac shook his head, but bent to give the tiny woman a kiss on the top of her head. "Thanks, Mom. I'll be a good boy and wear my seat belt."

"Don't forget me," Victor pleaded.

They were dropping Victor at Lambert in St. Louis for his flight to L. A. to do the Improv. And then, with several warrants in hand, they were headed for Springfield. Victor was throwing more luggage into the back seat for the dummy than himself.

"You sure you're feeling up to this?" Mac asked Chris gently.

She looked up at his ravaged face and thought how very interesting it would look now.

"Yeah," she admitted, even though she wasn't. Not

really. Not ever. "I have to know if she really did it."

Mac nodded, excluding everybody else at the periphery. "We may never know," he warned her again. "Not definitely."

No more than a week ago, that statement would have sent Chris's stomach skidding and her heart into overdrive. Now she just nodded. "I know. But I'm tired of losing sleep over it. It's time to face it head-on, just like Sandy said. And there's only one way to do that."

"In that case," Mac said with a smile. "There's only one thing left to say."

"Chris Jackson, have you found Jesus?"

Chris's reaction was pure instinct. "Yes, Harlan," she admitted, turning toward him. "I have. And He told me to give you a message."

Chris didn't even have to think about it. She just reared back for the swing of her life. By the time she got to the end of it, she thought one of the bones in her hand might have been broken. Her head spun alarmingly with the sudden motion, and Harlan was sprawled in the sidewalk, eyes stunned, jaw slack.

Chris didn't even wait for a reaction.

"There's only one thing to say?" she echoed, turning back to Mac.

There was dead silence in front of her house. Across the street, several pedestrians slowed to an uncertain stop, and Chris was sure she heard at least one strangled murmur of surprise. Her attention was all on Mac.

Mac didn't seem to notice that there was a man on the ground. He held out his hand for her and smiled. "Let's go."